BEFORE ANYONE ELSE

The Hashtag Series #8

by Cambria Hebert

Published by: Cambria Hebert Books, LLC

CAMBRIA
HEBERT

your key to escape.

http://www.cambriahebert.com

Interior design and typesetting by Sharon Kay of Amber Leaf Publishing
Cover design and photography by MAE I DESIGN
Edited by Cassie McCown of Gathering Leaves Editing
Copyright 2016 by Cambria Hebert

ISBN: 978-1-938857-93-5

DEDICATION

For the fans of *The Hashtag Series*.
You wanted a baby book…
So did Romeo and Rimmel.

Enjoy this last installment with our favorite family.

Special thanks to Jeddah Salera and Nathan Weller for embracing Rimmel and Romeo so wholly. The book trailer, the photos, everything you both have done to bring these two characters to life borders on perfection. I sincerely could not have asked for two better people to work with. Thank you.

BEFORE ANYONE ELSE

RIMMEL

Surprise (noun): an unexpected or astonishing event, fact, or thing.

I used to hate surprises.

In fact, I hated all unknown. I liked predictable. I liked safe. I liked books and quiet and knowing what to expect.

Romeo changed all that.

He changed my entire world, and frankly, it astonished me still. So to say I still hated surprises would be, in fact, like denying everything about life as I now knew it.

Some days—well, actually, *all* days I woke in this house, I was still caught by surprise. Lying in Romeo's warm embrace, with his heavy, muscled leg twined between mine and the feel of his smooth, chiseled chest rising and falling against my back was the best way to slowly arouse my conscience from slumber. Slowly, my eyes would let in the light of day, and slowly, they would adjust to their regular blurred state without my glasses.

I didn't need to see perfectly clear to be surprised.

The silvery white walls stretched up to the trey ceiling, which gave way to pure-white wooden trim. The design of the trey ceiling was multi-layered, having three different levels that recessed upward. The edge of each layer was trimmed out with more of the silvery-white paint that made them stand out against the otherwise pure white like shimmering bands of ribbon leading up to the cool-toned grey shade of the highest recess of the ceiling.

From there, my eyes would travel back toward the windows, which lined the side of the room and overlooked the sprawling property our family home was perched upon. Two oversized rectangular windows all trimmed out in white stretched from floor to ceiling on each end of the wall. In the center was not another window of the same shape, but instead a large, round one, also trimmed in white.

On either side of the two great rectangular windows hung deep-grey and white-striped curtains, which stretched the same floor-to-ceiling length as the glass and grazed the floor precisely.

Actually, not entirely precisely.

There was one curtain somehow slightly longer than the other three panels. It pooled on the espresso-colored hardwood and sometimes appeared slightly askew. The designer was horrified the second it was hung and wanted to send it back.

I told her no.

I liked it that way. A little less than perfect. A little bit a mess.

Just like me.

She thought I was insane.

In the end, I got my way. A girl couldn't be married for over a year to a man who always got what he wanted and not pick up a few tips.

The colors in here were serene, light, almost monochromatic... yet there wasn't one thing that was boring or that I didn't marvel at its beauty every time I looked at it.

From there, I'd turn my head and glance at the dark wooden side table beside the bed, the glass and silver lamp with an oversized, angular white shade and the few books I was reading at the moment taking up most of the surface area.

Just behind the table, on the wall, hung a mirror with more frame than actual mirror. The frame was some kind of glass that looked like shimmering pearls in a chevron pattern of white and grey.

Romeo's beside table looked the same, except his didn't have books. Instead, there were several copies of *GearShark* magazine.

Our bed was massive. The white tufted headboard was made of creamy-colored velvet and resembled a cloud with all the different tones of luxurious white bedding.

All the sparkly coordinating pillows were flung around the room, having landed wherever Romeo had tossed them the night before. I liked them best that way, scattered, not in the places they were actually supposed to be.

This was my house now.

Our home.

It was more than I ever even considered dreaming of. More than I asked for. Honestly, more than I wanted and, most assuredly, more than I needed.

However, my husband was a downright bossy man when he wanted to be, and giving me this home was something he refused to bend on.

So every morning when I opened my eyes, I took it all in. I gazed upon our room with brand new, slightly blurry vision. And I was grateful.

But never more grateful than I was for the man who took up more than half of this massive bed.

Romeo was my real home. Not the ultra-plush bedding, the paint on the walls, that breathtaking view out the windows, or my Range Rover parked in the five-car garage downstairs.

Him.

And now the little piece of him growing inside me.

Maybe that was the biggest surprise of all.

A baby. A life created from both of us. Something that was wholly his and mine—a person. I knew in the deepest part of me that this little girl was going to have the best of each of us, and hopefully none of my awkwardness.

The fact that I was pregnant wasn't a surprise. We wanted this baby, and Romeo worked very hard to make sure we got one.

Him working hard = lots of sex.

It wasn't such a sacrifice for either of us.

I think the biggest surprise was the instant, all-encompassing love I felt for a person I didn't even know. Someone who technically barely existed. Before our daughter even had a heartbeat, I was so completely in love it stole my breath.

I was used to love, to the bottomless kind, but this was wholly different. The love I felt for this little baby was unlike anything I'd ever known.

People always told me it would become even stronger when I held her for the first time. I couldn't even fathom that. But I hoped they were right.

Love was something I didn't think I would ever get enough of. Especially when it came to loving anything Romeo was a part of.

"You're doing it again," his gruff, sleepy voice whispered right above my ear.

I smiled. "What?"

"Staring at this room like you were kidnapped and opened your eyes to a place you've never seen before."

I giggled. "Well, if I was kidnapped and brought here, I probably wouldn't protest."

"You're killing me, Smalls." Romeo's teeth grazed over my earlobe and tugged.

I shivered even as I laughed.

"If you were kidnapped, I would burn the world down to find you," he vowed, breath fluttering across my ear and the husky quality in his promise making me squirm against him.

"I wouldn't stay willingly anywhere you weren't," I told him, even though he already knew. My hand reached up behind me to cup the back of his neck and pull him down.

His tongue was warm and languid, moving into my mouth without much haste, taking time to fully explore as if he hadn't already done this a million times before.

As we kissed, his hand slid over my side and across my belly, palming the baby and gently rubbing. I smiled into his lips, and he continued to kiss me.

"Your smile is my favorite flavor," he said, pulling back only slightly.

My heart tumbled over. "You have morning breath," I told him, smiling again.

"Is that your favorite flavor, Mrs. Anderson?"

I paused as if I were genuinely considering it. "I think I prefer pickles."

He threw back his head and laughed. When he glanced down, I caressed some of the blond strands of his hair falling over his forehead, brushing them away from his face, while I took in every single thing about him.

I did this almost every day. And every day, I found something new to gaze at.

I never wanted to stop looking at him like he was new to me. I never wanted to forget the way he made my heart sing.

"I love you," I whispered.

"I love you too, baby." His lips pressed to the tip of my nose, and I sighed.

I started to wiggle so he would untangle his limbs from mine. He made a sound of protest, and I glanced up. "Where the hell do you think you're going?"

"I have to pee."

This baby wasn't even that big yet, but it didn't matter. Apparently, my bladder was like the size of an acorn, because peeing was like my new hobby.

"Hold it," he commanded.

I gasped and opened my mouth to yell at him. How dare he tell a pregnant woman she couldn't pee!

I would kick him the minute he gave me my legs back.

Before I could do anything, he lifted the covers and disappeared. I screeched because of the way he moved quickly down my body and settled between my legs.

Entirely hidden beneath the covers, I felt his two very large hands span my middle and gently caress my rounded belly. He did this every morning, even before I started showing and my belly was flat.

I smiled and closed my eyes.

"Hey there, Pickle," he told my stomach.

I grinned up at the ceiling, still amused he called her that. It wasn't exactly original, but a girl didn't get to choose the type of cravings she got when pregnant. Mine was pickles. All the time. Every day. So yeah... Romeo dubbed our daughter "Pickle."

To be fair, he started calling her that before we even knew it was a girl. He'd been convinced this baby was going to be a boy, so when we found out (we didn't have to wait for the ultrasound at twenty weeks thanks to a new blood test they could do now) *he* was actually a *she*, my eyes went directly to my husband.

Not one ounce. Not one ounce of disappointment this wasn't a son. When he looked at me, I swear I saw his entire heart in his blue eyes, and it shimmered with tears. He'd never admit to the tears, but I saw them, and really, I didn't need to tell anyone.

He loved our daughter just as much as I did and, honestly, more than I ever thought a father could (you know, 'cause my father wasn't exactly award winning).

"It's time to start putting some meat on those bones," he told her, then paused. "Does she have bones yet, Smalls?"

"I think it's a little early for that. She still has quite a while to grow," I said, thoughtful. I should probably look that up, because really, I had no idea.

Beneath the blanket, Romeo grunted. I felt him pat my stomach. "Yeah, get on that. Well, what I mean is take your time, Pickle. You don't have to be that big, 'cause Daddy is big enough for the both of us."

"What about me?" I chimed in.

"I'm trying to talk to my daughter here, Rim," he scolded. Then lower and not to me, he said, "I'll have a talk with her about Daddy-Pickle time."

I giggled.

I felt him kiss my belly again. I wasn't really showing that much; my stomach was just more rounded out than usual, so his entire one hand covered the bump for another long moment before he tossed back the blankets and sprang out.

He wasn't wearing a shirt. His body was tanned, toned, and just as smooth as the day I met him in the library.

"Can I go pee now?" I inquired, trying to sound surly, but not achieving it at all. I was way to charmed by him to be surly.

He lunged forward but didn't give me any of his body weight. Instead, his arms took it all as he hovered over me. "Failing half my classes was the smartest thing I ever did."

I rolled my eyes. "That is not something to be proud of, Roman Anderson."

"It brought me you, didn't it?"

I didn't want to tell him it definitely was a good thing he was failing, so instead, I reached up and fastened my lips to his. When I finally pulled back, he grinned down at me like he knew I was trying to avoid telling him he was right.

It was maddening.

But also appealing.

"I'm taking a shower. Want me to wash your toes?"

"I can reach my own toes," I told him.

"It's good practice for in a few months, when you can't," he rebutted and jumped out of bed.

"I'll be there in a few," I called out as he disappeared into our massive adjoining bathroom.

I smiled to myself and sat up, dangling my feet over the side of the bed. I was only wearing a black lace bralette with a pair of matching boy shorts. Romeo liked seeing my barely-there belly, so I pretty much slept with it on display now.

I padded across the soft rug beneath our bed as I pushed at my knotted, messy hair. I felt stiff and sore this morning. I must have slept wrong. A warm shower would be like heaven.

The shower was on and steam was rising up from behind the glass doors as I moved past it and toward the water closet (that's a private room for the toilet). Romeo was standing at the sink, naked, with a toothbrush in his mouth and grinned, toothpaste all over his lips.

I laughed and shut myself in the small room.

It was then that life as I knew it changed.

Another surprise thrown my way… It was the kind that made me recall why I never used to like them.

Fear so raw pelted me it felt as if I were being physically ripped in half. It almost overshadowed the pain I noted in my body.

The pain that was *not* from sleeping wrong.

With unsteady hands, I finished up and stood there in the center of the room, hearing a loud buzzing sound fill my ears. I pushed past it, knowing I couldn't succumb even though I wanted to.

I flung open the tiny door and wobbled out into the bathroom.

Romeo was standing at the shower, with the glass door in his palm.

"Come on, slow poke." He called over his shoulder and threw me one of his trademark grins.

It died instantly on his lips. "Rim?"

He abandoned the door, and it swayed open behind him as he turned fully toward me.

I opened my mouth, but it didn't work. I tried again.

"Rimmel," he said, coming toward me, grasping me by the shoulders.

Cramping pain sliced through my lower half, and I whimpered and slumped toward him. He caught me, holding me back so he could look into my face.

"Something's wrong, Romeo," I managed.

I felt warmth between my legs and glanced down. Two rivulets of blood trailed down the inside of my thighs.

I started to cry, but not one sound came out of me.

I don't know much about what happened next. Romeo was there, our entire family was. I vaguely remember the sound of him shouting orders and the sound of the Hellcat's revving engine.

The memory that is clearest to me about the morning our happily-ever-after gave way to a budding nightmare was when the buzzing sound between my ears faded away and I was left sitting in a hospital bed.

And then there were two…

Pickle was gone before we even got to meet her.

Turns out Daddy might have been big enough for the both of them… but Mommy?

Mommy was the weak one.

DAILY NEWS

World - Business - Finance - Lifestyle - Travel - Sport - Weather

2016

THE WORLDS BEST SELLING NATIONAL NEWSPAPER

Issue: 240104

Monday 5th June

First Edition

World leaders meet in London to discuss the global economy.

July 27th is the day when representatives from the every country around the world will meet in London, England for talks to resolve the worldwide economic crisis. Everything from tax, interest rates, currency, import/export agreements, debt, commodity prices and private sector wealth will be the subject for discussion during this sculptural gathering of the worlds super powers.

Some critics are claiming that this will do nothing more than create further problems for poorer nations, but supporters of the initiative are quick to point out that, the forecast predicts nothing but a bleak financial future if things are left the way they are now. Heads of government face further criticism from protesters who insist that they should get their priorities in order and... *continued on page 2*

Climate change - Does recycling really make a difference or is history just repeating itself?

Recent studies carried out by institutes have revealed that recent weather phenomenons around the globe may be nothing more than nature behaving the way it

and he went on to explain that nothing we do today to protect the environment will have any effect on future atmospheric conditions, or to ensure that our children

THE INSIDE STORY ON FOOTBALL

No More Baby!

Who's to blame and will the football superstar stay with her?

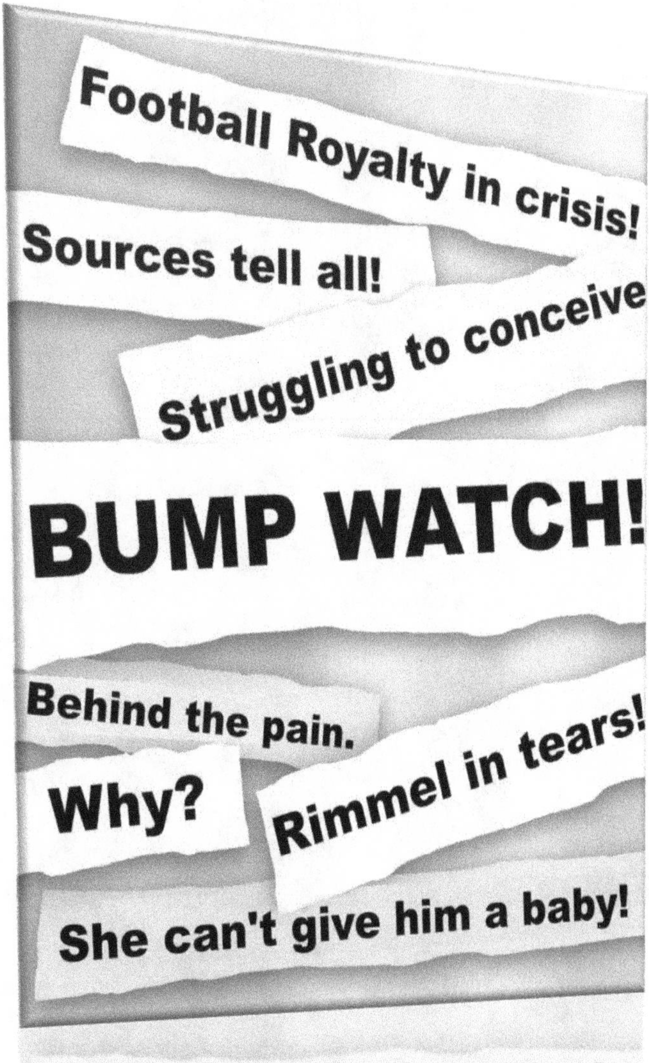
Football Royalty in crisis!
Sources tell all!
Struggling to conceive
BUMP WATCH!
Behind the pain.
Why?
Rimmel in tears!
She can't give him a baby!

THREE MONTHS LATER...

The Knights are off to a promising start! Will they be 2x SuperBowl winners?"

SPORTS DAILY

Chapter One

ROMEO

Kicking ass. Taking names.

Just another day in football. And in my normal, everyday life.

I was beginning my third season as a professional football player with the Maryland Knights, and it still felt like it was my first. Except, you know, I wasn't nursing an arm injury and I was the starter.

Oh yeah, and I had a Super Bowl ring.

I guess what I meant was I still felt the same rush when I put on the uniform. The same excitement pumped through me when I jogged out onto a freshly mowed and prepped field for the first snap of the game.

I knew my teammates now. I wasn't green to the NFL or as a football player. But my love for the game was still as pigmented as a fresh-off-the-printer dollar bill.

I hoped I always stayed that way. Passionate. Motivated. Hungry.

When I left for training camp over the summer, I had serious doubts. I wasn't feeling it. I still loved the game, but my motivation was lacking. Sometimes passion was diluted by life; other situations took precedence. I found myself packing my shit for camp and wondering if I would mentally be there this season. It worried me. It was the kind of worry I hadn't felt since my broken arm. As unenthusiastic as I was to play, the thought of *not* playing was equally disquieting.

Turns out playing ball, even just the preseason training and games, was just what I needed.

It was an outlet, a place to channel all the shit that caused me to feel so diluted. Being on the field reminded me of the things I loved most about this sport. When I was on the field, I could let go of everything else. The single-minded focus I always played with was a welcome reprieve.

So maybe I didn't "let go" of everything else.

That's where the kicking ass and taking names came into play. I brought it out on the green with me. I used it. I channeled it all into the game, into my arm, my throws, and the momentum with which I launched myself down the field.

I was really good at throwing a touchdown. I didn't often run the ball. I was bulkier than most quarterbacks; my muscle mass sometimes slowed me down.

Not this season.

This season, I was already making a name for myself as not only a QB who threw missiles into the end zone, but as one who bulldozed his way down the field with the ball tucked in close.

Good times.

There was a new aggression in the way I played. A fierceness that maybe wasn't there before. The coach said I was coming into my own. Experience was starting to show in the way I played. I didn't argue.

But he was wrong.

There was more to our kicking ass. More to the antagonistic way I performed.

I'd been simmering. Holding off a rolling boil until I finally let it rise.

The morning Rim stepped into my line of vision with her perfect, round belly on display and nothing but despair in her warm, brown eyes, my life was irrevocably altered.

Sometimes, the imagery was still all too vivid. I wondered if it would ever become less so. But here I was three months later, surrounded by the sounds of slamming locker doors, loud teammates, and the scent of sweaty balls permeating the space.

Secret confession of the locker room: Yes, sweaty balls had an odor. It wasn't a good one.

I still felt the high of our win tonight. Sweat still slicked my skin, and turf lingered beneath my fingernails.

It didn't matter.

The memories still seemed to haunt me at a moment's notice.

Rimmel with blood trailing down her inner thighs. The way her arms wrapped around her middle like a shield. How pain clouded her eyes and how fragile she felt cradled in my arms as I rushed her out of the house and into the car.

She told me once those first few hours were hazy, as if she'd been experiencing them through a veil. I never said it out loud, but sometimes I envied that.

My front-row seat guaranteed a really good view.

I never wanted to see something like that ever again. The fear that wracked my body that night was unmatched. So severe I was certain it altered me in ways I'd feel forever. Kind of how a scar marred skin that had been smooth before. My limbs shook with terror that night, my throat was tight, and breathing was no longer such a thoughtless task. It wasn't just fear for my daughter... but for my wife.

Sometimes I thought back to the night Braeden rushed Ivy to the ER. The night we all found out she was pregnant with Nova. I recalled how he looked standing alone in front of the viewing area of all the newborn babies.

The shadows beneath his eyes and the way my own chest constricted as we all stood around helpless, waiting to find out if there was or was not a baby.

I understood all too well how he felt that night, and as terrible as it had been...

What Rim and I suffered was so much worse.

You know, I was a pretty charming guy. A lot of people said I could talk a chipmunk out of the last of his nuts in the middle of a blizzard.

No one actually said that. But it didn't mean it wasn't true.

Anyway, I said all kinds of delightful shit to Rimmel over the years we'd been together. It was one of the millions of reasons she loved me (another was my, and I quote, "big ego"). I was entertaining and funny.

I wasn't a guy with a lot of regrets. Life was too short, and honestly, I was too fucking happy to care about anything that might have passed me by. However. I did regret this one thing I said once.

I'd like to place an order for one of these in blue.

The first time I held my niece, I'd said it. A jest, but not really. The idea of a tiny bundle made up of entirely me and Rim became tangible in that moment. The notion of becoming a parent, a father, bloomed somewhere deep inside me

I didn't know it at the time how one statement could weigh so much.

After that, it seemed like a clock I never knew existed started ticking. The press went into "Bump Watch" (FYI: a *bump watch* is entirely fucking stupid. A baby is not a bump. Just like a man bun is not a hairstyle. It's stupid.). People started asking when we were going to have a baby of our own. It seemed like almost daily, people would toss out the question.

I learned quickly a question like that could never be casual. A question like that held just as much weight as my off-hand "charming" statement that day in the hospital.

Not long after Nova came home, Rim and I started trying for a baby, even though we said out loud we wanted more time for just us. No one needed to know, just like no one needed to know we'd snuck off and married in secret before our wedding. Some things were just for us. Some things were so special they remained unspoken and sacred.

Then one unexpected day, I found my girl crying in the bathroom because she couldn't give me the bundle in blue I so charmingly ordered.

Fuuuckkk.

I hadn't been too worried about the months we'd been trying and hadn't been successful. I didn't know every month that passed and she didn't get pregnant was like a silent knife to her heart. Hell, the trying was enough fun for me.

• • •

Cambria Hebert

For Rim, it had been more. It turned into something she couldn't achieve. At least not in the timeframe she thought she should.

I hadn't realized how much pressure she'd put on herself until I found her that day, sniffling. Her eyes were red-rimmed, glasses slightly askew. Her hair was a mess, and she was sitting on the bathroom floor with tissues bunched in her hand. My name stretched across her back as she sat bundled in my Alpha U hoodie. It was still her favorite thing to wear.

She was mortified I'd found her that way.

It was a different time and circumstance, but that image of her brought me back. Back to the time she was sitting in the center of the animal shelter with a one-eyed cat in her lap.

I fell hard that day for Rim.

I fell for her all over again in the bathroom.

I sat down, scooped her up, and made her tell me. She thought she was somehow failing me. As if she ever could.

We had a talk right there on the bathroom floor about what I expected of her as a wife. It went a little something like this:

"Breathe. All I expect is for you to breathe."

It was a good talk. It got me a blow job and a smile on her beautiful face.

Not too much longer after that, I found her crying in the bathroom again. Seriously, a quick thought that our bathroom might be fucking cursed did cross my mind. Until I saw the smile beneath her tears. Between us, her arm was outstretched; in her palm, she offered me a stick. I really, really wanted to crack a joke about not wanting to touch something she peed on.

But I refrained. Her eyes were too sparkling for that.

She was pregnant. My baby was having my baby.

Life was good. *Better* than good.

The idea of our daughter folded seamlessly into our life. So many moments. So many moments we had to get used to the idea, to want her… to love her.

Then she was ripped away.

I've never seen pain like that in my wife's eyes. I still remember carrying her out of the hospital (like I'd let her ride in a wheelchair when my arms worked just fine.). She'd looked at me and said, "It wasn't supposed to be this way."

No. No, it wasn't.

But it was.

And here I was. Here *we* were.

In those first few weeks, I poured everything of myself into Rimmel and making sure we got through this. All of my anger, sadness, and frustration was restrained because it wouldn't help her and it wouldn't erase that void deep in her eyes.

In fact, I worried if she ever saw it, it would only make what she suffered worse.

The prep for the new season started, and an outlet presented itself. I unleashed it all on the field. During practice, at pre-games. Hell, any chance I got really. It helped. I still had Rimmel, my family, and I knew we'd have another child someday.

"We're the bomb dot com," B said, slamming his hand into the closed locker beside my open one. "We're taking the Bowl again this year."

I grinned. "Hells yeah."

"That was some nice throwing out there tonight," he said, leaning against the locker with his bare arms folded over his chest.

"Yeah? Well, you lived up to your name out there, too, *Hulk*."

Braeden flexed, lifted his biceps, and kissed them. "Sprinkles. Does the body good."

"Dude. Never say that again."

"Haters gonna hate," he retorted.

"Posers gonna pose," I mocked.

Braeden scowled. "You're an asshole. I'm hitting the showers."

I laughed. "I'd join you, but I wouldn't want to make you feel inferior."

Braeden stopped and turned back. The ends of the white towel wrapped around his waist slapped against his legs. "I'll whip it out right here, Rome. You know I will. We'll have a dick-measuring contest right the fuck now."

Several guys around us started cackling. "Keep it in your pants, Hulk!"

"Unleash the Kraken!" someone else hollered.

Braeden gave everyone the finger. I grinned and pulled off the rest of my uniform and wrapped a towel around my waist. Just as I was closing the locker door, my cell went off.

I reached for it, glancing at the screen. It was a text from Trent.

I pulled it up and stared down at the pic he'd sent through. Around the phone, my hand tightened, and all the muscles in my neck bunched. It didn't matter how hard I went out on the field tonight, this was all it took to make me ready to smash heads again.

I sucked in a deep breath and expelled it.

● ● ●

"What is it?" B asked from right beside me. His voice was low, all sense of teasing gone.

I held the phone out so he could see the screenshot of the newest article unleashed by the stalkerazzi.

Stalkerazzi = the press who wouldn't stop printing stories about me and my wife.

I actually really preferred to call them fucking photogs, but Rim didn't appreciate my "foul" language. I didn't appreciate the way they'd been torturing my wife. Still, I tried to tone it down when I was around my girl because it was the right thing to do.

B snorted. "What is this, your tenth divorce in the last three months?"

"Look at the fucking sub-headline," I ground out.

Braeden grabbed the phone and angled it more toward him and leaned around my shoulder. A low growl vibrated the air around us. "How is she?" he asked quietly, shoving the phone away from his eyes.

I pulled it back and texted Trent. *Rim seen it?*

His reply was instant. *Unfortunately.*

How is she?

A little quiet but fine.

They hovering? I typed back quickly, suddenly feeling like flying home tomorrow just wasn't soon enough.

Nope, he replied.

I found that surprising, but I didn't bother saying so. Thank fuck for Trent. Over my shoulder, B was reading the exchange. I let him. Less to reiterate later.

You home now? I typed out.

Yep. I'll hang for a while. I told her I needed cookies.

I felt my lips curl up. Rim couldn't resist a hungry family member. Even if she didn't feel like being "babysat," as she called it, the second Trent declared hunger, she'd make sure he was fed. Everyone called me the alpha of our family, but I considered her the head of us all. After the wedding, Rimmel really settled in. That ring might just be jewelry on her finger, but those vows, the papers we signed, it gave her something.

Security. A permanent family she'd never had. A promise we would never go away. The completion of the compound and having us all behind the gates together only made it stronger. Rim was the one who looked after everyone, who enforced pancake Sunday and proved loyalty and family was far stronger than blood.

She was our glue.

She was *my* glue.

It's the mother in her. The thought sent a pang of pain and regret through me, but I forced it away.

Braeden snorted. "Bastard always gets the cookies." Then he made a sound and muttered, "She better not feed him my sprinkles."

Thanks, bro. I'll call her when I get to the hotel, I typed out, then shoved the phone in the locker so I could go shower off in a hurry. I wanted to get back to the room so I could call Rim, hear her voice.

I missed her. It had been two weeks since I'd seen her last, and it was two weeks too long. If I was already missing her this much, this fast, it was going to be a hella long season of traveling.

Braeden was staring at me as I moved past. I kept going. He fell into step beside me as we headed toward the shower stalls.

"I'm getting really fucking tired of the press." My tone was short and gruff. Actually, I was already tired of the press. I was done the first time they printed something that hurt Rimmel.

B slapped me on the shoulder. "Dude, just say the word. I've got a bin full of fireworks and paintballs I'm just waiting to unleash on those gossip suckers."

I made a rude sound.

He was a little too silent. I glanced over at him.

He was staring back, straight faced.

My eyebrows shot up. "You serious?"

"All right, they're in the garage. Under lock and key."

It sounded like something we'd have done in high school, and then my mother would have lectured us afterward. We were grown-ass men now. With responsibilities. We didn't do that kind of thing. It was beneath us.

They keep torturing your wife.

The thought was like a drop kick to my nads. "Don't get rid of your stash just yet," I told him.

His eyes flickered with surprise. "It's not going anywhere."

Good, because I had a bad feeling the stalkerazzi weren't either.

Gossip +++ Buzz +++ Social Media Fren...
nation +++ News +++...
...ews +++ Information +++ News +++ Information +++ Information +++ N...

Celebrity News

"The BIG D!
And no, we don't mean dick."
-COMET ONLINE

Chapter Two

RIMMEL

Her name was Evie.

The meaning of her name was *life*.

It seemed appropriate somehow to give our daughter the name of something she wouldn't have. Evie never took her first breath. I never saw her eyes that surely matched her daddy's. I never got to hold her...

But she was a life.

My life.

Our life.

A life that never would be.

After I lost her, so much was unbearable, most of all the way people referred to her, the way they would whisper in hushed tones when they thought I couldn't hear.

She lost it.

That baby would have been gorgeous.

It. That baby. Would have.

No.

Evie. Ours. Is.

It didn't matter that we'd never get to hold her. I felt the crushing weight of her absence; I felt the hollowed-out core in my body where she used to grow. Empty. Lifeless.

How did I reconcile what was with what would never be? How did I let people know even though she technically never lived, she still existed and would never cease? I'd known loss. I'd known death.

This was so much worse.

Life goes on. That's what people said anyway. And in a sense, they were all right. Life did go on. Minutes passed, hours ticked by, and days dragged. Days turned into weeks and weeks into months.

The pain of losing her didn't dull. I learned to live with the stinging reminders every single day so they weren't as sharp as before.

Even though the pain dulled, the memory didn't. The blur of that day was still agonizingly vivid. It didn't even matter I was checked out for most of it, because even the emotions of events I suppressed haunted me.

Something else took over where the sharpest pain resided. Desperation. Almost total-consuming thought.

Wondering.

What if? Why? When? Again?

What if I'd never lost her? What if she was a bundle in my arms right now?

Why did this happen to us? Why was I being punished? Why was the press so brutally indifferent, so calculating and cold about my pain? When would it not hurt so much? When would I get pregnant again? Could I? Why wasn't I already? If I did… would I have a miscarriage again?

My brain was the internet, and I had one thousand tabs open all the time.

Time passed. I was stronger than the days following the loss. My family was my saving grace, a light in the dark tunnel I sometimes longed to escape into.

Romeo was like a screw drilled into a wall, into the stud behind the wall. An anchor, sturdy and immoveable. He held me up on days I couldn't stand.

And those first few days after, when both of us were pretty wobbly... he held me even then, as the family closed ranks around us both. Thank God for them all.

I didn't know why I lost Evie. No one did. The doctors gave us generic statistics and probable cause... I barely listened. What did it really matter anyway? She was gone. The answer wouldn't bring her back.

But I had a reason. A reason to keep moving, a reason to go on.

No. Not a reason. *Reasons.*

Romeo. Braeden. Ivy. Trent. Drew. Nova. My shelter. The animals. Romeo. (He's on the list twice cause he's the most important.)

The loss of our daughter was immeasurable, yet I still had more than my fair share. Somedays it was hard to feel grateful, but other... other days, I woke in my bedroom and opened my eyes and still felt the same wonder and surprise that this was my life.

That was something.

Romeo was everything.

It might seem strange, but as much of everything as he was to me before... he was more so now.

I felt closer to him than ever, but oddly, further apart.

I didn't understand, and mostly, I didn't think about it. I didn't want to. It was too hard, and there was already enough of that. Instead, I focused on the closeness. The way my heart sometimes beat solely for him.

I focused on his blue eyes and captivating smile.

On the life we shared, the family we had, and I tried not to fixate on what we'd lost. Most days, I was successful. Some days, I was not.

The sister animal shelter we were able to open after the hugely successful fundraiser put together by Valerie and myself was my refuge. Just as the one Michelle still ran across town had been when I was in college.

I loved it there. It was my pet project, my passion, and not a day went by that I ever once regretted foregoing veterinary medicine to stay here and run this shelter. It fulfilled me in so many ways. It made my heart full even on days it felt tattered and echoed with hollows.

This facility was larger than the one I used to practically live in, almost double in size. The building was located off the main road, down a winding side street, and boasted grass all around. The exterior was stone, the rough, uncut kind, the type that looked as if it were pulled straight from the earth. The muted brown and gray shades provided a warm feeling of welcome, which I loved because no shelter should feel cold and clinical.

This was home, albeit hopefully a temporary one, to the animals who stayed here. To the employees who so lovingly and willingly gave their time and care.

The windows were of normal shape and size at the front, trimmed out in white with wooden shutters. Not long after Evie went to heaven, I added flowerboxes to the front windows.

Well, I didn't add them. Me and tools didn't go to well together. Romeo hung them, and he did so that warm summer day without a shirt.

Three animals were adopted that day.

I'm pretty sure it wasn't the flowers I was planting that drew in the people... It was his shirtless, glistening skin. And the fact he waved and winked to every lady who walked up the pathway as he worked.

My husband, forever the charmer. But hey, it was for a good cause.

Anyway, in addition to the flowerboxes, I added potted plants at the front doors and made the place even more homey. Fall brought burnished gold and orange leaves that littered the grass and front walkway. The flowers were no longer cheerful and bright, but gone and waiting for the cold seasons to pass. Instead, there were pumpkins by the front doors, compliments of Ivy and Nova from the day we visited the pumpkin patch.

Side note: if you take Drew to a pumpkin patch, he's gonna want to drive the tractor that pulls the hayride. And when the man who's supposed to be driving recognizes Drew as *the* Drew who drives for the NRR, he's going to let him have the driver's seat. Tractors are not racecars... Someone needs to tell Drew. Well, wait, we all told him... at high volumes as he plowed through the corn fields with our wagon full of hay attached. If we had our pumpkins already, they would have been pie. Needless to say, Drew didn't drive us back to the barn.

Just inside the wide front doors was the open, welcoming reception area. Its tiled floors actually looked like real wood—all the pretty without the maintenance. The walls were painted a neutral shade of almond, and the windows were framed out with dark wood trim.

In the center of the room was the front desk. The front was done in stone the same colors as outside. It rose up to meet wide, granite counters, with the highest section being in the center, then a lower section on each side. Behind the desk, the wall was painted a shade of eggplant, the shelter's logo in the center in white.

On either side of the large reception desk and built into the purple wall were two doors. Each hallway led back to the animal quarters and back storage room and pantry.

The animals had all-tile "rooms" with solid floors (I despised the cage-type floors because little paws always got stuck in them) and glass doors that allowed them to see out clearly. The rooms were stacked on top of each other, which utilized vertical space.

Not every single room was like that, though. The larger dogs got tiled suites as well but with wrought-iron doors and all of them ground floor.

The wash and pantry rooms were basic but clean. The laundry facilities were all equipped with brand-new washers and dryers—a donation from Valerie and Tony.

Behind the shelter, outside, was a large fenced-in green space where the dogs could run and play. There were benches for the staff, and then off to the left was a separate fenced-off area, which was actually Braeden and Ivy's contribution last summer.

It was a dog pool. An in-ground, walk-in pool for the dogs to swim and exercise in during the warm summer months. Eventually, I hoped to have it enclosed so it could remain open all year round.

Yeah, I know. A pool. Pools are sort of my nemesis. All water, really. Braeden practically choked on his pancakes when I told him that's what I wanted to build with his donation money.

But this wasn't about me. It was about the dogs. And some of the older pets we had here really benefited from the nonimpact exercise.

I didn't oversee pool time; the other people who worked here did.

I was proud of this place. It was my home away from home. I spent a lot of time here and so did some of the animals.

It was already after closing, the doors were locked up, and the animals were secured for the night. When I closed, I always stayed about an hour after the place was shut down. I liked to clean up, straighten the pantry, and finish up the last bit of laundry. It was peaceful here at night, and sometimes I enjoyed the busy work.

Especially when Romeo was away for preseason.

He would be home in the morning, though, and just thinking about it made my stomach flutter. I didn't think I would ever not anticipate Romeo's presence.

It was another reason I was closing up tonight and making sure everything was done. I wasn't coming in tomorrow or the next day. This was it for Romeo and Braeden, the last bit of time off they would have before the season was officially underway. After this, it would be almost constant traveling, with little time off between games. If I could be home, I was going to be; nothing else was as important to me. Besides, the staff here was more than capable of running things.

I flipped off the back lights, making sure the night lights were all illuminated, and walked out toward the front.

Molly was still here, at one of the small desks at the side of the room. My eyes went right to her sitting there with her chin in her palm and a cup of what looked like tea at her elbow. She was one of two full-time employees we had here (besides me); the rest were volunteers from Alpha U and around town.

Molly was tall, nearly six feet. She had a slim build, and her blond hair was styled in this adorable pixie cut. I kind of envied it because she probably didn't even have to brush it when she got out of bed. The rumpled, messy look went with that cut.

I mentioned cutting my hair like that to Ivy once. She told me I was insane because my hair was gorgeous and gave me a really long lecture about hair care and hair texture, blah, blah… I never mentioned it again.

I mean, it didn't matter, because I didn't always brush my hair when I got up anyway. I smiled a little to myself at the thought. A wistful type of feeling breezed through me. I combed my hair a lot more these days than I wanted to.

'Cause, you know. Reasons.

"Molly! I thought you would have left by now," I said, coming around the large counter.

She jerked a little and pressed a hand to her chest. "Rimmel! I didn't hear you come out of the back."

I was slightly amused. "I didn't mean to scare you."

She blew out a breath and grinned. "I need to stop watching scary movies at night."

"Probably not a bad idea." I agreed. "Whatever you're finishing up, just do it tomorrow. No need to stay this late."

She cleared her throat and glanced down. A flash of something passed behind her expression, and my stomach tightened.

"I'm actually all finished. I was just waiting on you."

"On me?" I puzzled.

"Yeah, until your brother gets here."

It was a thing. A total embarrassing but necessary thing. When I closed or worked late, Romeo or Braeden met me to escort me to my car. Well, if Romeo was in town, he just drove me. If Romeo and B weren't here, then Trent or Drew came. If none of the boys were in town, I didn't close.

After everything the people in our family had gone through, me not being alone at night at work wasn't such a crazy request from Romeo. In fact, I kinda preferred it this way, too.

"You don't have to do that!" I said quickly. "Go home. Watch a movie that isn't scary."

Molly laughed. "I know I don't, but it's dark out and late…" She glanced toward the front doors. Funny she never worried about that when she left without an escort.

"Is something wrong?" I asked, pushing at the glasses on my nose. My hair was up in a wild bun—I was pretty sure there was a lost pencil in there from when I was doing inventory a couple hours ago—and my sweat pants had dog fur on them.

"Besides the fact that I have an overactive imagination from the movies?" Molly replied.

She was stalling.

I glanced down at her desk, where she'd been focused when I'd walked out. Looked like she had her iPad in front of her. A sour taste coated the back of my tongue.

"What are you reading?" I asked, stepping closer, trying to see the screen.

"Nothing," she said, moving her arms and cup of tea to cover it.

I was about to call her out on her craptastic lie when I heard a key in the front double doors. Both of us looked up to see Trent slipping inside and shutting the door behind him.

"Hey, sis," he called out, twirling the keys around his finger.

I loved when he called me that. It was kinda new for him, and every time he said it, warmth bloomed in my chest. I loved having a big family. It was something I didn't have growing up. Something I never really thought I would have. I definitely never imagined I'd have a bunch of self-appointed brothers who were bossy and maddening.

There was a time when Trent stayed in the background of our family, and then he started to slip away. It hurt, even though we weren't as close as I would have liked. But then everything changed, he and Drew finally admitted their feelings for each other, and Trent wholly embraced our family. He wasn't in the background anymore. We were closer now than ever before.

"Hey!" I called back, smiling.

"Sorry I'm late." He grimaced. "Got held up."

"Everything okay?" I asked, more suspicion rising inside me.

He nodded.

"Well, I'm out," Molly said, standing to shrug into a light jacket and pick up her bag, tea, and iPad. "Have a good couple days off, Rimmel. Enjoy your husband."

Trent was farther into the room now, closer to the desk. As she neared him, I saw her eyes lock on his face. "Lot clear?" she asked low.

That sour taste on my tongue exploded in my mouth.

"Molly," I said, and she turned. "Can I see what you were reading?" I stepped up and motioned for her iPad.

"It's embarrassing. Just a silly romance novel."

"You should never be embarrassed to read. It doesn't matter what it is."

Molly opened her mouth to likely make an excuse, but I took the iPad out of her arms and tapped the screen. As soon as it lit up, my back teeth slammed together.

"This is a new one," I remarked, unable to keep the annoyance out of my tone.

Trent moved to my side and looked down. "Fucking press," he muttered and moved to take the iPad. "Don't read that trash, Rim."

THE DIVORCE IS ON!
Romeo is on top on the field, but where is Rimmel?
Sources say the strain of losing a baby and her inability to conceive again
has put this once royal couple on a fast track to the big D.

My fingers tightened on the screen. My vision blurred a little, and a sick feeling wormed its way through my middle.

The gossip was never ending. The rumors never stopped swirling. The press was obsessed with us. They made the #BuzzBoss look like Barney. *That* was something I never imagined could happen.

Even now, three months after Evie... they wouldn't stop. I was beginning to think they never would.

Trent made a sound and ripped the device out of my grip. The screen went dark, and he thrust it at Molly. "Why the hell are you even reading that garbage? You know that shit ain't welcome here."

Molly looked guilty, her eyes sliding to me, then away. "I know it's not true," she offered.

Does she really? Or does some part of her believe some sliver of it?

"Outside is clear," Trent said, not as kind as he could have. "Thanks for waiting 'til I got here."

Did he call her and tell her to wait?

She nodded and glanced back at me. "Rimmel—"

I held up my hand. "No worries. Like I said, any reading is good reading."

Trent made a rude sound.

Molly left, making sure to glance out before slipping out into the well-lit parking lot.

"They were here, weren't they?" I asked.

"Fucking paps," Trent swore. "Took me a while to get them the hell off the property."

And that's why he was late and Molly stayed. Nothing like a new divorce headline to bring the vultures into the lot so they could flash their bright bulbs and hurl questions that bordered on insults at me.

"Thank you for doing that," I said sincerely. My chest felt constricted and my stomach vacant.

"You know I like giving those bastards hell." He flashed a quick smile.

Trent had become quite a shield the last couple weeks. It embarrassed me I needed one, but the truth was I could only handle so much of the press before I became overwhelmed.

They weren't nice to me. Sometimes they weren't that nice to Trent and Drew either, so the fact that Trent took them on during times he didn't really have to in order to keep them away from me said a lot about what kind of man he was.

I grabbed Romeo's Alpha U hoodie and my bag from behind the counter. As I was pulling the well-loved garment over my head, I paused the briefest of seconds to close my eyes and exhale.

Sometimes all the alone time a girl got to center herself was inside her husband's hoodie.

When I was finished, I glanced back at Trent and offered a smile before digging the keys to my SUV out of my bag.

He appeared before me and gently took the keys, tossing them back in my bag. "I'll drive you home tonight. You can come back to get your car tomorrow."

"Think they're waiting on the main road?" I asked, shoulders slumping a little.

"Probably. But that's okay. I've picked up some tips on driving fast from Drew."

I snorted. "Like you needed tips."

Trent slung his arm across my shoulders and led us toward the exit. I sighed and leaned into him a little more than I should have. It had been a long day. Actually, not really. Just the last few minutes had been.

His arm tightened around me, but he didn't say anything. Trent was a really good listener. He heard a lot more than most people, even when they didn't say a word.

His Mustang was at the curb instead of in a parking spot. He ushered me into the passenger seat, shut the door, and moved around the front toward the driver's side.

Don't let it get to you, I told myself. *Replace the thoughts with something else.*

It was a mantra I'd come to rely on in the months after losing Evie. The press was white hot, and after a few run-ins that left me shaken and burned, I pretty much stayed behind the walls of our compound, never so grateful we had the wall to keep them out.

Even though they were still obsessed, the media wasn't quite as rabid, which up until tonight gave me hope they were finally moving on.

I guess I'd been fooling myself. With the start of the NFL season and Romeo back out on the field, we were still a hot topic. The media loved their headlines, and Romeo and I starred in them quite often. I didn't go online much anymore, and I didn't watch those gossip shows on TV. Mostly, I avoided it all. I liked it that way.

Sometimes it slipped in.

Like tonight.

My mantra worked pretty well for me most days. Right now? Not so much. It was hard to replace the thoughts of what I'd read with something else when the something else mirrored the headline.

Something I'd just read preyed on my deepest subconscious thoughts that tormented me most recently. It was like opening Pandora's box and letting out a demon.

My greatest fear was once a pool. While I still loathed any body of water, the top spot it once occupied was now held by something else.

My inability to conceive.

What if Evie was my only chance to give Romeo a baby?

What if whatever made me lose her would also prevent me from ever getting pregnant again?

Celebrity News

"Sexiest Quarterback of the Year: Roman Anderson!"
TopShelf Magazine

Chapter Three

ROMEO

The tension that had parked itself between my shoulder blades the second Trent texted last night finally eased when the gates to our compound came into view.

B was driving; we were in his cobalt-blue Ford F-150 Tuscany Shelby Cobra. Since we traveled so much, we alternated between whose car we left at the team's airstrip. This was a badass truck, and it came in handy having something so big, with so much hauling capability (especially when we moved), but I missed my Hellcat and itched to get behind the wheel.

"I've missed this place," B said, his words mirroring my thoughts.

I grunted in agreement as my eyes swept the area near the gate, making sure everything was as it should be.

We moved here right before Rim got pregnant. The place had taken a while to build. But the wait had been worth it. Our home—our family compound—was everything I envisioned it to be.

• • •

I'm not talking about what colors the walls were or the type of appliances in the kitchen. Not that those things didn't matter. Well, shit, they didn't. Not to me. But Ivy and Rim cared, so that meant they were important.

I was more concerned with safety, privacy, and the security of our family.

You might think with so many people living on the same property, it might have been hard to settle on something, but it wasn't. It hadn't been hard at all.

We all wanted the same things. The girls just wanted them to be prettier than the rest of us.

My father told me about some land up for sale on the edge of town, not quite as far out as the back roads where B and Ivy went to have sex in the bed of his truck or where Drew and Trent went to speed, but in that general direction.

It ended up being perfect for what we wanted. Twenty acres of grass and trees, plus some rolling hills. It probably would have made great farmland, but we weren't farmers.

I was just a man who wanted as much privacy and security as I could get for my family. Besides the fact Braeden was like a vicious bear when anyone looked at Nova, Drew and Trent needed a place they could be without having the press up their asses.

But that wasn't all.

Rimmel was my main priority. I wanted to know, when I was on the road for football, she would be protected. And maybe, just maybe, something whispered deep inside me that she and I were going to need a place like this.

I was kinda sorry to be right.

The entire property was surrounded by a six-foot stone wall. Not the fake-looking shit made to look like stone either. Legit stone from the earth. It was sturdy and stable. Made for a nice barrier.

It wasn't cheap. In fact, it was fucking expensive as hell. I didn't care. You couldn't put a price on piece of mind.

Because the stone wall was made of natural stone, it blended in with the landscape of the property. Trees and large bushes hung over it and grew in front of it. The workers who built it bitched a lot because I wouldn't let them cut down all the nature. It made for an interesting work environment. Whatever. They were getting paid.

If I wanted a bare-ass wall with nothing around it, I would have bought in an overpriced subdivision. Trees were added privacy. Besides, Rimmel liked them. She especially liked when they changed colors and dropped those colors all over the property.

The gate itself was thick, solid wood, stained a dark brown with black wrought-iron accents at the top. We made it like that on purpose. Again, it was more expense, but we wanted something the stalkerazzi couldn't stick their lenses through to take pics.

It was a double gate; on each side was a thick stone column, and on top were two large lanterns. Since it was late morning now, they weren't illuminated.

B pressed a button on the remote inside his car, and the gates swung open, slowly revealing the interior of the property. Once there was enough space, he drove in and hit the button again. The truck sat idle while we waited for the gates to close behind us.

The compound sat back away from the gate, deeper on the property, thus giving us even more privacy. The road that led to the houses was freshly paved with dark tar, and it wound gracefully through the thick, green grass and mature trees.

As we drove, leaves that littered the pavement flew up and twisted in the breeze, scattering out around and fluttering behind in our wake. When we finally crested the highest hill on the drive, the house came into full view.

Being a guy who'd always known money, nice shit wasn't something new to me.

But this place was on a different level.

Since it wasn't just my and Rim's house, but the entire family's, a lot went into it. We all pitched in money, too. With me, B, and Drew having high-income contracts for sports, add in Ivy's high-profile job with *People* and the revenue from her YouTube channel (Seriously, people made a lot of moneymaking videos... Who fucking knew?), and Trent's job with the NRR, cash wasn't exactly an issue.

The front exterior of the home was stone, just like the wall. It was a mix of earthy tones like light and dark browns with some gray and deep blue. Actually, it wasn't a home.

It was a mansion.

Rimmel would shit a brick if I ever called it that around her. My girl didn't want extravagance. That's probably what made our place even better. It wasn't ostentatious or overstated. It was just huge. But so very homey and comfortable.

The stone home was European inspired; that's what the builder said. The girls basically pointed to a picture and said that's what they liked. I didn't really know what made it European. It looked like a big stone house to me. It was a sprawling two-story with lots of white-framed windows and chimneys. The roofline was multi-pitched and seemed to go on forever.

The front door was a huge, rounded-top, double wood thing with monstrous iron handles. The eave over it was also rounded and rose high, which made room for a large chandelier to hang and illuminate overhead.

On the right side of the house was a six-car garage. It was attached to the structure by a breezeway with the same stone framing but with glass walls. It allowed the family to move from the garage into the house free of the elements while still enjoying the view.

The house itself had eight bedrooms and ten bathrooms. The place also featured a huge home gym (obviously) with a sauna, a home theatre, and a game room with two bowling lanes.

On our side of the house, Rimmel had a library and home office where she often worked on stuff for the shelter. I found her there a lot in front of the huge picture window, sitting in a chair that would fit likely ten of her, with apple cider, a blanket, and a book. The fireplace operated on gas and lit with a single flip of the switch, so it was always on.

She always looked so tiny yet so cuddly, lost in the cushions, with her black-framed glasses perched on her nose and her wild, dark hair in a mess from hunkering down in the chair.

Note: I'd never admit to calling her cuddly. That shit would get my man card revoked.

Rimmel's library had accents of yellow, though.

Yellow was her favorite color. It reminded her of her mother.

It reminded me of her.

• • •

There was a cold breeze in the air this morning, sort of like the day hadn't warmed up with the sun, and the small evergreens planted between each garage door and dotting the landscaping in front of the house all moved a little with the way it blew.

The garage door opened as we approached, and Braeden drove right inside. I didn't spare a second, instead vaulting out of the cab, leaving my bags in the back.

I did throw a glance at my shiny green Cat on the way past. Since I was in such a hurry, I almost missed the fact Rim's Range Rover wasn't in its normal spot.

Almost.

What the fuck? Worry pierced through the relief I felt to be home, and I began to question if maybe I should have called when the plane landed. I'd thought to surprise her when I walked in… but now it seemed I was the one getting the surprise.

I didn't like that shit.

What if something was wrong? What if something happened?

Where the fuck was she?

"What's wrong?" B asked, coming up behind me.

"Rim's car isn't here."

"Maybe Trent has it, doing an oil change or something."

His thought process was a lot calmer than mine. Bastard.

"Yeah, probably," I said, refusing to show my concern. With renewed determination, I strode toward the door.

I'd been hoping to get home earlier. I always liked to sneak in when she was in still in bed and I could slip between the covers and wake her up with my body. It was already late morning, though, so I knew she'd be up, but I still anticipated seeing her likely drowning in sweats.

The way her eyes lit up when she saw me still made me feel like the man.

I'd never get tired of the way Rim made me feel.

Please, God, just let her missing car be nothing.

Me and B moved through the breezeway quickly and to the door leading into the house. I flung it open into the large laundry/mud room and barely registered a glance at the large washing machines, dryers, and deep sink.

"Rim!" I bellowed as I moved across the light-colored tile.

I heard her make a small sound of surprise from out in the open kitchen and grinned to myself. *She's okay. Everything is okay.*

Movement in the doorway caused my steps to quicken, and I braced myself for her slight weight to be flung in my general direction.

But it wasn't Rim that launched at me first.

It was a dog.

A dog that was not Prada or Darcy.

Yes, we had two dogs now.

Braeden and I both faltered and looked at each other, then back at the dog who was standing there sniffing the air in our general direction like it was trying to decide if we were friend or foe.

"Did you know about this?" Braeden asked.

"Why would I know about it?" I countered.

He made a rude sound. "'Cause your woman drags home animals on a daily basis."

The dog in question started barking.

I rolled my eyes.

● ● ●

In a flurry of movement, Rimmel rushed through the door, Darcy right on her heels. Darcy took one look at me and leapt forward, rushing right past my wife and nearly taking her out.

Rim made a sound and pitched forward, knocked over by the dog and her gigantic sweatpants. Braeden and I both lunged forward. I beat him and swung her up as she fell into my arms.

"Hey, baby." I grinned down at her as chaos literally reigned around my feet.

It was a typical day at the compound.

She looked up at me through her dark-framed glasses and past her wild hair. "You're home!" she squeaked, breathless.

"Tell me you missed me," I demanded loud, over the dogs jumping and barking.

"I missed you." Her hands wrapped around my neck, and she pushed close into my chest. I inhaled her scent, and instantly, all was right in my world.

"Tutor girl, what the hell is this?" Braeden wondered, interrupting my moment of sniffing my wife.

I made a mental note to get back at him later.

She perked up away from me a little and glanced over at B, who was scowling at the strange, rather large dog taking up the doorway while it barked its head off and refused to allow him through.

"You best move out the way, beast," he told it. "I got places to be."

Rimmel laughed and patted my chest. Reluctantly, I stood her on her feet but caught one of her hands in mine.

"It's okay, boy," she told the dog, stepped forward, and held out her hand. "Easy. They're friends."

The dark stopped barking and looked at Rim. "Come here." She snapped her fingers. Instantly, the large dog trotted over to her and licked her fingers.

She giggled.

"Rimmel…" I partially sighed.

She glanced up, a little guilty.

Braeden cackled, leaned over, and kissed Rim on the temple. "Hey, sis." He pulled back, glanced up at me, and smirked as he motioned at the dog. "Have fun with that. I got a wife and baby to kiss."

He disappeared instantly and left me alone with the dogs and Rimmel. Speaking of dogs. Darcy was dancing impatiently around my feet, so I dropped down and held out my hands.

Darcy was a black-and-white Border Collie that Rim brought home from work not long after she had the miscarriage. The life in her eyes when she sat on the floor to play with him was all I needed to see.

When I asked her what his name was, she promptly announced Mr. Darcy after one of the dudes in the books she reads so much. I wasn't about to call any dog *Mr.,* so we settled on Darcy.

Murphy was a little put off, but other than that, Darcy fit right in, and just like that, there were two dogs and a one-eyed cat in this house. It wasn't like I didn't expect our animal count to grow. Hell, that was one of the reasons I bought twenty acres.

"Hey, buddy," I said and scratched him behind the ears. He licked me in the face a couple good ones, and I winced. I noticed one of his toys nearby, and I picked it up and threw it out the door, somewhere into the kitchen. He rushed after it, and I stood.

Rimmel shuffled from one foot to the other and gave me a smile. She was wearing my hoodie, the sleeves so long they covered her hands. The dog in question was at her side, staring at me like he still wasn't sure what to make of me.

I dropped back down and held out my hand.

He came forward tentatively and gave my fingers a sniff.

"How long's he been here?" I asked.

"Five days," she replied reluctantly.

I laughed. "And you never mentioned him?"

"Someone brought him into the shelter just before closing the other night. It was during that terrible thunderstorm we had. They'd found him in the middle of the road, soaking wet and scared." She began.

I glanced at the dog, knowing where this was going.

"He was so upset from the storm. I couldn't just lock up and leave him there. Poor thing." The empathy in her voice was so sincere. The dog wagged his tail. It's like even he knew he hit the jackpot the second she laid her eyes on him.

My girl… Sometimes I wondered how the hell her heart fit inside her chest.

"So I brought him home and cleaned him up. Poor thing was starved! It was only supposed to be that one night. But he never left my side the next day, not even at the shelter. He stayed with me no matter where I went. When I was packing up to leave that afternoon, he sat by the door and looked at me…" Her voice trailed off.

I rubbed my hand over my face and hid a smile.

"What's his name?" I didn't even bother hiding the acceptance in my voice. Like I'd deny her anything.

"Really?" she asked, her voice hopeful.

I chuckled. "Duh."

"Ralph."

I blinked. "What?"

"His name is Ralph."

I glanced at the dog. He'd come closer to me, and I was scratching behind his ear like I'd done with Darcy. I had no idea what kind of dog he was. Frankly, he wasn't all that attractive.

Wasn't all that attractive = ugly.

He was adorned with plain brown fur, some white speckles on his ass, one white leg and ears that looked a little big for his head. One of those big ears had a literal chunk missing from it. Like someone took a big ol' bite out of it. Oh, and his eyes were two different colors. Not a nice green and blue either. More like a poop-brown color for one and then a more diluted yellow shade for the other.

Frankly, it was a little creepy.

His looks just made it seem even more unfortunate she named him Ralph. I patted him on the head, and he wagged his tail. Someone had to help this dog. Rim was obviously too kindhearted to understand the least she could do for an ugly mutt like this was give him a badass name.

I straightened and looked at her. "What the hell kind of name is Ralph?"

Rimmel gasped and rushed to put her hands over the dog's floppy, half-chewed ears. "Roman Anderson!" she gasped. "He'll hear you!"

"Baby, I'm sure even he thinks that's a terrible name," I said, dry.

She gasped again. "He likes it!" she demanded. "Just watch!"

She turned toward the dog. "What's your name, boy?"

He gave a bark. It was quite the ear-splitting sound… and *yeah*. It totally sounded like he said Ralph.

God help me.

"See!" She insisted and pointed at the dog.

I rubbed a hand along my jaw, then the back of my neck. "Welcome to the family, Ralph," I said.

Rimmel squealed and launched herself at me. I caught her as her legs wrapped around my waist. That was the stuff.

"I love you," she said and peppered my face with kisses.

Ralph barked.

Seriously. How the fuck was I going to call this dog Ralph?

"He likes you!" She bounced against me. Down in my sweats, my cock tingled. I was horny as hell. Her crazy antics were just making me want her more.

"And just what would you have done if he attacked me when I walked in, Mrs. Anderson?" I asked as I carried her into the wide-open kitchen.

"Trent and Drew have extra space. I'd come visit you," she deadpanned.

I jerked to a stop and stared down at her incredulously. She tried to hide her smile, and I lifted a single eyebrow.

She laughed.

The sound of her laughter fell away when my lips latched onto hers. I swallowed down the sound as I kissed her deep. Her happiness was the best flavor I'd ever sampled. Her shape was the best thing my hands had ever touched.

Her arms wound around my neck, her small body pressed as near as possible, and we melted together as my tongue swept into her mouth and explored as if it hadn't been there for years rather than weeks.

Around us, both dogs clattered over the wooden floor, the scent of coffee permeated the air, and I supported my entire life in my arms.

It was damn good to be home.

Celebrity News

Gossip +++ Buzz +++ Social Media +++ Information +++ News +++

"Porn star sues over rear-end collision!"
#OhNoSheDidnt
CELEB PIPELINE

Chapter Four

RIMMEL

There was nothing like being kissed by Romeo.

Trying to explain what he did to me was like trying to describe just how big the universe really was.

It was impossible.

There was power in his kiss. The kind of power that left not one inch of me untouched. The unfiltered authority and hunger in his body reached deep, beckoning every last piece of me, no matter how small.

We weren't strangers to one another anymore. The years we'd shared made sure of that. Now my body knew him, understood exactly how to fit against chest, exactly how far to tilt back to allow him in the deepest. I relished the roughness of his tongue versus the silkiness of his lips and the low growling sounds he always made when we'd been apart awhile but were finally back together.

Romeo was never in a hurry when he kissed. He always took his fill of me, but never without giving everything he got. He only drew back when he sensed I was no longer really present. Instead, I was drowning in the depths of the tangled web he'd woven me in.

• • •

With immediate protest, my body followed his as he eased away. Even though his mouth didn't lower again, the arms around me tightened, bringing me even closer, causing extra friction at my center when it rubbed against his toned waist. My teeth bit into my lower lip, and he laughed beneath his breath.

Romeo knew the exact effect he had on me. I couldn't hide it if I tried (good thing I never tried).

He carried me through the kitchen, past the massive, muted-turquoise island and under the stone archway to the wide sliding glass doors that opened onto the deck. He whistled as he walked, and both dogs clambered along after him.

When they were outside and the brisk autumn air mingled with the warmer air around us, he moved swiftly, catching me off guard and shaking loose some of the after make-out haze I was still wrapped in.

My back hit the glass door, and I made a sound because even through the sweats, I felt the cool temperature of the glass. It woke me up, and despite the chill in the air, my blood began to simmer.

Romeo used his large, powerful body to pin me there, my legs still wound tight around his waist. Both his substantial hands flattened on the glass on either side of my head, and I shivered in anticipation. I liked being surrounded by him.

He always made me feel entirely shielded, and it was his protective streak that called to me on a wholly basic level. Maybe it was because I'd often felt weak in life; maybe it was because I'd always been so in control of how I lived… It didn't matter.

I loved it.

When I was with him like this, I didn't mind being small. I didn't even mind feeling a little weak. His protection, the way his large body hovered over mine in the most intimate and promising way, was addictive.

I sensed rather than saw his fingers flex against the glass, and my tongue glided out to wet my lips while his bright-blue eyes gazed at me as if they'd never seen me before.

"I don't like being away from you, Smalls," he said, gruff.

"You're here now," I whispered.

He pushed the glasses up off my face, over my head like a headband, then returned his hands to the glass. His hips thrust upward, and my body slid up the door. My hands moved to his shoulders, my fingertips digging in.

"I got you, baby," he vowed, leaning in to nuzzle my neck.

He must have thought I was gripping him for balance or worry I'd somehow end up on the floor. I wasn't. I was holding on because the sensation of the stiffest part of him teasing the softest part of me left me reeling.

Goose bumps prickled my scalp as Romeo's lips whispered over my neck. The full width of his tongue licked slowly beneath my ear, causing my head to fall back.

"Why are we still down here?" I half moaned.

"If we lived alone, I'd take you right here, right now," he replied, scraping his teeth over my earlobe. "I'd press your naked body against this wall of glass and leave behind not only our fingerprints, but smudges from every last part of you."

My lips vibrated. Images of what he just spoke of flashed behind my eyelids, so vibrant and vivid it was almost like a show of lights. The grip my thighs had on his waist went slack. I didn't stiffen or try to recover. There was no need. He took my weight with ease, pulling us back off the door and striding through the house to the stairs.

Up in our room, he kicked the door closed and once again pinned me against the wall. This time, my shirt was ripped away, and his lips fixed onto my breast with skin-searing warmth.

I sighed and gripped his head, pushing him closer as I arched into his ministrations and whispered for him to suck deeper. He did, and pleasant pain bloomed at my core; little twinges of desire jolted between my legs and sent shockwaves into my lower abs.

Eventually, he relinquished my flesh, and I sank toward the floor in a quivering mass of give-me-an-orgasm-now. I made it to my knees before recovering enough to hook my fingers in his waistband and relieve him of everything covering his lower half.

His cock jutted from his center, and I wrapped my hand around it as he groaned and kicked away his pants. He was hard and unbending beneath my palm, silky smooth and ready. I pumped the wide length, noting the way his balls drew up before I leaned forward and took him deep.

He murmured something as I sucked, and I pulled back only enough to lick across his head. My fingers dug into the sides of his hips, and I picked up the pace, driving my lips over his throbbing cock and enjoying the slightly salty flavor coating my tongue.

When he started to draw away, I released his quivering cock and pushed it up against his abdomen. My lips caressed the underside of his balls and licked up the interior of his thigh.

Seconds later, his hands slipped under my arms and lifted. In seconds, I was eye level with him, like it wasn't even work to hold me so high.

He searched my eyes, both his blue irises bouncing between my brown ones. Even though my vision was slightly blurred, I knew what he was searching for. I wanted to give it to him. I craved it.

Still, a part of me held back.

It wasn't a fun thing to be at war with oneself. It didn't matter who won, because a part of me would still lose.

"Rimmel?" he asked. It was a question I knew well now. One I hated, yet I loved him for it.

I swallowed, staring at my husband, so desperate to say yes but unable to form the word. Almost imperceptibly, I shook my head.

"I love you," he replied immediately. My feet hit the floor with gentle care, and one hand left me when he reached for the sweats he'd kicked off only moments before.

Always prepared.

That was Romeo, always ready to give me exactly what I needed.

What about his needs?

I felt myself slipping deep, away from him and this moment and into the prison of my own mind. I felt a tug on my hips and glanced up. Romeo was sitting in a nearby chair, the throw pillows already scattered at his feet.

I smiled because he was too impatient to go just a few feet more to the bed. His impatience brought me back to the moment. When I was completely naked, I straddled his bare thighs. I closed my palm over his head, giving it a light squeeze. His eyes flared, and he ripped open the foil packet he'd just fished out of his sweats with his teeth.

I watched Romeo roll the latex down over his cock, and a hint of sadness washed over me.

"Hey," he murmured, lifting my chin with the backs of his fingers. "I missed you so goddamn much."

I smiled at the husky quality to his words. My glasses were lost somewhere in my shirt, but I didn't have to see clearly to recognize the heavy spell my husband was under.

I might be a small girl, but right now, I wielded a lot of power. Even if there was a condom between us.

Slightly calloused hands settled on my hips as I slid down over his length with serious care. I liked this part, when he first entered me. Inch by inch, my body accepted him, stretching so my inner walls sheathed him with the perfect amount of pressure. Romeo's body went slack against the back of the chair, and I began to move. At first I slid up and down with slow, methodic movements, essentially teasing us both, but then I needed more.

With one swift movement, I sank all the way down, taking him as deep into my core as I could and holding him there. Romeo's palms moved to my thighs and squeezed. I rocked slightly.

My moan filled the room. I loved him this deep. I loved the way he felt rubbing against my inner walls, against that tender spot deep inside.

My forehead dropped to his shoulder, and I moaned again. With a jolt of energy, Romeo took over, surging up and rocking into that magic spot. All the muscles in my body tensed; I wanted release, searched for it.

"Romeo," I begged, climbing just a little closer against him.

He didn't say anything. He just tilted up a fraction more, and mind-numbing pleasure stole all thought and reason from my body. I shuddered over him, wave after wave of ecstasy poured through me, and his cock began pulsing. My name ripped from his lips, and his hands tangled in my hair.

We rode the waves together. When I began to come down, I continued gently rocking in his lap until Romeo fell back with a sigh. My cheek pillowed against his chest, both his arms locked around me, and I rested against him, listening to the sound of his erratic heartbeat.

I wished we could stay like this forever.

Of course, no moment, no matter how sweet or sour, lasted that long.

Tenderly, he lifted my body, and I made a sound of protest.

"I know, sweetheart. Hang on."

Instead of setting me aside, he adjusted and hugged me close for long moments, then pushed up out of the chair, taking me with him. On his way to the bathroom, I was deposited on the end of our luxurious bed. After pressing a kiss to my forehead, he disappeared into the other room to clean himself up.

Alone, my previous haunting thoughts returned. How ironic that I sat in the center of this beautiful room, during a beautiful moment of my beautiful life. I had more than I ever dreamed possible, more than I ever thought to ask for…

Yet still…

Still I sat here and wished for something I didn't have.

* * *

It seemed such a shameful waste. How much longer was I going to do this? How much longer would Romeo continue to ask what I wanted before he gave up completely and just stopped asking?

I thought I was getting better. Actually, getting better was a crappy way of putting it. I wasn't sick. I didn't have an illness like strep throat or an infection some pill would chase away.

What I had was a chronic condition for which there was no cure. A gaping hole where part of me used to be. I didn't want that hole to close up, because it was all I had left. So even though I tried to "move on," part of me still clung to that place, because the second I let go, I would have nothing.

So yeah, every single day, I put one foot in front of the other. I combed my hair (okay, not always), put on a smile, and dressed up my pain so no one else could see it.

What was that saying, though? One step forward, two steps back? Something like that. It seemed every time I felt a little stronger, there was always something there to challenge my strength.

I wanted to be strong. I *was* strong. I even wanted to move on.

There was a problem with moving on, though. In order to move on, you had to leave something behind.

How would I do that when that something was my *daughter?*

Romeo appeared in the doorway, and my heart squeezed. His blond hair needed a trim, which was the way it always seemed to look. I loved the way it curled up and stuck out a bit at his neck. His jaw was shadowed with light-colored stubble, as if he couldn't be bothered to shave, so that coupled with the unruly hair gave him a roguish air this morning.

The long length of his muscled body drew my eyes. Watching his muscles work beneath his skin was fascinating. Everything about him was fierce but graceful. A few years of playing pro football had only honed his physique, making him more confident in his own skin (as if he needed additional help with that!), and in some sense, he seemed more mature.

Age, even just a few years, looked so good on Romeo. It was almost unfair the way he became more of who he already was.

Before coming to my side of the room, he flipped on the double-sided fireplace in the corner of the room (you could also see it from the bathroom), and flames flickered to life. The wall of windows was uncovered; the view of our property stretched before us, and morning light spilled into the room. Multicolored leaves floated from the trees as the fall breeze blew, and the sky was crowded with clouds, which meant the sun wasn't blindingly bright.

Romeo started flinging pillows all over the room, and I sighed. "I just made the bed."

"You knew I was coming home," he pointed out like I should have known better.

I did.

I just liked watching him sling them around.

When all the throw pillows were gone, he flung back the covers and slid between them. His long arm reached out and grabbed the corner of a furry blanket draped across the foot of our bed and pulled.

Since I was sitting in the center of its softness, I went with it… right into his arms. Our bodies sank into the mattress. Cool sheets and blankets cocooned us together, and Romeo's muscular leg wedged between mine.

I lay on my back, staring up at him as he gazed down at me. We were pressed together, completely naked. His scent, masculine and clean, mingled around, so I inhaled deep.

"So what's new around here? You know, besides R?"

"R?" I puzzled, feeling my forehead wrinkle.

"I can't do it, Smalls." He shook his head sadly. "I can't call that poor dog Ralph."

I reached up and squeezed his nipple.

"Ow!" he said dramatically, even though I knew for a fact it didn't hurt.

"R is the name of a zombie," I told him.

"Well, Ralph is the name of a serial killer cab driver in Brooklyn."

I gasped. "It is not!"

His lips twitched. "I bet if I Googled it right now, I'd get a hit."

I couldn't help it. I laughed out loud. When my laughter died away, I noticed him watching me, his expression soft.

"What?" I prompted.

He twirled a finger in the length of my hair. "I love the sound of your laugh. I don't hear it enough."

A shard of pain pierced my chest. "Romeo…" I started softly, regret heavy in my tone.

"I saw the headline," he spoke before I could say whatever I was going to say.

I glanced away. Gentle pressure wrapped around my chin and pulled my face back. "I just want to make something clear."

I nodded.

"The only *big D* you're getting from me is my dick."

"Romeo!"

He wagged his eyebrows. "You like that? Maybe I should call the press and have them quote me."

Oh my goodness, he was in rare form today! I pressed my lips together and shook my head quickly. Laughing would only encourage him.

"That's one headline I'd like to read." He gazed off into the distance as if he were in fact imagining a full news article about the impressive size of his... ah... man parts.

A giggle burst from between my lips, and he glanced down. Another leaked out, and before I knew it, I was full-on laughing again.

"Tell me about football," I said when I could talk.

This was sort of our tradition when he came home from traveling for away games and training. He'd carry me upstairs, we'd go at each other like teenagers, and then we'd lie in bed and fill each other in on everything we missed.

Yeah, we talked every day when he was gone, but it wasn't the same. It wasn't the sound of his voice so close by or the expression of his features when he told me about something one of his teammates did.

I'd learned a lot about football this way, and I'd also learned all the team gossip. Who knew men talked so much in the locker room?

As he talked, I pressed my palm against his chest and took in everything about him. I'd seen him a thousand times; I knew every nuance of his face intimately. Even still, watching him was never boring. There was something about Romeo no one else had.

Some people might call it magic, and I supposed that could be true. To me, though, it was more. Not everyone believed in magic, but I'd never known anyone who didn't believe in him.

After a while, his stomach grumbled. "Someone's hungry." I noted.

He made a sound and pulled me closer into him.

"Coffee?" I suggested, sort of in compromise. Coffee I could do without leaving this room.

"Sounds good." He agreed, so I slipped out of bed. The cool air brushed over my bare skin, and I shivered.

My furry white slipper boots were on the floor, so I quickly shoved my feet in them before moving off the rug across the hardwood. We had a coffee bar built into our room, and I quickly put some on to brew.

As it did, I grabbed the shirt he'd been wearing when he got home and tugged it over my head, then dug around for my glasses.

My hair was pretty ridiculous, so I pulled it up into a sloppy bun without even looking in a mirror.

I'm sure it looked really fab.

After adding some flavored creamer from the mini fridge to our mugs, I carried them over to the bed where he was propped up against the headboard, watching me. He took both mugs while I climbed back into the bed and tucked my legs beneath me.

His shirt dipped off one shoulder, exposing a lot of my skin, but I didn't bother adjusting it. Instead, I wrapped both hands around my mug and smiled.

"Why didn't you tell me about the article?" he asked after taking a sip.

"If I told you about every headline or article written about us, that's all we'd ever talk about," I retorted mildly.

"It hurt you." The words ripped out like they'd cost a lot to utter.

"I know it shouldn't." I lowered the mug away from my face, toward my lap. It battered my already overburdened heart that something as trivial as gossip had the power to harm me.

His voice was gentler this time. "Who says?"

I faltered. *No one says. It's how I feel.* "There have been far worse stories written about us."

"I really thought they'd have moved the fuck on by now," he growled.

The first few weeks after Evie, the press was relentless. They camped outside the gates, at my job… at the hospital right after I lost her. Every headline that could be construed was. Gossip and rumors flew.

Some of the things they said cut deep, so deep I'd never even talked about it.

At first, it was hard not to look. Our phones were going off day and night; they were calling the house and our family. Romeo and I couldn't go anywhere together without practically tripping over anxious people vying for a shot that would make them a lot of money.

They called Romeo's parents, and one time they followed me into a grocery store. The flashing bulbs, unflattering pictures online, insensitive questions, and lingering stares became too much. How were we supposed to grieve when we were smooshed so tightly beneath a microscope?

A family meeting was called.

Romeo loved his family meetings.

Pretty much all sources of press were banned from this house (except *GearShark* of course). We all got new phone numbers, which no one gave out. All the volunteers and employees of the shelter were asked not to bring the stuff to work. I hadn't been to one pregame or practice for the Knights this season. I missed sitting in the stands and cheering.

Foolishly, I thought the press were backing off. I started to think it actually might be okay for me to go to some season games.

Then last night happened. It made me rethink sitting in the stands anytime soon.

I wasn't a football darling anymore.

Well, maybe I was. I was the darling they wanted to destroy.

And Romeo? He was my victim.

"I can't hide forever," I said, uncomfortable. "It's just making it worse."

Romeo paused, set his cup on the bedside table, then did the same with mine. His body turned so he was directly in front of me. "Who said you're hiding?"

I shrugged one shoulder. "Me."

"Rim, is that how you feel?" he asked.

I shrugged again. I did that a lot these days. It seemed easier to shrug off a question, the way I really felt, than to say the words out loud.

He waited, not accepting my signal, but not asking again.

I sighed. "I don't really feel like I'm *hiding*. You know I've never been one for the spotlight anyway. But it's sort of what I'm doing. The media is going to keep inventing stories about us the more secluded I stay. Maybe we should just do an interview, shut everyone up."

"No," Romeo said, flat, his mouth drawn into a thin line.

"Why?"

"The press has no right to our lives, Rim. They have no right to *you*. What we've been through is no one else's business. Making you relive that…" He stopped, and I noted the way his hand flexed in his lap.

I reached out and covered it with mine.

He exhaled.

"So we don't talk about Evie." My stomach dipped a little when I said her name. "Maybe we just make it clear we aren't getting a divorce. Satisfy their curiosity." Or maybe going to sit in the stands at a game, no matter how hard it would be, could portray a silent message. A sign of my support and love for my husband.

He barked a laugh that was not humorous. "You know damn well they'd never accept that. They'd say whatever to get us into the studio, then fucking assault you with questions about the baby, and…" His voice fell away. A low curse slipped from his lips, and his free hand rubbed over his hair, mussing the blond strands.

"And they'll ask me why I'm not pregnant again." I finished softly. Yes, it had only been three months. In the media world, three months was forever, and it must mean I was unable to conceive.

Deep down, I had those fears, too, even though we hadn't even started trying again.

"Fuck them!" he growled, chest heaving.

"Do you ever wonder?" I whispered, the words rushing out so fast I barely understood them.

Romeo stilled. Beneath my hand, his own jolted. "Rimmel."

I looked up, beckoned by the way he spoke my name. Surprised yet also sad.

Tears crowded my eyes. I blinked furiously, holding them at bay, silently screaming for them to stay where they were.

"I know why you aren't pregnant yet, sweetheart. I'm always present when we have sex," he replied with a half-smile.

I shoved his shoulder lightly. "I'm serious."

"I know." All traces of his attempt to help me chase away the tears vanished. "You're not ready." He tucked a stray strand of hair behind my ear. "And that's okay."

"Are you?" I glanced up, staring into his azure eyes.

"Not until you are."

He was sweet. Thoughtful. So caring.

Still, I couldn't help but feel he only said that because he thought it was the right thing to say. Deep down, I felt like Romeo was ready to try again.

But I wasn't.

And I didn't know if I would ever be.

Celebrity News

Romeo is HUNG!
His dick is legit.

·BROUGHT TO YOU BY·
ROMEO'S WISHFUL THINKING

Chapter Five

ROMEO

There was a barrier between us, and I wasn't talking about the condom.

Not that I really liked the condom.

Not really liking it = wanted to throw them in the trashcan and light them all on fire.

I'd grown way too accustomed to slipping into Rimmel bareback and feeling her silky heat envelop me. I missed it. I missed the friction of her skin on mine and the spontaneity of not having to wrap it.

Not that the sex still wasn't good. It was better than good. Sex with Rimmel would always be my vice. She would always be who my body craved.

The condom was just temporary anyway. After Evie, she didn't go back on the pill. It was unspoken that we would eventually try for another baby. But not right away. Her body needed time to recover. Both our hearts needed some time to mend.

I never really thought that three months later, I'd still be buying the latex in bulk, but I was, and there wasn't one damn word I'd say against it. She wasn't ready, not even for the possibility of becoming pregnant again. I heard the truth in the vulnerability of her voice when we were talking about the press.

I saw the war in her eyes before, when I asked her, as I always did, if the condom was still needed. She wanted to say no, but her heart wouldn't let her.

That was the barrier I meant.

It wasn't physical. It wasn't even tangible. Sometimes I thought I imagined it, but then there were other times, like today, when I saw the battle in her eyes or felt a great distance even when she was at my side.

There were times in the past when distance threatened to separate us. The reasons then and now might not be the same, but the result was. I didn't like it.

Oh, hells no.

I really wasn't sure what to do about it, though. This wasn't something I could fix. I could have a restraining order served, deck a guy in the face, or even just profess my love. Rim knew I loved her.

And I was learning sometimes love didn't fix everything.

In a way, what held us sort of separate was something we'd not faced together yet. Loss like Evie was permanent. It was irrevocable, and as I was coming to realize, it wasn't something that even truly healed.

Rimmel was taking it hard… maybe harder than I realized.

Harder than me.

The guilt of that might haunt me forever. It was also something that likely kept some space between us.

I missed my wife. I missed having our souls touch even when we were miles apart. I might not know how to fix everything, but I did know something.

I wasn't giving up.

Maybe what we needed was time together. Not talking about the press. Not worrying about condoms or even the detachment I knew we both felt.

We needed quality time. Low-key time. Time for me to remind her even though we'd lost something, we still had each other. Maybe once I saw the shadows in her eyes lose some of their darkness, the guilt gripping my chest wouldn't be so heavy. *Hopefully.*

I didn't have much time before B and I were off again. The season was already underway, and soon we'd be on the road way more than we'd be home. I'd just have to make the most of the time we did have and then, after that, all the moments in between.

After Rim and I ate plates of bacon, eggs, and fruit, I dumped all the dishes in the sink and snatched her around the waist before she could try to wash them or put them in the dishwasher.

"C'mon, let's go for a walk," I said against her ear.

"I need to clean up," she retorted, leaning back into my chest.

I nipped at her ear. "Later."

Since her back was to my chest and my arms were wrapped tight around her waist, when I started walking, she had no choice but to follow. We left the bright kitchen and walked into the mudroom, where there was a huge wall-length built-in bookcase-type thing. Except it didn't hold books.

It held shoes.

Why women needed so many damn shoes I'd never know. Hell, even Nova, and she could barely walk.

Leaning down, I scooped up Rim's favorite fur-lined boots and held them in front of us.

Rimmel grabbed them and stepped away so she could push her legs into them. Before we'd finally left the bedroom, she'd put on a pair of leggings that hugged her body and a long, oversized gray sweater.

Her hair was down, and I knew she brushed it because as she did, I'd heard her in the bathroom muttering to herself about it.

I slid on some sneakers and whistled for the dogs. Both of them came lumbering into the room like a pair of idiots. Rimmel laughed at their antics, so I supposed their idiotic behavior was worth something. I opened the door, and they rushed out into the garage before us.

"Where we walking to?" Rimmel asked.

I turned back as she was sliding a chunky knit cap over her head and ears. It was gray, just like her sweater.

I loved her. Everything about her. So much that sometimes it still caught me off guard.

Sometimes it still scared the hell out of me.

I shrugged. "Does it matter?"

"No," she said, her voice softening as if she'd read my thoughts.

There was a door at the back of the garage that led behind the house, past the huge deck, the massive play structure we'd had built for Nova, and the stone fire pit with benches.

The dogs barked and ran ahead with gusto, and the autumn breeze picked up strands of Rim's hair and fluttered it around her shoulders.

I walked a few paces in front of her and crouched down, offering her my back. "All aboard."

She laughed and flung herself onto my back. I straightened, hooking my arms beneath her knees, and set off across the property.

The sun was high in the sky, but the air was cool. It smelled crisp, like damp leaves and acorns.

"It'll be a good night for a bonfire," I told her.

"We haven't had one of those in a while."

"All the more reason to have one," I replied.

Her chin settled on my shoulder right next to my head. We walked (well, I walked; she rode) in silence a while, the crunching of leaves underfoot and the rowdy dogs barking in the distance the only sounds.

I could feel her heart beating steadily against my back. The rhythm calmed me in ways nothing else could. Not even football and bashing heads on the field.

Trent and Drew had their own house on the property. It wasn't as huge as the main house, but it was still big, with four bedrooms, and had the same look as our house. Beside it was a huge garage, and when we got close enough, I saw the doors were open. Seconds later, I saw them moving around the Fastback inside.

"Let's go tell them about the bonfire tonight," Rim said.

We set off in that direction.

I ducked under a tree, and Rimmel reached out and plucked a yellow leaf off a nearby branch. "I love fall," she said soft, holding the leaf out to study it.

I grabbed her hand and pulled it close to kiss it before tucking my hand back beneath her knee.

Trent saw us coming across the grass and stepped out of the garage and waved. Then he wiped his greasy hand down the side of his jeans, leaving a black trail.

Rimmel snorted. "That's never gonna wash out."

"You guys made it back," Trent called.

Drew heard him and came out from around the Fastback to stand beside him. Trent shifted automatically, angling just slightly closer to him. They didn't touch, but just the way they inclined their bodies when close said a lot.

They were happy, something that was fucking good to see. After everything that went down last spring and the way those two fought against their feelings, I honestly started to wonder if they'd ever surrender.

But they did.

Them becoming official locked this family into place.

Someone asked me once in an interview what I thought about having two gay men in my family. I told them I didn't even think about it. It was simply the truth. I didn't care my brothers were gay. I only cared they were happy.

Besides, bitches be tripping, and I didn't exactly relish the thought of those two bringing home two bitches I'd have to watch circle around my girl.

And yeah, bitches were exactly what they'd have brought home, because Trent and Drew were meant to be together, just as much as me and Rim. Anyone else would have been completely wrong and a choice made out of denial.

Trent was happier than I'd ever seen him in the past five years since we met. He wasn't as guarded anymore, at least not around us. It was like he finally stepped up and accepted the place he'd always had in this family.

He and Rim had grown closer, something I was grateful for. B would probably always be her number one big bro, but B was gone a lot with me. At least this way I knew she had someone at home she could go to if shit hit the fan and I wasn't around.

The changes in Trent were all thanks to Drew, who was the reigning champ of the NRR. We'd all been in the stands for the championship race. What a rush it had been to see him cross the finish line first.

It was right up there with the day B and I won our first Super Bowl.

"What's up, guys?" I asked, holding out my fist for a round of bumps.

Rim patted me on the shoulder, and I crouched down so she could jump off my back.

Drew reached out and mussed the hat covering her head. "There's my style sister," he cracked. Rimmel laughed and adjusted the hat on her head.

Drew was wearing the same style hat, except his was black and a little tighter on his head.

Trent rolled his eyes and smiled.

"People are already talking, saying the Knights are out to keep their champ status," Trent said.

I smiled. "Hells yeah."

"So what's going on?" Drew asked, wiping off a car part with the rag in his hand.

"Bonfire tonight," Rimmel said.

"Sweet. We should be back by then."

Trent tossed him a look over his shoulder. There wasn't much to it, but it had the muscles between my shoulder blades bunching. I couldn't help but feel like the off-hand comment was something Trent didn't want us to hear.

"Where you going?" Rim asked.

"Need some car parts," Drew replied easily. "Want me to get some marshmallows while we're out?"

"Like you even have to ask." Rimmel laughed. "Better get double because Braeden will eat half of them."

Darcy and R came bouncing over, and Rimmel laughed, dropping down to pet them both.

"What's going on?" I asked Trent, keeping my voice low.

He glanced over at Rim, then quickly back. "Nothing major."

He knew better than to say that shit to me. He made a sound, then walked a few paces farther from Rimmel, the dogs, and Drew. "The press is hanging around again. I chased them off the property at the shelter last night."

"You said they weren't there," I ground out low.

"They weren't, 'cause I showed them the door."

"Dirty bastards," I growled. "She didn't say anything to me."

"She didn't see them, so there was nothing to say. Her car is still at the shelter. I'll pick it up for you when we go out later."

Ah, that explained her missing car. I hadn't even asked her about it because it didn't really matter. All I cared about was she was home and safe.

"To get car parts," I said dubiously, not believing for one second they were actually going out for parts. Shit, their garage was practically an Auto Zone.

Trent's eyes held all the answer I needed.

"Where you going?" I asked, folding my arms over my chest.

"What are you two whispering about over there?" Rimmel called out, then started our way.

Trent's eyes cleared. "Later," he said, then shifted to smile at her. "We, uh, aren't really going out for car parts," he said, like he'd been caught.

I shifted back onto my heels, waiting to hear what he would say.

Rimmel's nose wrinkled. "Then where are you going?"

Trent blanched. "We, uh, forgot to pick up Nova's b-day present."

"You were supposed to do that days ago!" Rimmel scolded him.

She was cute when she admonished people.

"I know," Trent replied. "That's why I didn't want to say."

"Don't be telling Ivy, Rim," Drew pleaded, joining in. "You know she'll give me a lecture that lasts until the party starts tomorrow."

Tomorrow was Nova's one-year birthday party. Ivy had been planning it for a month.

Rimmel snorted. "Your secret's safe with me."

Trent tossed his arm around her and pulled her in for a quick hug. Over her head, our eyes connected.

Liar, liar pants on fire.

There's no way Drew hadn't already picked up Nova's birthday present. Hell, they'd probably already bought her half the damn store.

Trent's eyes promised to clarify later, and they also promised two other things:

1.) Obviously, it wasn't something he wanted to say in front of Rim.

And

2.) I probably wasn't going to like whatever the fuck it was.

Chapter Six

"Exclusive!
NRR studs caught on
camera in a rare PDA-filled
moment!"
-PMZ

RIMMEL

Boone's Farm was flowing.

Well, just into my and Ivy's glasses. All the guys were drinking beer because, you know, Boone's Farm was "lame" and "tasted like Kool-Aid."

But I saw Braeden sipping it out of Ivy's glass, and there was also the fact that he was the one who brought home the bottles.

Uh-huh, I had his number. It was 1-800-I'm-A-Big-Phony.

"Hey!" Ivy scolded, snatching back her glass and making the light-pink liquid slosh around. "Get your own!"

Braeden made a face and stuck out his tongue to wipe it off with the sleeve of his hoodie. "That shit is just as bad as I remember."

"I think you like it," I teased. "You just don't want to admit it."

"You wound me, tutor girl." He placed a hand over his heart and rounded his eyes. "That you could think so low of me..." His words trailed off with a dramatic sigh.

• • •

I rolled my eyes. "You're the one over there trying to steal it."

"Not steal," he admonished. "Just taking a sip of some memories." I watched him lean over Ivy and kiss her on the temple.

She smiled and leaned into his lips. Her perfectly polished hand came up to rub at the side of his jaw. "That was a good night."

"Yes, it was." He agreed quietly and kissed her again before pulling back.

Ivy smiled up at B. Her blond hair wasn't as long as it used to be. With her crazy schedule with her YouTube channel, her column with *People,* and being an amazing mom to Nova, she announced one day she didn't have time for all her long, thick hair, so she chopped it off.

In a very fashionable way, of course. Ivy didn't do anything unless it was fashionable.

Now she wore it as a long, graduated bob. It was shorter in the back but then grew longer in the front. The front section still reached past her collarbone, so I considered it pretty long, but it was shorter than she used to wear it. The strands were still blond and shiny. Sometimes she wore it blown out and sleek, which really showed off the steep angle of the cut. Other times, like tonight, she added some texture and wave with a curling wand and some kind of salt spray.

Beside her on the bench was a cordless baby monitor. Through the speaker, Nova made a sound, and Ivy cocked her head to the side to listen. Nova made another sound, a short cry, and Ivy stood.

Braeden put a hand on her shoulder and gently pushed her back down. "I got this."

Ivy shuffled on her feet, as if she were considering just moving past him. B made a sound. "You've been doing it for weeks while I was gone. It's my turn."

Her blue eyes softened, and she smiled. He handed her his longneck and strode across the deck and into the house.

Braeden was an incredible dad. Probably the best I'd ever seen.

Romeo would be even better.

The thought stung, and I took a sip of the blue liquid that really shouldn't even be considered alcohol. I had to agree with my BBFL; this stuff was terrible.

Or maybe it just tasted that way because of the feelings suddenly worming around deep inside me.

Ivy sank back onto the bench, trading his beer for her wine glass. "Earth to Rimmel," she said, taking a sip.

I glanced up, shoved the empty feeling down deep, and smiled. "Good night for a bonfire."

"Sure is." She tucked one jean-clad leg beneath the other. She was dressed perfectly in a pair of dark skinny jeans and a silky, loose, wine-colored long-sleeved shirt. Expertly draped around her neck was a cream-colored, cable-knit scarf, which paired perfectly with the thick, knee-high, cable-knit socks on her feet. The sides of the thick socks were lined with round, wooden buttons.

"So where are you?" She rested her chin in her partially sleeve-covered hand, even in the nighttime lighting and with the fire sparking with orange and red flames, I felt her clear, blue gaze settle on me.

I laughed lightly and held up the glass filled with Blue Hawaiian Boone's Farm. I admit I picked it because it was blue. It reminded me of Smurf Balls.

• • •

"I'm over here thinking Braeden was right. This wine—and I use the term loosely—is lousy."

"You're totally right." Ivy grimaced and abandoned her glass.

I did the same, and we both giggled.

"You ready for tomorrow?" I asked, thinking ahead to my niece's first birthday party.

"No… I can't believe it's been a year," she mused.

Before I could reply, the lights on the baby monitor lit up and sounds came through. Nova started fussing again, but almost as fast, Braeden's voice cut through her cries. "Now don't be doing that, Critter. Your momma's gonna come up here and accuse me of not knowing how to handle ya."

Ivy made a rude sound, and I snorted.

Nova's cries stopped, and I heard his faint footfalls moving across the room. She made a sound I recognized as the same one she always made when she held up her arms to be picked up.

"Da-dadadadada," she part cried, part babbled.

"All right now," he said soft, and I imagined him reaching into her crib to pull her into his arms. "Tell Daddy what's going on."

Of course the baby said nothing.

"Gonna make me guess? You women are all the same. Always wanting us men to read your minds," he muttered, but affection was heavy in his voice.

It was a little heart-melting for such a big, rough, and sometimes hotheaded man to turn into such a big ball of mush when faced with a little dark-haired girl.

"I'm just gonna get right to the daddy duties. C'mon, then. You can help." He went on. "Let's check the closet first." The sound of a door opening and closing came through.

I glanced across to Ivy. Her head was turned toward the monitor as she listened to her husband and daughter, her eyes soft and her lips pulled into a small smile.

Oblivious to the fact we were listening to his entire interaction with Nova, B continued. "Nothing in there. Let's look under the bed." He made a grunting sound as they looked under the bed and then a few corners of the room.

As I listened to the entirely adorable moment, my stomach started to feel a little heavy. I fidgeted on the bench, tucking both legs beneath me tightly so I was sitting Indian style.

"All clear," he announced. "Nothing in here to be upset about, baby. C'mon. Back to sleep with you. Tomorrow's a big day."

I imagined him nudging her head down onto his shoulder as he rubbed her back with a hand that was so much bigger than her. The sounds over the monitor went quiet except for the slight rocking of the chair near her crib.

I cleared my throat and unfolded my legs, about to stand. Suddenly, sitting still was just too hard.

Ivy reached out and clicked off the monitor, the lights on the front went dark, and the faint hum of static ceased. "Rimmel, I—" She began, and I got to my feet.

Romeo appeared soundlessly (how can someone so big be soundless?). I almost ran right into him as I fled. "Ladies," he said, flashing his famous charming smile. Not far behind were Trent and Drew.

They were holding hands.

A simple act that really wasn't that simple for them. It took a long time for my two brothers to be comfortable touching each other in any way when any of our family was around. They did it more often now, and it made me feel proud.

Proud because, clearly, the family we all built together was strong enough for them to finally be themselves without worry. Simply seeing them hand in hand seemed to bring me back to the moment. The cool fall air, the crackling fire, and the scent of burning wood.

"Brought you something," Romeo said. I loved his voice. So familiar, yet it still affected me like it was brand new.

There was a mug in his hand. Against the night backdrop, I could see the puffs of steam curling up from the liquid inside. Cinnamon and spice tickled my nose, and a feeling of utter calm washed over me.

"You brought me apple cider?" I asked, reaching for the white mug.

"You hated the Boone's, didn't you?" he mused.

I snorted and pushed my glasses up my nose. "How'd you know?"

The warmth from the cup seeped into my fingers, making me realize how chilled they were. I lifted the drink, inhaled the scent, and let the heat brush under my nose.

"You're not a Boone's kinda girl, Smalls. You're a cider kind."

He was totally right.

"Well, don't tell Braeden. He'll never let me live it down," I muttered, sipping the drink.

Romeo caught one of my hands and tugged me along, back toward the bench, but then we bypassed it to walk around the fire to a large wooden Adirondack chair. His big body filled it completely, and he tugged me into his lap.

I tucked in close, hugging the mug into my chest and closing my eyes for a brief moment when the back of my head cradled against his shoulder.

Trent sat where I'd just been, and Drew tossed some more wood onto the fire before sitting right beside him.

A moment later, Braeden came out of the house and across the deck. Ivy glanced around at him. "All's good," he assured her and straddled the bench she was on. Quickly, Ivy turned the monitor back on.

I gazed up into the inky sky at the stars marring the otherwise dark canvas. Romeo's arm slipped around my waist, holding me just a little closer.

The sound of a phone going off pulled my eyes from the view. Ivy lifted up her smartphone, the illuminated screen casting a bright light over her features as she glanced down at it.

Remember how I said Romeo passed down a media ban on the house? Ivy's phone was the exception. It was part of her job to stay in the know on all the celebrity news, etc.

"Really, princess?" Romeo asked, lifting his beer. "Can't take a break for one night?"

"I thought I silenced this thing," Ivy grumbled, but then her attention was caught on whatever she saw.

She glanced across the fire pit at Drew. His mouth flattened, and the air around him shifted.

"What is it?" I asked.

"Apparently, our two studly brothers were caught in some PDA today," Ivy dished.

Behind my glasses, my eyes lifted. "What?" I glanced over at Trent and Drew.

"Fucking gossip hounds," Drew spat.

"What happened?" Ivy asked, darkening her screen, then setting the phone facedown beside her.

"Nothing," Trent replied. "We were out. The press was lurking and got a shot of us kissing."

"Did you at least give it a little tongue?" B cracked.

Ivy elbowed him in the side.

"Ow!" he hollered.

"Idiot," she muttered.

"This just happen?" Romeo asked.

Trent nodded. "While we were out getting marshmallows."

Mmm, roasted marshmallows.

"I'm sorry," I told them. Why couldn't the press just leave us all alone?

Underneath me, Romeo seemed tense, a direct contrast to how he felt just a moment ago. I lifted my chin to gaze up at him.

His face turned down, his lips brushing over mine lightly. I couldn't help but feel like he was offering me comfort.

It worked.

"It's not a big deal," Trent said. "Not the first time they caught us. Won't be the last." He seemed a lot less annoyed about it than I would have expected. In fact, Trent had a hate-hate relationship with any stranger with a camera these days.

I couldn't even say I blamed him.

"How about those marshmallows?" I asked, wanting to change the subject and get back to what tonight was supposed to be about: family time, relaxation, and fun.

"I left 'em on the kitchen counter," Trent replied.

I hopped up from Romeo's lap and brought my cider with me. "I'll see if we have everything for s'mores while I'm in there."

"I'll help." Ivy jumped up.

As we walked toward the house, I heard the rumble of Romeo's voice. I couldn't make out what he was saying, his voice so low and kind of quick.

I didn't really need to hear his words, though, to understand something. Romeo wasn't too happy with the newest headline, which I admit wasn't a surprise at all.

What was a surprise was the way my intuition whispered there might be something more to this, and judging by his tone, I wasn't the only one who felt that way.

"Fisherman arrested for using wife as shark bait!"
#SheBurnedHisDinner
STUPID CRIMINALS

Chapter Seven

ROMEO

Something stunk.

And it sure as hell wasn't me.

The stank of information I didn't know but needed to had clogged the inside of my nose ever since I saw Trent in front of his garage.

It was all I could do to wait to hear it and not demand instantly to be in the know. The only thing that held me back—the only thing that always seemed to anchor me in a place of patience—was Rim.

She came first, and judging by the way Trent acted earlier, I was afraid whatever this was would likely hurt her.

I watched her small, perky ass disappear into the house, along with my sister, and decided there would be no more waiting.

"What the fuck is going on?" I asked, sitting forward, elbows on my knees.

The sound of Braeden's beer bottle hitting the bench seemed to punctuate my demand. "What?"

Trent and Drew glanced at each other, and I growled. My patience was used up. Rim would be back any second, so he needed to spit it out.

"I chased the press off the shelter property last night," Trent said to B, then looked at me.

"Vultures," Braeden muttered. "How the hell did you clear 'em out?"

"I made a deal. Offered them something they couldn't turn down."

"Such as?" I pressed.

"Exclusive guaranteed photos of me and Drew."

"Man-love PDA," Braeden mused, tipping his bottle against his lips.

I stood and paced in front of the fire. "You threw yourself at the press to protect Rimmel?"

"It's not that big of a deal," Trent replied. Beside him, Drew didn't seem so convinced.

I let a few choice words fly. It *was* a big deal. Trent and Drew hated being put on display in front of the world. The bigots and haters never shut up, and quite frankly, it put targets on their backs every time they were seen out together touching, even in the most innocent ways.

Trent was a private guy; he was very protective. Experience had taught him to be extremely cautious about who he let into his life, who he showed his true self.

I locked eyes with Drew. "Was it bad?" He'd be a little more blunt about what the camera-wielding devils were like today.

"It was worth it," he replied.

"That's not a fucking answer."

Sensing my agitation, B stood. "How much did you give them?"

Trent shook his head once. "Not much. A kiss, some hand holding. I told them where to be today and what time. They were there. We performed, then got in the car and sped home."

"Why the fuck did you show up?" B asked. "You could have blown them off."

"Because next time it wouldn't have worked. They would have just come at Rimmel harder."

"What else happened?" I asked, sensing there was more. Rim was followed a lot. The press was already outright brutal, so if Trent was worried they were about to get worse, there was a reason.

He scrubbed a hand over his face.

"I got a call," Drew said. "I was offered a lot of money to spill some family secrets."

My body stilled. "What?" I growled.

"They mostly wanted dirt on you and Rim. They asked about Rim's past, her miscarriage..." Drew went on.

The edges of my vision started to go a little dark. Rage was like a black cloud, rolling in with a massive storm, threatening to consume me.

They had no right. No right to Rimmel and her private pain.

"Obviously we told them to go fuck themselves." Trent spoke up. Maybe he sensed I was about to blow. "No amount of money would make us turn on family."

"Christ." I fumed and dropped back into the seat. I drained about half my beer in one swallow, then finished the rest.

"How much?" B asked.

Drew hesitated, then replied. "Two million."

I shot up again. Two million dollars! That wasn't just a bribe for family secrets. That was a goddamn bounty.

They put a bounty on my wife.

Hells no.

"Not long after the call, the newest divorce headline was up, and the wolves were camped out when I pulled up to escort her out of work." Trent went on. "I figured they might be extra vicious if any of them knew how much any kind of dirt was worth, so I shooed them the fuck out."

"I'm surprised they went," I muttered. Trent and Drew were a good front page story, but pics of two dudes kissing weren't worth two mil.

"Some of them needed a little extra convincing," Trent intoned and cracked his knuckles.

Drew made a sound and drank more beer. I knew by the look on his face he wasn't happy. Trent basically inserted himself between my wife and the press. He'd been through a lot, and the last thing he needed was to get into a fight with a pack of money-hungry assholes and take them on by himself.

Even knowing all that, I couldn't feel sorry.

I pushed out of the chair, stepped up to Trent, and stuck out my hand. He glanced between me and my palm. A heartbeat went by before he stood, placing his palm in mine.

"Thank you," I said, shaking his hand. "I'm sorry you had to do it, but I'm grateful. Rim just… She's…" I hesitated to call her fragile, even though, to me, she was.

She'd hate it. And really, she wasn't weak. Rimmel was the strongest woman I knew. Maybe that's why she was fragile in my eyes. I know. It was a complete juxtaposition. Sometimes Rimmel was too strong; she was so strong it made me fear she might shatter at any moment. Especially if she was hit in just the right spot.

"I know." Understanding laced his tone.

I offered my hand to Drew, and he accepted it. We locked eyes, and I apologized for the position he and Trent had been in. He nodded once as if to say he understood.

Across the deck, Rimmel stuck her head out the door, marshmallows piled in her hands. "Anyone need a beer?" she called out.

"Yes!" all of us answered at once.

She laughed and disappeared back inside.

My gut clenched. "I'll call tomorrow and put a bodyguard on her."

B made a whistling sound. "That didn't go over too well last time."

That was an understatement. She was so opposed to it I called it off. Not this time. I wasn't taking any chances with her safety.

"Two million dollars is way too much motivation for dirt," I replied. I glanced at Drew. "Do you think that offer was just on the table for you because you're family, because you're close to us?"

Drew shrugged. "Could be. But I wouldn't bank on it. If it was good enough, they'd probably write anyone a check."

Braeden made a rude sound. "Rim's so innocent. There ain't even anything in her background worth two mil."

The second the words were out of his mouth, we looked at each other. I actually felt some of the blood drain from my face.

"You don't think…" B whispered.

We stared at each other, both reliving the nightmare in Florida when I basically got shot trying to clean up the mess Rim's father made, all for the sake of money.

"What?" Trent demanded.

I swallowed and shook my head once. "He's clean, hasn't been gambling. Hell, he's barely out of rehab."

"Rimmel's father?" Trent said, thoughtful. "You really think he'd sell a story for a payday?"

"As long as he isn't in debt up to his ears or thinking about his next score, no," I said.

"Time to check in on Daddy Dearest," B quipped as the girls stepped out of the house with their arms full of supplies.

"I'll make a call," I vowed, then glanced at Trent and Drew. "Thanks for the heads-up and for not spilling it all in front of Rim."

"We're family," Trent replied.

I knew I was going to have to make my girl aware of what was going on, but not tonight. Hell, not even tomorrow. These next few days were ours, and I was going to safeguard that like no other.

"Who wants s'mores?" she called, joining us by the fire and dropping all the ingredients on a long, stone counter just outside the circle.

I caught her around the waist from behind and lifted her off her toes. "I got all the sugar I need right here," I growled and attacked the side of her neck.

She made a squealing sound but didn't try to get away. My girl knew better than that. She wouldn't have gotten very far if she had.

Laughing, she turned her face so I could lock our lips together. Her tongue tasted like cinnamon and clove. Mine likely tasted like beer.

Braeden cleared his throat loudly. "That's shit brothers don't need to be seeing."

Rim kissed me softly one last time before pulling back just a little. "I want it browned. Not burned," she informed me.

"What am I, your slave?" I joked.

Her nose wrinkled. "You roast better marshmallows than me."

"You better do it, Rome. We still have a burned patch in the deck from the last time she tried to roast her own." Braeden cracked.

He was a wiseass. I grinned widely because he was a funny wiseass. I'd never forget the look on my wife's face when her marshmallow damn near exploded in flames. Frantically, she tried to put it out but ended up flinging the thing through the air, where it landed in a still-blazing, messy heap just behind where I was sitting.

Rim grimaced. "He's right."

I threw back my head and laughed before leaning in to press a kiss to the tip of her nose. "One perfectly browned, not burned marshmallow coming up."

"Gooey on the inside," she added with a faint smile.

"Whatever you want, baby," I whispered, kissing her again.

I spent the rest of the night feeding her sugar, holding her close, and kissing her lips every chance I got. Inside, I still churned from the information Trent and Drew delivered, but I flat out refused to let it show. I knew I did a damn good job of keeping it under wraps by the happiness in Rim's brown eyes and the languid way her body melded into mine.

There wasn't anything I could do tonight about the bounty put out on our lives, so it was just going to have to wait.

Celebrity News

Gossip +++ Buzz +++ Social Media Frenzy +++ Information +++ News

"Daddy's little girl turns 1! A look back on the first year of Nova Walker's life."

—CELEB FAMILY

Chapter Eight

RIMMEL

Today was a big day.

An exciting, happy day. Yet I didn't feel those things. Instead, I stood in my grand walk-in closet, with its giant marble-topped island and beautiful antique lantern overhead, and felt a restless sort of energy coursing through my limbs.

I tried to ignore it. I told myself I was just excited and anxious to celebrate the first birthday of my only niece. It kept me moving. I went through my two racks of clothes and ruffled through my drawers several times.

I didn't really see the clothes, though. Even though I told myself I was looking to put an outfit together and pulling out things that matched, I wasn't. It was an excuse. An excuse to feel normal. An excuse to pretend I wasn't feeling out of sorts and almost frightened.

I didn't like this feeling. It wasn't the first time I'd known it the past few months. Each time my limbs started to tingle and my stomach jittered, my gut whispered. I closed my ears to the whispers, though, and pushed on.

My heart pounded a little too fast and too hard, and my mouth was a little too dry.

Anxiety.

Stress.

Panic.

I knew what these things were, but I shunned them. I told myself I was way stronger than something so filled with trickery. It was as if my body and mind were rebelling against what I knew to be true. The feeling of sickness coating my innards wasn't really real. It was what my mind was doing to my body.

I hated it. I rebelled against it.

Unfortunately, it only made the way I felt worse. Like a vicious cycle, the more I ignored it, the more those feelings insisted they be known.

I dropped down on a nearby tufted bench and sipped at the coffee I'd carried in here from the coffee bar in the kitchen. Trying to pick out an outfit was almost hopeless. Most definitely exasperating. If Ivy wasn't already so busy with party prep, I'd go beg her to pick something for me.

I was tired, but I knew my lagging only stemmed from the feelings attempting to consume me. I took a deep breath, exhaled, then pushed to my feet.

What I wore really didn't matter. It certainly didn't require so much thought and effort. I snorted to myself because it was practically ridiculous I was even standing in here stressing about my outfit.

It isn't your outfit you're worrying about.

Abandoning my coffee to the white marble top, I plucked out a pair of distressed, light-colored, straight-legged jeans and tugged them on. Next, I grabbed a white and black stripped, long-sleeved top that felt really soft and comfortable (which were my two favorite things). Once it was on, I realized how loose it was and mentally groaned. Romeo's parents would be here today. Ivy's mom and Braeden's mom.

I didn't want to look like I didn't bother at all.

But I didn't want to change either.

Blowing out a breath, I grabbed a yellow lace bralette and pulled it on over the bra I was currently wearing but beneath the T-shirt. Frankly, the fact I managed that without falling over should have earned me a gold medal.

Once that was done, I glanced back up, grabbed a handful of the hem at one of my hips, and tied it into a knot. I stepped back to look at my attempt in the large floor mirror leaning against the wall.

Good enough.

It was super casual, but this was a one-year-old's birthday party. It wasn't a night at the Met. The knot made the shirt not so loose, and the lacey yellow strap from the bralette that showed at my shoulder was a nice accent.

At least I hoped it was.

I shoved my feet into a pair of white Converse and left the closet with my coffee. At the counter in the bathroom, I traded the caffeine for a hairbrush and studied the haystack on my head. Just the thought of trying to comb it out overwhelmed me.

I noticed again the pounding of my heart and the slight tremor in my fingers.

I wanted Romeo.

I was being silly. Stupid even. I didn't need his arms right now or the comfort of his presence. I was in my own home, wearing my own clothes, and I had nowhere I had to go today outside the walls of the compound. It was a family day. I loved family days.

Romeo was already downstairs, helping Braeden set up a bounce house in the backyard. I smiled to myself because I was sure it was quite a spectacle, and I knew I should hurry to go down to see it.

Since trying to brush out all the knots in my bird's nest wasn't in the cards, I decided instead to comb it up and secure it into a messy knot on top of my head.

Ta-da! #Fancy.

Darcy and Ralph were lying on the foot of our bed, and when I stepped out, both their tails wagged. A little of the restlessness I felt went away when I looked at them. I paused to scratch behind both their ears, then called to them as I left the room.

Both dogs followed along behind me like shadows as we trodded downstairs. In the kitchen, Ivy was issuing orders to Drew and Trent.

"Don't hang it like that! My God, think of the pictures!" She gasped.

I stopped and watched them with full-on amusement from beneath the stone archway that separated the kitchen from the great room.

"Your niece is going to look back on this day, not to mention the freshly painted walls—"

"Rimmel! Save us!" Drew interrupted Ivy when he saw me lurking.

Ivy made a sound and spun. "Thank God! A voice of reason! Just look. He's trying to staple the banner to the ceiling. *Staple!*"

I giggled and looked up at Drew, who was indeed standing on a chair with a stapler in his hand.

"A stapler might not be the best way to go," I told him with a wide smile.

"Little traitor," he muttered.

"We're outnumbered," Trent told Drew.

"We can take 'em," Drew intoned.

From her highchair, Nova squealed and fed all the food on her tray to the three dogs who sat patiently at her feet.

"This place is a zoo," Ivy muttered.

I laughed and went over to a nearby junk drawer, pulled out some Scotch tape, and carried it over to Drew. "Here, don't use half the roll. It should come off okay later."

I stepped over to Ivy, who looked flustered and gorgeous all at the same time. Her blond hair was straight this morning, her makeup glowing and natural, and she was wearing a T-shirt-style dress made in dark-blue lace. On her feet were a pair of dark-brown suede, knee-high boots with no heel.

"Have you had any time to breathe this morning?" I asked.

"In between issuing orders!" Drew cracked.

"Andrew Wayne!" Ivy snapped.

Trent guffawed.

"Not funny, frat boy," Drew growled at him.

"Get some coffee. Relax a few," I told her, giving her a gentle push toward the coffeemaker.

Nova had cleared her tray of food, and the dogs were looking mighty satisfied.

"Did any of that make it into your belly before you shared it all with the puppies?" I asked her.

She smiled and held up her arms.

I lifted the baby out of her seat and cuddled her close for a long moment. She laid her head against my shoulder, and I rubbed a hand over the soft strands of her thick, dark hair.

My stomach dipped, but I ignored it. "Let's give Mommy a break," I told her when she pulled back and looked at me.

As usual, she reached for my glasses. I evaded the move by taking her hand and pressing a kiss to it. She smelled like Cheerios.

Nova looked a lot like Braeden, with lots of dark hair and the same shape face. Her eyes were all Ivy, though, round and blue. She was a happy baby, always ready with a smile, and she liked to climb in your lap when you read.

At my feet, Prada stood staring up, waiting to see where I would go with her favorite friend. Because Prada was still pretty young when Nova was born, the pair sort of grew up together. I was surprised at how tolerant the Chihuahua was of the baby, especially when Nova would tug on her ears and tail.

"Done," Trent announced as he and Drew stepped down from the chairs. We all turned to look at the colorful, giant Happy Birthday banner stretching across the room.

"Looks good, guys. Thank you," Ivy said.

"Anything for my favorite girl," Drew said, poking Nova in the belly lightly.

She laughed very enthusiastically and looked at him expectantly. Drew obliged and tickled her again.

She was still laughing when Drew turned to Ivy. "Can we go change now, before Mom gets here?"

She waved them off. "Yes. Thanks for helping me in here. I appreciate it."

Both guys saluted her, then went to the door.

"Don't come back here in sweats!" Ivy yelled after them.

I grimaced. I wasn't in sweats, but I wasn't wearing a dress, either. "Should I change?" I asked.

Ivy laughed. "No. You look great! I just like to give him hell."

Murphy sauntered in the kitchen, stopped in the doorway and stared at the three dogs, and flicked his tail. I went to the sliding doors and shooed all the pups outside.

"Want to help me feed the kitty?" I asked Nova, carrying her along with me.

She pointed at Murphy and nodded. I moved around, getting out his plate and a fresh can of food. I sat Nova on the counter, making sure I stood directly in front of her so she wouldn't fall, and popped open the top of the can.

Nova lifted the spoon and was swinging it around, about to put it in her mouth.

"Here," I told her and showed her the food. "Put some of this on the plate."

Nova looked between me and the food, then dipped in the spoon. Of course she didn't really scoop up the food, just got the spoon messy, then touched it onto the plate.

"Good job!" I praised her. "Murphy's gonna love this." As I spoke, I wrapped my hand around hers and the spoon and scooped out the food onto the plate. Every so often, she would glance up at me as we worked, and the weight of her innocent blue eyes seemed a little heavier than usual.

"All done," I said and set aside the can and spoon.

Nova made some sounds and held out her arms. I lifted her, and we put the plate on the floor for Murphy, who was already at my feet and purring as loud as a lawn mower.

Nova clapped when he started eating. "He likes it!" I told her and patted her belly. Nova wiggled to get down, so I stood her on her feet but held her hands to steady her.

She wasn't quite walking yet. She was close, but we'd yet to see her first independent steps.

"Rimmel," Ivy said, and my heart sank. I just knew from the sound of her voice and the way she watched me with Nova this was coming.

I wished I could deny it or fake it. I'd already been trying to hide it. Clearly, I failed.

"Yeah?" I said a little brighter than I felt.

"Today is hard for you, isn't it?" She went right for it. I admired that. At least this way the conversation would be faster.

"Is it that obvious?" I asked, soft.

She smiled sadly. "Not really. It just seemed like last night you were a little lost in thought, and with the party today…"

"Some days are just a little harder than others, you know?"

Ivy nodded, a remorseful look crossing her features. I didn't want that. I didn't want her to feel like she couldn't celebrate her daughter just because I'd lost mine.

"Today is Nova's day," I told her confidently. "A happy day. We shouldn't let anything put a dark cloud over it."

"You know I'm always here if you want to talk, right? No matter what," she told me, and I nodded, unable to speak.

Ivy nodded once, then straightened away from the counter and held her arms out to Nova. "Why don't we go see if Daddy and Uncle Romeo got the bounce house up without killing each other?"

Nova stepped toward her mother, and I helped steady her as she walked over.

A buzzing sound cut through the kitchen, and Ivy glanced up. "Someone's at the gate." I was about to offer to buzz them through, but she was already moving to the corner of the kitchen where the house "control panel" was.

The panel consisted of a large monitor that allowed us to view various positions around the property thanks to cameras. There was also a tablet where everything from music to locks were controlled by a few taps on the screen. One of those taps had the ability to open the gate and allow in visitors.

"Oh, it's my mom," Ivy chirped and pressed the button to open the gate. It was on a timer and would swing closed after a few seconds passed to allow the car to drive in.

"Grandma's here!" Ivy told Nova.

Nova grinned and started to sink toward the floor. Guess her little legs were tired of standing. I lifted her back into my arms.

"We'll go check on the guys. Give you a second with your mom when she gets up here."

"You're sure?" Ivy asked, searching my eyes.

"I'm sure." I nodded.

"Thanks," she replied. "I'll call down and let Drew know she's here. He hasn't seen her since the day my father kicked him out."

Ivy's father wasn't invited today because he'd disowned his oldest son for being in a relationship with another man. Ivy had been so upset he treated Drew this way she cut him out of her life, so by extension, the life of his only grandchild, too.

Ivy was upset and angry with her mother, too. After all, she hadn't done more to protect Drew from their father, but Ivy hadn't been able to bring herself to keep her from Nova. I understood, and since their mother was a little more accepting of Drew's relationship (note: she didn't totally cut him out, but made no effort to speak to him), Ivy invited her for the family party.

"Do you think Drew and Trent will be okay?" I asked, concerned.

Ivy nodded. "I pretty much told our mother if she said or did anything to upset him, she would be asked to leave."

I let out a breath. "Good."

The last thing any of use needed today was drama.

I was already wound tight enough for all of us.

"Let's go find Daddy," I told Nova as Ivy walked out of the kitchen in the direction of the front door.

Outside, there was a giant pink and purple bounce house in the shape of a castle taking up most of the yard near the house. Nova was the only child at the party today, so it was an awfully large house for one, but even so, I'd have done the same for my daughter.

My arms trembled a bit as I carried her across the deck, and my tongue felt thick against the roof of my mouth.

"Beat this!" Braeden's voice carried through the air, but I couldn't see him. He gave a shout. Then the walls of the pink castle shuddered.

"In the bag," Romeo's voice retorted, and then the castle shuddered again.

Oh my word, what a bunch of boys. They were playing in the bounce house!

"I totally beat you," Romeo shouted.

Braeden immediately started arguing, and the pair began hurling some fairly colorful insults at each other.

I was closer now and could see through the windows, which were lined with thick, black netting.

They were wrestling.

Two grown football players were wrestling in a pink castle bounce house.

I guess this toy wasn't for one child after all, but three.

"What kind of example are you setting in there!" I called out.

Romeo froze in the middle of pinning B to the air-filled floor, and his head jerked up. "Hey, baby," he said, as if what he was doing were completely normal.

"Get in here, sis!" Braeden yelled from beneath my husband.

"Da-da!" Nova yelled.

Braeden jolted up, shoving Romeo off. "You trying to teach my daughter her daddy is a pansy, Rome!"

Romeo fell back onto the floor and laughed.

"There's the birthday girl!" B said, bouncing over to the door. Yes. Bounced.

As previously mentioned, he was an overgrown child.

"Look at the big castle. You wanna come in here with Daddy?"

Nova practically dove out of my arms when he reached through the mesh doorway.

"What the hell are you wearing, Critter?" B remarked, holding her out. "A dress? How are you supposed to bounce in a dress?"

Nova laughed. She was wearing a pink dress with a full skirt that looked like a tutu. Over top was a small, white cardigan with a hot-pink flower on the side.

"She looks like a little princess in her castle." I admonished him.

B kissed Nova sloppily on her belly, and she laughed. "Rome! Hold my girl."

Romeo appeared and lifted Nova into his arms. She grinned up at him as he pushed the dark strands of hair off her forehead. "Looking pretty cute today, sweetheart."

My throat constricted, and I tried to tear my eyes away from the sight. Somedays—most days—it didn't bother me to see Romeo and his niece.

Today it hurt.

It hurt a lot.

Thankfully, Braeden's form filled my vision, cutting off the sight of Romeo with a baby in his arms. "Get in here, tutor girl."

"What?" I gasped. "No way."

"No choice," he ordered and held out a hand.

I lifted my chin stubbornly.

I must not have done a very good job intimidating him, because he threatened me. "Come willingly, or I'll toss your tiny ass in here."

I flung out my hands and allowed him to help me inside. Obviously, it felt odd underfoot because the floor was filled with air and sank under my weight.

I planted my feet a little wider than normal, trying to maintain my balance. Braeden let go of my hands but kept his out, expecting me to fall.

When I didn't, I grinned at him.

I caught the last-minute flash of orneriness in his eyes, but it was too late. He leapt forward, bouncing right in front of me.

I shrieked and lost my balance. Braeden laughed, caught me around the waist, and jumped as high as he could. He didn't let go of me. Therefore, I went up in the air with him.

"Braeden James!" I yelled as we hit the floor and wobbled around.

B threw his head back and laughed, pulling me in for a hug.

My already unsteady stomach felt even more so now. Served him right if I barfed all over him.

Nova was clapping and making a bunch of babbling sounds. Romeo laughed. "You wanna bounce, too?"

Nova tried to get down, so Romeo put her on her feet, facing him, and held her hands. Her little body shook as she tried to stand, and he bounced just enough to give her a wobble.

She laughed like it was the greatest thing ever.

Romeo grinned, the kind of smile I'd only ever seen on him. The azure in his eyes sparkled as he watched Nova while they "bounced."

Without thinking, I leaned into B a little farther. Braeden's arms tightened around me, serving as a wake-up call.

I stiffened and pulled back. He let me go and didn't say anything.

"I should probably take Nova back to the house. Ivy's mom was pulling up when I came out."

"I got it," he said. "I better go see if Ives needs anything."

"I need my kid, Rome," B said, going over and swinging Nova up in the air. Romeo waved to her as she watched him over B's shoulder. Her attention was immediately diverted when Braeden bounced them out the door. Her laughter floated behind them.

Romeo stepped toward me and snagged me around the waist. "Ever do it in a castle?" He wagged his eyebrows at me suggestively.

"One filled with air?" I joked. "No."

The next thing I knew, he fell backward, bringing me with him. His back sank into the floor, and I sprawled across his chest.

I rubbed my hand over the side of his jaw and went in fast for a kiss. I pressed my lips wholly against his, looking for all the contact I could get. He groaned and wrapped both arms around me and rolled.

His weight pressed me into the floor, creating a cocoon around us, as his tongue wrapped around mine. Small sounds vibrated the back of my throat as my hands strained against his back and tugged at his shirt.

We kissed without lifting our mouths, changing direction by sliding our lips one way, then another. I explored him deeply, seeking something I didn't quite understand but knowing with him was the only place I would find it.

His body moved against mine, and it was like a spark to my chest. Like a jolt to a drained battery. I groaned, my head fell to the side, but Romeo kept kissing. His lips moved across my jaw, trailing over my neck and down so he could lick over the lacey strap of my bra.

"Romeo." I sighed, wrapping one leg around his hip.

He chuckled.

"What?" I asked, my voice breathless.

He lifted his head. "I think someone is missing what I didn't give her last night."

"You must not remember last night too clearly, then," I purred, rubbing my hand up his back. "Because I recall getting an awful lot."

The backs of his fingers brushed over my cheek, and he smiled down. He still did it. He still looked at me like I was all he saw, like I was the sun and the moon all wrapped up into one.

A little of the panic I'd been struggling to shake since I woke up slipped away. Romeo made me feel so full of love that there just wasn't room for all the anxiety trying to take over.

"You liked it," he said, smug.

"So did you." I could be smug, too.

Last night after the bonfire, we'd escaped to our room, and I got in the shower to wash away the scent of burning wood. Of course, I didn't get in the shower alone. Things got heated, as they always did with Romeo. But we didn't have sex.

He'd told me in a rather brazen and sexy way he wanted me to come across his tongue so he could taste it. He made it impossible to deny. His lips, his tongue… the pressure of his mouth when he sucked. It was my undoing.

I thought maybe once I'd come apart, he'd slide into me like he always did. Instead, he lay down beside me, gathering me close.

When I glanced up with questions in my eyes, he'd smiled. "No sex. Just play."

I kinda liked the idea of just playing, so I slid down his body and did just that. He wasn't the only one who had the pleasure of making someone come across his tongue.

"You miss me," he said, bringing me out of last night's memory and back into the bounce castle.

"Always," I whispered.

"Why are you trembling, baby?"

"Because of you."

"You were shaking before I even touched you." His lips brushed across mine briefly.

"Today makes me think about Evie." I confided, squeezing my eyes shut. "It's just…"

"Hard." He finished, understanding in his tone.

I nodded. "Seeing you with Nova…" I began but couldn't finish.

"I'm sorry, sweetheart." He rolled onto his back so his arms could tuck me along his body, my head pillowed on his chest.

"I wish it wasn't so hard," I whispered, a weight pressed on my heart.

We lay there in the center of the pink and purple castle without saying a word. He just held me, stroking my back as I listened to the sound of his heart beating beneath my ear.

I finally accepted the fact I was really struggling today, and with that acceptance, it became a little easier to breathe.

"I'm better now," I whispered a little while later.

I felt his lips on the top of my head.

"We should probably go in the house. Everyone's probably here."

His arms tightened around me.

I sighed. I could stay here another minute.

The sound of what sounded like a door slamming and the rumble of low voices had me sitting up. Romeo followed, keeping one arm around me.

Trent and Drew were on the back deck, their body language stiff.

"Something's wrong," I said immediately.

All thoughts of myself and my feelings were forgotten as we started for the door.

"Women line up to give Romeo the baby his wife can't!"

-GALAXY

Chapter Nine

ROMEO

You know what pisses me off?

When good days are ruined by bad shit.

And no, I'm not talking about Rim. Of course today was going to be hard for her. Fuck, it wasn't that easy for me either. She had a right to her pain, and so did I. She wouldn't be the sensitive, deep-feeling woman I loved if our niece's birthday party didn't make her think about the child she lost.

I saw it last night; she didn't know it, but I did. The closer we came to today, the more anxious she became. It was one of the reasons I took sex off the table last night. I didn't want the pressure of the condom. I didn't want to ask her and for her to have to say no, but at the same time, I didn't want to not ask and make her wonder. So no sex. No condom. No worries.

Besides, there were other ways, hella good ways to get it on.

Rim didn't go around shoving her pain down people's throats (unlike other people who shall soon be named), causing more hurt and making a thing out of something that wasn't supposed to be a thing.

• • •

121

In fact, my girl went out of her way to stuff it down. She tried so hard her body shook with it. I loved her. So goddamn much. It killed me she hurt like this. I lay there holding her, trying to come up with some way to make it better.

I could give her another child, but she had to let me.

Just when I felt some of the tension leave her body, drama came to the hood. You know, I thought having a gate would keep that shit out.

Clearly, I was wrong.

Trent and Drew were still on the back deck when we walked up.

"What's the matter?" Rimmel worried, hurrying over.

"Everyone's here," Drew said, his voice oddly void, and stared out across the view.

"Who's everyone?" I asked, my tone steely. I had a bad feeling I knew what he was going to say.

"Drew's father," Trent replied, his eyes meeting mine. They were shadowed and angry at the same time.

If there was one thing I'd learned over the past few years, it was life wasn't easy. In fact, at times, it was fucking brutal. Family was supposed to be the exception. Family was supposed to make life easier.

It wasn't always that way.

Guess that's why the six of us formed our own family. A family by choice and out of loyalty.

"He wasn't invited." I crossed my arms over my chest. I wasn't above kicking someone off this property.

"Didn't stop him from coming," Trent retorted.

Rimmel heard something she didn't like in his voice and went to his side. He draped an arm over her shoulders, and she peeked around at me with a frown.

We didn't need this. Rim had enough going on inside her without worrying herself sick over Trent and Drew. And my brothers deserved to be at peace in their own damn home.

I strode toward the house. There was some shit I couldn't fix, but I could do something about this.

"Wait." Drew stopped me.

I turned back.

"He's Nova's grandfather."

"He gave up that right," I countered.

"I don't want a fight," he said quietly. "I don't want to be anything like him."

Trent made a sound and stepped up to Drew's side. "You aren't. You are *nothing* like him."

"Just let him stay. I'm not putting my sister in the middle of this. Or my niece."

"I'm pretty sure Ivy didn't ask him to be here," I said.

Rimmel shook her head, agreeing with me. "Definitely not."

Drew rubbed a hand over the back of his neck. "No, but he came anyway."

"This is your house. Our house," Trent said. "He's not welcome here."

"I'm sorry, frat boy," Drew told him. "It won't be like last time. He says one thing to you, even looks at you cross-eyed, and I'll toss him out myself."

"Don't worry about me, Forrester," Trent spoke. "This isn't about me."

"It's always about you," Drew replied, almost too low for me to hear.

Rimmel glanced around at me again, her heart in her eyes. I shook my head. I was getting pretty fucking tired of feeling helpless. I wasn't, but some of these situations sure played with a man's head.

What the fuck kind of father did this to his son? It was amazing to me the man in my kitchen right now could be so cold to his own blood. That he would put his own happiness before his child's. And why? Because he didn't agree with who his son loved. I'd never treat my kid that way. Never.

You sure about that?

I shook off the thought. It was bad shit.

"He's out," I said, not in anger, just in truth. I wanted to toss him out. Fuck, my fingers itched for the fight. I just wanted him gone. I wanted everything he represented gone.

"No," Drew said after a moment. "Today isn't about me." He glanced at Trent. "As long as he keeps his bigoted opinions to himself, doesn't say anything to T, and overall acts like a decent person, then he can stay. But after today, he's out."

I nodded once, respecting his choice. "You change your mind, just say the word." My eyes met Trent's and held until he nodded. I wanted him to know if or when he had enough, then I'd show our unwanted guest the door, regardless of Drew not wanting to upset his sister.

"Your parents are here," Trent told me after a few seconds of silence.

I nodded, holding out a hand to Rim. "C'mon, Smalls. Let's go make nice with my mother."

Rimmel glanced back at Trent and Drew. Drew gave her a smile. "I'm fine. Go ahead. We'll be there in a few."

Inside, the kitchen was fuller than when I left it earlier. My parents, B's mom and the man she'd been dating a couple years, and Ivy's parents were all there.

The island was piled with brightly wrapped gifts, and a bouquet of balloons floated nearby.

Nova was the center of attention in her frilly, girly dress, wrapped up in Adrienne's arms (that would be Ivy's mother). Ivy was standing not far behind them, a frown on her face as she stared at her father.

Braeden stood at his wife's back. He looked up, and our eyes collided. I made it perfectly clear the way I felt when I stared back. Judging from the way he returned my glare, he was feeling the same.

"I wish you wouldn't have done this today," Ivy said, watching her parents fawn over Nova.

"Done what? Come visit our granddaughter on her birthday."

"It's not technically her birthday yet," Ivy retorted as if she weren't sure what else to say.

Nova's actual birthday wasn't for a couple weeks, toward the end of September, but because of the football season schedule, Ivy and B decided to have a big party early, before all of us were going in different directions.

"I could have just brought her to visit you."

"Nonsense," Burke said, brushing off the evident concern in his daughter's voice.

Anger flared in Braeden's eyes. He was caught in the middle, too, not wanting to cause a scene at his daughter's birthday party, but also not wanting anything to hurt his wife.

I stepped forward, releasing Rim's hand and using my size to tower over Ivy's father. I wasn't one to actually try to intimidate someone. Frankly, I never really had to. Usually, my presence was enough, but I wanted this man to know exactly what he was dealing with.

"You say one word, you even breathe in a way I don't like, and I'm going to personally remove you."

"That won't be necessary," Adrienne was quick to say, glancing up from Nova.

"I suggest you spend some time with your grandchild, then get the hell out of my house."

Burke turned his full gaze to me. I saw some anger there, even protest. But it didn't matter. He was no match for the turmoil bubbling inside me.

He realized it in seconds and cleared his throat.

"Is that a bounce house outside?" Adrienne exclaimed to Nova. "Why don't you show Grandma how you jump?" She started walking toward the back door. "Burke, why don't you come play with us?"

He gave me a lingering stare. I didn't budge. A small, cool hand wound its way around my middle, and I covered Rim's fingers with mine but didn't look away from Burke.

"Romeo," she whispered.

Burke walked away, joining his wife, and they took Nova outside. Seconds later, Trent and Drew came back in.

Ivy rushed to her brother and threw her arms around them both. "I did not invite him! I'm so sorry. I shouldn't have invited Mom."

"We know, sis." Drew assured her as he one-arm hugged her.

Braeden bypassed everyone and quietly went outside. Through the windows, I noted the way he stepped to the edge of the deck and stood watching over his in-laws with his baby daughter.

Ivy pulled back and faced everyone else, who were all standing quietly.

"Who's hungry?"

"I'll help you get everything set out, honey," Caroline told her daughter-in-law.

"I'm always ready to eat," John said from her side. Everyone laughed, and B's mom elbowed him in the side.

"Well, she asked," he defended, rubbing at the spot.

After that, things started up again, and the tension drained away now that the offending couple had gone.

"Roman," my mother said, coming forward. "Rimmel, how are you both doing?"

"We're good, Mom," I said.

"It's good to see you again," Rim replied politely.

"Get over here," my dad said, holding his arms out to her. She smiled and stepped into his embrace. "Good to see my favorite girl," he whispered loudly into her hair.

The sound of Rim's light giggle eased a lot of the tension inside me.

"Tell us all about preseason," Mom said, including Dad and Rim in the conversation. "Then tell us about the shelter, Rimmel."

These days, my mom and Rim had a polite, bordering on friendly, relationship. Mom tried to make up for all the shit she pulled before Rim and I got married, but the wounds cut deep. I couldn't blame Rim for being so cautious.

I never once tried to help my mother's cause in rebuilding a relationship with my wife. As far as I was concerned, Mom made her bed and if/when Rimmel wanted more than a friendly understanding, that was up to her.

We talked for a few moments, mostly about football and the fact we had another dog, before Mom and Rim went to help Caroline and Ivy set out platters of food and set up a large crystal bowl of punch.

The afternoon passed in a flurry of family, food, and baby stuff. Nova got a shit ton of new presents, one of which was an electric, pink Barbie car Trent and Drew put together in the yard. We sang "Happy Birthday," and Ivy helped her blow out the candles on her giant rainbow cake covered in sprinkles.

The top layer was reserved especially for Nova, so when Ivy set it in front of her, a giant mess was a given. I had to admit my niece looked pretty cute covered in icing.

After a while, the kid started getting fussy, tuckered out by all the activity. Ivy and B disappeared upstairs to clean her up and put her down for a nap while the rest of us hung around downstairs. It was awkward at times with Burke there. I felt the tension between him and his son and the anxiety Trent had about the entire situation.

Burke kept his trap shut and pretty much acted like Drew wasn't even there. I wasn't sure which was worse really—ignoring him or saying something that pissed us all off.

Even though I kept an eye on the situation, most of my attention centered around Rimmel. I watched her closely, making sure today didn't become too much. I looked for any indication I might need to pull her out of the room, maybe give her a little extra space to breathe.

My girl did well, though. I only saw the worst of the shadows when everyone was singing and watching Nova blow out her candles. Rimmel didn't let it hinder her day or take away from the fact her niece was turning one. She was just as hands on with the baby as always, and if she hugged her a little tighter than usual, I think it was only me who noticed.

A short while later, B sidled up to me, offering me a beer from the pair in his hand. I took it and watched my mom and Rim across the room. They were doing some dishes together, and I noted Mom talking quietly to her.

"How's she doing?" B asked in his own low tone.

I took a sip of the beer (my first and only of the day—training, you know) before replying, "She's tough."

"There's another article circulating online," he said, turning so his back was to the room and he faced only me. "Saw it on Ivy's phone when I was upstairs."

"How bad is it?"

"It's stupid shit," B replied. "But it's stupid shit that hurts women."

I gave him a look.

He sighed. "It's a long list of women who have offered to give you a baby." He cleared his throat and leaned in. "They're saying Rim can't."

It was like a punch in the gut. I didn't want her seeing that. "Don't these vultures have anything better to do? Like I'd want some ho's baby," I griped. "It ain't true, you know. We haven't even been trying."

B nodded. "Dude, you ain't gotta tell me, but yeah, I figured as much."

"Don't mention the headline to her," I said. "She doesn't need to know about it."

● ● ●

"Already cleared off Ivy's phone."

I took a pull on my beer, enjoying the way it slid into my stomach and bloomed into my bloodstream. I glanced back at Rim, thinking ahead to my impending travel schedule. I wasn't ready to leave. How was I supposed to be when the buzzards circled overhead, just waiting to swoop in?

Speaking of buzzards, thoughts of Rimmel's dad filled my mind. Thoughts of the two million-dollar payout a story with even the slightest ounce of truth would provide.

"I gotta make a call," I told B and left him and the rest of the family to step out by the fire pit.

I was skeptical if he would even answer. In fact, if he did or not would probably be more telling than anything he might actually say.

"Hello?" He picked up on the fourth ring.

"Brock, this is Romeo," I said, skipping the pleasantries. This guy hurt Rim so much. He failed to protect her when she needed it most and got me shot. I didn't feel like asking him how his day was going.

"Romeo, is my daughter okay?" Worry laced his tone, and I took that as a good sign. Or a lie.

"She's fine. There's nothing wrong." I assured him.

"Well, I'm surprised you called."

"I'm sure you've seen the headlines circulating about Rimmel and me." I began.

"Well, yes. They're hard to miss." He agreed.

Gee, don't sound too worried about your only daughter. Douchebag.

"Look, I want to know if the press has contacted you. If you've spoken to them at all."

There was a poignant silence on the other end of the line. "You think I'm selling gossip about my daughter to the media?"

He seemed surprised.

I didn't take too kindly to people thinking I was stupid.

"We both know you probably aren't above it," I deadpanned.

He made a sound.

"I didn't call to insult you. I called because I'm protecting my wife."

"Well. There are worse things." He allowed, still an unhappy note in his voice. "They haven't contacted me. And no, I haven't sought them out."

"Keep it that way," I said. "Don't betray your daughter because a skeezy magazine offers you a pile of cash."

"I would never." He was indignant.

"Are you still clean?" I cut in. "Still not gambling?"

He sighed. "I'm still sober. Still going to my meetings and therapy. I haven't gambled since everything happened."

"That's good to hear. Rimmel will be proud."

"How is she?" Brock asked. "Is she pregnant again?"

My back teeth slammed together. Didn't fuckers realize how intrusive that question really was? Why did people think they had a right to ask that, a right to know?

"No. She's not," I said, terse.

"Oh, that's a shame. I'm looking forward to holding my grandchild."

So many things. I wanted to say so many asshole things. "Yeah, well, we aren't ready yet. And if you love

● ● ●

131

your daughter and want to hold any future grandchildren at all, you'll make sure you stay clear of the press. Not one word."

I felt his anger through the phone over the fact that I was dictating and basically threatening to keep him from my wife and child, and I knew he was likely going to say something that would piss me off.

I pulled the phone away from my ear and hit END.

Fastest way to not hear what someone has to say? Hang up on them.

Did it make me an asshole? Sure did. Did I give a rat's ass? Hells no.

"Romeo?" Rimmel's voice called to me from behind. I glanced over my shoulder and smiled. "Hey, baby."

"What are you doing?"

I held up my cell. "Phone call."

"Everything okay?" She came closer as I shoved the device into the pocket of my jeans.

"Even better now that you're here."

She smiled. "Everyone's leaving." She hitched her thumb over her shoulder toward the house.

"'Bout damn time," I muttered. "Thought they'd never leave."

She laughed. "Did you have plans?"

I caught her around the waist and lifted her. Her legs wound around my waist. "I got a hot date with my wife."

She lifted a brow. "Do you?"

I nodded slow, stroking my thumb over her side. "What do you say, Mrs. Anderson? How about some one-on-one time with your husband?"

Her hands cupped my jaws. "I love that idea."

"It's a done deal." I confirmed.

Her laugh floated behind me as I carried her into the house.

Chapter Ten

"Stadium SELLOUT! The Knights will have a full house for their first home game this season!"
—MARYLAND SPORTS

RIMMEL

Never in a million years would I have thought life might bring me here. 'Course it wasn't really life that had my Ranger Rover pulling up this familiar drive.

It was circumstance.

For three months, I'd been frozen in time. I remained where I was while pages on the calendar turned and changed. Leaves on the trees morphed into colored jewels, then were gently shook free to leave behind bare branches that would, in time, bud with new life.

I wanted to be like the trees on our beautiful compound.

I wanted to gently shake away the chains that held me in place. I wanted to bud with new life, with change. No longer could the days and weeks pass me by, because that wasn't living.

Even though I wanted to desperately claw through the veil between life and death, to reach out and find my daughter and pull her close, it was impossible. Right now, I existed between the two. Between life and death.

Caught wanting to live, but also not knowing how to loosen my grip on death.

Everything seemed so unattainable. It was why I'd come to realize I'd remained this way for six long months. When one needs to do everything, one chooses to do nothing.

However, just because everything felt—at times—unfeasible, it didn't mean it was. I had Romeo. He was already mine. And while I loved my lost Evie so deeply, the past week had made me realize something. Something I was terribly ashamed to admit I'd lost sight of.

I chose him.

Romeo.

I would always choose him no matter what choice there was.

I just needed a little help. Someone to show me how to shake free of the old so I could bloom with the new—but do it in a way that I could still bring the memory of my daughter with me.

To be frank, I didn't trust a therapist. My reality was I would go there to heal and spill my deepest pain and thoughts… only to have them all sold to the highest bidder and wind up as front page news.

Dramatic?

Unfortunately, no.

We learned that the hard way the night I lost Evie. Someone on the hospital staff leaked the news to the media. It was the reason we were attacked by paparazzi on the way out. I didn't have the luxury of being anonymous. Our pain was something others paid to see, a fact I would never be able to comprehend.

I parked close to the house, glancing in the rearview, making sure no one followed me up the drive.

A car followed me the entire way; the tail started the second I hit the main road by the compound. It slowed when I turned onto this street, but I knew it was likely parked down on the road.

The press knew better than to step foot on my in-law's property. Tony would eat them for lunch in court. And Romeo... Well, I wasn't sure how much more he could be pushed before he retaliated, too. My husband was not the kind of man who tolerated what he considered threats to his family.

In fact, he'd been relatively mild in handling everything they'd put us through. If you considered mild a huge stone wall around twenty acres of private land, some sort of family escort to and from my job at the shelter, a media ban, and unlisted phone numbers for everyone in our family.

Even though I was almost sure the reporters following me hadn't come onto the property, I checked the mirrors before expelling a relieved sigh.

I shut off the engine and tucked the keys in my bag, but before getting out, I glanced across the way, to the white, stately looking pool house where Romeo used to live. So many good memories in that little house.

I heard a sound, sensed movement near the main house, and turned. Valerie was standing in the backdoor, holding it wide, looking at my car with surprise on her face. I smiled sardonically to myself.

I was probably the last person she expected to see today.

Since it was clearly too late to chicken out and run away, I pulled up my big girl panties and stepped out of the car, taking care to hit the locks from the inside since I already stashed my keys.

"Rimmel!" Valerie called. "Is everything okay?"

"Everything's fine," I assured her. "Romeo's fine."

She watched me walk the short distance to the house, then stood back to permit me inside.

"Is Tony here?" I asked, turning to see her close the door behind us.

"He's at the office," she answered. "I just put on some tea. Would you like some?"

"Sure."

Valerie waited while I pulled off the navy boyfriend-style blazer I wore. It was from Topshop. Ivy picked it out, as she did all my "presentable" clothes. Yes, I was actually wearing real clothes today. I figured a visit with the monster-in-law warranted it. After all, the last thing I needed was to see the judgement in her eyes about my state of dress and be totally pissed off before I even said what I came here to say.

Besides, it was good for me to get out of the sweats and comb my hair. I hadn't been doing that much at all lately. Since I hadn't been doing appearances with Romeo or out anywhere really, dressing nice hadn't been a priority. After all, the animals at the shelter didn't care what type of pants I wore, as long as there were treats in the pockets.

They were my kind of crowd.

I hung the blazer on a nearby hook, then placed my handbag on the one beside it. It was a Kate Spade, something else Ivy picked out.

I moved to tug off my tan fur-lined boots, but Valerie waved me away. "Just leave them. I know how you love your boots."

"They keep my feet warm." I smiled. In addition to my usual fur-lined footwear, I was wearing a pair of white skinny jeans and a taupe V-neck tee that felt like silk against my skin. It was a longer length so it covered my butt, which made me feel okay about wearing white jeans.

"So you keep saying," Valerie replied and moved toward the kitchen. "I've been looking online for a pair for myself. There are so many to pick from. How do you ever choose?"

Valerie was going to buy a pair of the boots I wore?

I glanced around to make sure I was in the right house.

"Honestly?" I said, evilly anticipating her reaction. "I got these at Target. They were on sale." She probably didn't even know Target sold shoes.

"Oh really? That's where I buy my paper towels."

See.

"I'll have to see if I can find a pair next time I go."

That surprised me. I thought Valerie Anderson would scoff at the thought of buying a pair of shoes at Target.

Maybe she was working on turning over a new leaf as well.

These days, things between Valerie and me were cordial. We were friendly at family dinners, football games, and anytime else we were together. She came to the house the day after I lost the baby, something I wasn't prepared for at all. I was almost convinced I'd see some kind of disappointment or even condemnation in her eyes.

There wasn't any. Not even a hint. It was that morning I recalled a conversation we'd had a long time ago about her struggles with having a child. I'd thought about that talk a lot in the days since, wondered about it. About her.

I didn't dislike Romeo's mother, not anymore. Disliking a mother for wanting to protect her son seemed really trivial these days.

But I would never forget some of the things she'd done to hurt me. In all truth, I was scared to be here right now. I felt as if I were opening myself up for additional potential hurt. There was a time long ago when I thought she and I would have a relationship.

That was before she announced my father killed my mother. That kinda put a kibosh on things.

She'd worked hard over the last two years to rebuild some kind of relationship with me. I think she finally conceded that Romeo truly loved me and I truly loved him. The beautiful wedding she put on for us (and B and Ivy) was her way of extending the olive branch, and I accepted it.

But today was a first.

I'd never driven over here on my own, knowing Tony wouldn't be here, with full intentions of spending time with her.

Healing.

That's what this was about, and if there was anyone who understood the loss of a child, the desperation to have one, it was her. Perhaps in my quest to heal the deepest of my wounds and reconcile my future with my past, I would also begin again with my mother-in-law.

"Roman's in Texas right now, correct?" she asked, interrupting my thoughts.

"Yes, then he'll be back here in Maryland for a home game this weekend."

Valerie nodded as she poured me a mug of hot tea and added the exact amount of sugar I always took.

She'd been paying attention. "Anthony and I are driving down for the game."

They went to almost all of Romeo's home games. I thought it was sweet. It made me miss going as well. I'd grown to love football over the past few years.

"He's grateful for your support," I told her, accepting the mug when she held it out. "I am, too. He should always have family there to support him."

Valerie tilted her head a fraction. "You're welcome to join us in our box anytime. The press is kept out."

"I'll keep that in mind." I wrapped my hands around the mug, allowing the heat of the tea to seep into my cold fingertips.

"Let's sit." She gestured toward the small table in front of a few windows on the other side of the kitchen. "I have to say, when I heard a car coming up the drive, you were the last person I expected to look out the window and see."

I set the tea down to run my fingers through the blown-out strands of my hair. It was sleek and silky feeling against my skin and, in many ways, a little jarring. I hadn't worn it straight and down like this for quite a while.

"I was hoping we could talk." I fidgeted some more with my hair before abandoning it for the mug. "I don't really have anyone else to, um, go to."

"I'm always here to talk, anytime you want," she replied gently. Valerie was a perceptive woman, and I was certain she knew coming here today had been a challenge in itself.

"It's about the baby," I blurted out, not knowing how else to bring it up.

"I figured as much. I wanted to call you so many times, but after everything…" She paused, then forged on. "I didn't want to push or pry. I know we haven't had the easiest of relationships."

I laughed lightly. "That's putting it politely."

Valerie smiled. I could only hope to age as gracefully as she had. As usual, she was dressed perfectly in a pair of black skinny pants and a cream-colored silk blouse that tied at the side of her neck in a fashionable bow. Her hair was cut into a shoulder-length style that showed off the thick, blond strands, and her makeup was so seamless it practically looked airbrushed.

In addition to her wedding ring, she had several other statement rings on various fingers and a diamond tennis bracelet around her wrist.

"Well, I am a lady," she retorted with a slight twinkle in her eye.

Was she joking? Did Valerie Anderson actually want to wear boots and joke?

I resisted the urge to glance out the window for signs of an impending apocalypse.

"I'm glad you came by," she said, her voice taking on a more serious tone.

I swallowed thickly; my throat felt stuffed with cotton, so I drank some of the tea. It didn't help, but it did stall for time.

"How are you doing?" Valerie asked, giving me a nudge.

The mug made a light thudding sound when I set it on the table. "Not very good," I whispered, staring down into the dark liquid. I didn't want to look at Valerie. I was afraid of what I'd see.

Pity. Sorrow. Understanding.

Even though I was here for the understanding, to be honest, I still didn't want to see it reflected in her eyes. My pain felt singular. Unique. In many ways, the pain was the last connection I had with Evie. If I saw understanding in Valerie's eyes, I was terrified it would somehow take away what little I had left.

No one can take away Evie. She is and always will be your daughter.

How easy the thoughts come; how very difficult to believe them.

"I feel stuck," I elaborated. "Like I can't move on. I want to, but it feels disloyal."

Valerie reached across the table, her perfectly manicured hand settling over mine and squeezing.

"It hurts," I admitted, emotion welling up inside me until my own skin felt stretched tight. "It hurts all the time."

"It's always going to hurt, sweetheart," she answered.

I wasn't expecting that, and I looked up.

She offered me a ghost of a smile and nodded. "There will always be an empty piece inside you that Evie took when she was lost. There will always be days when you look at the calendar and mentally calculate how old she would be that day. You'll always seek out her face in children who look the way you imagined she would."

My breathing hitched because she knew.

She knew my thoughts without me having to voice them.

"You keep waiting for the pain to dull, but it hurts a little more every day. People have probably told you it's been long enough now. They've tried to put a limit on your grief."

I nodded.

She knew.

"People do that because your pain makes them uncomfortable. It's hard to see. Look at me, Rimmel," she asserted.

I did because Valerie wasn't a woman you ignored.

"The love you feel for Evie is not quantifiable; therefore, neither is the time it will take to feel human again. I've taken a long, silent look at you over the past year, my daughter-in-law, and I've learned quite a lot. But at the top of that list, I have learned your capacity to feel is unlike anyone I've ever met. It's a blessing and a curse for you. A blessing because when you love, it's with everything inside you. A curse because when you hurt, it's almost crippling."

I lifted my hand to brush away a tear trailing over my cheek.

"The good news is you learn to adapt. You learn to live with the loss of your daughter."

"It feels like I'm betraying her memory," I whispered. "To move on."

"I know. But that empty spot I said she took with her?" she asked, and I nodded. "She has that piece of you. And that place inside you? That's not nearly as empty as it feels. That's her place now, and she's going to be there forever."

More tears fell. She was with me. Always.

"It was my fault." I wept. "I'm not as strong as Romeo. I couldn't keep her safe."

Valerie made a sound and came around the table. The next thing I knew, both her arms were around me; she was hugging me tight.

"I know it feels that way. I blamed myself for years and years, just like you. It isn't your fault. These things, these horrible things just happen."

I grabbed her arm where she hugged me and held on. For the very first time since I came out of that shock-induced haze at the hospital, I felt it all at once.

The weight of it all was so cumbersome I thought I would crumble.

I didn't.

I cried. I felt helpless. I felt guilty.

But I weathered the storm of emotions; that in itself made me feel stronger.

After a while, I pulled back from Valerie's hold and wiped at my face with the backs of my hands. She released me to rush off and get me some tissues (that she probably got from Target) and set them at my elbow. I took a few minutes to clean up my face and sip at the tea before glancing up.

"Can I ask you something?" The hoarse way I spoke jarred me.

"Of course."

"You told me once the doctors said you'd never have children. And that you tried for years." Valerie nodded, so I continued. "Romeo was your miracle baby, but did you ever have a miscarriage like me?"

She smiled sadly. "Two of them. It was after those that the doctors told me I'd never have a child."

Two. Just the thought of having to survive something like this more than once was enough to make me never want try again.

"We were devastated, much like you and my son." She cleared her throat. "Losing a child isn't something I would wish on anyone. Not even my worst enemy."

"It still hurts you?" I asked. "Even after all these years?"

"It does. I've just learned to live with the pain, and over time, I've come to accept it wasn't anything I'd done. It just wasn't meant to be."

I digested her honesty for a few moments before speaking again. "Romeo wants to try again." I admitted. "He says he isn't ready until I am, but I just know."

"My son wants you to be happy."

"That's what I want for him."

Valerie smiled. "Have you talked to Roman, told him how you feel?"

"We've talked." I hedged. "After your first miscarriage, weren't you afraid it would happen again?"

"Terrified. Then when it did happen, I thought I somehow manifested it to come true because I'd been so worried."

"Oh, but that's not true," I rushed out, instantly feeling empathy for her.

Valerie smiled. "If only you'd let yourself off the hook that easily."

Yikes. She had a point.

"Having another baby, trying to get pregnant again doesn't take anything away from your first one. And yes, there is always the risk of another miscarriage, but the chances are slim. And for me, when I weighed the potential pain against the potential joy of holding my baby in my arms, the joy always won."

I let everything she said to me sink in. We sat and drank our tea in silence, but it wasn't awkward or uncomfortable. I didn't think about all the things she'd done to me in the past and how skewed our relationship had become.

She wasn't that person to me anymore.

She was a mother. A woman who understood pain and loss. An ear and a confidant.

And what was most remarkable?

I hadn't forgotten a single thing she'd put me through. She was just more than that now.

It made me feel like maybe I could have more, without forgetting about Evie.

"I should have come here sooner," I finally said.

Valerie laughed. "I never thought I'd hear you say that."

I snorted. "I never thought I'd say it."

"You came when you were ready, and I'm glad you did."

"Me, too," I whispered.

"Talk to Romeo," she said, calling him by his nickname for like the first time ever. "Really talk. Don't be afraid to tell him the things you worry about the most. I think you may realize you have more in common than you think."

"I think I may be ready now."

"And if I may suggest something?"

I nodded.

"Go see your doctor, talk to her. Maybe have an exam. Even an ultrasound, if it gives you peace of mind. Then you'll know everything is as it should be in case you and Roman decide to try again."

I hadn't thought of that. I'd been so lost inside my own worst thoughts; I'd forgotten I had some control.

"I think I will." I nodded.

After that, the conversation went to lighter things. Mostly talk about Romeo and his father. She asked me again to come to the home game and sit in their box, and I agreed. Getting out would be good for me, and any excuse to see my husband was a good one.

A few hours after I walked in, I was shrugging back into the boyfriend blazer to walk out. But on the way out, I felt a little less heavy, a little more unburdened.

As I was stepping out the door, I stopped and turned back. "Thank you, Valerie. I truly mean it. You're a good mother."

Her face softened, and she pulled me in for a hug. "Thank you for trusting me enough to talk to me."

I pulled back and smiled.

"Tell Romeo I said hello!" she called after me. "And Rimmel?"

I glanced over my shoulder as I pulled open the door to my car.

"You may be half the size of my son, but your strength matches his."

That was probably the nicest thing she'd ever said to me.

It was also the first time I'd ever felt grateful she was in my life.

ROMEO

The familiar sound of my cell caused my arm to fling out in my sleep. The ringing didn't quit when I flipped it over.

It was then I realized it wasn't the alarm.

"Yeah," I said into the phone, my eyes still closed.

Rimmel's voice filled my ear. "Are you still in bed?"

I jolted upright, the sheet falling around my waist, and blinked open my eyes. "Fuck, what time is it?"

"It's only seven," she replied, amusement in her tone. "Aren't you usually training by now?"

I groaned and fell back onto the pillows, making sure I kept the phone at my ear. "Game day," I murmured. My eyes flew back open. "Rim? What's wrong?"

My heart started to pound, breath quickening, and I shoved myself up on one arm. She never called me this early.

"Nothing!" she replied quickly. "I'm fine."

"You're sure?" I asked, still unable to calm down. Flashes of her tearstained face and the pain in her features that night at the hospital months ago assaulted me.

"I promise," she vowed. "I just missed you. Figured you'd be up by now."

"Don't do that shit to me, baby," I grumped and lay back on my side, the phone tucked against my ear, held in place by the pillow and my head.

"I have a surprise," she said, anticipation in her voice.

"Yeah?" I smiled. "Let me guess. We got another dog. And a cat."

"Romeo!" she admonished.

"A hamster, then." I teased.

Her giggle filled my head. My chest swelled with love, and I mentally counted the days until I would be able to go home to her.

"No, I didn't bring home another animal."

"This time," I muttered.

She giggled again. "I'm coming to your game tonight!"

"Huh?" I responded, my brain still not fully functioning. Well, that and her words were about the last thing I expected to hear.

"Your parents asked me to sit in their box with them."

"You're going to be here tonight?" I clarified, wanting to be sure. Excitement pumped through my veins and woke me the rest of the way.

"Yes! I'm packing a bag right now. We're leaving in thirty minutes to drive down there."

"Fuck, baby, that's so good to hear." All her words caught up to me. "Wait. Did you say you're sitting with my parents?"

"Valerie invited me. Their box doesn't allow press."

You know it's bad with the media when Rim chooses to sit with my mother. Usually, my girl sat in the stands, as close to the field as she could. She told me she enjoyed sitting where the fans did, and it was more exciting that way. Plus, she had a closer view of the field.

I knew that really meant she just wanted a close-up of my ass in my uniform.

It was a fine-looking ass.

"You're sure you're up for it?" I asked, putting aside my own intense desire to have her here to think of what this might cost her.

I still hadn't told her about the two million-dollar payday or the fact the stalkerazzi was actively looking for dirt. I didn't tell her I called her father either.

I should have. I could now. It was hard to pile more on her already full plate. Plus, we got so little time when I was home. I was there and gone. I just wanted us to be normal for a while, enjoy each other.

"Up for seeing you kick ass on the field? Uh, yeah!"

I chuckled. "I'm up for seeing your ass in my bed tonight."

"Perv," she clowned.

"You love it."

Her voice softened, and I could picture her standing there clutching the phone, looking like a mess, with a soft smile on her face. "I do."

I hated to bring us out of our little bubble, but I had to. Pushing up on the mattress, I leaned back against the headboard. It was hard as fuck. I glanced back at it, scowling. I missed my house. Being in a different hotel room every week sucked balls. It was easy to forget what city I was in if the games were too close together.

Technically, I really didn't have to be in a hotel right now. Not here anyway. Since this was a home game and we were here at home base, I could have gotten my own place. B and I talked about getting a small apartment for when we were in town training, doing press, and games. However, I didn't so much like the idea.

I had a home already, one I wasn't eager to replace. Or add to.

Point was any place Rim wasn't was no place for me. That apartment would have been just as cold as this hotel room.

And yeah, if we had an apartment, we'd have to clean and shit. Here at the hotel, we had room service, housekeeping, and someone at the front desk who respected our privacy and didn't give out our room numbers. It worked, and if it wasn't broke, I wasn't about to try and fix it.

"Rim, I want you to come. I miss you. But you gotta know the press will still be around. They always are. They'll be out of the box but still everywhere else."

She sighed. "I know. I can't hide forever, Romeo. I don't want to miss your games. You're my husband, and I want to support you. I already told you I think if I stop hiding, they may just see we're fine and move on."

I really didn't think so. It was too much money. I wanted to keep her locked away, safe from prying eyes and idiot questions… but how reasonable was that? Would hiding even help, or would it only serve to isolate her more—to the point she could only dwell on the reason she was staying out of sight?

Fucking convoluted thoughts.

Thank God I got to run the field tonight. I had a feeling I was going to need it.

"I'll make security aware you'll be in the stadium. They can make sure you aren't hassled on your way to the box."

"I miss you," she told me.

"Ah, baby, me, too. This hotel bed is going to be a lot more comfortable tonight with you in it."

We talked a few more minutes before she had to go finish packing so they could leave. Apparently, Ivy and Nova were coming, too. All of them would be in the box tonight. The girls were all driving down together, meeting my parents.

The day passed by quickly, as it always did, but I still glanced at the clock every now and then, wondering if Rim was in town yet. We did some press, some warmups, and headed to the field. Tonight's game had sold-out seating, so it was going to be a roaring crowd.

After we were suited up and ready to head out onto the field, I checked my phone to find a text from Rim.

Full house tonight! We're already in the box. Kick ass, and I'll see you later #♥

I smiled, shoved the phone in my locker, and joined B, who was waiting. "Dude, you better not be this damn slow on the field tonight."

I gave him the finger.

"Girls here?" he asked, not even batting an eye at my gesture.

● ● ●

"Why you playing like you didn't check your phone, too?" I cracked.

He grinned.

"Decent of the 'rents to have them in the box tonight," B said as we huddled up in the center of the locker room for a motivational speech from the coach.

"Might need to talk to Gamble about getting one of our own. Sitting in the stands isn't the best idea right now."

"I'm sure your mother would love to have them in there all the time."

Oh, I'm sure she would, too. Anything to try and get a little closer to Rim. Hell, when we told her she was going to be a grandma, I could have sworn for a second she liked Rim better than me. Her own son. What kind of horseshit was that? Second fiddle, that's what I was going to be the minute my kid was born.

If I ever had one that is.

It became even clearer to Mom that if she wanted the kind of relationship I knew she did with me and any kids I might have, the only way she'd get it was to be kind to my wife.

Did I think all her effort to be close to my wife was for that reason? No. But it sure as hell didn't hurt.

When Rimmel miscarried, I was nervous, even suspicious Mom might back away from her like she had the first time they'd been close. She didn't. If anything, she seemed more determined to make their relationship right.

Maybe Rimmel accepting the invite to sit in the box was her way of taking the extended olive branch.

"All right, listen up, meatheads!" the coach roared, and everyone went silent.

All thoughts of Rimmel and my mother went away as I focused on the game.

The team rushed the field, the crowd went nuts, and the game got underway. A few times, I glanced up at the box I knew my parents sat in, even though I couldn't see through the glass.

I hoped the press wasn't too vicious when they entered the stadium. I hoped Rim was having a good time.

I played hard, wanting to impress the fans and make our first home game this season pretty epic. It also helped my mojo that my wife was so close. I'd forgotten how much it meant to me when she was at my games, what kind of mental high-five it was knowing she was close, and the reward at the end of a go-hard game was a rubdown from Rim.

Braeden was on fire tonight. Hell, the whole team was. We started kicking ass right out of the gate and hadn't stopped when halftime rolled around.

I thought briefly of rushing up to the box to claim a kiss but knew I'd get mobbed and it would turn into a circus.

Back in the locker room, spirits were high, the coach was fucking thrilled, and the team didn't have to endure a lecture about our pansy asses sucking.

Coach and his assistants disappeared into his office to analyze the first half and make adjustments where needed, and the team got a much-needed piece of downtime.

A few of the guys actually headed for the showers. We had one player we dubbed Dirt because, ironically, the dude hated to get dirty. He showered every halftime. He always said a clean body was more efficient.

Dude had issues.

"Don't forget your body wash, Dirt!" B yelled, and I laughed.

I grabbed a Gatorade out of the fridge and then tossed one to B before uncapping it and swallow some. Next, I pulled off my jersey and equipment from the waist up. It felt good to breathe a little.

Braeden was already sitting by our lockers with his feet up, so I palmed my phone and joined him. I tuned out the loud players around me and Dirt singing at the top of his lungs in the shower (Seriously. That dude should *not* sing Brittney in the shower. Just wrong.) and checked my phone.

So proud of you! Rimmel texted. *Killin' it out there!*

I smiled as my fingers flew over the screen. *2 quarters left. Then you're all mine.*

I tossed my phone in my lap and leaned my head against the cold metal of the lockers.

B stared down at his phone, shaking his head. I smacked his arm. "What?"

He glanced up, his mouth in a thin line. "Nothing," he muttered and tossed the phone onto his legs.

"You see that shit Drumbo pulled out on the field?" he said about a player on the opposing team. "That dude is asking to meet my fist."

"That guy ain't even worth your time," I said, acting like I was totally distracted by his talk. "He's such a douche. I give him four games before he's out with an injury the rest of the season."

Braeden made a rude sound. "Ass munch."

I laughed but reached out and snagged the phone off his lap. He dove sideways to yank it back, but he missed. "Gotta be quicker than that," I said and lit up the screen.

A couple screens were pulled up, one of them being coverage of the game. Sometimes we checked the sports channels to see what they were saying about us or even the opposing team. Every once in a while, we got lucky and pulled some info that we used to our advantage on the field.

Only today's coverage was less about the actual game and more about who was in attendance. Rimmel was in the house, and everyone damn sure knew it.

I seriously would never understand why the press was so freaking fascinated by my wife. She was mine. Everyone else needed to mind their own damn business.

Ass munches.

I learned that from Braeden.

Everyone was clamoring for a look at her. Some speculated she came against my wishes, and that's why she was hiding. Others thought she was hiding because she was hiding a bump. Some said she was too scared to show her face.

Since when did the game become about what the wives of the players were doing? Why was it about their clothes, their ability to pump out kids, and where they sat at games?

This was football. *Football*. Not a fucking soap opera.

"Jesus Christ," I muttered and handed B his phone.

"I asked Ivy if everything is okay up there."

"What'd she say?"

"Said it was all good."

Rimmel didn't seem upset in her texts, so maybe she didn't know the stir her presence but lack of being seen caused.

I pulled up my phone and shot out another text.

You and Ivy leave the stadium a little early. Less traffic. We'll meet you guys at the hotel. I left a key at the front desk 4 you.

I didn't want Rim hanging around, waiting for me after the game.

See you then.

"We'll meet at the hotel after," I informed B.

He nodded. "Smart."

I leaned my head against the locker and shut my eyes. It seemed only seconds passed when Coach was yelling for us all to hustle back to the field. As we went, the familiar thunderous and echo-y sound of the crowd hummed around us. It served as a surge of adrenaline and signaled to my conditioned brain it was game time.

I knew Rim was okay in the box. My parents were with her, and security in that area was tight. People could talk shit online all they wanted, but it was just words.

The game resumed, and I jogged out on the field and called a play. My teammates and I fell into position; the ball was snapped into my capable hands. In the span of a few heartbeats, I scanned the players, looking for an opening. I bypassed one because dude was seconds away from getting trampled.

Hopping on one foot, I pulled my arm back, feeling the usual tingle in my muscles as I prepared to launch the ball.

I saw my opening, releasing the ball.

It spiraled perfectly right down the field. My receiver leapt up and caught it, the football folding right into his waiting hands. He turned and launched forward, rushing down the field.

I watched, hoping for just another step, another yard.

Finally, he was forced out of bounds, but not before he managed to advance us near the end zone.

The crowd went nuts, cheering and screaming. B came rushing up to smack me on the helmet. "That was a sweet-ass throw, Rome!" he yelled.

I spit out my mouth guard and grinned.

Along with our other teammates, who were celebrating, I turned to regroup. I leaned in to call another play.

"What the fuck?" Trumbly muttered and glanced up out of the huddle.

The rest of us followed suit when we noticed the same thing. The crowd was still going nuts. Now don't get me wrong. There was always cheering and a roaring crowd at games, at all times.

I'd just thrown a sweet pass and got everyone's juices flowing, but it should have died down some by now. They should have been anticipating the next snap; they should've been holding their breath for a touchdown.

Why weren't they?

"Uh, Rome," someone said, and I straightened.

One of the guys slapped me on the back and turned me toward the giant screen broadcasting the game.

Oh. Shit.

I lifted my arms and signaled for a timeout.

Celebrity News

Chapter Twelve

"Too ashamed to show her face!" FORUM

"He deserves better!" TEXTER

"Rimmel in hiding!" FRIENDBOOK

RIMMEL

Sometimes a bitch just snaps.

I wasn't a bitch.

Far from it, actually. But there was also a limit to how much a fairly mild-tempered girl like me could take.

I was damn near that point. Like a rubber band being forced around a too-fat stack of papers, I was thinking about snapping.

I guess that's how I knew I wasn't a bitch. I highly doubted bitches thought about it before they snapped.

That probably stung harder for whoever was on the receiving end. No matter. I could sting, too. I was married to Romeo after all, and my big brother was a hothead.

I felt stronger today. And the day before. And the day before that.

I glanced over at Valerie. She noticed me and smiled.

Ever since that day I'd shown up at her door and we had tea, I'd felt stronger. It was like just getting permission from someone who wasn't me, who wasn't my husband who loved me so unflinchingly it wouldn't matter what I said or did, lifted a weight off my shoulders.

Permission for what?

To forgive myself. To understand that maybe, just maybe, Evie's loss wasn't my fault. It was okay to hurt and cry. It was okay to want so desperately to try for another piece of Romeo but just as desperately not want to, also.

It was okay to be a mess.

I am allowed.

My goodness, I hadn't noticed just how sore my shoulders were from carrying such a load. How bruised my heart had become.

It was worse than even I'd known.

Was I better now? Completely healed?

No.

I still ached for my daughter. Some moments I still blamed myself for the loss of that little baby. I still looked at Romeo and wondered if he thought I failed him, even though he told me I hadn't.

I was still scared.

Those were moments now, and as all-consuming and engulfing as they were, I was able to tell myself those moments would give way to new ones.

And they did.

Now, along with those dark times, there were lighter ones. I thought of my mother rocking my daughter in her arms. I thought of her singing her the songs she'd sung to me. I thought hopefully of the child Romeo and I would be blessed with, the one whose eyes I would look into and see his father reflected back.

I was stronger.

Not healed. I would never be "healed." I didn't think there was such a thing for a person who'd lost a child. It was simply learning to live incomplete.

I still had a very long way to go, but Valerie helped me realize I didn't have to go that distance alone. It was one of the reasons I was here today. I wanted my husband. To gaze into the bottomless azure of his stare, to feel his lips beneath mine and be calmed by a presence only he provided. I wanted to show him I was coping and to support him in everything he did.

I chose Romeo. So I was here.

Everyone knew it, too.

That's where the snapping came into play.

There was a special entrance for those who had box seats at the stadium. More private, if you will. Celebrities, well-to-do business owners—Ron Gamble and company—owned box seats, so I supposed it was a necessity for discreetness.

When we arrived, we parked near that entrance. Romeo's parents were just behind. Security was waiting at the door. I had no doubt Romeo had them all on guard. It didn't matter, though, because the press was still there. They might not be allowed into the boxes, but nothing stopped them from being outside the entrance.

Ivy and I had glanced at each other. I felt a dip in my belly because I knew what was coming. I glanced down at what I was wearing.

"Should I have dressed better?" I worried.

Ivy flipped the long, blond ends of her hair over her shoulders. "Honestly? It doesn't matter what you wear. They're going to say crap no matter what."

True. "Well, it's a good thing I went for comfort."

Ivy smiled. Of course she looked perfectly posh in a pair of skinny jeans, a funnel-neck sweater, and a green army-style jacket with studs on the shoulders.

And me?

I was in my usual. Jeans and a hoodie. Not my Alpha U hoodie, though, my Knights one. It had Romeo's name and number on the back, too. My hair was down, though, instead of up in the usual bun. Ivy had blown it out for me last night, and it was still nice and smooth, so I figured I'd give Valerie a treat and not look like a total troll.

Wasn't I a nice daughter-in-law? :-)

There was a sudden knock on the passenger window, and I jumped, pressing a hand to my chest. Tony was standing there with a guilty look on his face when I whipped around.

He motioned for me to get out of the car, then glanced around at the descending press.

Ivy was already on the move. She'd put her Range Rover in park (yes, we drove the same kind of car, just different colors) and climbed into the backseat where Nova was strapped in.

"Lots of pictures," she said, trying to make it sound like a game. My resolve strengthened, likely because of anger. We shouldn't have to play a game with our children so they weren't alarmed by the vultures.

"Get out on Tony's side," I told her. "He can help shield Nova."

"Okay, ready," she said, a diaper bag on her shoulder and Nova in her arms. The doors on my side of the SUV popped open at the same time, both of us scurrying out.

Tony put his arm around me, but I motioned to Ivy. "The baby."

He seemed torn, glancing between me and Nova.

"She's just a little girl," I told him.

He nodded once and went to Ivy, wrapped an arm around her shoulder, and started forward. Valerie fell into step beside me as the four of us moved toward the entrance.

Reporters and paparazzi crowded around. The sound of snapping pictures and the constant flashes threatened to blind me.

"Rimmel!" someone yelled. "Over here!"

"Get a picture of her stomach!" someone else yelled.

"Are you pregnant?"

"When's the divorce?"

"What do you have to say about the list of women offering to give Romeo a baby?"

My rushing footsteps halted. Everything inside me stilled.

There are women offering to give my husband a baby?

In the words of said husband, *Oh hells no!*

Valerie made a sound of distress and took my hand. I looked up at her. She had her chin high and a stubborn, intimidating look on her face.

Be like that.

With a sniff and, if I do say so myself, rather on-point hair flip, I marched ahead, holding my chin high.

"Is it true you can't conceive?" someone shouted.

Cameras flashed.

I felt my resolve waver, but I forced it back in place. Thankfully, security officers shoved through the press and flanked Valerie and me. After that, we were whisked into the building where Ivy and Tony waited.

• • •

Valerie gave my hand a squeeze before releasing it. I could have sworn I felt a little pride from her at the way I handled that.

I did better than I thought. Perhaps the weakness I was so afraid of was more perceived than actual. It didn't matter my insides quivered, my stomach was in knots, and all the muscles at the base of my skull felt like they'd been slammed with a wrecking ball.

Unfortunately, my well of tolerance for handling things seemed to dry up quickly, so it was uncertain how much more I'd be able to withstand today.

The box Romeo's parents had was beautiful. There was seating for over ten people, a large flat-screen TV that played the game, another smaller TV above the full bar showing coverage from SportsCenter or something, and a wide glass front that looked down over the field.

The bar was stocked with a ton of drinks (alcoholic and non), and there was a full spread of game day eats across the counter.

A few of Tony's colleagues would be joining us, but other than that, it was just us four and Nova.

It was definitely a pampered way to enjoy a live football game. And bonus! It was climate controlled, so that meant the cold autumn air wouldn't freeze my fingers into numbness.

Still, I preferred sitting in the stands.

It was more real to me. More normal.

The first quarter was fun and relaxing. We munched on snacks, drank apple cider and hot chocolate (Ivy and I didn't drink at games… Ivy barely drank at all), and played with Nova.

Valerie and I even cheered on Romeo together.

It's never just that easy, though.

Word got out that I was here. Pictures of me entering the side doors were already popping up online, and posts were flying. If I thought the questions the reporters screamed at me were invasive, well… They looked like pretty lacey panties compared to the stuff online.

You'd think we'd miss all the fun posts about my life and marriage inside this swanky box, but no. Even the sports channel started covering it. The announcers for this very game mentioned me.

Several times.

The end of halftime signaled the end to my tolerance.

When two male announcers who were supposed to be talking football suddenly changed topic and started debating if I was in a box and not in the stands because I was either afraid to face reporters or I was upset because of the women in the stands, things got a little hard to avoid.

Anger started bubbling up inside me. It was a relatively new thing for me. Sure, I'd been angry before. Lots of times. But this was different.

This was the kind of anger that started as a small flame and grew brighter and hotter until, at its core, it was so white hot it burned blue. The kind of anger that bespoke of a mother bear protecting her cubs. I might not have any cubs to protect, but that instinct was still there.

The need to protect myself, my husband, and the life we had together was impossible to deny.

"What girls?" Ivy muttered after we'd both stared at the TV, nearly slack jawed from the announcers' dialogue.

I had no idea. Perhaps being on a complete media blackout hadn't been wise. Perhaps burying one's head in the sand only got eyes full of dirt.

Ivy was the first to turn away from the bar and stalk to the window. "Where are these supposed women?" Her hands planted on her hips as she stared out. Nova stood beside her, hands on the glass, while she made a bunch of sounds and said Da-da over and over.

I joined her, and we both peered down into the stands. "Is that them? Right down there?" Ivy asked dubiously, putting her finger on the glass to point. "That girl has enough bleach on her head she could be a human flashlight."

I snorted.

"And here they are folks," the announcer said in the background as the coverage continued. "Look at those women. Should we call them Romeo's Roadies, Robb?"

I spun. Heck, everyone looked up at the TV.

The cameras were zeroed in on a row of women all dressed to the nines, with their hair all done up like they were at the Oscars and not an outdoor football game. Their cleavage was exposed, their earrings could cover a continent, and their lipstick was layered on like armor.

They all held Knights flags, waving them around like they were at a pageant. Oh my God, I thought I was rid of girls like this after college. Clearly, some women never grew up.

One of the women, tall, thin, definitely too blond, who looked like a model was holding a giant sign: **I'll Have Your Baby!**

I gasped.

Remember how I said I wasn't a bitch?

I lied.

I was done with the rumors, the accusations, and the dirty, no-good hos hitting on my husband. I always knew Romeo was going to be a magnet. I always knew women would fling themselves at him at impossible speeds.

But a baby?

This was going way, way too far. What if I truly couldn't give him another child? What then? These women would be making a mockery of my deepest pain. They acted as if my lack of procreating somehow made me not good enough for Romeo. It implied he would be so shallow as to literally pick a woman out of a crowd and impregnate her.

Ew.

Like moldy blue cheese ew.

"Rimmel!" Ivy called behind me. Up until that point, I hadn't even realized I'd moved. "Where are you going?"

I spun from the door and glanced back, taking in everyone in the room. Valerie was watching me with wide eyes, and Tony looked like he wasn't sure what to do.

"Everyone is so desperate for a picture of me… Well, I'll give them one."

"Give 'em hell, girlfriend," Ivy stated proudly.

I yanked open the door and strode out into the hallway. I noted the security officers hanging out nearby; they all straightened the instant I appeared.

I gave them a wave. "Boys."

"Uh, Mrs. Anderson, where are you going?"

"To watch the game," I replied sweetly and strode away.

I gathered some attention when I stepped out of the private hallway. A few photographers were lounging on their asses, propped against the walls. The second I marched by, they snapped to it, blinking widely as if they couldn't believe what they saw.

Morons. Every last one of them.

I went past the concession stands, the vendor booths, and the public bathrooms. Toward the end was a wide hallway that led out into the stands. I walked through as the volume of the game grew and grew.

The second I stepped between the rows, I stood at the bottom and scanned the crowd. I looked toward the general area where Ivy pointed before. I figured I'd know them when I saw them… You know, the sign offering to have my husband's child was like a giant YOU ARE HERE insignia.

The photographers were right with me, taking pictures and on their phones. They hurled questions, too, but I ignored them. I was drawing attention, but really, what was new?

Then I saw them.

The I "heart" Romeo fan club.

Groupies.

Malibu Football Barbies.

I walked along in front of the bottom row of seats. The railing was at my side, and I stayed with it, keeping my eyes locked on the women.

I started hearing my name murmured; people started pointing. I glanced out over the crowd and waved and smiling.

Act like this is entirely planned. Like you aren't partly dying inside and your smile is more real than those bitches' boobs.

Fans waved back. That part was kinda nice.

By the time I reached the section the women were in, I'd drawn a crowd and a harem of people following along behind me. From above, a camera crew appeared. They had the great big cameras and headsets strapped on their faces and started down the stairs in my direction.

I waved at them, posing a little right there with the field as my backdrop.

Then I turned to the wannabes.

They were all giving me dirty looks. You know the kind of look you see on the movie *Mean Girls*. The kind every other woman who isn't your friend gives you when you go out in public. Judgement. They were measuring me, trying to decide how hard I'd be to get rid of and wondering what it was Romeo saw in me. They snickered at my clothes, my glasses, and the lack of makeup masking my face.

I strode up some steps and stopped beside their row. They were all openly staring now.

"You're embarrassing yourselves," I said loud enough for the sections nearby to hear.

"The only embarrassment I see right now is your wardrobe." The woman closest to me snickered.

So original.

I gave them my best *Mean Girls* smirk, pinching the fabric of the Knights hoodie between my fingers. "Oh? You mean this old thing? It's a team hoodie. It has my *husband's* name on the back."

"Quit trying to hold on." One of the girls stood and faced me. "A man like that doesn't want half a woman."

Okay. *Ouch.*

Sometimes the worst insults are the ones that prey on our deepest fears. Even though I tried not to let the fear haunt me, tried to reason it away… I was deeply afraid I'd never get pregnant again and it would make me less than.

I didn't even openly acknowledge the comment. Instead, I angled toward the one with the sign. "Put it down," I growled.

Yep, I growled.

Go me!

She laughed.

I lunged forward, past a couple fangirls (who, my God, used WAY too much perfume), and grabbed the sign to yank it away.

The woman was ready and kept her hand on the corner. We ended up getting in a tug-of-war over a stupid sign right there in the middle of the row.

Not my finest moment, but how much disrespect could a girl take?

"Get off her!" a girl behind me screeched. I felt her talons dig into my shoulders.

Talons = acrylic nails that were frighteningly long.

I lost the grip I had on the sign and stumbled backward. I knocked into the girl yanking me, and we both fell into her seat, with me directly in her lap. I scrambled up, making sure I stomped extra hard on her stiletto-clad foot.

She howled, and I felt sick satisfaction as I righted the glasses on my face.

Security came rushing forward, trying to get through the press crowding me from every angle.

The noise from the crowd suddenly burst into my wild mood, and I realized what the hell I was doing.

Stooping to their level.

And I wasn't doing a very good job. I was getting pushed around by Barbies.

This was going to be in every magazine for a month at least.

I stood and moved along the row, back out into the stairwell.

"Security!" the men in uniform yelled as they pushed closer to us.

"Ow!" one of the hos pouted. "That was assault!"

I rolled my eyes. Beneath my resolute exterior, the anger and upset I felt drained away. It circled around my feet before running off and leaving me there alone and shaken. My knees were trembling; my fingers ached. Everything inside my brain became foggy, and an overwhelming sense of panic stole over me.

What have I done?

Security was going to reach me any second. All these girls were going to blame me, and they wouldn't exactly be wrong.

Romeo was going to have to bail me out of jail.

He was going to be so mad.

Good thing Tony was in town. I was probably going to need a lawyer.

Around me, people started yelling and gasping. It took a minute for it to penetrate my own internal dialogue.

I blinked and followed where everyone was pointing. A giant uniform-clad football player was jogging this way. In one running leap, he jumped up on the wall and straddled the rail.

I stared as the larger-than-life athlete reached up and yanked the helmet off his head. Blond, messy hair flopped over his forehead, and impossibly blue eyes locked on mine.

My lungs remembered how to breathe. I sucked in air, not even realizing how badly my body needed it.

● ● ●

"Romeo!" people yelled and surged forward.

"Excuse me," he said, and the crowd literally parted.

The girl beside me made a sound, then elbowed me. "Bye, Felicia."

That wasn't my name... Who in the world was Felicia?

"What the hell is going on here?" Romeo asked as he jogged the short way up the stairs.

"Romeo, I—" I balked. I had no idea what to say.

The blonde on the end actually stepped in front of me and offered her hand to him. "I'm—"

He held up a hand. "I don't care."

Without touching her, he reached around and held out his hand.

"C'mon, Smalls. This is no place for my girl."

My hand slid into his. He felt like a furnace. My fingers curled in close to his palm.

I stepped around Bright Lite Barbie ('cause you know, her hair practically glowed) and gave him a sheepish smile.

"Baby, what did I tell you about putting the smack down on fans?" he asked and blinked down at me.

"They had it coming," I grumped.

He threw back his head and laughed. The crowd cheered.

He could do no wrong. Literally. I think it said so in the laws somewhere.

"Can't leave you alone for five minutes." He shook his head sadly. "This is the second football game I've had to stop for you."

"Well, I didn't tell you to come charging up here," I retorted. He smiled like my sass amused him. I sighed. "I'll go back to the box," I vowed, aware of everybody watching. I didn't even have to look to know our image was being broadcast on the jumbo screens.

"Oh no you don't," he drawled.

Next thing I knew, he swung me over his shoulder like a sack of potatoes. His shoulder pads were hard against my middle.

"Roman Anderson!" I yelled. "You put me down right now!"

"Can't do that, baby. Security is coming for you. You don't want me getting in a fight defending your honor, do ya? I have a game to finish."

I tried to kick him. It didn't work.

He started down the stairs, bringing me with him. I tapped his back. He paused. "Yes?"

"That sign," I growled. I'd be damned if I watched the rest of the game with that hooker waving around that insult.

"What sign?" he asked, clueless. Seriously. How could he be so oblivious?

He spun, and my head went wonky.

"Romeo," I intoned.

"What the fuck?" he muttered and stalked back up the stairs. He set me on my feet right beside him. I felt like the smallest person on Earth standing there at his side. He was even larger than usual with all his football gear on. Right now, he was easily three times my size.

"Ladies," he charmed. "Is that sign for me?"

They giggled, and my upper lip curled.

"I just wanted you to know"—the bitch slid a glance at me, then back at him—"that you have options."

Romeo reached for the sign. She gladly surrendered it.

A few self-satisfied looks were thrown my way.

Romeo lifted the sign and ripped it in half. The girls all gasped. I smiled like I'd won the lottery. He dropped the pieces at his feet.

"Sorry, ladies. I'm taken, and that ain't changing, *ever.*"

Romeo reached for my hand and tugged me down the stairs. At the railing, he vaulted over and landed as gracefully as a cat. He looked up at me, holding out his hands. "C'mon, then."

My mouth fell open. "What?"

"Get down here." He crooked his finger at me.

"I'll go back to the box."

He shook his head adamantly. "Oh no you don't, you little troublemaker."

I put my hands on my hips and scowled. I show one act of defiance in my entire life and now I was labeled a troublemaker. As if.

"No."

He laughed. "Now, baby. Don't you want to watch the game from the sidelines?"

Well, it did sound appealing.

Not to mention it would a great big neon sign to all women on the list of potential baby mamas that I wasn't going anywhere.

He chuckled and held out his arms. "I'll catch you."

I hesitated, then thought, *What the hell.*

I jumped off the railing and landed in Romeo's arms. The next thing I knew, he was running across the field to where his team waited, bringing me the whole way.

"One a scale of one to ten…" I began as he ran. "How bad is this?"

His lips curled up. "A ten."

I groaned and dropped my head against his chest. The team surrounded us, and I was congratulated on my "scrappy" skills.

Oh my goodness. They were going to call me Scrappy now.

That might be worse than being on the news.

"What the fuck do you think you're doing, Anderson?!" Coach yelled as the team parted. "That was a valuable timeout."

I peeked up from Romeo's chest at the coach.

"Sorry, Coach. Had to collect the wife."

Pretty sure I was in danger of dying from embarrassment.

The coach muttered some very inventive choice words and pointed to the field. "The game! Get back to the game!"

Romeo rushed forward and deposited me on the bench. Before jogging off, he snagged his heavy team coat off the ground and slung it around my shoulders. I snuggled down into it. His lips brushed my forehead.

"I kinda like the jealous side of you," he said.

I groaned.

"Sit tight, baby. I gotta game to win."

I stared at his butt when he ran back onto the field.

Please. You would have, too.

I spent the remainder of the third quarter and the rest of the fourth right there on the bench. The players entertained me, and Romeo kissed me between his turns on the field.

It was the best seat in the house.

Celebrity News

Chapter Thirteen

"Rimmel's jealousy!" MYPLACE

"He's taken! That ain't changing!" POSTDECK

"Romeo's Timeout!" SWOONREPORT

ROMEO

Scrappy wife. Happy life.

Rim was a fighter, tougher than she looked. Most of that strength was internal, though. People took one look at her, and she was dismissed faster than a room full of boys who never showered and farted too much.

Hell, even I was guilty of looking at her and worrying about her fragility.

But then she went and pulled something like she did today.

One minute I was throwing passes into the end zone, and the next I was rushing the stands because my girl was taking on a pack of mangy wolves.

Here's the thing: when you back a wounded dog into a corner, it's going to come out fighting.

Rimmel was starting to fight, ignited by a most surprising source.

Jealousy.

Ah, the sweet taste of watching her get all riled up because some ho thought holding up a sign would make me notice her.

While I might be hella amused she was riled up over skanky women I wouldn't even think twice about, I knew it went deeper than that. She'd seen the media coverage and was likely also subjected to the press when she pulled into the parking lot.

I appreciated her scrappy will. I did.

But seeing her being pushed around, stumbling into someone's lap, while the paparazzi circled like buzzards wasn't something I found entertaining.

It was one of those moments I saw her vulnerability. I'd be damned if some bitches would break her.

No one was going to break her while I was around.

It was pretty much unheard of to pull a wife or anyone down on the sidelines during a game. Didn't stop me from doing it.

Ron Gamble wanted higher ratings. He liked that Rim was a draw for a new kind of crowd. Well. He got what the fuck he paid for tonight.

I didn't do it for that, though. I did it for her. It was a public display of *I'm with her*. Didn't think I could get much clearer than that.

When the game was over (we smashed it and took home the win) I had post-game shit to do, and she couldn't come hang around the locker room. If she did, she'd likely be scarred for life.

Seriously. Some of the dudes were akin to wild animals.

I escorted her back to the box, then had security accompany them all to the cars. I went to the locker room, where I was ribbed mercilessly for the stunt I pulled. I was a big boy; I could take it.

Anything for Rim.

● ● ●

By the time B and I arrived at the hotel, I was pretty fucking spent. Done with the press, the game, the people. I just wanted my wife and a quiet room.

B and I were on the same floor. Ivy and Nova were waiting for him, so the second we stepped off the elevator, we pounded it out and separated.

"Tell my sis I think she's a badass," B called over his shoulder as I moved on down the hall.

I laughed.

She was sitting in the center of the bed when I walked in. She glanced up, a red licorice twist falling from her lips. Behind her black-rimmed glasses, her brown eyes went wide, and she tugged on the neck of the T-shirt she wore because it exposed more than it covered.

I dropped my duffle at my feet and leaned against the door, crossing my arms over my chest.

Her hair was down in a waterfall of dark silk. It looked like she brushed it out about a thousand times, which was a thousand more than she usually did. She was nervous, likely fidgety in that clumsy way of hers, probably wondering just what I'd say when I stepped into this room.

I was hot all over, flushed from toe to head. My body was lethargic from the physical demands the hours of football had extracted. I didn't feel tired, just lethargic. Heavy.

My veins were thick with desire, need almost overwhelming.

Almost. Not quite.

Rimmel sensed my mood, the prowess with which I watched her from my steadfast position against the door. The room hummed with silence, with singular energy.

Her stillness was overcome by the aforementioned restlessness, and I watched with sharp attention as she wiped her palms over the caps of her bent, bare knees. Beneath the thick fabric of the T-shirt she stole from my bag, her chest rose and fell with uneven movement, and I knew with certainty the rhythm of her heart was madly irregular.

She was small in the center of the king-size bed, but her presence was anything but. She filled this room like she filled my chest. Absolutely. Undeniably.

She adjusted the falling shirt again. Her teeth sank into her lower lip as she watched, waiting for whatever it was she thought I would say.

"Take off your shirt," I rasped. The tone of my voice made it sound like I had a three-pack-a-day habit and I inhaled every single time.

Her stare flew to mine, surprise flickering behind the glasses.

"Lose the glasses, too."

Not one word slipped between the fullness of her lips, but she moved to do my bidding. The glasses went first, slid away carefully. A long stretch of bare skin was bared when she leaned over to place them on the bedside.

I didn't move.

I stood and stared.

Rimmel returned to her Indian-style sitting position, and her small hand delved between her legs to disappear. My breathing quickened at the sight. One second passed before she pulled it back up, bringing with it the hem of the shirt.

The fabric peeled away, revealing patches of pale, creamy skin as she moved. Once it was gone, she rose onto her knees in the center of the blankets and held out the material, releasing it to fall on the floor.

She wasn't wearing a bra.

Her small, perky breasts were on total display, which caused my mouth to water. I knew exactly how she tasted. Exactly how she felt.

All she wore were white cotton panties with large cutouts on each side, which exposed even more of her slim body. Her stomach dipped in slightly on each side, just above the soft flare of her hips. There was a space between her thighs, a place that didn't touch… It was a place where I belonged, as if her body were built with me in mind, predesigned for this.

I stared at her a long time, not saying anything, and she let me look. The trance she put me under was broken when she picked up something off the bed and brought it to her lips.

Blood drained from my head and into my jeans when the long, red twist slid between her parted lips, her tongue licked across the candy, and her teeth sank in to take a bite.

I shoved off the door, my stride only halted when my thighs came against the side of the mattress. Rimmel smiled, a slight naughty curve to her kissable lips, and held the candy up to mine.

I let her push the licorice between my teeth, and sweetness hit my tongue. It was good, but she was better.

With a wicked smile and glint in my eye, I bit into the soft, chewy snack. I watched her as I chewed, then snatched the rest of the licorice away and ever so lightly trailed the end across her collarbone and down to the fullness of her breast.

● ● ●

Her nipple tightened, puckering with anticipation, and there was a catch in her breath.

The candy disappeared over my shoulder, hitting the carpet with a soft thud, but I didn't hear. My body surged forward. I caught her around the waist and tumbled with her onto the mattress.

She was warm and supple under me. Our eyes met. I looked at her for the millionth time and couldn't wait to see her a million more.

Her lips parted, and I knew she was about to whisper my name, but she didn't have to utter a sound. I already heard; deep inside, our hearts already whispered.

The distance between us condensed to none. My lips overtook hers as we sank into one another. I explored every inch of her with my fingertips and tongue. The feel of her body straining against mine under the weight of the seduction I laid heavily across her skin made my own hum.

I lifted my head from her breast, glanced down into her dazed expression, and smiled. Her hands clutched me closer, then tugged at the fabric that still covered my body. I'd practically made love to her, and I was still fully clothed. I'd explored every single inch of her. Between her legs was already dripping with silk. The skin across her chest was flushed.

Slowly, I licked down her body, pulling away an inch at a time. When our skin no longer touched, my pace quickened. Swiftly, I shed my clothes, abandoning them where they lay. Rimmel watched me with heavy eyes, swollen lips, and need dripping from her very pores.

I didn't ask the question. It just didn't matter right now… I thought maybe it wouldn't matter ever again.

The condom I rolled over my rock-hard cock wasn't the barrier I'd originally thought. It was the words, the thoughts... the unspoken wall we'd unintentionally placed between us.

I lay on the bed and reached for her. Rim straddled my body, and I reveled in the way she looked above me.

Her body accepted mine the way I knew it would. Rimmel was an extension of me now. Where I ended, she began. Her soft sighs were my biggest triumph, and even though she rode me, I still moved against her.

The curtain of her hair fell behind her shoulders when her chin tipped back, the creamy skin of her neck exposed. I caressed it, trailing down over her chest to cup the breasts on full display. Her hips bore down, and soon, both of us were panting.

Rimmel bent forward, collapsing against my chest, so I wrapped her tight in my arms. Her nose pressed against my neck, and I surged into her, claiming her release.

Hers wasn't even over before mine began, so we climaxed together, clinging to each other in the center of the bed as if we were each other's gravity.

I don't know how much later it was when I grasped her head and lifted it so I could look into her face. "I really fucking love you."

"I really fucking love you."

I really loved when she said fuck. It was the dirtiest word coming out of the most innocent lips.

My tongue dipped into her mouth for one final taste before I had to gently lift her off my body and slip out of the bed. Once I was cleaned up, I stepped back into the bedroom, not bothering to rummage for clothes.

Rimmel was lying in bed, eating another licorice twist. I laughed. "Where the hell are you getting those things?"

She scowled. "You threw one on the floor."

"I'll buy you another bag, baby." I chuckled and slid in beside her. There was a whole pack of the stuff right there, halfway under the pillow.

I snagged one and took a bite. "Reese Cups are better."

Without a word, her hand disappeared beneath her pillow and pulled out a king-size pack of my favorite candy.

I lifted an eyebrow, and she stole my red twist and stuck it between her lips, where it hung out like a long, red cigarette, and put the chocolate in my hand instead.

I ripped open the end with my teeth, unwrapped the first chocolate cup, and shoved the entire thing into my mouth. I made a sound of appreciation as the milk chocolate and peanut butter melted in my mouth and exploded across my tongue.

"I definitely didn't expect that kind of greeting," Rimmel said, giving me a sidelong glance.

"What can I say? Seeing you 'roid out on them bitches in the stands made me hot."

She made a choking sound. I glanced up mildly as I shoved another entire cup in my mouth.

"'Roid out!" she exclaimed. "I did no such thing."

I grinned, showing off all the lumps of chocolate and peanut butter in my teeth.

She rolled her eyes and smacked my chest. "You're disgusting."

"Here I thought all those people at the stadium were cheering for my epic throw. Come to find out my girl fight was getting all the love."

"It wasn't a girl fight either," she muttered, taking another chomp on the candy. Her head tilted, causing her glossy hair to slide over her shoulder. "Fine. Maybe it was a little."

"You saw all the press coverage, huh?" I asked, dropping my voice and taking on a more serious tone. I loved teasing my girl, but this wasn't all a joke.

She snorted. It was still just as adorable today as it was the first time she did it. "Are you kidding? The sports announcers were talking about it. The *freaking* announcers!"

I propped myself against the headboard, using a pillow as a cushion, and draped the sheet over my lower body. "Yeah, I saw some of the shit being reported."

She scowled. "Did you know there's a list of women who have volunteered to have your baby?"

I shrugged, pointing to myself. "They want a piece of this."

Rimmel dropped the candy onto her lap and stared at me, astounded. "You knew!"

"I do spend a lot of time in a locker room with a bunch of dirt bags, baby," I countered.

"You said nothing." Her lips thinned.

Oh shit, she was not amused. I wasn't going to charm my way out of this one.

"How would you feel if there was a list of men who were offering to get me pregnant?" She sniffed, crossing her arms over her bare chest.

A low grumble filled the room. My chest vibrated from the sheer force of it. "I think you know," I intoned.

I'd kill.

I'd sit in jail for the rest of my life.

"Well, not only did you *not* tell me about this list, but I had to hear about it during a national televised game, in a room with *your parents*."

I'm sure my parents already knew about the list, but I didn't bother pointing that out. That definitely would have made things worse.

I opened my mouth, but she stuck her finger between us.

Dayum… Smalls was sassy tonight.

"Not to mention I got to look down in the stands to see an entire row of glow-in-the-dark bobbleheads holding signs, offering their services."

Glow-in-the-dark bobbleheads? Original.

I laughed.

She planted her hands on her hips. "Those women were so bleached out I'm shocked they even had hair left. It was probably all extensions."

"I'm not interested in anyone but you, baby," I told her, trying to hold on to my shit. If she said one more adorably cute thing in anger, I was going to piss myself from laughter.

"Don't you placate me, Roman Anderson."

The hotel landline rang, saving me. I dove to the side and picked it up. "Roman Anderson," I said briskly.

It was the hotel staff. "Mr. Anderson, this is the restaurant downstairs. We were getting ready to close up tonight and noticed you haven't ordered your usual room service. Would you like us to put that order in?"

There was one perk of staying at the same hotel for every home game. The staff here knew me very well.

I made a sound of appreciation. "Actually, that would be great. Running a little behind tonight and forgot to call."

● ● ●

I felt Rimmel staring at my back and glanced around. "Could I add a slice of that chocolate cake you guys make and some coffee to that usual order?"

I heard once that if your lady was in a mood, the best course of action was to throw chocolate at her and back away. I wasn't backing away from Rimmel. I'd rather take the heat of her anger and be at her side. But chocolate might be a good idea.

"Of course," the man on the line replied smoothly. "We'll have that right up, Mr. Anderson. And congratulations on your win this evening."

"Thank you," I said, then hung up the phone. "I got you some cake," I told Rim.

She sighed wearily. "I'm sorry about what I did. That definitely wasn't the time or place. And I only made the press more rabid and embarrassed us both."

I grabbed her around the waist and lifted, placing her in my lap so she was facing me. I noted the goose bumps along her upper arms, so I tugged the sheet out from under us and pulled it up around her back. Her hands grasped the sides and tugged it closer, holding it there.

"You did *not* embarrass me. I don't think you ever could."

Round, brown eyes with flecks of gold fell on mine. "I marched into the stands, knowing the press would follow, and literally confronted those ho-bags. I didn't do a very good job either. I fell into one of their laps!"

I chuckled. "A couple things… Those *ho-bags* had it coming." I lifted a finger as I listed things. "And maybe I should show you a few moves to make you a little less… clumsy and a little more effective."

She muttered, "I'd probably kill myself, and we both know it."

"There will be no dying," I said, allegedly in jest, but there was an underlying note of steel in my voice. I didn't let myself think about why.

"What about the press?" she asked.

"What about them?" I scoffed. "They can't get any more zealous then they already are."

She worried her lower lip. I used my thumb to stop her and smoothed out the soft flesh.

"A list, Romeo," she said again.

"Baby, stop worrying about some stupid list. How many lists do you make every single day, and how many do you walk out of the house or shelter without, making them useless anyway?"

She giggled.

That's because the answer was all of them. Rim and her lists. She made them, but she never actually looked at them.

"This is a list of women who want to have my husband's baby." Her voice caught. The underlying pain she'd lived with since Evie was evident.

"That's right. *Your* husband. I belong to you, Rim. Always. I don't want anyone but you. I haven't since the day you spilled pencils everywhere, in your lesbian sweater, and gave me a list of rules."

A laugh bubbled up in her, but it didn't quite make it out.

It killed me to see her like this. I felt the storm raging inside her. I understood now that today pushed her past her limits; her breaking point was exceeded. I had no idea how to reassure her. I didn't know how to downplay what the press was saying. The fact was it sucked. There wasn't much I could do about stupid lists and bitches with signs (except tear those signs in half).

I glanced at the top of her head, which was right in my line of sight because her chin was dipped, lying against her chest.

"What if I can't?" she whispered.

"What if you can't what, sweetheart?" I murmured, brushing away some of the hair concealing her face.

Her breath hitched. My chest clenched.

"What if I can't give you a baby? What if Evie was our only chance?"

An audible click echoed through me. That one sound held a lot of answers.

It also let me know I was an idiot.

No clue… I had no idea she felt this way. As if the guilt I knew wasn't enough already, it doubled.

"Rimmel." Her name sounded more like a sigh, a slight admonishment. It brought her eyes up to mine. They were watery, tormented, and her chin wobbled.

Shit. Carefully, I hooked an arm around her, pulling her close. She collapsed against my chest, and a deep sob broke free. I'd only heard that kind of sound from her once before. The night she lost our daughter.

That sound haunted me, rattled around inside me with all the other ghosts of that night… In many ways, I'd become a haunted house. I became fearful of that sound and if I'd ever hear it again.

Her tears were wet against my chest. I felt them slide over my pec and disappear somewhere between us.

I was an alpha. Always in control, always the solid one everyone looked to for answers. I fixed shit. That's who I was.

I didn't know how to fix this.

How had I missed that my wife was still so deeply in pain? How had I not known she was terrified of never holding a baby in her arms?

I tucked her closer, tightening my grip, because at the moment, the least I could offer was my strength. God knows I wasn't sure what else I could.

She snuggled closer, and in a tortured, tear-disrupted voice, she spoke. "It took me months and months to get pregnant. Longer than most women my age. I started to even doubt I could, but then Evie…"

She cried again, her words interrupted by the agony in her heart erupting and flowing out like hot lava from an active volcano.

"I was so happy. We were so happy. And then I lost her… I wasn't strong enough to carry her. My body didn't protect her. I didn't protect her like I should have. Now she's gone… and I'm scared, Romeo." She pulled her head up, looking at me with red eyes. "What if I can't get pregnant again? What if I do and I lose the baby again? What if giving you children is just something my body can't do?"

She sniffled and rubbed at her face, wiping away the worst of the tears. Little gasping sounds shook her as she tried to rein in the emotion taking over her body.

God, she carried so much. Too much.

I grabbed her face, looking directly into her eyes. "Why didn't you tell me you were torturing yourself this way?"

She shrugged. "I thought maybe with some time, I'd stop thinking like this, my fear might go away. But it didn't. It's been over three months, and I still tell you to wear those stupid condoms."

"I don't care about the goddamn condoms," I growled. "I told you I understood you aren't ready to try." *I just haven't understood enough.*

She shook her head sadly, twisting the sheet in her hands. "I am ready. I'm just so scared. Scared I won't be able to get pregnant but also scared I will."

I nodded, understanding lighting my brain. "It's a lot of what-ifs. A lot of unanswered questions. What if you can't get pregnant?" I repeated. "What if you can and miscarry again?"

More tears slid from beneath her lids as she squeezed them tight.

"But, baby, what if you can? What if what happened was just a terrible thing? What if we try again and it turns out better than you imagined?"

"Are you afraid?" she asked, her eyes wide and innocent.

I smoothed a hand down the side of her head. "Every day."

"Really?"

I smiled. "Hard to believe, huh? It's just because I'm a badass."

Her lips lifted.

I grabbed her face again. "I will love you no matter what, Rimmel. Baby or no baby. The only thing in this life I can't live without is you."

I'd said this before. Months ago. I thought it sank in, but it hadn't. Sometimes words needed repeating.

"And this shit about you not being strong enough to protect our daughter…" I shook my head, adamant. "Stop it."

She laughed. "You can't just command my feelings."

193

"I can, and I will," I demanded. "You are the strongest woman I've ever met. You might be small, and you might be kinda awkward." She pinched me, and I winced. "But your body"—I reached between us and put a hand on her stomach—"is perfect. I don't know why Evie couldn't stay with us, baby. But I do know her loss was not your fault. She knows it, too."

Her eyes filled again. I really fucking hated when she cried.

Rimmel whispered, "I like to think she's with my mother."

A lump formed in my throat. I swallowed, trying to dislodge it. "I think she probably is."

There was a sudden knock on the door. "Room service!"

Rim straightened with a little shriek and whispered yelled, "We're naked!"

I rounded my eyes. "Thank God you told me! I'd have answered the door and showed off all our goods to the waiter!"

Rim scrambled off my lap, trying to leap off the bed for her clothes. She ended up tangled in the sheet and half dangling off the mattress.

"Just a minute!" I called, loud enough for the guy in the hall to hear.

"You're killing me, Smalls." I reached down and supported her twisted form as she fought to get free.

With her feet finally on the floor, she straightened to her full shorty height and glared at me. I kissed her on the head and jammed her shirt over her head. "Out of sight, woman." I smacked her playfully on her bare ass.

She took the shirt and disappeared into the bathroom, and I pulled on my jeans but didn't bother with a shirt. I let the waiter in with the rolling cart, added a big tip to the slip, and signed it.

"Have a good night, Mr. Anderson."

I held the door for him, and when he was gone, I threw the lock and pushed the cart over toward the bed. Rimmel appeared in the doorway of the bathroom, wearing my old shirt.

"Your cake is here." I lifted a silver lid off a small plate to reveal a giant-ass piece of cake dripping in chocolate.

She came over and poured herself a mug of coffee and added cream and sugar. I flipped off the lid on my plate, which held a huge steak, a pile of roasted vegetables, and a skewer of grilled jumbo shrimp.

"C'mon. I'll share with ya," I told her and lifted the plate to get back in bed.

"I'm not that hungry," she said, sipping at the coffee.

I scrutinized her as I sat and shoved a shrimp in my mouth, patting the mattress beside me. It pleased me when she picked up the cake and a fork and joined me. The plate filled with chocolate rested on the bed in front of her drawn-up legs, the mug cradled in her palms.

"Romeo?" she asked quietly.

"Hmm?"

"Do you think it's disloyal to Evie to try and have another baby?"

I set down the fork and then the plate, turning to her. "I think your heart is so big we could have ten kids and you'd love them all equally as much, including the one who isn't here."

"Really?"

"You keep bringing home dogs, ugly ones at that, and you love them all just as much as Murphy," I quipped.

"Ralph is not ugly. He's unique," she scolded.

Sure was. Uniquely ugly.

"It's not disloyal, baby," I said instead of arguing about the R's attractiveness. "You know how I feel about loyalty. Especially where family's concerned. We won't ever forget about Evie."

She nodded. "Valerie said something similar."

The shrimp between my fingers paused midway to my mouth. "My mother?"

Her eyes crinkled around the corners with her smile. "I went to see her earlier this week. We talked."

I threw the shrimp back onto my plate and pressed the back of my hand to her forehead. "You feeling okay?" I joked. "First you get into a brawl at the game, and now you tell me you went to visit my mother."

She wagged her eyebrows at me. "*We had tea.*"

I gasped dramatically, then went back to eating the shrimp. I was starving. "You for real went to see my mother?"

She nodded, setting aside the coffee. "I thought she might understand how I felt better than most people…" Her voice faded away.

She was right. If anyone understood exactly what Rim was going through, it would be my mother. I'd always hoped someday they would find a way to move past all the shit Mom did, but this wasn't the way I would've chosen for them to do it. Maybe this was a silver lining in the otherwise black cloud that hung over us.

I took her hand and laced our fingers together, silently offering support.

"How did it go?" I asked, slightly wary.

"Really good. Just hearing what I was feeling was valid and normal from someone who'd been there really shifted something inside me."

"In a good way?"

She nodded. "I feel stronger now."

Her words cut me even though I knew that was the last thing she intended. I felt like shit I hadn't known she was still blaming herself and fearful of losing another child. "I wish it had been me that made you feel stronger."

Her fingers tightened around mine. "I wouldn't have been able to get to this point if it weren't for you. I never thought anyone could ever love me the way you do, Romeo. I truly thought it wasn't possible. But you do."

"I'll never stop," I vowed.

"In an odd way, I think hearing the understanding from someone who doesn't love me like that, from someone who actually debates if she even likes me, is what made the difference."

"I get that." I leaned close and kissed her softly. "But you know my mother loves you."

Rim made a sound; I wasn't sure if it was acceptance or denial, but I let it go. This conversation wasn't really about my mother.

"She told me to talk to you, you know. Tell you how I felt."

"I'm glad you did."

She swallowed and took a breath. "I'm ready to try again."

I stilled. Did she mean what I thought? I looked into her eyes. They were so wide, so innocent... yet so knowing. Her head bobbed, as if telling me yes, I was exactly correct in what I was thinking.

"Rimmel, don't let the things the media is saying get to you. That goddamn list either. We aren't on a schedule; there's no pressure for this. It hasn't been that long." It had only been a little over three months. In terms of the outside world, I supposed that felt like forever.

But in terms of the heart?

It was like a passing second.

She tucked her hair behind both ears, holding my searching gaze steadily. "It's not because of the press or anyone else. It's because I want to. I want your baby, Romeo. I want a part of you growing inside me."

I still recalled the way she looked with just a slight swell to her stomach. She was so tiny she started showing almost immediately. There was something primal about it, about knowing my child was growing inside her. Usually, it was just the woman's hormones that changed with pregnancy, but it changed mine, too. It made me even more protective, as if it were a sudden awakening to just how fragile life really was.

I cleared my throat. "It's not something that needs to be decided tonight."

"I've been thinking about it a while. Since before you left for the season. Then I talked to your mom…" Her voice trailed away.

I don't know why, but her sudden readiness made me a whole lot less ready.

You know why.

"But there is something I want to do first." She went on when I said nothing.

I leaned around her for the coffee. "Name it."

"I was thinking about going to see my doctor. You know, get an exam, maybe some bloodwork, make sure everything is as it should be. I thought it may give us, well me, some extra confidence that this pregnancy may work out better."

"That's a real good idea, baby. You call the doc and let me know when the appointment is. I'll be there."

"But football," she protested.

I made a sound. "Fuck football. You come first."

Rim leaned forward and kissed my cheek. "I love you."

"Me, too," I said, then gestured to the cake. "Eat your chocolate."

She chuckled and reached for the plate.

She seemed lighter now, like, as she said, the last couple weeks had shifted her thinking. I was grateful for that. So damn grateful. I wanted her happy. I'd give anything to make sure she was.

Even at the risk of my own peace of mind.

Cambria Hebert

Chapter Fourteen

RIMMEL

I dreamed of repeated knocking. Until I woke enough to realize I wasn't dreaming; the knocking was real. And it was annoying.

"Whoever that is, is an asshole," Romeo grumbled and slid out from beneath me. I made a sound as my body connected with the mattress.

The knocking continued, even as Romeo rustled around for something to put on and promised whoever was there an untimely demise.

"Took you long enough!" Braeden's voice boomed into the room the second the door swung open.

I smiled into the pillow, imagining Romeo scowling.

"What the shit, man?" he grumped.

"Pancake Sunday," he announced, ignoring Romeo's combative tone. I heard the light sound of glass on glass and lifted my head to see him wheeling in a giant room service cart covered with white linen.

"It's Monday," Romeo growled.

Ivy, who was carrying Nova, stopped in front of him as she walked in. "I tried to tell him he was being a moron."

Nova held out her arms for Romeo and leaned forward.

"Uncle Romeo is tired," Ivy told her.

Romeo grunted and reached for the baby. "Never too tired for you, lady." She settled in his arms with ease and gave him a short-on-teeth smile.

She looked pretty adorable this morning, with white and pink striped tights and a white onesie with the words *My Daddy Plays Football* in gold glitter. Around her head was a pink striped headband with a floppy bow on top. The strands of her dark hair stuck out around it like she'd been playing too hard already and hadn't thought about her hair at all.

She got that from Braeden.

Or maybe me.

On her feet were a pair of gold-glitter tennis shoes. Seriously, baby-size shoes had to be one of the cutest things known to man. I had no idea where Ivy found half the stuff Nova wore, but I swear she could open her own boutique and be a highly sought-after business overnight.

As Braeden clattered around the room (and seriously, I mean clattered; oh my word, he was loud!) and Ivy told him to be quiet, I lay my head on the pillow and stared at Romeo and Nova. It was the first time in a long time seeing him with her in his arms only made me feel one type of way.

Want.

Lately, it had been want coupled with guilt, anxiety, sadness, and loss.

Don't get me wrong. I still felt those things. I always would. Losing a child was something you lived with, not something you got over. But for the first time in a very long time, I allowed myself to solely want another child with my husband and not be overcome with everything else.

Hope swelled inside me. It was sort of like sunshine after a rainstorm that lasted for days.

A pair of sweatpants-clad legs stepped into my line of sight. I glanced up, past the T-shirt and crossed arms, to look into the face of my scowling big brother.

"I got a bone to pick with you, tutor girl."

I raised an eyebrow, which made me wonder where my glasses were. "You just burst into my room at the crack of dawn, and *you're* the one with the bone to pick?"

"It's after nine," he said, dry, and handed me my glasses, which were on the table beside him. He knew me too well.

"So you become an overnight sensation for brawling in the stands, and suddenly you're too good for pancake Sunday?"

I shoved the glasses on my face, then pushed at the mass of hair threatening to attack my entire head. "It's Monday," I told him, even though Romeo already had. "You guys weren't home for pancake Sunday yesterday."

"Excuses," B reprimanded.

"Wait," I said, heaving up into a sitting position. "Did you say overnight sensation?"

"You're trending on TweetDeck," Ivy said from across the room. "And just about every other social media site."

I groaned. "The clip of you in the stands yesterday has over a million hits on YouTube already."

I fell over, letting my face bury into the pillow.

"My sister, the unexpected bruiser."

"I'm never going to hear the end of this," I groaned into the pillow.

There was another knock at the door.

"What the fuck is this? Grand Central Station?" Romeo muttered and went to the door.

"You watch your mouth when you're holding my kid," Braeden told him.

"He hasn't had his coffee yet." He really shouldn't teach her such bad words, but I would defend him anyways.

Braeden glanced at me and winked. I sat up once more and shoved my fist under my glasses and rubbed at the sleep still clinging there.

"Heard there was coffee up in here!" Drew announced, waltzing into the room.

Surprised, I glanced around B. "Drew! Trent!"

"Hey, sis." Trent smiled.

"Everyone's here!"

"It's pancake Sunday. Monday edition," B said.

"It's a family tradition." Trent nodded.

"You guys drove all the way here to eat pancakes with us?" I said, surprised. I glanced at Romeo. "Did you call them?"

He shook his head. "Nope."

"We saw the game." Drew guffawed. "Thought you might need someone to bail you outta jail."

Oh, for heaven's sake.

"It was a rough night. Figured you could use some family time," Braeden said low, tugging on my hair.

My eyes misted up. I held out my arms to him for a hug.

He wrapped me up, squeezing me tight. Before pulling back, he whispered in my ear, "I love ya, sis, but you gotta put on some clothes. This just feels wrong."

I gasped and laughed at the same time.

I was wearing a T-shirt, but that was about all. The blankets did cover me from the waist down; it wasn't as if I were exposed.

"You better get your girl, Rome. One slight move and all her tidbits could be exposed."

Romeo grabbed B by the back of his neck and pulled him away. "Dude, get the hell away from my wife."

I waved at Nova and shoved the covers back.

"Clothes," Romeo said, planting himself in front of me like a shield.

I grabbed my bag and darted into the bathroom. Outside, I could hear everyone talking, the sound of plates clattering, and the scent of maple syrup and bacon wafted through the air.

I smiled as I pulled on a pair of black leggings, a loose button-up chambray shirt, and added a chunky knit cream-colored cardigan (that was too big, my favorite) over top.

The blown-out, sleek strands of my hair were long gone. In their place was my usual wild style. Well, it was nice while it lasted.

I'm sure by now you know what I'm going to say.

I didn't bother with it. I pulled it up into a massive knot on top of my head. Because I still had some flyaways going on that looked like horns, I fished out a yellow polka dot headband I sometimes wore when I washed my face. I used it to make me look less like Satan, then called it a success.

No, I didn't care that the headband didn't match.

I was just about finished when Romeo let himself into the bathroom, paused on his way past to kiss me on the temple, then went to the toilet to pee.

And this was marriage, folks. The real kind. Not the kind in romance novels.

Romeo had no qualms about peeing in front of me. Or doing any other bodily function, no matter how gross or stinky.

"Hey, baby," he called, and I rolled my eyes.

"*No*, Romeo. I do not want to hold it for you."

Men.

"You really didn't call them?" I asked, putting my pajamas and hairbrush I didn't use back into my bag.

"Didn't have to. They're family," he replied simply.

Even after all this time, I still was surprised by the people I got to call family.

After he finished up and washed his hands, Romeo grasped me around the waist. "I wish I could come home with you today."

I tilted my head back. "Me, too."

"Rim!" B yelled from outside the door. "Your phone is going off!"

I wrinkled my nose. "Who would be calling me?"

I left the bathroom, and Braeden was there, holding out my phone. "It's my dad," I said because I knew Romeo was curious.

"I'll make you a coffee," he said on his way past.

"Dad?" I answered. He didn't call very often, and when he did, it wasn't this early in the morning. It made my stomach twist.

"Hi, Rimmel, honey," he said. There was no trace of alarm in his voice.

"Is something wrong?"

"No, no. Everything here is fine. I'm still working, and I haven't missed a rent check."

"Oh, well, that's great to hear," I told him. Ever since my father lost literally everything and went to treatment for his severe (and frankly, deadly) gambling addiction, he'd been trying to rebuild some kind of life.

For a while, he stayed at my grandparents' home while he searched for a new job (which wasn't too easy to find after all the press coverage).

But then he got hired on at a construction site as one of the crew (must have been a bitter pill to swallow considering he used to be a foreman for his own business) and was able to save up to rent a small, one-bedroom apartment.

I hadn't been back to Florida since everything happened. I'd only seen my father once (at our wedding), but I did still try to talk to him every week or two.

Up until now, I was uncertain whether or not our relationship could ever be salvaged. Sometimes I still doubted it. But if I could get to a better place with Valerie, then there was hope for my father.

There was an awkward pause between us while I waited to see why he called. He cleared his throat. "I just wanted to let you know I've been contacted by the press."

"What!" I squeaked.

I felt several pairs of eyes turn to me from across the room.

"Don't worry." He reassured me. "I told them to shove their pile of cash where the sun don't shine."

"They offered you money?" My eyes found Romeo, and he frowned.

A spidery feeling crawled up the back of my neck.

"Yeah, just like Romeo said. And I know he was concerned when I talked to him that I would sell out my own daughter, so I just wanted to let you know I didn't. And I'm not going to. You're more important to me than money."

What in the world was he talking about? Romeo talked to my dad? When?

Romeo was watching me carefully, almost as if he were afraid I might explode. I could have. Well, not explode. That wasn't my style. Unless of course bobbleheads were holding signs for my man. But I could have asked my father for details, found out everything I wanted to know just then.

The problem with that was loyalty. I was just as loyal as Romeo. I would never throw him under the bus like that. I would show a united front and pretend I knew what Dad was talking about. Romeo was my husband, and I trusted him. Sure, sometimes he did bonehead stuff (like whatever this was), but I still had his back. Always.

"I appreciate that, Dad," I replied. "I'm really glad to know you're doing well."

"How about you? Everything okay there? I saw the game last night."

I groaned. "That won't happen again."

"I figured. Those gossip hounds have been giving you hell. I was glad to see you giving it back."

That surprised me. "You were?"

"'Course. You're a fighter, Rimmel. You always have been."

I was a fighter. It was becoming more apparent to me every day.

I asked about my grandparents, and then we fell silent again.

"Well, you'll let Romeo know what I said?" he asked, sensing the conversation was coming to an end.

"I'll tell him." My eyes found my husband once more.

He grimaced.

Before we got off the line, I said, "Hey, Dad. Out of curiosity, what did the press want?"

He made a sound. "Anything that would make a good story. And they were willing to pay big money for it, too."

"How much?" I asked.

"If the story was juicy enough, over a million."

The choked sound I made caused him to chuckle. "Don't you worry. I told them no. I'm clean now, sweetheart. I plan to stay that way."

"That's great, Dad. I'm proud of you."

After I disconnected the call, I spun, taking in my entire family sitting around with plates piled with eggs, bacon, and pancakes. I put my hands on my hips and pinned Romeo with a hard look. "Care to tell me what that was about?"

B whistled under his breath. "Scrappy makin' a comeback."

"Romeo," I said, ignoring my brother.

Romeo didn't balk; he just gave it to me straight. "The press put a bounty out on you, Rim. They want dirt. Anything they can get."

I felt my shoulders slump. I wasn't surprised, but I was weary. "How do you know that?"

"Because they called me," Drew put in.

I looked at Drew. "They called you?"

He nodded, and Trent's face went sour. "They offered me and T two million dollars for a no-holds-barred exclusive tell-all about you and Romeo." He cleared his throat. "Mostly about you."

I felt lightheaded. Two million dollars!

That was insane!

"They're willing to pay that amount of money just so they can continue to basically bully me in the media?" I asked, my voice slightly hoarse.

B stood, but Romeo was closer and came to my side. "That's why I didn't tell you right away, baby. I didn't want you to get upset."

"I am upset!" I exclaimed.

Nova made a sound, and I felt contrite. "I'm sorry, sweetheart," I crooned, stepping away from Romeo and lifting her out of Ivy's arms.

Ivy smiled at me encouragingly.

I kissed Nova on the head, and we found her a clean spoon and an empty plastic cup to play with. It always amazed me that kids would rather play with random stuff than a bag full of actual toys.

Once she was settled with her new discoveries, I turned back to everyone. Ivy sat forward and cleared her throat. "Rim has a right to be upset."

"Did you know?" I asked her.

She shook her head slowly. "Not about this. Of course I know the media is always looking for a story. I do work at *People*. But they usually don't talk about our family in front of me. I think they know it wouldn't go over very well." She paused, then cleared her throat. "I do know, though, they would pay a huge sum of money for any kind of exclusive with you guys."

"And my father?" I turned to Romeo.

"I called him. I wanted to know if the press called him, too. I was concerned."

"Concerned the addict in him would see all those dollar signs and jump back into gambling."

"It's not a stretch," Romeo said.

"No. It's not." I relented. I wouldn't defend my father. He lost that privilege the second I found out he basically let my mother pay for his gambling debts... with her life.

I pinned Romeo with a stare. "You should have told me." Then I glanced at all three guys. "You *all* should have told me."

Ivy made a sound of agreement. "Mm-Hmm."

We girls had to stick together. We were outnumbered.

"Look," I said, lowering my voice and trying to sound reasonable. "I know I haven't been myself since, um, since Evie. But I can't hide forever. I need to know about this stuff. Otherwise, I get caught off guard, like yesterday at the game."

Braeden snickered.

I gave him a dirty look. It only made him laugh harder.

"And then again this morning with my father. From now on, no more shielding me. Let's all just deal with this together, as a family."

Romeo wrapped his arms around me from behind and hunched in around me. "You got it."

All my brothers made sounds of agreement.

"Now, is there anything else no one has told me?" I asked, going forward to the coffee Romeo made me.

"I have an ingrown toenail," Braeden announced and shoved a piece of bacon in his mouth.

"I think my underwear might be too small," Trent added and shifted uncomfortably.

"Just go commando," Braeden cracked. "Drew would be thrilled."

Drew wagged his eyebrows, and Ivy made a sound. "There are some things you just shouldn't say out loud," she announced.

I laughed and went over to the huge cart with the food. My stomach rumbled. Romeo came up behind me, resting his chin on my shoulder when I reached for a plate. "We good?"

I tilted my head back. "We're good."

"I was just worried it would be too much."

I nodded, understanding. "Did you make a plate yet?"

"I was waiting on you."

I kissed him, then started piling eggs on the plate in my hand. "No pancakes," he whispered in my ear. "It's bad enough I ate candy and half your cake last night."

Romeo was strict with his diet during the season, something I just didn't envy. I bypassed the carbs and sugary syrup for bacon and fruit to go with his eggs. When the plate was full, I handed it to him, along with a fork.

"Thanks, baby."

Quickly, I made my own plate, which was the opposite of Romeo's. Two pancakes with maple syrup and butter and a side of fruit.

All the chairs in the room were taken, so I sat on the bed, stretched out my legs, and used my lap as a table.

"So the press called your dad?" Romeo asked when everyone was quiet.

"Offered him over a million dollars," I said, cutting into my pancake.

"I really fucking hate the press," Drew muttered.

"He said no, right?" Romeo wanted assurance.

"That's what he said."

He nodded, looking a little worried. I understood. It wasn't as if I didn't feel the same. My father was a good liar. "I'll call my grandmother later. See what she says."

Romeo nodded.

Braeden pushed out of his chair and came over, flinging himself onto the mattress beside me. The next thing I knew, he confiscated my fork and started eating my pancakes.

"Get your own carbs!" I exclaimed.

"Can't," he said, taking another huge bite. "They don't count when I eat them off your plate."

I glanced at Ivy. She shook her head. "I can't help you. I've tried to fix him. It's impossible."

"You know you love me, Ives."

Nova laughed from the floor. B grinned. "Tell your mama!"

"Drew..." Ivy began in that sisterly tone only she seemed to have. "Did you even comb your hair this morning? Or yesterday? You need a haircut."

He groaned. Beside him, Trent snickered.

"Rim doesn't comb her hair either," Drew muttered.

Braeden was still inhaling my breakfast, but he paused to pat me on the leg. "You're prettier than Drew."

"At least she attempts to fix hers!" Ivy retorted.

Nova pulled herself up using the side of the bed and peeked at me and her father.

"Hey, Critter, want some pancakes?" Braeden leaned down and picked her up. She settled on the other side of me so I was sandwiched between her and my BBFL.

"Help yourselves," I muttered but cut off a small piece and held it up to Nova's lips.

She sucked it into her mouth and smiled. My heart turned over. She was so beautiful. I caressed the side of her cheek while she chewed and then laughed when she pointed at the plate for more.

As I was feeding her (and Braeden was still helping himself), I felt Romeo's stare. Our eyes connected.

Ivy was giving Drew a fashion lecture, Trent was laughing, Braeden was food stealing, and my niece was waving her spoon around with a mouthful of pancake.

We smiled at one another. Everyone else fell away.

Today was a good day.

Celebrity News

Chapter Fifteen

"Yo momma is like a squirrel. She can't keep deez nuts out of her mouth."
—LockerRoomSmackTalk.com

ROMEO

Another state, another game. Another practice.

Rim was home. She and Ivy drove back to our compound not long after we finished up pancake Sunday (in disguise as Monday). Drew and Trent followed them.

It was probably torture for them, considering they never drove the speed limit, but the girls did.

After the night Rim and I had and the way she finally opened up, I just wanted to be home. I wanted to spend time with her. I wanted to make sure all the ground we recovered didn't crumble away.

I loved Rim—more than myself. Our marriage was still work, though. All marriages were. We might have the perfect love, but life wasn't perfect. It seemed it came at us, tested us, tried to pull us apart. Usually, circumstances—*life*—pushed us together.

Losing Evie didn't push us apart, per say, but it didn't push us closer either. It left us in this stagnate state that we had to fight to get out of.

The way we sometimes circled the issues taking up space in our minds made it seem we weren't fighting at all. We were. I'd always fight for her. For us. Some battles were just quieter, and some took more time.

I was practicing hard today, running the ball more than usual. It felt good to run, to power down the field and exert so much energy.

By the time practice wound down, I was drenched in sweat. My arm quivered from throwing, but it didn't worry me. It would hold out. The way it felt now was normal; it wasn't so exhausted I wouldn't be able to recover. In fact, I'd be better in the next game for it.

We didn't practice much during the actual season, mostly one good practice a week. Sometimes it was nice to just get out here and fuck around. Blow off steam. B and I were like magic out there tonight. He sensed my aggression, and it seemed to power his own.

So why did I play so hard?

Because that's how I was. Go hard or go home.

<insert manly grunt here>

Well, mostly that. Then there was this other small reason.

Rimmel opened up to me about her own dark thoughts. She was brave, wanted to try again even though she was still scared.

Made me feel like a coward.

I didn't relish this feeling. In fact, I fucking hated it.

It tasted vile. It smelled like rot, and it darkened my mood.

I hadn't done the same. I'd kept quiet about my biggest torment. What would she think of me if I'd spilled? Would she still respect me? Would she still look at me with the same warm brown eyes that made me feel like I hung the moon?

I was protecting her; I'd reasoned with my subconscious. It was a pansy-ass excuse. She didn't want protecting. She'd announced as much during pancakes, when everything came out about her father and the press.

I should have pulled her aside and confessed it all.

I didn't.

The loud drone of the music playing in the background brought me back into focus. These thoughts didn't belong here right now. Right now, it was football time.

On the sidelines, I watched our players go at it. Practice tonight was an ass-kicker.

"Romeo!" My name floated through the noise, along the breeze.

I didn't pay much attention. My name was yelled a lot during games and practices… and in general.

"Anderson!" The use of my last name had me glancing around. No one ever called me that, at least not fans. Or hell, even the team. Anderson wasn't even on the back of my uniform. I was simply Romeo.

Note: watch out for imitations. There is only one.

And it's not that guy Shakespeare wrote about either.

One of the team staff members was rushing toward me, a headset perched on his head, a Knights jacket around his torso. He carried a clipboard and pen. In his hand was a phone.

"Romeo!" he called out again as he drew closer.

I turned my back on the team and stepped forward, leaning down so I could better hear whatever he had to say over the noise.

"Urgent phone call." He shoved the phone between us.

Urgent phone call?

I didn't even have a chance to panic—you know how your stomach drops and you automatically assume the worst because the word urgent was being thrown around? I didn't have any of that.

It was like my mind was suddenly stuffed full of cotton. I felt my blood pressure spike, but even that was muted.

I grabbed the phone. "This is Roman Anderson."

The voice on the other end of the line was strange and unfamiliar. He spoke fast, and it took my muddled brain a second to catch up. I pressed a finger to my other ear, trying to mute out some of the background noise so I could focus on his words.

All the blood drained from my face.

"What!" I yelled.

He started talking again, rambling really... All that blood that drained from my head? It rushed right into my chest. Adrenaline spiked inside my body so fast my head spun.

I stopped hearing. I barely even thought.

The phone hit my foot when I dropped it, but I didn't pick it up.

I started running. Not out to the field where I was supposed to be, but away. People called my name. I didn't even pause.

I ran as fast as I could; I ran for my life.

Celebrity News

"IVF Shocker! Desperate to conceive, Rimmel Anderson takes drastic measures!"

—CELEB PIPELINE

Chapter Sixteen

RIMMEL

To go or not to go? That was the question.

The day after Ivy and I returned home from Romeo's game, I called my obstetrician. I spoke to her nurse and requested the doctor herself give me a call back when she had a free moment.

That free moment came the next day. Have you ever waited for a phone call and every minute, every hour seemed extremely dragged-out until you thought you might scream? Yeah, it's no picnic.

I was at the shelter when my cell finally rang. I told her exactly what I told Romeo—I wanted to come in. I wanted to be sure everything was as it should be. I wanted peace of mind.

I requested an appointment for early the next week, when I knew Romeo would be able to make a quick trip home between games. Unfortunately, my OB was going to be out of the office all next week.

Apparently, she was going to Bora Bora.

It was very inconvenient. I refrained from telling her that, though.

The thought of waiting another full week and a half to feel I was finally out of limbo and at least trying to move on honestly threatened what ground I was finally gaining.

Side bar: Why did the saying *move on* feel so wrong? It was like those two words implied I was simply walking away, forgetting about whatever I was moving on from. I wasn't. I was just trying not to allow it to hold me hostage. I needed a better term.

Dr. Crawford must have heard the disappointment and underlying anxiety in my reaction because she offered to fit me in before she left. By fit me in, I mean she offered to stay late the day after tomorrow (since her schedule was already beyond booked).

One problem: Romeo wouldn't be home by then.

If I didn't take the appointment, I'd have to wait until after she got back. Who knew if that would even fit with his schedule? To go or not to go?

In the end, I accepted. It was just some tests, possibly an exam. Romeo didn't really need to be there, other than for emotional support. I could handle the appointment. Then when she returned from vacation, she could review all my lab work with both of us. It was going to suck waiting that long for the results, but at least the tests would be done.

It was incredibly generous Dr. Crawford offered to extend her hours for me. I wasn't naive enough to think she was doing it just because she liked me. It was because of who my husband was. Because of my "celebrity status." I usually hated that.

Not this time.

This time I was glad, and I had no qualms about using it to my advantage to get a special appointment. After all, it seemed a lot of drama and "bad" came with that status of ours… It was kinda nice to get something positive out of it, too.

An added bonus was the offices and lab would be more private. Since the media was sniffing around so viciously, that was a definite silver lining.

I thought about asking Valerie if she would come along, but in the end, I decided to go on my own. I was a big girl; I could handle it. I could have asked Trent. I probably should have… Romeo likely expected it. But I wanted to do this on my own. It felt really personal to me. Like something I needed to do for myself.

It was late afternoon when I walked into the office. It was quiet, sterile, and clean. The receptionist looked up and smiled brightly when I appeared.

"Mrs. Anderson," she said. "How good to see you again."

"Thank you," I replied, signing the clipboard at the desk. "I'm here for Dr. Crawford."

She nodded once, the dark, short curls on her head bobbing. She hit a button on the phone and then spoke into it. "Mrs. Anderson is here."

I didn't even have time to sit down. A nurse wearing dark-blue scrubs opened the door to the back. "Right this way."

I followed her back and did the usual: weight, blood pressure, blah, blah. I was pretty sure I weighed about a thousand pounds more because of all the water I drank before arriving. I was hoping she'd do a sonogram, you know, just to make sure all was well. Sonograms worked better with a full bladder.

"Rimmel." Dr. Crawford appeared from a long hallway. "You look well."

"Thank you," I said, shifting uncomfortably.

"Ahh, I recognize that dance," she said warmly. "Hoping for an ultrasound?"

"If you think that might help?" I asked. I really had no idea what to ask for. I'd told her what I wanted on the phone, but she didn't detail everything she planned to do.

"Sure, we can do one. Come on back. We'll do it first. That way you can empty out that bladder."

Again, I found it convenient that Romeo and I were "celebrities" and everyone knew he made an insane amount of money. Doctors didn't question the things I wanted—like extra sonograms—because they knew we had the money to cover it and wouldn't have to fight with insurance companies. I didn't care about the money Romeo made, but it was a true blessing when it came to the health and well-being of my future child.

After the sonogram, I peed in a cup, got a basic exam, and went to the lab for some lab work. Of course, it seemed like they took half my blood volume, and honestly, it made me a little queasy. I didn't complain, though.

Once I was fully dressed and had a small container of orange juice in my hand (to replenish some energy and sugar), I was led to my doctor's spacious office, where she was already sitting behind her desk in her white coat.

She was an attractive woman with long, dark hair, green eyes, and a kind smile.

"Have a seat," she said, motioning to the chairs in front of her desk.

I did, suddenly feeling very nervous. During the sonogram, she pointed out things and generally told me everything looked wonderful, but it seemed I was sitting down right here to be given the final verdict on the chances of me conceiving again.

I'd also like to note I realized there were a lot of women out there who suffered worse than me. More miscarriages, years upon years of struggling to conceive or even not being able to have a child at all. I realized some might find it silly I was so frazzled and worried about conceiving because it took over six months to get pregnant, and then when I did, I lost her during my first trimester.

But how did you put a rating on pain? It wasn't really a competition and certainly not one I would ever enter. The pressure I put on myself to get pregnant, coupled with the loss of not carrying her to term and feeling as if I failed Romeo… well, it cut me. Deeply.

"I've gone over everything from your previous pregnancy, the sonogram we did today… I made a few notes from the exam," Dr. Crawford said.

I nodded, feeling my heart thud beneath my ribs.

"Of course I won't be able to go over your bloodwork until after next week," she added.

"Yes," I replied, wishing she'd get to the point.

"I see no reason to believe you won't conceive again and go on to have a healthy pregnancy."

My eyes filled with tears, but I blinked them away. The relief was almost overwhelming, but even so, there was a part of me afraid to believe. "Are you sure?"

She smiled kindly. "I cannot guarantee you won't have another miscarriage. Sometimes they just happen for reasons we don't always know. What I can tell you is everything I've seen and based on your age, health, etc., you will be able to have the baby you and your husband very much want."

I let out a silent exhale. "And the bloodwork?"

"I'll call you as soon as I get back and go over your file. I can tell you right over the phone if you want."

My nod was eager.

"I do not anticipate anything to show up, no red flags or reasons to keep you from getting pregnant. I see no reason why you and your husband can't start trying again as soon as you like. Your body is healed from the miscarriage. It's able to do what it needs to do."

"Okay," I replied, nervous and excited all at once.

"I know getting pregnant after a miscarriage is very frightening. I also understand you may feel some guilt. I strongly encourage you to talk to someone, anyone who is willing to listen and support you. And start taking prenatal vitamins now. That way you have all the nutrients in your system before you conceive."

I made a mental note to go pick up a brand-new bottle on the way home.

"Anything else?" I asked.

"Relax," she implored. "Getting pregnant is easier when you aren't so stressed. Stress is taxing on the body. Get lots of rest. Be kind to yourself."

"Right." I agreed. I knew that was coming. If only relaxing weren't so difficult.

"It might also be good to get in the habit of not lifting anything heavy. It won't cause you to miscarry, but it's better safe than sorry. You are a small woman."

After a few more moments of talking and her basically reassuring me, our appointment came to a close. I thanked her and walked out of the offices feeling better than I had when I walked in.

For the first time in a long time, the possibility of a baby excited me, and it didn't seem so out of reach.

I thought back to before I lost Evie, to the joy both Romeo and I felt. The way he used to talk to my belly and bring me pickles. The way we browsed baby boutiques to look at tiny clothes. I was even looking at pink. How could you have a little girl and not look at pink?

Even after what happened to my mother and the negative feelings I had about the girly color, Evie had given it new meaning again. That feeling was gone now. If anything, pink was even more abhorrent to me now, and I don't think even another baby would change that.

But that was okay. Not all little baby girls had to wear pink.

Looking back, maybe it had been a mistake to get the early blood test to find out it was a girl. But on the other hand, knowing her sex was just one more thing I had of her. It was a blessing but also a torment. Even still, the blessing outweighed the negatives.

The entire office was quiet and empty now as I walked toward the front door. When I stepped out into reception, I was taken aback when the receptionist smiled from behind the counter.

"All finished?" she said, chipper.

For some reason, her chipper-ness made me feel odd.

"Yes, thank you. Is there anything I need to do to checkout before I go?"

She glanced at the computer screen before her and shook her head once. "No, it looks like everything is fine. We'll bill you any portion owed."

"Okay, great," I said, shifting the Kate Spade bag in my grip. "Have a nice evening."

"You, too," she called out as I walked away.

● ● ●

In the elevator, I pulled out my cell and checked the time. Romeo was probably still at practice, so I figured I would wait to call him when I got home. On the way, I'd stop and get a bottle of the vitamins the doctor recommended as well.

Nerves filled me once more at the thought of trying to have another baby. Desire also swelled deep inside me. I would be able to feel all of Romeo again, no thin layer of latex between us. I couldn't wait for that moment, so I started brainstorming ways to make the night he came home special.

The elevator opened. I stepped out, still daydreaming about my husband, his body, and the night he'd finally arrive home. I moved through the lobby without really paying attention, then pushed through the wide glass door and onto the sidewalk opening up to the parking lot.

I got about four steps outside and instantly regretted not paying attention.

Fantasizing about my husband was all well and good… but it probably shouldn't be done in public.

The sounds of pounding feet, shouts, and the glare of flashing cameras caught me completely off guard. I groaned out loud because the disappointment and surprise at seeing the vultures was so real.

How did they know I was going to be here? I'd been so careful on the way, making sure no one followed me. I told no one I was coming, and I even came after hours!

I felt like stomping my foot on the ground and having a hissy fit right there.

"Mrs. Anderson, can you tell us what you were inside for?"

"Rimmel! Is it true this is your doctor's office?"

"Are you having IVF treatments because you can't get pregnant on your own?"

Oh my God! Did these people have no morals? No respect for others? What kind of people would literally sit outside a doctor's office so they could harass someone and shout the most insensitive questions at them on the street?

I turned so I could go back in the building, but I was surrounded. It was as if I were in a bubble of people. People I was seriously considering kicking.

I turned back and started forward, thinking I would just push past them all and make a run for it. It wasn't parked far; I could make it.

Everyone moved as a unit around me. It was overwhelming, and in only a few seconds, a minute tops, my limbs were shaking.

They yelled my name, hurled questions, and continued to take pictures.

"No comment!" I yelled, trying to push through the swarm as I walked.

"What do you think about the list of women offering to give your husband a child?" someone yelled.

I gritted my teeth.

At the edge of the sidewalk, I paused because the thick line between me and the pavement was congested. I locked eyes with a photographer, a man with a greasy man bun, ratty jeans, and a bad shave, and gave him my best intimidating stare.

"Excuse me," I half growled.

"Answer some questions for me first," he intoned. "Can I get a shot of your stomach? Turn sideways."

"No!" I shouted. "Move!"

He laughed, as if he thought my display of annoyance were fun. I turned from him toward the next wall of man and pushed out my arm, using it as a battering ram to hopefully get through.

He and the greasy man bun stepped toward each other and forward, which caused me to bounce back. I tripped and nearly fell. My handbag landed on the sidewalk, and I quickly bent to retrieve it.

This was mortifying. It was incredibly demeaning, and frankly, if I didn't get through, I was afraid I might cry out in frustration. Some days, I would give anything for Romeo's size and muscle mass.

Sure, I could stand there and pose for a few pictures, maybe answer a couple questions. It wouldn't help. They would just want more and more.

Do not engage. That was the way my family and I had come to operate with the press. It worked, for a while.

Clearly not anymore.

Maybe I should have brought Trent along…

"Rimmel!"

I snapped out of it, and my body went rigid. Like a cannon, I shot forward, plowing right between two paparazzo, and managed to squeeze through. I stumbled out of the crowd and ran to my Range Rover, unlocking the doors and leaping inside.

Once there, I hit the locks immediately and collapsed against the leather with a heave. My body was shaking, my chest squeezed with panic, and my mouth had gone dry. After a few short seconds, I placed my bag in the passenger seat, trying to ignore the flashes and knocks on the windows.

They were all tinted, so I had some privacy. Except of course the windshield.

Once I had my keys in hand, I started to turn toward the wheel. A loud thump sounded in front of me. I shrieked and spun, gripped the steering wheel. The man with the greasy man bun was lying across the hood, taking pictures through the windshield!

He seriously needed to get a life.

I had a moment's thought to call the police. I even looked down at the phone in my lap. But that would require sitting here longer.

I wanted to go home.

The Rover started up with ease, and I glared at the man on the hood. With an evil little thought, I turned on the windshield wipers and held down the button for the washer fluid. It sprayed everywhere, including on the man and his camera.

He gave a shout and leapt back. Actually, he slipped off the hood and hit the pavement.

Gee, I hoped he wasn't hurt.

Not.

I gunned the engine, still sitting in the same spot, and threw the car into reverse. The man who fell off the car stood with an angry look on his face.

"You broke my camera, you bitch!"

No. You broke it. You asshole!

I resisted the urge to stick out my tongue. Instead, I started backing up. The movement of my car forced some of the paps to move. It took me a little longer than usual to back up, but I did, and once I was clear of the spot, I laid on the horn aggressively to give fair warning to everyone in my way.

Before hitting the gas, I glanced around for greasy man bun, but he was gone.

Probably gone home to lick his wounds about his camera.

"Buh-bye," I said and drove forward. A quick glance in my rearview showed some of the people rushing for their cars.

I sighed. I hoped that didn't mean they'd be following me.

Guess I'd have to put off getting my vitamins. I think that bothered me more than anything. What kind of life would I be bringing a baby into if I couldn't even safely and peacefully go to the store for vitamins when I needed them?

What if I'd had a baby with me tonight? What would I have done?

Horror assaulted me. Horror and dread. Doubts assailed me. Was I doing this for all the wrong reasons? Would it be better if I didn't have another child? Any baby of ours would be relentlessly pursued. I couldn't even protect myself. How would I protect an innocent child?

You couldn't before...

A sob formed in my throat; my vision went a little blurry with unshed tears.

Bright headlights shone into my rearview mirror, and I winced, averting my gaze. I blinked and glanced up, looking to find a car right on my bumper.

The wheel jerked in my hands. In surprise, I tore my eyes away and back to the road. Once I was straight, I glanced back up to see if I could tell who it was chasing me.

Another car swerved alongside mine, and my head whipped around. Because this one was right beside me, I could see into the car better. It was one of the vultures, the one who nearly knocked me down with the help of greasy man bun.

I'd bet a million dollars it was him behind me.

I felt a slight tap on my bumper, causing my car to jerk. I screamed and gripped the wheel, trying to keep on track.

The car beside me swerved closer, and I sucked in a breath. Panic made me weak; my breath came in gasps as I struggled to decide what to do. I could pull over, but would they pull over, too?

Was it safer to keep moving so they couldn't at least get to me? Or was it safer to pull over and take my chances?

I hit a button on the dash and yelled, "Call local police!"

The sound of my Bluetooth registering and the call going through nearly made me weep. I focused on the road in front of me as I drove, hitting the gas a little heavier than I probably should, but fear and adrenaline gave me an overwhelming desire for flight.

The operator on the other end answered, and I just started talking, not even bothering to listen to her introduction. "My name is Rimmel Anderson. I'm on Fleet Street, heading away from Dr. Crawford's office. I'm being chased by two men who I believe are paparazzi. They're in two separate cars." Something hit my back end again. I screamed. "They're trying to run me off the road!"

"I'm dispatching a unit now, Mrs. Anderson. Is there anywhere you can pull over until help arrives?"

"I'm scared to pull over! What if they attack me?"

"Can you give me a description of the vehicles?"

I called out as many details as I could as my car drove down the street and I white-knuckled the wheel. It wasn't much. I was almost to the point of not being able to think. Just then, the man behind me laid on his horn, the disruptive sound blaring through the night.

I heard the acceleration of his car behind me and braced for impact, but none came. When I glanced in the mirror, I couldn't see his headlights anymore because he was so close.

"Please hurry," I whispered.

"We're on our way. Can you pull over?"

I glanced up ahead. There was a gas station with lots of overhead lighting a couple blocks away. "There's a GoGas station up on my right. I'll pull in there."

"I'll direct the officers."

Tears ran down my cheeks. I hadn't even felt them. My stomach and body was so tense it cramped, and the feeling reminded me of the day I lost Evie.

Just thinking about her, just reliving even a fraction of something from that day broke something inside me. A cry ripped from my lips, and I leaned over the steering wheel.

The car beside me swerved in again, and I tried to avoid him. My Range Rover fishtailed a bit, and I fought for control. The lights of the gas station drew closer, offering me some kind of safety. I focused on them, but all I saw was flashes of the press and all I heard was the screeching of tires.

The car at my side slammed over again, this time catching me off guard. I cried out and jerked the wheel, trying with everything I had to avoid getting sideswiped. The car behind me clipped my bumper. I heard it rather than felt it.

The next thing I knew, the Rover was out of my control, skidding off the road and toward the gas station I'd been so desperate to reach.

The huge overhead lights that had once seemed like a beacon and promise of safety, turned out to be just the opposite.

The Range Rover collided head on with one of the cement lamp poles. The ear-splitting sound of crunching metal and the airbag exploding at my face was all I knew.

Burning pain burst across my entire body as dust and debris clogged my airways.

Everything went dark.

Chapter Seventeen

ROMEO

"Mr. Anderson?" the voice on the other end of the phone said.

"This is Roman Anderson," I said, a feeling of dread worming its way through my guts.

"This is Paul Ryken. I'm a first responder in Maryland. I'm calling to let you know I'm here with your wife,"

"What!" I yelled. My fingers went numb. I fumbled to hold the phone. Black spots swam before my vision as I struggled to hear everything.

"She was involved in a car accident tonight. We're at the scene now. I wanted to let you know she's being transported to Primary Hospital—"

The phone hit my foot. I didn't even know where it went after that.

Now here I was in a helicopter, on my way to the hospital. I had no idea what Rim's condition was, but it didn't matter.

I was scared.

More scared than I'd been in my entire life.

Including the day we'd lost Evie and I watched Rimmel nearly crumble.

Never again. I didn't want to do that ever again.

A fine tremor worked through my joints, always there, reminding me nothing was steady, nothing was solid. It wouldn't be ever again until I saw my wife, until she looked at me with clear eyes that weren't wracked with pain.

"Almost there," Braeden said quietly at my side.

My eyes flicked to the window. All I saw were lights. Lights that blurred together.

I should have asked what her condition was. I should have asked to speak with her. Anything. I should have demanded any shred of information that would make this ride just a little more bearable.

Braeden's leg was bouncing, his own agitation showing.

The second I rushed off the field, he'd been right at my heels. I couldn't even tell him what was wrong. I'd just looked up from grabbing my shit out of the locker and said her name.

He knew.

He knew from the tone of my voice, from the rigid set of my body… There was nothing else on this planet that could make me lose my shit like this.

He hadn't asked for details. He didn't say anything at all.

Instead, my brother made a call to Gamble himself, roused the man out of a closed-door meeting, and spoke quietly into the line. I was already running toward the exit of the building. Just before I stepped out into the lot—I'd run if I had to—B grabbed me, yanked me back, and pointed to the stairs.

He still spoke, but I didn't listen. I ran the stairs without even stopping. I took all ten floors double-time.

When I hit the door that led to the roof, I burst through and stared at the sky.

Braeden slid his phone away. "Any second now. You're going to have to tell the pilot where to go."

I did. The hospital name ripped right out of me, and Braeden took the news like he'd been punched in the face.

Here we were… the chopper descending out of the sky toward the giant X on a large building.

The second we touched down, I was out, despite warnings from the pilot. The wind was so strong it was like running against gale-force hurricane gusts.

I withstood it.

Nothing, not even wind brought forth by our creator himself, would keep me from getting to her.

Braeden kept pace but fell behind me. Even he knew not to get in my way. I burst into the ER like a man with a bomb strapped to his chest. People stopped what they were doing and stared.

"Where is she?" I bellowed to no one and everyone.

A nurse behind the station rushed around. "Follow me."

I ran after her. She glanced behind me at B, and I growled. She turned back without another word. I wasn't putting up with any kind of rules from the staff. We were both going in. No arguments.

It seemed I went down the longest hallway ever, despite the speed at which we walked.

The nurse pointed to the very last room at the end of the hall, and I rushed past. She was smart because she got the hell out of my way. I didn't hesitate at the door. I didn't debate on the sight I might find.

I didn't care.

Please just let her be breathing.

There was a curtain drawn around the bed, still hiding her from sight. It pissed me off, and I grabbed a handful of the material and ripped it back.

"Rimmel!" I roared as I yanked. The sound of seams ripping and metal groaning against metal filled the room.

A nurse looked up from the bedside; her loud gasp didn't even register.

Rimmel's body jerked with shock. The bed was in a sitting position, her body relaxed against the mattress. Her eyes went wide like saucers, and her too-pale cheeks began to bloom with faint color.

"Romeo!" Her voice was muffled, and she grabbed at the oxygen mask covering her face.

An oxygen mask.

I had a brief moment of tunnel vision when all I could see was that thing covering her mouth and nose. A thing helping her breathe.

She's supposed to be able to breathe on her own.

A sound I'd never heard before ripped from deep inside me. I dove at her. My entire body wrapped around hers, and I pulled her close, squeezing her as tight as I dared. Half her body was lifted off the bed. I supported almost all her weight.

She was small. Fragile. So easily broken.

She's having trouble breathing.

My face disappeared in her neck. The strands of her naturally unruly hair threatened to suffocate me, but I barely noticed. She smelled like home.

She was my entire life.

A tremor racked my chest. I felt it move beneath my ribs.

Her hands splayed out across my back, gripping with strength I thanked God for. A few seconds went by, and she tried to pull back, but I refused to budge. I wasn't letting go.

Her head wiggled, but I still didn't move.

"Sir," the nurse said from the bedside.

I growled.

"Rome," B said, kicking me lightly. "You're squishing Rim's mask."

I pulled back only inches, enough so she could reach between us and pull down the mask so it hung around her neck.

"Don't worry. I'm not pregnant." She hurried to assure me. The tone of her voice nearly severed the only thread that was still holding me together.

But then her words sank in.

I drew back, staring down into her eyes. "Why would you say that to me right now," I demanded, anger punching me in my already scrambled and twisted guts.

"I…" Her mouth opened and closed, her features surprised.

Did she really think I cared about that more than I did her? What. The. Fuck?

Did she care about that more than herself? Again: What. The. Fuck?

I made a sound, unable to even process that shit. I grabbed her close again, holding her tighter than I should. "It's you I'm worried about, baby. Only you."

I felt her hands on my face, my cheeks; she was smoothing her cool fingers over my overheated skin. "I'm okay. Everything is fine."

"You need to put the oxygen back on," the nurse told Rimmel, stepping closer.

● ● ●
239

My head whipped around, my arms yanking her back into my chest. Daggers flashed from my eyes. I felt them piercing her busybody skin. She took a step back. I actually saw a look of fear cross her face.

"I got her," I intoned.

"But the doctor—" she protested.

Was she really fucking speaking? Oh, hells no.

I started to pull back from Rim, my spine rigid, eyes locked on a nurse who should have just turned around and run.

Once again, Braeden intervened. "Why don't you go get the doctor, ma'am? We'd like to talk to him."

He physically guided her away from my wife. I stared at her the entire way. Braeden was muttering some shit about how I was half out of my mind and how the long ride messed with my head…

Bunch of bullshit.

She left the room, and all my attention zeroed back in on my wife. I glanced down. She was literally plastered against me. I gentled my hold and pulled her back a fraction.

"Is anything broken?" I asked, praying to God there wasn't.

"No."

I shifted, lifting her completely, and slid my body under hers. She settled between my legs, her back against my chest. I locked my arms around her waist and pushed her head back against my chest.

Braeden came back in the room and looked Rim up and down. "Tutor girl, this shit ain't funny."

"Good thing I'm not joking," she said. Her voice was weak and strained. She sounded a little high. There were some red, aggravated cuts and scratches on her face… and her glasses were missing.

I didn't like it.

Her body felt like rubber against mine, like she was too weak to even hold herself up.

Braeden came forward like he was going to lean in and kiss her.

"I wouldn't if I were you," I rumbled. B shifted back and dropped into a chair right beside the bed.

"Roman Anderson!" Rimmel scolded, but it lacked her usual charm and heat.

It made my heart squeeze.

"It's all right, sis. I'll touch you later. When it ain't a threat to my life."

"What the hell happened, Rim? Why did I get a call from a stranger that took about twenty years off my life?"

"Maybe you should put the mask back on your face," B said, leaning forward, his eyes intent on Rimmel.

I leaned around her, scrutinizing her face. It was pale. Her lips were cracked, and her eyes seemed even larger than normal.

I cursed low and gently lifted the mask, pressing it over her nose and mouth.

She rolled her eyes.

"Hush," I told her and adjusted the straps so they held it around her head. After I smoothed her hair back, I leaned back, bringing her with me. "Just breathe," I said. "You can tell us later."

I wanted to know now, but it wasn't the most important thing.

The doctor came in the room, wearing green scrubs and a lab coat, a stethoscope hanging around his neck. The nurse hovered in the doorway, unsure if she should come in.

"Mr. Anderson?" he said, staring at me in the bed.

"Yes." I dared him to tell me to move.

He didn't.

"I'm Dr. Westfall." He gave me his hand. I released Rim long enough to shake it.

"Tell me what's wrong with my wife."

She pulled the oxygen off her face again. "I'm fine," she said. "Just shaken up."

The doctor glanced at Braeden. I made a rude sound. "He's her brother."

Dr. Westfall nodded brusquely. "Your wife was involved in a car crash this evening. Her vehicle ran off the road and hit a cement light post."

My body went rigid under hers. Braeden jerked up in his seat. "How the hell did that happen?" I demanded.

The doctor cleared his throat. "The airbags deployed. Rimmel was hit in the face and chest. Even though the impact was heavy, she sustained minor injuries, including bruising from the seatbelt, a sore chest from the airbag, a bloody nose, and some superficial cuts and scratches to her face from her glasses shattering."

Her glasses shattered against her face. "A bloody nose…" I murmured. The mental image of Rim with blood on her wasn't something I ever wanted.

"As I already discussed with her, she may have a rash tomorrow from the airbag hitting her face, and a slight cough is a common occurrence for the next day or so, as a lot of dust is usually inhaled when an airbag deploys."

"Is that why she's on oxygen?" Braeden asked.

I wanted to know, too, but I was still trying to get past the fact she was in her car when it slammed into a fucking cement pole. Thank God I made her get a Range Rover. If she'd been in something smaller, less safe, this could have been so much worse.

Maybe for her next car, I'd just buy a damn tank.

"No, that was because she had a severe panic attack when she first arrived," the doctor replied.

Rimmel glanced down. I noted the way her head tilted as if she were embarrassed.

"It's okay, baby," I whispered, hugging her close. Her hand slid around my forearm and gripped. What the fuck happened that caused her to have a panic attack? The accident? Or was it something more?

"The oxygen will help open up her lungs, though, so it might prevent a cough," the doctor said. "I can't say for sure."

"Did you hit your head?" I asked, reaching up to gently probe her scalp.

"No, I didn't."

"No concussion, and I see no reason for her to stay overnight." He glanced at Rimmel. "Are you feeling better? Do you feel like you need to stay?"

"I'm better now. I'd like to go home."

"If you start feeling worse or have a terrible headache, anything like we discussed, come back to the ER immediately."

"I will."

"Okay, well, if there are no other questions, I'll have the nurse bring in your discharge papers."

I held my hand out to the doctor. "Thank you."

"My pleasure," he returned, then took his leave.

"Your driving has officially hit a new low, tutor girl. You're supposed to stay on the road," Braeden cracked when the doctor was gone.

"They ran me off the road!" Rimmel wailed and promptly burst into tears.

A few things happened at once:

1.) I told Braeden he was a fucking moron and I was going to nut punch him.

2.) I grabbed Rimmel up into my lap and pressed her tearstained face into my shirt.

3.) I got really, really fucking furious.

She just said someone ran her off the road. As in they deliberately tried to hurt her.

"All right now, baby." I tried to calm her down. It was like she'd been holding it in until the nurse and doctor left.

Braeden was on his feet, pacing right beside the bed. He gave me an apologetic look, and I glared at him. Without even considering the fact I was going to beat his ass, he sat on the bed, practically taking up all my space.

His hand went to Rim's back. "Hey, I'm sorry, sis. I was just joking. Guess it was too soon. I'm an asshole. You're a good driver."

She sniffled, rubbing her face into my shirt.

"Rimmel…" Braeden tried again.

"Back off." I warned.

She pulled away from me and hugged B. He hesitated a second before enclosing her in his arms.

The nurse walked in. "I have your—"

"We're busy!" Both B and I snapped.

She backed out of the room, and we ignored her.

"I'm sorry." Rimmel released Braeden and hiccupped. I pulled her against me once more.

"Baby, did you say someone ran you off the road?" I asked, trying not to push her but really freaking desperate to find out what the fuck was going on and why we were sitting in this ER.

"You guys came all the way here from… Where were you again?" She lifted her head and looked at me. It was like she hadn't even heard my question. She was lost in her own thoughts.

"We were in New York. Thank fuck it wasn't Cali," I muttered. That was where I'd be soon. Hell, just thinking of being on the other side of the country made me break out into a cold sweat.

"How did you get here so fast?" she asked.

"I called Gamble. He was in town, and we used his chopper," B answered.

"Thank you for coming." Her voice was so sincere.

"As if we wouldn't." B scoffed.

I couldn't talk. It was like all the words I wanted to say crowded in my throat and choked me, making it impossible to get anything out.

There was so much I wanted to tell her, so much I wanted to know.

She noticed my silence. I wasn't sure she understood it. But I think she thought it was her fault. I hated she thought she was somehow to blame. But in way… she was.

Her words when I first rushed in this room echoed inside me. Taunting me.

"I'm sorry that guy called you. I begged him to let me do it. He wouldn't. He recognized me right away, and you're the top contact in my phone." She made an angry face. "I think he actually wanted to call you, speak to *Romeo Anderson* himself. I hate people forget you're a person, that you have feelings and you're more than a football god."

I rubbed a hand up her back. "It's all right, baby. As long as you're okay."

"I don't even know where my phone and bag is." She frowned.

"It doesn't matter. We'll get you new stuff."

"I think my car is totaled." She started to cry again. "The police had it towed away."

Braeden and I exchanged looks. The police.

"Don't worry about the car, sweetheart. It's okay."

Rimmel cuddled back into my chest, pulling her knees up with her. Her clothes were kinda light considering it was dark out and it was cold out at night. Why the fuck was she out at night?

Alone.

Then I remembered. I cleared my throat and forced out the words. "Didn't you have a doctor appointment today?"

"Yes, and I didn't even get my vitamins!" Her voice wobbled, and she sniffled. Oh fuck, did the appointment not go well?

"So this was after the appointment?" I questioned. I had no idea where to even start.

"It wasn't an accident," she intoned, tipping up her head to look at me while wiping away her tears. "They ran me off the road. The police have already been here."

Braeden's eyes narrowed, and we glanced at each other once again.

"Who ran you off the road?" I asked carefully.

"The paparazzi," she replied, flat. "They ambushed me when I walked out of the doctor's office."

I was going to need blood pressure medicine before I left this fucking sick ward. I took a steadying breath; I didn't want her to feel my extreme need to do bodily harm.

"Explain, Rimmel."

So she did. She told us everything.

Every goddamn detail.

Chapter Eighteen

"Drunk man steals a boat, tells police he's Jack Sparrow!"
-DUMB CRIMINALS

RIMMEL

It wasn't often Romeo was speechless.

In fact, usually, he wasn't at a loss for words. If anything, he just bellowed the F-word and as many other foul things he could think of.

Right now, he was quiet.

Quiet Romeo was a scary Romeo. It was like the calm before the storm. Or an empty football stadium.

I wasn't scared of him. I wasn't intimidated either, but in this moment, I saw why others often were. Romeo was not a man you wanted to piss off. He was levelheaded. He could be reasoned with.

But...

There was a point when a man like him had enough.

Sort of like when a bitch just snaps. Except guy style.

I hadn't seen Romeo reach this point very often. He'd come very close when Zach was torturing us and we ended up in the hospital. Even then, he'd acted semi-responsibly and allowed the police to deal with him.

• • •

After he knocked him out and busted up his face of course.

Oh, and got him kicked out of Alpha Omega.

He'd also threatened to cut ties with his mother, but between you and me, he wouldn't have. He may have put her on ice for a while, but he'd never remove her from his life. And honestly, I'd never allow him to.

I don't know if anyone else inside this SUV noticed his almost deadly calm that was entirely deceiving, but if they did, no one said a word.

We were in the back of Ivy's white Range Rover. Trent was in the passenger seat, Drew driving, and Romeo, Braeden, and me were in the back. Ivy and Nova were home, but since this car would fit us all more comfortably (versus Trent's and Drew's Mustangs), he brought this one to the hospital to get us.

Romeo wasn't the only madman in the car.

Trent was, too. He didn't say so, but oh, I felt it.

He was angry I didn't ask him to come to my appointment. Angry I didn't call him when I was admitted to the hospital.

<Sigh>

I loved my family, but three overbearing brothers was a lot to handle at times.

I didn't want to make any of them mad, but sometimes a girl had to be her own woman. Having an escort (aka babysitter) everywhere I went was just stupid.

Of course, if Trent had been driving earlier, we probably wouldn't have plowed into a pole.

Oh my. I was turning into a girl who needed a babysitter.

God help me.

As if my night wasn't shitty enough, I had to go and get sucker-punched with that little gem of realization.

Boo.

Romeo turned and glanced out the back window for about the hundredth time.

"We aren't being tailed," Drew said, not even glancing from the road. "If we were, I'd lose them. Trust me."

Romeo sank back into the seat.

"Compound is locked down?" Braeden asked.

"Yes," Trent said immediately. "I made sure."

"One of you could have stayed behind with Ivy," I commented.

They all snorted. Like all of them. At the same time.

How rude.

"How long you here for?" Drew asked, still not taking his eyes off the road. Every now and then, I'd see his glance flick up to the rearview before returning to the windshield.

I was tired, drained really. I was also mildly embarrassed. I had a panic attack. A full-blown body meltdown, when I first arrived at the hospital. It hit me so fast and so unexpectedly.

I didn't know they could be like that. It was as if one minute I was fine, and the next my body and mind had completely turned against me.

A cold sweat broke out over my body; my mouth ran so dry my tongue stuck to the roof of my mouth. I was shaking, not trembling as I'd been since I crashed. Full-on rattling that made it impossible to sit still. Everything around me went blurry; it was like I was living in a haze. I felt dizzy, nauseous, and my stomach cramped painfully.

The doctors saw it, even as I panicked worse, thinking something was seriously wrong. I was strapped with an oxygen mask, and a needle came at me with rapid force.

I'd twisted and evaded the stick, though. I was still enough in my right mind to deny the medicine. "No drugs," I insisted loud enough they heard me through the mask.

"It's just to help calm you down," they'd said.

"No." I refused.

If I was going to try and get pregnant, I didn't want anything like that in my system. I didn't care if it would be long gone by the time I actually had a baby inside me. The doctor's visit today put me in a mindset, a committed one.

I would do everything humanly possible, no matter how small, to make sure any baby conceived after Evie was protected.

Maybe it was irrational. I didn't care. It's what I wanted. It was my body.

Everyone else could suck an egg.

The doctor frowned, but I held firm. In the end, I stuck with the oxygen, and they put me in a quiet room. Of course, it only stayed quiet for less than five minutes before nurses and doctors and exams ensued.

"Don't know," Romeo answered Drew's question, rousing me out of my own head.

"You have a game on Sunday," I said, glancing up at him. Everything was blurry because my glasses were gone. I wasn't a fan of muddled vision, but I took comfort in the fact I had an extra pair of glasses at home.

A clumsy girl like me always had a backup.

He shrugged, not seeming to care about his game.

I glanced at Braeden, who was on my other side. He patted my leg but said nothing.

The rest of the ride to the compound was quiet. I laid my head on Romeo; his arm stayed tucked around me tightly. He was warm, and I was cold. He was strong, and I was small. I knew he was angry. I knew some of that anger was directed at me. Probably because I went out alone.

But even angry, he didn't shove me away. Rome held me close.

The exterior of our house was lit like a Disneyworld attraction. I didn't think there was a single shadow within yards of the house. Drew pulled into the garage immediately, and we all sat there, unmoving, until the door was shut behind us completely.

Once it was, the door leading into the house swung open, and Ivy filled the doorway. Her face was clean of makeup and her hair was pulled away from her face. Worry marred her features, as she shifted from foot to foot, waiting for us to get out.

Braeden glanced at me. I smiled. "Go on."

He leaned in to kiss me, and Romeo pushed his head away. "You're pushing it," he rumbled.

"If you need protection, come get me," Braeden whispered, loud.

"Get out of the car," Romeo snapped.

I put a hand against his chest as if I would restrain him. Actually, I *would* if I needed to. He was threatening my BBFL.

Braeden got out of the car. He didn't seem the least bit offended. Ivy was bouncing right beside the passenger door where he exited. I watched him lift her off her feet and kiss her cheek. She smiled, her arms tight around his neck.

Then she pulled away and peered into the still-open door. "I've been worried sick! If Nova wasn't already in bed, I'd have driven to the hospital, too!"

"You don't need to be out at night!" Braeden and Drew snapped at the same time.

Romeo and Trent made sounds of agreement.

Ivy met my eyes. "They're like this tonight, huh?"

I nodded dramatically.

She sighed, resigned. "C'mon. I made cider."

I started to slip away from Romeo, to scoot across the backseat toward the door. I didn't get far. He lifted me, held me on his lap, and exited the backseat on his side, all while lifting me into his arms.

"I can walk," I told him.

"No."

I looked at Trent for help, but he crossed his arms over his chest.

Traitor.

Everyone filed in the house. Prada, Darcy, and Ralph all danced around excitedly. Ralph leapt up toward me, and Romeo jerked.

I gave him a look. "Don't you yell at my dog."

"Who wants a bone?" Ivy called from farther in the kitchen, and I heard a bag of dog treats rattling.

All three stopped what they were doing and raced away.

"Here you go," Ivy said as she passed out the treats. "Go lie down."

All three dogs trotted off toward the living room, content.

Romeo stood in the middle of the spacious kitchen and made no move to put me down.

"Here's your cider." Ivy brought me the mug and handed it to me.

"Hi, Romeo," she said, giving him a smile.

"Princess," he replied, gruff.

"Coffee's on," she told him.

I mouthed, *Thank you,* and she smiled.

"How badly are you hurt?"

"Not much, just bruises," I replied.

Her blond head bobbed with relief. "Thank goodness. What happened?"

Romeo went rigid, and I glanced up at him, worried if I went into the whole story again, he'd really flip. When I first told him and Braeden, they'd both went deadly, calm silent.

"She's been through a lot, baby," Braeden said. "I'll fill you in upstairs."

Ivy glanced at Romeo, then away. "Okay." Her eyes found mine again. "You're sure you're okay? Can I get you anything at all?"

I wiggled to get out of Romeo's arms. He didn't budge. I made a sound of annoyance and held out my hand to Ivy. It was the closest I could come to a hug. "I'm fine. Thank you."

"We'll talk in the morning. Have coffee."

"No leaving this compound," Romeo declared. "Both of you."

Ivy sighed. "Well, we have coffee here. Since all four of you want to be such cavemen, you can watch Nova while Rimmel and I drink our caffeine in peace."

With that, she turned away. But beneath the archway of the kitchen, she pivoted back with a sigh. Her footsteps carried her to Drew first. She slipped her arms around his waist and hugged him close.

"Love you," she whispered.

● ● ●

Drew hugged her back. "You, too, sis."

Ivy then went to Trent and did the same thing.

Afterward, she held her hand out to B, motioning for them to leave the room. Braeden took her hand but glanced over at Romeo. That was the true measure of brotherhood. I'd only ever seen it between the four men in this room.

Romeo was like a bear with a butt rash tonight. He threatened Braeden's man parts, smacked him in the head, and growled at him more times than I could count. But he was still here. He wasn't pissed. He was reluctant.

Reluctant to walk out of the room in case his brother needed him.

"I'm straight," Romeo told him. "Thanks for everything tonight, man…" His voice faded away. "For getting us here."

"Anytime, Rome."

He said his good night to Trent and Drew, then allowed Ivy to lead him from the room. Their quiet voices floated off as they went.

Drew went over to the coffee pot that had just finished brewing, poured two mugs of coffee, added the creamer that was sitting nearby, and then turned toward us. "If you need anything, just call. We'll come right up."

"Will do."

"C'mon, frat boy," Drew said to Trent. "Let's go home."

Trent was looking at me like he wanted to say something, but at the same time he didn't.

I looked up at Romeo. "Put me down."

His upper lip curled, but the tone in my voice was not to be defied. The second I was on my feet, I surrendered the mug to my husband and closed the distance between Trent and me. My legs felt kinda like Jell-O.

"I'm really sorry. Please don't blame yourself. This was not your fault," I told him quietly.

His arms fell to his sides. "You shoulda called me."

"I should have." I allowed.

He wrapped his arms around my shoulders and hugged me close. My eyes fluttered closed as I hugged him back. He pressed his lips to the top of my head. "I'm glad you're okay."

I tightened my hold. "Thanks."

After that, both Trent and Drew stepped out onto the back deck so they could walk down to their house.

Romeo and I were left alone.

"You're mad," I said.

He lifted an eyebrow. "You have no idea why."

"I could guess," I whispered.

"You'd be wrong."

I stepped close to him, so close I had to tip my head back to look up into his flaming blue stare. "Then tell me, Romeo."

He stared at me for the span of two heartbeats. I know exactly because I counted. Silently, he went to the coffee pot and turned it off. There was a small light on above the sink. He left it and started for the door. On his way, he picked me up again. He was so incredibly graceful. Not one drop of my cider spilled.

Our two dogs trailed along behind him (Prada went with Ivy) as he climbed the staircase and turned toward our wing.

"Bed," he ordered both dogs the second he stepped into the bedroom, and they followed the command, lying in their gray, velvety beds.

They never listened to me like that. In fact, when Romeo wasn't home, they slept in our bed. They hogged most of it, too!

Gently, he placed me on the bed, my legs dangling over the end. He took the untouched cider and set it away. Romeo dropped to his knees in front of me, pulling off my shoes.

"I need a shower. I was mid-practice when the call came in," he spoke, setting them aside.

"Okay."

I expected him to move away, to leave me on the bed while he went to the shower. Instead, he stood, picked me up for the thousandth time tonight, and brought me into the bathroom.

"What are you doing?" I asked.

"You're showering, too."

"I've had just about enough of your bossy attitude tonight," I intoned.

"You have dust and powder all over you from the airbag," he uttered right back. "And there's blood on your shirt."

Of course there was.

He cleared his throat, speaking in a softer, more vulnerable tenor. "And I'm not letting you out of arm's distance. Don't ask me to do that, Rim. Not tonight."

My heart tumbled beneath my ribs. "I'm right here."

The shower wasn't eventful, at least not in the sexual sense. True to his word, he didn't leave my side. He touched me. He washed me. He ran his fingers through my wet hair... but it wasn't because he was turned on.

It was almost as if he were reassuring himself I was here.

I returned the caresses and stuck to him like glue. I washed his body and used my slick hands to knead the muscles of his back and neck. He was so tense he felt like granite beneath my hands.

I was tired, yes. But never so tired to give him what he needed. Right now he needed this. *Me.* It wasn't often Romeo was like this, so I wanted to make sure he knew when he was, it was okay, and I would always, *always* give him what he needed.

Afterward, we dried quickly, and I smoothed some moisturizer on my face. The skin there burned a bit, and I knew just from the feeling I'd likely wake up with some kind of rash from the airbag.

Romeo dressed in nothing but a pair of loose, ratty light-gray sweats. They hung low on his hips, accentuating the prominent V-shape at his lower half.

The ends of his wet blond hair curled up at his neck and stuck out. He looked tired. Worn out. Something I wasn't used to seeing.

I pulled on an old Alpha U T-shirt and then picked up my brush to try and get through my hair. Behind me, Romeo took the brush and started working it through my ends before moving up to brush the entire length.

I shut my eyes as goose bumps raced over my scalp. The worst of the night drained away. Well, no. Not the worst.

The worst was he was angry with me.

"Tell me why you're mad," I said, opening my eyes to gaze at him through the mirror.

"I'm not just mad," he replied, still brushing.

"Then what are you?"

His mouth flattened into a thin line. "Guilty."

Guilty! What in the world would he be guilty of?

"My accident was *not* your fault."

He shook his head once. "That's not what I'm guilty of."

"Then what?" I pressed.

He glanced away. Then in the mirror, our eyes met again. "Guilty of loving you more than I loved our daughter."

Celebrity News

Gossip +++ Buzz +++ Social Media Fre...

...nation +++ News ++...

...ews +++ Information +++ News +++ Information...

Chapter Nineteen

"How to give him the best BJ he's ever had!" *with details!*

LADY BOSS MAGAZINE

ROMEO

The truth comes out. It always does.

Not that there had ever been a lie. I'd just kept quiet about some of my deepest thoughts. I wanted to protect her.

To protect myself.

I felt guilty. Painfully so. Like the worst kind of man.

But these were my burdens to bear. It wasn't her responsibility to know the weight I carried. My job was to carry it all... and hers as well.

The look on her face said it all. Of all the words I could have strung together, those never even crossed her mind.

What must she think?

What would she when I finally confided my own despair?

I guess even sometimes the strongest fought battles that threatened to bring them down. But I was still standing. My sword might be dull, my armor scuffed, but I wasn't done fighting.

Cambria Hebert

I would never stop.

However, the time had come for this silent battle to become pronounced.

"What?" Rimmel echoed as if in shock. Slowly, she turned away from the mirror, gently grabbed my wrist, and took the brush from my palm.

It made an audible click on the stone counter when she set it aside, but our eyes remained on each other.

I nodded. "I feel guilty, Rim, so goddamn guilty. I didn't want you to know."

She made a slight sound of distress, rushed the centimeters between us, and wrapped her arms around my waist. Her body pressed in close, gripping me like she was on a rollercoaster and I was the safety bar.

I was surprised. I didn't expect a hug. I actually didn't know what I expected.

Maybe part of me expected her repulsion.

It was irrational, though. Rim wasn't like that, and she never would be. I knew this. Still, sometimes it was hard to reason with emotions that tried to break you down.

"C'mon," she whispered, took my hand, and led me from the bathroom.

The bedroom was dim. Only the light from the bathroom filtered in. Both dogs were snoring but stopped and beat their tails against the floor as soon as Rim came into sight.

It made me realize something.

She was a collector of lost souls. The forgotten, the bypassed, the most beautiful at heart. Rimmel saw beauty no one else saw, and even though how she made others feel was amazing, it was nothing compared to the way it made her shine.

She would love me through this, *in spite of this,* because though my feelings were ugly, she would see beyond them.

I hit the switch for the fireplace, the subtle whooshing of flames catching with gas filling the room. Firelight shimmered through the room, giving everything an elusive glowing cast.

She perched on the side of the bed, her legs so short they hung off the side like she was a kid sitting in one of those folding movie theater chairs that half folded up on them because they weren't heavy enough to keep the seat down.

Damp hair cascaded down her back, some thick, dark strands falling over her shoulders to frame her pale cheeks. They had a lot more color now. The pink was a little too pronounced. It reminded me of her taking an airbag to the face just hours before.

In the shower, I'd seen the bruises. A purple, mottled stripe covered her chest and collarbone from where the seatbelt had locked around her body. Her knee was bruised, too. She said she didn't remember how it happened. My guess was she smacked it into the dash on collision.

There were more random bruises all over her. I tried not to look at them too long beneath the spray. They made me sick.

"God, when that call came through," I said, my voice sounding choked inside my head. "I didn't know how bad you were, what had happened… just the possibility of losing you, Rim." I couldn't finish. Instead, I shook my head.

"You didn't." She held her hands out to me. I stepped up. Rimmel leaned forward, pressing her forehead to the center of my stomach. My hands fell to her shoulders, one cupping the base of her neck.

"I don't think I could survive it."

"We survived Evie," she whispered.

Beneath her head, my abs rippled as my muscles flexed.

"That's the thing, Rim. The thing I can't forgive myself for. I didn't want you to know."

Her head lifted off my skin, dark eyes imploring mine. She wasn't wearing her glasses, so I saw right in. "Of course. You didn't get the chance to meet your daughter."

I made a sound, pacing away. "No." I leaned forward, placing both hands on the mantle and leaning forward. I didn't want to look at her when I said this. I stared at the flames instead.

I spoke three words. Three words that were not *I love you*. Three words that had stayed tucked inside me as the ultimate plague. "I was relieved."

"Relieved about what?" she puzzled. Fuck, the innocence in her voice; it was almost too much.

Maybe that's why I'd been so afraid to admit this to her. She was so innocent, so unconditional… This was why I was so afraid she wouldn't understand.

Rimmel would never feel like this. I didn't think she was even able.

The vile thoughts raced through my head and propelled me around. I jerked, staring at her from across the room. "Relieved it was Evie that died and not you."

Rimmel sucked in a breath.

I pushed on, afraid if I didn't spill it all right now, I'd never do it.

"I still remember," I whispered. "The way you looked that morning, stepping out into the bathroom with blood smeared between your legs. It wasn't even that much, but to me, it seemed like buckets."

As I spoke, Rimmel tucked her knees against her chest, locking them close with her arms. Wide, brown eyes peered at me from over them.

"You doubled over. The way you clenched your body like the pain was ripping you in half. You felt so small in my arms when I ran through the house with you, and then the empty way you stared off at the hospital. You didn't cry at first. You didn't say anything at all. Tears ran down your face, but it's like you didn't even notice."

"Romeo," she whispered, despair in her voice.

"The way the doctors hovered around you. The pain on your face from whatever was happening inside you… It scared me. It fucking tore me to the bones. All I could think was there could be complications, that whatever took Evie might take you, too."

Rimmel unfolded herself off the bed and hopped down. I was lost in the memory of that day. I didn't notice her approach until her arms wound around me and the warmth of her cheek hit my chest.

"Keep talking," she whispered.

"I prayed. Outside your room that day while you were being examined, I prayed to God. I asked him— no, I begged him not to take you. I actually told him if he had to take someone, to take our daughter… anyone but you. Then the doctor came out. He shook his head at me, and I nearly crumbled. I grabbed him by the front of his scrubs you know. I slammed him up against the wall."

I felt her shock at the confession. She'd had no idea of my idiotic behavior. A nurse ran down the hall, called for security, but the doctor waved her away.

"'My wife,' I'd growled, almost like I dared him to tell me you were gone. 'Your wife will be fine, but your daughter is gone.' That's what he told me."

I hugged him then. I went from one extreme to the other. I hugged a man I'd never met and just threatened with bodily harm, right there in front of everyone. "You know what I said to him?"

"What?" Rimmel asked.

"I said, 'Thank God it wasn't Rim.'"

"That doesn't make you a bad man." Rimmel began.

I made a sound. "I walked into that room and looked at you. My whole world came back together… Then I realized your entire world had just fallen apart."

I tucked my arms around her, holding her against me.

"It sank in what I'd done, that'd I'd literally been praying, bartering for your life over my own daughter's. What the fuck kind of father does that make me? What kind of man? You cried so much that night it killed me."

"You loved our daughter," Rimmel said, absolute. "I know you did."

"I did. I loved her so much, but I love you more. I will always love you more than anyone, Rimmel, even any child we create."

"It's a different kind of love, Romeo." She took my hand and led me toward the bed. "The love you have for me is a different kind of love than the kind you have for a child."

"I chose you." I rubbed a hand over my face.

"It's okay," she murmured, pressing a hand to my chest. "I can't imagine what it must have been like for you that day."

"I don't want to do it again," I said, hard. "And then I got that call earlier…"

"That's why you were so mad," she said, almost to herself.

"No," I bit out, my mouth thinning. "I'm mad because of the first words out of your damn mouth."

Her mouth formed a little O.

"*Don't worry. I'm not pregnant.* That's what you said to me. As if I were only rushing there because I thought my kid might be inside you."

I shoved away from the bed, pacing some more. I felt agitated, hot… misunderstood.

"I've been living with this constant voice in the back of my head since Evie, this stupid nagging worry that you might be ripped away. That day I came home and your car wasn't in the garage? Yeah, I damn near pissed my pants because I was afraid you might not be here."

She made a sound, half strangled, half alarmed.

"Do you remember what I said to you when I found you crying on the bathroom floor?"

Her teeth sank into her lower lip, and she nodded once.

"What?" I demanded. I wanted her to say it.

"All I had to do was breathe."

"I meant that." I nodded once. "It's all I care about. As long as you breathe, as long as you're here with me, then everything else is just details."

"I thought you wanted a baby," she whispered.

"I do. But I want you more. You could tell me right now that your doctor said you couldn't ever have a child, and I wouldn't care. It's you I want. Before anyone else, Rim. That's what you are to me. Forever. You come *before anyone else*."

Tears fell over her lashes, dripping down her cheeks. She wiped at them and made a sound that was half hiccup and half snort. "I love you before anyone else, too. It's why I've been fighting so hard to come back to you. I choose you, Romeo Anderson."

I rushed across the room and grabbed her. Her legs locked around my waist as I held her, and my mouth crashed over hers. I kissed her deep and hard. I was rough, likely too rough, but I didn't think about that. I only thought about getting inside her, feeling her... tasting the words she just spoke before they evaporated off her tongue.

I was still attacking her mouth when her fingertips dug into my head and pulled back. I felt half drunk when I tried to focus on her. I just wanted back between her lips.

"I can have a baby."

I glanced up, gaining some of that focus I'd been failing at.

She gave me a timid smile. "The doctor said she saw no reason we can't have another child."

"What's the risk to you?" I asked.

"I'll be fine."

I set her away from me, even though my body screamed in protest. "You still want my baby? Do you still think I'll make a good father? After everything I just told you?"

"Oh, yes. You already are the most amazing father ever."

I shook my head.

Rimmel took my face in her palms, forcing my head down so she could look up into my eyes. "I blamed myself every day for losing Evie. I blamed my body, my luck, even all the stupid pickles I ate. I still blame myself sometimes. I know I always will."

"That wasn't your fault," I ground out. I didn't want her blaming herself.

"It wasn't yours either."

My eyes flashed to hers.

"You begging God for my life even at the expense of hers was not what made me miscarry. She was gone before we even left the house that morning. You were scared. I would have done the same thing."

I snorted. "No. You wouldn't."

"I went into the stands at a football game to stake my claim over you to a bunch of Lite Brite bobbleheads. I was prepared to throw down," she said, matter-of-fact. Almost as if she were a little badass. "If I'm willing to do that over a stupid list, imagine what I'm capable of if I were truly afraid you were being taken from me."

Warmth suffused my chest. I chuckled because she thought she was going to throw down at the game. Like I'd have allowed that.

She still loved me. The same way she had an hour ago. I saw it in her eyes. I felt it in my soul.

"I forgive you, Romeo, even though there really is nothing to forgive. You loved Evie, and I know if she were here right now, you'd be wrapped around her little finger, and she would be a daddy's girl."

She forgave me.

Her hands rested on either side of my waist. "But it isn't my forgiveness you need. It's your own. It's okay to be human. You don't have to be alpha all the time."

"I am." I argued.

She smiled. "Well, yes, you are. Even now. That's how I know you have the strength to forgive yourself."

"I'm not sure I can." I admitted. It seemed like I would be letting myself off awfully easy.

"I know. It won't come overnight. I'm still working on it, too. We can do it together."

"I really fucking love you."

"I'm sorry I scared you tonight."

"I shouldn't have gotten so pissed about what you said. I just… Don't ever put yourself behind anyone else, baby. Never. You are irreplaceable to me."

Her lips made contact over my heart. She pressed in, kissing deep. My eyes drifted closed.

Rimmel pulled away and crawled up onto the bed and into the center of the one million pillows. She lay back, sinking right into them all.

I crawled up alongside her, but that shit was lumpy and uncomfortable as hell.

I made a rude sound and started flinging the offending pillows all over the room. Rimmel lay against the comforter and watched; I felt her eyes like the most sensual caress.

"Kiss me," she demanded.

I kissed her. I always did what she told me.

Well, when it involved using my tongue.

I felt lighter somehow, like the worst of the storm had passed and all that remained were some storm clouds with a rainbow peeking through.

Rim was the rainbow.

I pulled back, pressed our foreheads together, and lazily perused her face. My body pressed hers into the mattress. I loved the give in her body when I was on top of her. Her fingertips danced along my spine, exploring the expanse of my back.

We stayed like that a long time, just staring at each other, her hands grazing along my bare skin.

When the tension became too much, our lips met again. I stroked into her mouth, made love to it with mine. Our tongues slid against the other, and I sucked her lower lip into my mouth.

Her fingers tightened against my back. The nipples beneath her T-shirt grew firm. Desire blanketed the room like freshly fallen snow.

It was almost like the first time all over again, as if I were experiencing her body like I hadn't already a million times. She trembled under me, her leg slid between mine, and her fingertips played in the hair at my nape, tugging and pulling me closer.

When air became essential, I tipped her head back to scrape my teeth down her neck and suck her collarbone between my lips.

She moaned and arched against me.

I pulled back, rolling off her. "You need to rest."

Rimmel sat up, peeled the T-shirt over her head, and revealed to me her completely naked body. "I want you." She lay back down beside me, her breasts on full display.

As I took in my fill, her hand found the tie on my waistband to slowly tug it free. I was already hard, painfully so. My body begged to claim her; after everything tonight, the urge to fill her was powerful.

A small hand delved into my pants, brushed against my swollen head, and wrapped around my rod.

I sucked in a breath because it felt so good.

Rimmel stroked me for a while as I stared at every inch of her body before me. Usually, I was all over her, but tonight, I used my eyes. I let my stare do the talking. It worked as well as my hands. Because she pumped me a little harder, the skin on her chest became flushed and her limbs grew restless.

When she started pushing at my pants, I rolled on top of her, settling between her widespread legs. My hand dipped between us, and I stroked upward, my fingers instantly coated with her arousal.

I smiled, dipped my head to her breasts, and lavished attention on the pair with wild abandon.

Rimmel strained against me. "Please, Romeo." She panted.

My vision was hazy, my brain drunk. The room smelled like sex, and I hadn't even entered her yet. I pushed down my sweats, not even bothering to kick them off completely. My cock sprang free, and Rimmel reached for it. I lifted so it was just out of reach.

She made a sound, and I smiled.

Slowly, I shifted, rocking so the tip teased her entrance. I groaned because her liquid coated me instantly, a feeling I hadn't known in a long time.

I only allowed myself that one slip, not even entering her, just sliding along her slit. Resting on both elbows, I took her mouth again, kissing her lazily as her hips searched for what it wanted.

Desire pumped in my blood, so strong it made my heart pound. Even though I moved slow and languid, it felt like I'd just done an hour of cardio.

It's just what she did to me.

She moved against me until she hit the spot she wanted, and I slipped inside.

Both of us moaned. Even though I held my body still, my cock twitched. I couldn't help it. I stroked into

• • •

272

her a little farther, fully sheathing my dick in her silky, tight heat.

"Christ, baby," I swore.

She made a small sound and wiggled so I was even deeper.

My eyes rolled back in my head.

But then reality came a'knocking.

I wasn't wrapped.

Fuck. Fuck. Fuckity.

I wanted to stay where I was. I longed to pull out and sink back in again. I craved the way it felt to be this close.

I started to pull out.

She caught my hips, opening her eyes. "Stay."

"I forgot—"

"I know."

"Rim…"

"Stay."

I surged back in. Pure instinct took over. I reined it in, moving slow at first. This was a feeling neither of us had known for a long time. It was new again, so I tried to prolong it.

I kept it slow, painfully so. I made love to her with my body and my heart. Eventually, our unhurried pace just wasn't enough.

Eventually, we both needed more.

With all my weight on my hands, I pumped into her, hard and fast. Her hands gripped my biceps as her hips surged up to meet mine with every plunge.

I knew when she was close because her hips tilted down and her movements quickened. I let her have control as she basically speared herself on my cock, over and over.

My name fell from her lips when her body tightened and convulsed. No longer able to thrust against me, I moved my hips, making sure to hit the sweet spot I already knew by heart.

The little sounds of pleasure she made were like music to my ears, and within seconds, my own release started to work its way up my shaft and threaten to coat her insides.

I started to pull back, but she grabbed me.

"Stay."

I fell onto my elbows, my face pressed into her neck. My dick pumped deep inside her, spilling out warm seed and making me mutter incoherent words.

Rimmel rocked gently against me as I came down. Aftershocks rippled through me, and a feeling of satisfaction I hadn't known for so long kidnapped my limbs.

Leaving myself inside her, I used the last of my strength to roll us over so she was draped over me and I accepted all her weight.

Neither of us moved. I stayed inside her, even after I'd gone soft. Her head stayed pillowed on the center of my chest, and I stroked her back with languid caresses.

Eventually, she shivered.

I realized we hadn't made it beneath the blankets.

She weighed practically nothing when I lifted her off. "Please don't go," she murmured.

"Wouldn't dream of it."

I yanked the blankets back and slid beneath, guiding her to do the same. Our bodies spooned together, and she sighed a contented sigh.

"Darcy, Ralph!" I called, making sure I had a good hold of my girl.

• • •

The mattress rocked when both dogs leapt up onto our king-size bed. One settled on the other side of Rim by her knees, the other at her feet.

"It's perfect," she whispered into the night.

She was right.

Celebrity News

Chapter Twenty

"Inside Ivy Walker's Closet!" #StyleGoals

RIMMEL

Murphy was on the counter when I stepped into the kitchen. The second he saw me, his purr tripled in intensity.

"Murphy the lawnmower," I sang on my way past and stopped to scratch behind his ears. He only put up with it for so long before giving me a loud, "Yowwl," because he was tired of waiting for his treats.

Behind me, Darcy and Ralph were clambering through the living room. The sound of something being knocked over had me wincing as I was pulling out the cat snacks.

I didn't bother looking. I probably didn't want to know anyway.

Murphy was watching me intently when I crossed to him and put two small, soft treats in the palm of my hand and held them out.

He ate them gingerly, like he had all the manners in the world.

I guess he did compared to the two dogs begging at my feet.

Once Murphy was finished, I scratched him again before he sauntered off down the island and hopped onto the floor. The dogs didn't even bother trying to chase him. Instead they hammered their tails against the floor and stared at me longingly.

I laughed and grabbed the dog bones next.

"Shake," I told Darcy, who immediately held out his paw for me. "Good boy," I praised and gave him the snack.

Next, I did the same for Ralph. He didn't give me his paw. He rolled over and showed me his belly. "Close enough!" I declared and gave him the bone.

Once the coffee was on, the dogs were at my feet again, begging, so I shooed them outside. The morning air was crisp; the scent of fall floated on the breeze. I shivered a little, snuggling down into my hoodie, and settled in the open doorway to gaze out over the property.

It was so beautiful here. Wide open, secluded, and quiet. I watched a few sunny-colored leaves swirl downward before settling in the grass. My cheeks were upturned; the air bit at them, but it wasn't uncomfortable. I felt refreshed, like I hadn't been able to enjoy this much of my surroundings in a long time.

Last night had been… Wow.

The feel of him inside me… and then again this morning. Romeo was everything I could ever want.

It surprised me that he seemed to be just as tormented as me the past few months. All this time, we'd been suffering alongside each other, trying to shield the other, when what we should have been doing was working through it together.

No more of that, though. It was all out in the open. I knew it. I could feel it. Last night felt a whole lot like the air tickling my cheeks right now. A fresh start.

Not a do-over.

Not forgetting.

Just beginning again.

Beginning didn't seem too overwhelming with Romeo at my side.

"Morning!" Ivy chirped from behind.

I turned from the doorway as she stepped into the kitchen. "Hey." I smiled and pulled the door closed.

Prada was dancing around Ivy the same way Ralph and Darcy had done me. Ivy laughed and gave the dog her bone, then headed for the coffee.

Her hair was wavy today. I don't know how she got it to look so good. Her face was free of makeup but had the soft sheen of moisturizer. Unlike me, she'd changed out of her pajamas.

Hey, I put a hoodie over mine. That kinda counted as getting dressed... right?

She was dressed in a pair of pastel-pink leggings, gray slipper boots, a slouchy gray T-shirt, and a mint-colored duster that hung down to her knees. It looked soft to the touch and sort of floated behind her when she walked.

"Did you have some yet?" she asked, holding out her mug.

"Not yet."

"Oh good, then. I'm just in time."

"Where's Nova?" I asked, glancing around like I expected her to just walk right in.

"With Braeden. I'm pretty sure he took her to go bother Romeo."

I snickered.

"Girl time." She smiled.

• • •

We hadn't had girl time in a while. I missed it.

I took the creamer and a bowl of washed berries out of the fridge, set them on the island, and went for the coffee. Ivy reached into the pantry and pulled out a loaf of pumpkin bread she'd made sometime yesterday.

Ivy was actually a really good cook. Better than me... but I would hopefully learn.

Once we both had our coffee the way we liked it, we sat at the bar with the berries and bread in front of us. We didn't bother with plates, something we wouldn't ever do if the guys were in the room.

They'd see us once and think they'd never need to use a plate again.

So ridiculous.

I popped a raspberry in my mouth and savored the slightly tart flavor on my tongue. Ivy sipped at her coffee but then got up to let Prada out once she finished her bone.

"How are you feeling?" she asked, coming back to sit down again.

"Sore," I answered honestly. Especially my chest area. "And my face burns. Stupid rash."

"I have cream that will clear that up," she said. "I'll put it in your bathroom."

Ivy had a cream for everything. It was a talent.

"Braeden told me what happened." She began, and I nodded.

"Stupid paparazzi," I muttered.

"They really have become obsessed with you guys," Ivy remarked, breaking off a piece of the bread and popping it into her mouth.

"I know." I sighed. "I can't believe they called my father."

"Two million dollars is a lot of cash," she said.

"Do these tabloids really pay that?" I asked, seriously.

"Oh yeah, if the story's big enough."

"Well then, I don't think they'll be abandoning their stalker ways anytime soon."

"I don't think so either." She frowned. "I wish there was something I could do."

"I really don't think there's anything any of us can do. Romeo was making noise last night about filing a civil suit against the men who ran me off the road."

Ivy's eyes widened. "Do you know who they are?"

"No. I gave the description of the cars to the cops, though. They were out looking last night. Part of me hopes they found them, because what they did to me was so scary…"

"But?"

"But the other part is worried about what Romeo will do, and it may be better if they just disappear."

"All four of them are going to be overbearing idiots for the next few months," Ivy said, forlorn.

"I know."

"Braeden actually told me I should cancel my trip to New York this morning." She made a rude sound. "As if! What am I supposed to do? Call *People* magazine and say, *Oh, sorry, my husband won't let out of the house because he hates reporters?*"

"I forgot that trip was coming up," I said, sipping the coffee. It tasted good, slightly sweet and warm. It felt amazing against my throat, which was sore and a little scratchy. Absentmindedly, I rubbed below it, the bruise on my chest aching.

"It's just a few days," she said. "I'll be in meetings and photoshoots mostly. Just stuff for my column."

"It's the best feature in every issue," I said, and I meant it. I always read her column, even if skipping past some of the stories and photographs of me sometimes gave me a stomachache.

"My channel on YouTube just hit one million subscribers." She flashed a straight, white smile.

"Oh my God! That's awesome! Why didn't you tell me right away!" I leapt up and threw my arms around her.

She laughed and hugged me back. There was a time when I was more reserved with physical affection—hell, affection of any kind—but not anymore. Not with my family.

"We have to celebrate!" I insisted. "Should we have a party?"

Ivy laughed. "I think we have enough going on right now. Maybe for two million."

I didn't like that idea. I made a mental note to talk to Braeden so we could at least come up with something special for her. She'd worked so hard over the past year and a half. Even with having a baby, she still made time to get her career off the ground. Now here she was with a huge style channel online and a monthly column in one of the biggest magazines in the country.

"I'm so proud of you. Everything you've done," I told her.

"You, too," she insisted. "You practically built that shelter from the ground up. It's the nicest facility in this entire state."

"I want to do more," I said, then realized I was downplaying what I'd achieved and told myself to knock it off. "It's a great place. I do want to expand a little, offer a veterinarian clinic."

"Oh, I like that idea. Are you rethinking vet school?"

"Somedays." I admitted. "But I like where I am right now. I like being able to work with the shelter animals, in a way make my hours. I plan on doing a lot more fundraising this year as well. I can't do all of that and hopefully have a family with Romeo *and* be in school."

Ivy set down her mug with a thump. "A family." She picked up on that little slip right away. "Are you…?"

I shook my head quickly. "No. But I think I'm ready to be."

This time Ivy hugged me. We both laughed because we were being total girls. "I'm so excited! Nova will have a playmate!" Then she pulled back. "Wait, are you okay with it? How are you?"

"I'm doing better. I went to the doctor yesterday." She nodded because she'd known about the appointment.

"I thought you going after hours would have helped keep away the press." Ivy scowled. "Did they follow you?"

"I didn't think so." I puzzled. Up until now, I'd been so upset over the accident and everything with Romeo last night, I hadn't given it much thought. How did they find out? I glanced at Ivy. "They were shouting at me, saying I was undergoing IVF because I was desperate to conceive."

She made a choked sound. "Ugh! I'm sorry."

I shrugged. What they said really wasn't the issue, although it did make me mad because they acted as if IVF were something bad or to be ashamed of. It isn't.

Not at all, and if I were doing that, they had no business trying to make the situation harder.

Where would they even get that idea?

Suddenly, the mental image of the receptionist sitting at the desk as I was leaving flashed into my mind.

I knew. *I knew.*

"It was her," I muttered, feeling like an idiot.

"Who?" Ivy insisted.

"The receptionist at the office. I didn't really think much about it before, but it seemed a little odd she was still there as I was leaving."

Ivy's blue eyes narrowed. "The dirty bitch probably called the press and got a payday."

"Wonder how much my car accident earned her," I said, bitter. It hurt me that I couldn't even trust my doctor's office. Was nothing private anymore?

"It's definitely a headline today," Ivy muttered.

I rolled my eyes and picked up my coffee. "I don't want to talk about it anymore."

Ivy's eyes twinkled, and she leaned forward to whisper, "Wanna talk about babies?"

I giggled. "There's no baby to talk about... yet." I felt my own eyes widen. "Unless!" I glanced at her midsection.

"Oh no!" Ivy shook her head. "I'm not pregnant."

"Are you going to have more?"

She averted her gaze, picking at the fruit.

"Ivy?"

"Braeden wants to."

"But you don't?" I pressed.

"No, I do... I just..."

A lightbulb went off overhead. "It's because of me, isn't it?" I whispered.

"No! No, I…" Her shoulders slumped. "I can't think about having more kids right now when you've been struggling so much. It seems cruel."

I grabbed her hand, giving it a squeeze. "I would never want you to put your own family on hold because of me. I would never be hurt by you and my brother having more children."

It touched me more than I think she would ever know that she considered my feelings when contemplating her own life choices. It also made me feel a little guilty, as if I were holding her back.

"You're our family, too," she insisted. "Besides, I'm busy with work right now. Nova is a handful. It's your turn. Yours and Romeo's. Maybe next year will be ours."

"But what if I can't?" I said, voicing the same redundant fear that always seemed to come up and bite me.

"You can," Ivy said, her voice absolute.

"Yes. I can," I echoed, more for myself than her. "But promise me you won't put your life on hold for me. And if and when it happens, I want to know. Don't not tell me because you think it will break me. I love Nova, and I will love any other little Braedens you have."

"Girl!" Ivy scoffed. "You may be little and the guys might argue with me, but I know you aren't so easily broken. Neither of us is." We both laughed. Then she turned serious. "Thank you."

"So…" I began, lightening up this girl time. "When do you leave for New York?"

"In a few days."

"Are you taking Nova? Want me to watch her?"

"Actually, I'm bringing her with me. My mom is flying in. She's going to stay at the hotel with Nova when I'm in my meetings. Then we'll hit up a couple kid museums."

"Just your mom?" I asked, thinking of the birthday party disaster.

She made a sour face. "Oh yes, I made sure of that. I can't handle my father right now."

"He still hasn't come around at all?" I murmured, thinking of the hurt I saw on Trent's and Drew's faces.

"No." Ivy's voice was hard. "And I just can't understand it. I gave him a piece of my mind when he showed up here, and it wasn't a friendly piece either."

"I don't understand either," I said, slipping into my own private thoughts. It was way too soon for me to think I couldn't have children; it wasn't totally out of the cards for me. However, being a woman who just went through the loss of a child, it seemed unfair. Why would someone who was blessed with not one, but three children be foolish enough to push one away while other people out there would kill for the chance to have just one and love them no matter what?

I cleared my throat. "Was your father upset when you read him the riot act?"

"Of course. He tried to lecture me. I wasn't about to listen to it, and we got into an argument. Of course, Braeden heard, and you know how he is. The second he heard my father raise his voice at me, he was showing him the door."

"I'm sorry." I laid my hand on hers. "I know what it's like to have a rocky relationship with a father."

She smiled. "Good thing we have each other. I figured this trip would be a chance for my mom to see Nova, because we won't be seeing her during the holidays. It's neutral territory, and I'll be busy so there won't be much time to get into it about Drew."

"The holidays," I mused, realizing they were creeping up on us. "We'll make it special, really decorate the compound," I vowed.

"Definitely." She smiled.

After that, our chatter turned to clothes and other light topics. The dogs all raced back in from outside and danced around our chairs, hoping for dropped morsels of food.

It was good to be like this with her. It wasn't the coffee shop we used to go to in college, but it was still nice. And at least here we didn't have to stand in line. Or run the risk of running into people we hated... like Missy.

Ew.

A horrible stampede sounded on the stairs overhead, and we glanced at each other and groaned. Seconds later, from the other room, I heard, "What the shit? Who knocked over the coffee table?"

I winced. Then not one second later, Braeden hollered again, "My shoe! Who the hell chewed my shoe?"

Well... I guess I knew what got knocked over earlier.

"Ralph!" Romeo growled.

"You gotta get control of your mutt, Rome," Braeden muttered.

As if he knew, Ralph came racing into the room and sat at my feet, looking up at me angelically and stoically all at once.

I patted his head. "Just ignore them. You're a good boy."

Ivy giggled.

Both guys appeared. Romeo was carrying Nova; Braeden was carrying his chewed-up, slobbery shoe, which he held up like he was presenting evidence.

"I told you not to leave your shoes lying around," Ivy remarked as she sipped her coffee.

"That's enough out of you, Blondie." He shook the shoe at her.

I laughed. B swung his scowl to me. "This is your fault. That dog"—he gestured to Ralph—"did this."

"I'll buy you some new shoes," I told him, still petting my dog.

Nova held her arms out to Ivy, and Romeo surrendered her. Once Nova was in her mother's lap, she reached for the dog, and Ralph licked her fingers.

I batted my eyes at Braeden.

"Jesus!" He tossed his shoe in the trash. "We're so whipped. This house is a freaking circus."

Romeo stepped up close, Ralph still sitting between us. He gave the dog a look, and I poked him in the stomach. When he glanced up, I pursed my lips.

He chuckled and leaned down. The kiss lingered... just the way I liked it.

"We have to fly back to New York today, baby," he informed me.

I tried not to show my disappointment. I knew it was coming. This was his job, and he really wasn't supposed to be here now anyway. It still sucked, especially after last night. Especially since I felt so close to him.

"What time do you leave?" I asked, wondering how I was going to drive them to the airport. My car was gone. After last night, he probably wouldn't hand me the keys to the Hellcat.

"*We* leave at one." He kissed my nose and pulled back to head for the coffee. On the way, he snagged my empty mug so he could pour me more.

"We?" I said.

Ivy gave me a *here we go* look.

"You're not staying here alone. Ivy's going to New York."

"I have to work," I rebutted.

"You can get someone to cover."

"No. I want to work. All I'll do at your game is dodge the press and hide in the hotel room."

"I'll be there." He acted like that was the deciding factor.

It almost was. I wanted to be with him, but I really did have some things I needed to get done at the shelter.

"How about I stay here this week? I promise to not go anywhere without Trent or Drew. And when you go to California in two weeks, I'll come with you."

"We'll all go to California!" Ivy suggested.

"Works for me," Braeden said.

Romeo stared at me. I knew he didn't like the idea, but he was outnumbered.

"I'll be fine." I assured him. "California is farther away; it's a longer stay. I'll get all my work done these next couple weeks and have time to find someone to cover for me while I'm gone."

"If someone even *looks* at you funny, you're on the first plane to New York or Chicago, whichever city I'm in."

Chicago was his next stop after Sunday's game in New York.

"Promise," I vowed.

After a minute of him pouring and stirring coffee, he returned to my side, then sat beside me. "Fine."

I wrapped my arms around his neck, kissing his cheek.

Next thing I knew, I was in his lap.

"Get a room," Braeden griped. "Brothers don't need to see that nasty."

"Good idea." Romeo stood.

He left our coffee where it sat and carried me out of the room and toward the stairs.

"See you down here at one!" he hollered back to Braeden.

We spent the rest of the morning in bed.

Celebrity News

Chapter Twenty-One

"Ratted out by those she trusted! #FootballRoyaltyBetrayed"
—MARYLAND GAZETTE

ROMEO

Do not engage.

It's a pretty common sense rule when it comes to dealing with the gossip mongers.

Until they nearly kill my wife.

No, she wasn't seriously injured. But she could have been killed.

Now, do not engage didn't seem like common sense. It seemed stupid as fuck.

I wasn't sure how to fight against an entire community of stalkers out to take her picture. I wasn't sure how to stop them. Technically, following her on the street in any public place was legal.

Running her off the road was another story.

If I had been there that night, I'd probably have snapped some necks.

Seriously. I'd been walking around with the bitter taste of fear in the back of my throat. Seeing her the way I had the day she lost Evie ignited it in me like nothing had before. Even Zach.

How did I deal with these assholes?

I couldn't sue them all. I couldn't be with Rim night and day. Even if I put a bodyguard on her, they'd still harass her from afar. That is *if* I could find a bodyguard I trusted enough to follow her around. I couldn't, despite the many calls I'd made. None of them were good enough.

I needed action. To set an example. A standard.

I needed to send a message.

Don't fuck with my wife, or I'll fuck with you.

I liked it. It was very decisive.

Don't you think?

Braeden and I flew to New York, then on to Chicago. The Knights were playing well. So far, we'd won all our games. I wasn't naïve enough to think we'd get through the season without any losses at all, but we could make it through with less than a handful.

Chicago had been a tough game; it was my worst game so far this season. Even at my worst, I still played well. We still won.

I craved my wife. The sound of her voice, the scent of her skin, the feel of her body. I had her three times the day I was home after her accident.

Three times bareback.

I wanted her again. And again.

I also wanted her safe.

I called my father between traveling, football, and press shit. I'd dodged questions left and right about her accident and the state of our marriage. It was a bunch of bullshit. I played football; I didn't run a damn gossip rag.

The two assholes who ran my wife off the road had been arrested; the cops had actually caught them the night of the accident. My father was pleased about that because the cops seized their cameras immediately.

There were photos of my wife on them, photos of her outside the doctor's office and getting into her now-totaled SUV. We were pressing charges. They weren't going to walk from this. They would be example number one.

I also had him draw up some documents, which sat in my wife's lap in a discreet manila envelope as we drove into town.

Have I mentioned lately how much I fucking loved my Hellcat? Best car in the world.

She still purred over the road just as perfectly as the day I got her.

Rimmel was quiet during the drive, and when I pulled into the lot and killed the engine, I turned to face her. "You can stay in the car if you want."

She gave me a withering look and adjusted her glasses. "Maybe *you* should wait in the car."

"Give me a kiss with that sassy mouth, woman," I growled and leaned forward.

I was smiling when she leaned in, but her lips didn't meet mine the way I expected. Instead, she kept her lips out of the kissing and licked across my mouth.

My eyes shot open. She licked me lightly again, lingering where my top and bottom lip met, teasing, enticing me to open.

I did. She stroked deep into my mouth, and I palmed the back of her head to deepen the kiss.

The loud sound of a slamming car door caused her to jump back and spin around. "It's just someone over there," I said quietly, still feeling the slickness from our kiss on my lips. "It's not a reporter."

She grimaced as if her reaction embarrassed her.

"Let's do this," I said. What we were here for would empower her, and I was all about that shit.

She nodded once and climbed out of the Hellcat.

No baggy sweats for my girl today. Today she was dressed something fierce. When she stepped out of the closet, I knew she meant business, and it was just proof she had come a long way since the day we lost Evie.

I knew Rim would never be the same. Hell, neither would I. It didn't matter. I loved her no matter what.

But I sure liked it when she got all angry kitten.

I admired the way she looked coming around the back end of the Hellcat toward me. Tight black jeans that hugged every line of her frame. Black boots—not her usual fur lined; instead, these had a heel. The top she wore was also more fitted than her usual fare. It was plain white, body hugging, and sexy as hell. Over it, she wore a black leather jacket.

Her hair was straight, sleek, and fell right down her back. When it was blown out like that, it hung halfway down her back. I couldn't remember the last time she had it cut.

The envelope of papers was tucked under her arm, and as she approached, the clicking of her heels on the pavement stuttered as she pitched off to the side.

"Whoa." I stopped her from the downward spiral. "You look hot in heels, Smalls, but you can't walk in them."

"I know," she grumbled, straightening away. My hands hovered at her sides in case she decided to fall over again. Without another word, she marched forward. Every two steps for her was one for me.

Our fingers threaded together as we walked. I didn't let go even when I opened the door and allowed her in first. We held hands in the elevator and were still connected when we stepped off and into the lobby of the doctor's office.

Rimmel stiffened when her eyes swung to the reception desk. She glanced up at me. "That's her."

"Mrs. Anderson," the woman said, "and Rom—I mean, Mr. Anderson! Good to see you today. I didn't realize you had an appointment."

"We don't," Rimmel said, her voice nothing like the friendly, innocent one she was known for. "I figured if I called ahead, you would have made sure the press was waiting downstairs when I pulled up."

The lady paled. "I'm sorry?"

I made a sound. Rim put her hand on my waist, effectively restraining me. Instead, she stepped forward and rose to her full, short girl stature. But damn if it wasn't something to see.

"I'm pretty sure you're not sorry," she replied. "I'm here to see Dr. Crawford. I just need a moment with her in her office."

"She's fully booked—" The receptionist began.

"Call her." Rimmel cut her off. "Tell her I'm here."

I could see the calculating wheels in this bitch's head turning. She was already trying to figure out a way to make it look like she called back but couldn't get the doctor on the phone.

"You can do this the easy way or the hard way," I intoned.

Her eyes flashed to mine.

I smiled.

Her throat worked. She picked up the phone and spoke quietly into it.

"She's in her office now," she said. "You—"

Rimmel didn't even wait for her to finish talking. She dismissed her and strode through the door, back toward the office and exam rooms.

● ● ●

Before going back, I leaned on the counter, near where the woman was sitting. "Hope your resume is nice and polished up, 'cause you're gonna need it."

"I didn't—" She started to protest.

"Save it." I slapped the words at her. "I don't know how much you got paid for almost getting my wife killed, but it probably wasn't enough." I pulled away, then turned back. "By the way, you may want to move to another city... preferably another state. You're gonna have a hard time finding work around here. Unless, of course, you like flipping burgers."

I sauntered through the half-open door Rim had just disappeared through. She was standing in front of an open door, waiting for me, so I quickened my step to join her.

"Mr. and Mrs. Anderson," Dr. Crawford greeted us when we stepped into the room. "I'm surprised to see you."

"Thank you for agreeing to see us," Rimmel said politely.

"Of course. Did you have additional questions about the blood test results?"

We'd already gotten those results. Everything was good.

"No," Rimmel replied.

"I read about your car accident. You aren't having any kind of pain, are you?"

"I'm not having pain, but I am here because of the accident."

The doctor motioned for us to sit down. Rimmel did, but I was slower to join them. I thought long and hard about just staying on my feet so I could tower over the doctor, but in the end, I decided that was probably the wrong move.

I was an asshole, but not all the time.

Besides, I'd like to believe this woman hadn't known what was happening under her nose. I'd give her the benefit of the doubt until she gave me a reason not to.

"I'm afraid I don't understand."

"One of your employees, the one out at the desk right now, is the person who tipped off the press that I was here that day. She's the one who called them and brought them all here."

The doctor shook her head. "That can't be. My staff knows our patients' privacy is of utmost importance."

"She pretty much just admitted it to me out in reception," I said coolly.

Dr. Crawford picked up her phone and dialed for the receptionist. After several long moments, she hung up. "She's not answering."

I laughed. "I'm sure she's already hightailed it the hell out."

The doctor frowned. "Helen," she called. A nurse appeared in the doorway. "Can you tell me if Bethany is out front?"

We all sat there in awkward silence while we waited for Helen to come back and tell us what I already knew.

"She's not there," Helen said, coming back into the room. "And all her stuff is gone."

The doctor paled. "Thank you. Close the door on your way out."

When we were alone, she straightened in her chair. "I'm shocked and very embarrassed. This is completely unacceptable, and I want to apologize profusely to you and your husband on behalf of myself and this entire office. Putting you in danger is the last thing I would ever want. I'm a healer."

I studied the doctor as she spoke and then for several minutes after she finished. When I was done, Rimmel and I looked at each other, and I nodded once.

Rimmel pulled a stack of legal documents out of her folder. "This is a legal and binding nondisclosure agreement. I understand you are bound by doctor-patient confidentiality, but clearly, your staff doesn't understand that." The woman looked between my wife and the papers, but my girl just kept right on going. "I think you are a good doctor, and you know my history with the miscarriage… I would like to continue on here with you as my OB-GYN. However, I can't do that unless you and your staff sign these."

"You want me to sign an NDA?" The doctor seemed slightly offended.

"Yes. If you refuse, I will be transferring to a new, more discreet practice."

"And I'm going to file a suit against this practice for endangering my wife."

"You won't win that case," the doctor said, visibly upset.

I shrugged. "Probably not, but just the press will ruin your business."

"How dare you!" The doctor jumped up from her seat. She glanced over at Rimmel. "I've always tried my best to accommodate you and give you the best care."

"I realize that," Rimmel said. "And that's why I'd like to stay. But I can't do that if I'm worried someone on your staff is going to tell the press my every move. If… when I get pregnant again, it won't be just me, but my baby."

The doctor sank back in her chair. "I'll need to have my attorney look over these."

"Fine. You have one week to sign them and return them to Anthony Anderson's law firm. If you have any questions, you can contact him directly via the number on the documents," I replied.

Rimmel stood, keeping her back straight. "Oh, and just for transparency, I'm pretty sure that receptionist was also the one who called the press the day I miscarried my daughter. She's the reason they were outside the hospital."

"She wasn't at the hospital." Dr. Crawford argued.

"No. But she knew I was because I called your office on the way to the hospital. I spoke to her."

Realization dawned in the doctor's eyes.

"I'm so sorry," she whispered.

"I know," Rimmel said, kindly.

I wasn't feeling too kind. I didn't know how the hell my wife had so much compassion for other people.

"Please look over the papers," she added.

Dr. Crawford nodded.

Rimmel went to the door. After giving the doc another long, lingering stare, I pushed out of the seat and joined my wife at the door.

As soon as we stepped into the hall and the door snapped shut behind me, Rimmel looked up. "I can't come here anymore." Her quiet voice was forlorn.

It just pissed me off even more.

I brushed a hand down the back of her head. "I know, baby."

I'd known that since she told me she suspected the receptionist. I'd never let my wife be seen at an office that put her life in danger. *Never.*

But Rim had to come to that realization on her own. I couldn't order her. It would have caused a fight. I had to let her see what I already knew. Plus, I really did want those papers signed. Not only would that NDA cover any contact Rim or I had with the office from here on out, but it covered all the care Rimmel got here in the past.

I figured with two mil up for grabs, I'd make sure none of my wife's records were "accidentally" leaked to the media.

There was some movement in a nearby door, and I glanced around. Two nurses were peeking at me from around the nurses' station.

Back in the day, the college days, I would have flashed them my smile, laid on the charm.

Today, I ignored them.

Snooty bitches.

I hated snooty bitches.

"C'mon, Smalls." I draped an arm across Rimmel's shoulders and guided her to the exit. "Let's go get some ice cream, then buy out Pet Warehouse and take treats to all your lovable mutts at the shelter."

She gasped. "Really!"

"Duh." I rolled my eyes.

She loved buying stuff for those animals. Even something as simple as rawhide bones just made her so happy. I admit I liked it, too. Dogs were pretty simple creatures, and even just a snack and a pat on the head made their day. Their joy was infectious.

She started rambling animatedly about one of the dogs and how she had the perfect treat in mind for him. I listened to her prattle on, warmth filling my chest.

When she tripped over the stupid boots, I swept her up and carried her the rest of the way to the car.

"Maybe I should have brought my regular shoes," she told me, staring down at her stiletto-strapped feet.

"Already ahead of you, Smalls. They're in the backseat."

She laughed. "You know me so well."

I did, but even still, Rimmel managed to surprise me. She did so just moments ago, inside the doctor's office. She'd handled it like a total boss. I was just the muscle.

(Good-looking muscle at that.)

After I made sure she was buckled in the Cat and the door was shut behind her, I whipped out one of those single-use cells and hit a pre-dialed number.

Soon as the asshole picked up, I spoke in low, muffled tones, with my palm over the receiver. "Word is Rimmel's doctor's office is the one who tipped off the paparazzi of her appointment that day. So much for doctor-patient confidentiality."

"Who is this?" the person asked.

I ended the call, dropped the cell on the ground, and stomped on it. I didn't leave it lying there. I'm not an idiot. I picked up the broken pieces so I could toss them in the trash at our next stop.

Was it wrong of me to rat out that doctor, especially since I didn't think she knew what had been going on right beneath her nose? Probably.

I didn't fucking care.

Rim's shady ex-doctor had just become example number two.

Chapter
Twenty-Two

RIMMEL

Four days in California just wasn't enough. It was beautiful. Sunshine, warm breezes, and palm trees.

Everyone was gorgeous, too. I was beginning to think it was a prerequisite to live here. It was probably better we were due to fly home to Maryland soon, considering my penchant for sweats.

Funny how when I first moved to Maryland from Florida, the winters were a shock and the cold temperatures were bitter. I still wasn't a fan of the cold or anything to do with the snow, unless I was looking at it through a window.

But I loved the seasons now. I loved the way everything changed and bloomed. I even loved the way everything fell away in the fall. Being here in Cali reminded me of that, because I found myself lying there in bed, looking forward to the crisp air when we got home.

This turned out to be a great family trip, even though technically we were here because of work and the fact Romeo wasn't willing to be on the other side of the country from me right now.

I didn't go to their game here. I was afraid it would be a circus with the media, considering the last game I attended, my accident, and now the impending charges against the two photographers who ran me off the road.

Instead, Ivy and I went shopping. Trent and Drew were our unfortunate bodyguards. I say unfortunate because I was sure they'd rather be at the game than walking behind us down Rodeo Drive like security guards.

In our usual fashion, Ivy shopped like a boss while Nova and I followed along and looked at the sights and in the windows. I got a few nice things, most of them Ivy picked out, but there was this one thing I chose for myself, a pair of designer leggings.

They were black and looked like leather; they weren't shiny, though, like I belonged in some eighties hairband. They were butter soft with a matte finish, and they hugged my body like they were made just for me. They weren't even too long (a rare thing). The fabric stopped at my ankle in a stylish flare. Even I knew they were the perfect length for a pair of cute shoes.

Not heels. Maybe wedges.

Or maybe studded sneakers… Ohh yeah. Those.

I also picked up a few things for Valerie. With Christmas coming up, I figured it would be nice to choose a few really nice things to wrap up.

I'd seen her a few times since our talk that day about the miscarriage. We had lunch, and I'd asked her to help me plan another fundraiser. I was more open to our relationship now, more willing to set aside the past to move on to the future.

Our talk that day really helped me; in some ways, it helped heal me.

I was so grateful I'd ordered her a beautiful pair of Uggs, had them gift-wrapped, and sent them to her house. I wasn't sure she'd actually wear them, even though she said she'd been looking for a pair. But it was a gift solely from me, a gift I never would have considered sending before because I would have thought she would have been offended.

She called me the day they were delivered. She exclaimed over the quality and couldn't believe they could be bought at Target. I didn't bother to tell her I'd gotten her the designer brand and those weren't from Target.

Valerie said she loved them, she couldn't wait to wear them, and she was so touched I'd thought of her. Things were good between us, and I sincerely hoped they stayed that way.

It was nice in California. We blended in a little better. People here weren't as "star struck," because celebrities were a dime a dozen.

I even saw one of the most-photographed stars walking down the opposite side of Rodeo Drive with a gaggle of cameras blocking her path.

Admittedly, when I first looked up and saw the spectacle, my entire body tightened and I froze. Anxiety that they would turn to me, understanding of what the celebrity must have been feeling, and memories of everything that happened most recently rendered me immobile for a few long seconds.

Ivy hadn't noticed at first; she'd been going on about a window display and a pair of sunglasses, but then she realized I wasn't there.

The family surrounded me. Ivy gently took the handles of Nova's stroller, Drew angled his body in front of mine so I couldn't see the circus, and Trent wrapped his arm around me and tugged me into his side.

We ducked into the closest boutique. Drew stood at the door with his arms crossed over his chest, watching out the glass like he would physically deter anyone with a camera from entering this shop, while Trent stayed glued to my side.

I had the best family, and I found myself blinking back tears because I was lucky enough to call them that.

In between the football games, the training, and Romeo's busy schedule, we managed to take Nova to the beach, go out to dinner, and Romeo and I snuck off to a movie for some alone time.

It felt almost more like a vacation than anything. I was more relaxed now than I'd been in so long. I'd literally forgotten what it had felt like.

I was still lying in bed when I heard the key in the door.

"Smalls!" Romeo called when he walked in. This hotel room was like a small apartment, and his voice echoed through the room to reach me.

"Back here!" I called.

He appeared in the doorway, leaned against the doorjamb, and grinned. The purple Knights T-shirt he wore stretched across his chest and biceps with the team logo dead center on his chest. He kinda looked like a superhero.

It kinda turned me on.

"How was the team meeting?" I asked.

"Endless." His eyes roamed the bed and blankets covering me.

"That's it, though, right? You have a little time off now?"

He nodded. "No game this coming weekend. I'm all yours."

"I like the sound of that."

"You been in bed this whole time, Smalls?" Romeo half smiled. I liked the way the smirk met his eyes. He was in a playful mood.

"It's hard work being married to you," I jested. "I'm tired."

"Whatcha got on underneath those blankets?" He wagged his eyebrows.

I wagged mine. "Why don't you come over here and find out."

I almost bounced off the bed completely when he took a running leap and landed dead center in the mattress. I squealed as my body flew up, but he locked an arm around me, anchoring me in place.

Laughter filled the room as he ripped back the blankets and scowled.

"You led me on, Smalls. You told me you were naked."

"I did no such thing!" I gasped. "Your dirty mind just assumed I was. I don't lie around naked, you know."

"You should," he muttered and stuck his head beneath the T-shirt I was wearing.

I started to speak, but my mind went blank when his lips grazed up my middle and latched onto my breast.

I groaned as familiar heat pooled between my legs. My fingers yanked at his shirt. Because it was so snug, it didn't slip off so easily, and I groaned in frustration.

His laugh vibrated against my skin before he appeared from beneath my shirt. "Impatient this morning, are we?"

I narrowed my eyes at him. "Yes, so get naked."

The sound of his laugh was muffled by the insistent beating on the door.

"Go away!" Romeo shouted and reached for me again.

"Romeo!" Ivy yelled, still knocking on the door. "Romeo!"

He vaulted out of bed, a low curse following him as he moved quickly through the suite. The urgency in her voice alarmed me as well, and I jumped out of bed and adjusted the shirt I was wearing and reached for a pair of pajama shorts nearby to hastily pull them on.

"Ivy, what's wrong?" Romeo demanded the second he swung open the door.

"Thank God!" she burst out, and I stepped into the sitting room as she rushed into the room.

Her hair wasn't styled, she didn't have makeup on, and I was pretty sure she'd forgotten to put on pants. Unless Braeden's old Alpha U shirt was so long it hid them.

I'd never seen her so... looking like me before.

Romeo glanced out into the hall behind her, likely looking for Braeden. But she was alone. "Where's B?" he demanded. "What happened?"

"I have news!" she held up her phone like it was evidence.

"Ivy!" Romeo grabbed her by the shoulders and forced her to look at him. "Is everyone okay?"

I could see the concern on his face, the way his body was tensed and ready to react. It wasn't very often Ivy came rushing to him. So obviously, the fact she was, plus the absence of Braeden, made him worried.

It worried me, too. So much that I rushed past them and into the hall toward their suite, which was on our floor.

Their hotel room door swung open, and I was so intent on finding my brother, I collided into him and Nova.

"Whoa." He steadied me with one arm.

"Braeden," I said, relief strong in my voice. "You're okay."

I collapsed against him, wrapping my arms around his waist. Nova patted me on the top of the head.

"I'm fine, sis." He assured me. "I told Ivy to calm down. She was gonna get everyone all worked up."

"What's wrong?" I glanced up, still hugging him. I wasn't ready to let go yet.

He shrugged. "I don't know. She didn't even tell me. She just started yelling, *Oh my God,* and ran from the room. Took me a minute to finish wrangling Nova into clothes."

"But you're okay?" I asked, wanting to be sure.

"I'm perfect, just like always."

Obviously. His big ego was still intact.

A little farther down the hall, another door opened. Trent stuck his head out. "What the hell is going on?" he demanded.

"Ivy is having a breakdown," Braeden deadpanned.

"Something's happened," I said, elbowing B in the side.

"Forrester!" Trent called behind him. "Family meeting!"

Braeden and I went back into our room, leaving the door open for Trent and Drew. Romeo was standing in front of Ivy, who was waving her phone around. "I can't believe it!" she was saying.

"What the fuck did you do to my sister, B?" Romeo drawled when we walked in.

"Like she needs my help to be insane," he muttered.

"Hey!" I exclaimed. When Ivy said nothing, I glanced over at her, but she was still beyond occupied with whatever she needed to tell us.

I looked at Romeo, then pointedly at her.

He sighed, dropping an arm around her shoulders. "C'mon, princess, tell me what's going on."

"I'm so sorry," she told him, her voice calming as he led her farther into the room.

"Don't be sorry. It's not the first time someone's knocked urgently on our hotel room door."

She shook her head. "Not for that, for what I have to tell you."

Drew and Trent came in the room, shutting the door behind them.

"Ivy, what's wrong?" Drew asked, his eyes going right to her.

Nova was fussing around in Braeden's arms, wanting down. There were a few toys still in here from the day before. Braeden sat her down with them, and we all turned to look at Ivy.

She gave me a regretful look, then turned her eyes to her phone. "After Nova ate this morning, she was playing and watching cartoons, so I was going through my email—you know, checking to see what I missed while I was here and what needed my attention when we got home."

Romeo shifted, crossing his arms over his chest.

"Blondie, the point." Braeden tried to hurry her along.

She nodded and looked at me. "Remember how I said I wished there was something I could to do help with the press stalking you?"

I nodded.

"When I went to New York and had those meetings at *People* headquarters, I nosed around, talked to some of the staff... put out some feelers to see if anyone knew who it was that was offering such an insane amount of money for any big story on you."

I didn't like the way this was sounding.

"And?" Romeo asked.

"No one knew anything. Of course they heard about the pay, and they always had their contacts looking for stories, too."

"Ivy," Romeo growled.

"I'm getting to it!" she snapped. "Well, apparently, some of the people there kept digging around. And they found something. It's all right here in this email."

"What does it say?" I asked, my stomach twisting.

"It's not good, Rimmel." She actually looked like she might cry, which made me incredibly nervous. "They finally found someone who was willing to give up a story on you."

"Who?" I frowned. *Please don't let it be my father.*

"There's an exclusive story that's going to be a huge headline. It's actually being shopped around right now... The bidding is insane."

The room was silent; everyone was holding their breath for this latest bombshell.

"It's Jonathan Kane," she whispered.

I gasped. All the blood drained from my head. A slight buzzing sound was all I heard. I stared at her without really seeing... memories coming at me full force... terrible, shameful memories I'd worked really hard to put away.

Strong arms came around me. I gave them all my weight as I fought against the feelings and emotions swirling inside me.

"Who the fuck is Jonathan Kane?" Romeo roared.

I forced my eyes up. It took a moment to focus on his face. "It's him," I whispered. "The guy who took my virginity." *When I was only thirteen years old.*

Oh my God, everyone will know.

"Oh, hells no!" Romeo yelled.

The next thing I knew, he was gone, and I was being supported by Braeden. Romeo was pacing the room like a caged lion.

"Why would the story of your lost virginity be worth so much money?" Braeden asked the room.

Only Romeo and Ivy understood.

I hadn't told anyone else; it was too embarrassing.

I cleared my throat. "Because—" I began, and Romeo made a sound.

"You don't have to tell them."

"They're family," I said.

He rubbed a hand over his face.

I felt all three of my brothers stare.

"After my mom died... I went through this phase... I was, um, really different than I am now. I fell in with the wrong crowd, some older kids... One of them told me he loved me, and I believed him."

Braeden remained silent. I didn't look at him. I was afraid to. Instead, I looked at Trent and Drew. Their mouths were drawn, but Trent looked at me with acceptance, and it gave me strength.

"I gave him my virginity. I was only thirteen." Braeden sucked in a breath. I kept my eyes on Trent.

"After that, he refused to talk to me. Everyone acted like I didn't exist... That's how... It's why I was so guarded when I first met Romeo."

It's how I became a #nerd.

"I'm so sorry, Rimmel. I didn't want to tell you, but this is something you needed to know."

"This isn't your fault, Ivy," I said, trying to regain some composure.

Braeden was so tense it was actually making me uncomfortable. I knew he'd never hurt me, but it was like he was holding it all in because he was about to blow.

I patted his arm and stepped away. Reluctantly, he let me go. He joined Romeo in the mad pacing across the room.

"Who bought the story?" Romeo demanded. "When's it running?"

"It's still being bid on. *People* was given an option to bid. That's how I found out. He actually hasn't done the interview yet... He's giving it today."

"Today!" I burst out.

Ivy nodded miserably. "If only I'd checked my emails a few days ago, I'd have known about this sooner."

"Where is he?" Romeo replied, deadly calm. "Florida?"

Ivy glanced down at the email, running through it again. "He's here, in California. She probably flew him out here to stay at some posh place to butter him up."

"She?"

Ivy's face fell, and she nodded. "I'm afraid that's not the only bad news I have. This gets worse."

"What is it?" I asked, steeling myself.

"I found out who the person is behind the interview, who's behind the bidding war and searching around for all the dirt."

"Who!" Romeo growled.

Ivy bit her lower lip, a flash of disgust, even fear flashing in her eyes.

Oh no. *No. It can't be.*

"It's Missy."

Missy.

The #BuzzBoss was back.

Chapter
Twenty-Three

Thank you for making
#BuzzBoss.com the
fastest growing source
of Buzz for two years
running!

ROMEO

Five.

That's how many phone calls I had to make to find out which swanky-ass hotel Jonathan Kane was staying in.

It was good luck for me he was on the other side of Hollywood.

But it was going to be a very, *very* bad day for him.

I'd hated that guy from the first time Rimmel told me about her past. If he had lived in Maryland, I would have already hunted him down and beat his ass. I always thought maybe it was a good thing we were states apart.

But now...

Now the douchebag had a name. I also had an address.

Most of all, I had renewed motivation.

This wasn't going to happen. This exclusive story he planned to sell to the highest bidder was dead. And I planned to bury it twenty feet under.

* * *

Rimmel had been through enough in her lifetime. I didn't know why bad shit kept happening, but I was done with it.

I hadn't been there back then to stop this motherfucker from hurting her, but I was here now. I was tired of doing everything by the book, too.

Legal. Proper. Upstanding.

Clearly, those things were ineffective when dealing with some people.

Some people just needed punched in the goddamn head.

This Jonathan Kane didn't know it yet, but he was about to become example number three. The rest of the world hopefully wouldn't see this example, but he'd feel it, and the ripples of it would spread out to the most unsavory people in the underground belly of celebrity secrets, and they would know.

And Missy?

Apparently she'd gotten off too easy the last time we dealt with her. We assumed because she kept Braeden from getting charged in Zach's death that she was done with her bitchy college ways.

Wrong.

Maybe she should be example number four.

Point was when we boarded a plane for Maryland and I took my wife home, all this shit was going to be over.

It wasn't going to hang over our heads. It wasn't going to be something that threatened to drag Rim down or put that god-awful distance between us.

We'd been through worse. It was time for some happy shit.

It was time for some peace.

If I had to force it, so be it.

After all the bad news had been laid out, Rimmel excused herself to the bathroom to change out of her pajamas, and Ivy went to do the same (I really think she was so upset she didn't realize she hadn't been wearing pants).

Us four guys were left sitting in the suite, looking at each other. Soon, as both girls were out of earshot, I announced, "I'm putting a stop to this today."

Five calls later, I had the name of the hotel, and Drew hacked into the hotel's database and found out his room number.

"I'm going over there," I said, pocketing my cell.

"We're going, too," Braeden announced, standing. Trent followed suit. Drew was still hunched behind his computer, his fingers flying over the keys.

I rather liked the idea of four big guys showing up unannounced at this shithead's door with a special message, but I didn't like the idea of involving them.

"You should probably stay. I'm not going to be just talking." I flexed my fists, so ready to put them to use.

"No shit?" B chimed in. "We thought we were going for tea and crumpets."

"Fuck off," I ground out.

"Whoa…" B reared back at the underlying edge in my voice. "Look, we're all just as pissed this fucker is messing with our sister. We're all going."

Trent and Drew nodded solemnly.

"Whatever, but if we all end up in jail, don't get pissed at me." I paused. "And I get first, second, and third punches."

"It's all you." B spread his arms.

Even though I wished beating this punk's ass was going to be enough to make him walk from the story, I knew better. I needed more than brute force. I glanced at Drew, who was a freaking hella good hacker. I never realized just how good he was until he started messing around with some guys who fucked over Trent.

It was a skill I needed right now.

"Drew, I know it's really short notice, but do you think you could find out anything, any kind of dirt on this Kane guy? I just need anything to help convince him to back off."

"Already on it," Drew said from behind his laptop.

I blew out a breath, my hands actually shaking from the intensity of my anger. To no one but all of them, I said, "She can't deal with this right now. She was just starting to seem like herself again. This shit needs to stop. I'll walk from the NFL if I have to."

I felt the silent stare of three sets of eyes. All three of my brothers looked shocked and partially disbelieving.

I nodded, grave. "One way or another, this story is DOA."

"Consider it gone, Rome," Braeden said. "We're all behind you. Family takes care of family."

Drew went back to typing, Trent watched over his shoulder.

"I'm gonna go check on Ivy before we go. She was pretty upset. She was running around in her damn panties, for fuck's sake."

I nodded and glanced toward the bathroom.

B slapped me on the shoulder. "Go check. I'll be right back."

"Hurry up," I ordered.

He nodded and left the room.

I left Drew to his computer snooping and let myself in the bathroom. Rim was sitting on the closed toilet seat, just staring at the wall.

"Rim." I crouched in front of her.

Her light-brown eyes met mine. "I don't feel so good."

"I know, sweetheart," I murmured and picked her up to sit down with her in my lap. When she tucked her face into the crook of my neck, a lump formed in my throat.

"Don't make yourself sick over this. I'm taking care of it. That story won't see the light of day."

"I'm not sure you'll be able to stop him."

"I'll stop him," I said, not an ounce of give in my voice.

She looked up at me, and I felt her worry.

I pushed her head back into my neck and hugged a little tighter. "It's all going to be okay, Rimmel. I promise."

I didn't make a promise lightly. She knew this.

I felt her inhale, then slowly let it out. "I'm sorry."

"Why are you apologizing?"

"Because if I hadn't... had sex with him, this wouldn't even be an issue right now."

I made a sound, and as much as I loved the feel of her against me, I pulled her around so she was straddling my lap and I could look directly into her eyes.

Her glasses were slightly crooked from leaning against me, so I adjusted them before addressing her words.

"I couldn't give two shits that you slept with him," I announced. "That story could go national—hell, it could run internationally—and I would still be the luckiest bastard in this world. I would still stop football games for you. I would still love every ugly dog and cat you drag home. I would still walk down the street holding your hand and tell everyone who asked exactly where my heart resides." As I spoke, I pressed a palm to her chest, right over her heart. "This story coming out only upsets me because it upsets you and because it makes you relive something you shouldn't have to ever think about again."

"I made a bad choice," she whispered, tears in her eyes.

"You were thirteen years old. You were a *child*. He was older and manipulated you. Frankly, in my eyes, that fucker raped you."

"He didn't—"

"You defending him?" I asked, no challenge to my words, but I did lift my eyebrow.

"No." Her voice was forlorn.

"You've been through enough. I'm putting a stop to it. I can't make the press stop reporting on us, but I'm going to make it a lot less desirable. By the time I'm finished, everybody in this business is going to know they don't fuck with my wife, and if they do, they're going to get a face full of me."

"I like a face full of you," she mused.

"This isn't your fault," I insisted. "It's that bitch Missy's."

"I hate her," Rim whispered.

"Yeah, you and about a million other people," I muttered. "Don't worry about her either. I'll take care of it."

Before she could tell me no, I changed the subject. "I need to ask you something. I don't want to, but it has to be done."

"Anything." Her wide, brown eyes were innocent, open. Honestly, just looking at her made me even more pissed.

How anyone could take advantage of someone so good and hurt them deliberately was so beyond me.

"Can you remember anything about Kane? Anything he might have done or if he had a record... a reputation? Anything?"

Her brows furrowed together like she was really thinking about it. "I'm pretty sure they did some drugs; they definitely drank... maybe some light shoplifting."

"Anything else?" I asked, not wanting to make her feel like I was pushing.

She frowned. "I don't think so. I was young, and I didn't ask any questions. When he turned his back on me after, I kinda shut down. I tried to forget."

"Okay," I said gently, pulling her back into me and wrapping my arms around her back. She was trembling. "Have you eaten anything yet today?"

I felt her shake her head.

"I'll order some room service, have it sent up."

"I'm not hungry. I feel sick."

"How about coffee and juice?"

She made a sound, and I smiled. It wasn't a no.

"I'm going out with the guys for a while. You and Ivy hang out here with the baby. We'll be back in a bit. Don't open the door for anyone."

"You're going to find him."

Oh, I'd already done that. I sighed. Rim wasn't stupid, and I could sugarcoat it all I wanted, but she'd see right through me.

"I'm not going to let this go," I said honestly.

"I figured." She pulled back. I noted how tired she looked. "Just promise me you won't get arrested."

● ● ●

"I'll do my best."

She rolled her eyes, clearly not believing me.

"You done in here?" I asked and stood, bringing her with me.

When she nodded, I carried her out into the bedroom, sitting her on the side of the bed with the pillows at her back. I handed her the room service menu and the remote for the TV.

"Ivy!" I hollered.

She appeared with Nova and Braeden on her heels. She looked a lot less harried than this morning, but if I were being honest, she'd definitely looked better. It was like just bringing Missy up had a way of putting shadows back in her eyes that I thought had long since gone away.

Behind her, Braeden looked pissed, so obviously he'd seen them, too.

"You two stay here. Watch some chick flick and make sure you order food. Get the whole menu if you want. I don't care."

Ivy nodded, not bothering to argue. She'd probably already done that with Braeden.

"Don't answer the door for anyone," I commanded.

"What about the room service guy?" she said, glib.

Two could play at that game.

"Have him leave the cart in front of the door and open it when he's gone."

"If you go to jail, I'm not bailing you out," she told me, walking past to hand Nova to Rim and climb onto the bed.

"I feel the love."

Rimmel snorted. I glanced around at her and winked.

"I'll see you in a while," I told her.

She nodded, her face unsure. I closed the distance between us and kissed her head.

I walked out of the room without looking back. All three of my brothers followed.

"Tell me you got something," I said to Drew once we were in the rental.

Trent was driving, and Drew was in the passenger seat with his laptop still open. "Sure did," he replied, smug.

It seemed like it took forever to get to the other side of Hollywood and to the hotel where Kane was staying. When we finally arrived, I practically jumped out of the rental before it was even fully stopped.

Trent parked around back, not at the main entrance, and I pulled a baseball hat over my head. In fact, all of us wore one, figuring it was better to at least make us not quite as recognizable.

There was a side entrance to the hotel, but you needed a key to get entry. We got lucky, though, because there was a large carpet cleaning van parked right nearby, and the giant hose they used to clean with was in the door, propping it open.

No one saw us walk in and round the corner for the stairwell. Kane was on the third floor. No one said a word as we moved up the stairs.

We didn't have a plan. We didn't really need one. We were family, and we would operate as one unit regardless.

The anger was still so intense inside me; it hadn't dulled at all on the trip over here. If anything, it had only grown worse.

I didn't hesitate at his door. I knocked on it swiftly as my three brothers stood at my back.

About two seconds ticked by before I heard the door being opened.

I stood with my feet planted on the carpet, fists at my sides, and chin down, using the brim of my hat to conceal my face.

The door swung open. I looked up.

He knew.

He knew the instant our eyes met who I was and why I'd come.

I enjoyed the fear that flashed across his face. I reveled in the fact I was twice his size and he realized it instantly.

I smiled. It was an unfriendly gesture that, once delivered, made him step back.

The little chicken shit tried to slam the door in my face.

He was funny.

My palm slapped against the solid wood and pushed. The resistance of my one arm outdid his full body throwing into it.

He knew it was a lost cause and abandoned it to turn and run.

The motherfucker turned and ran.

What kind of man ran from a beating he fucking deserved?

It didn't matter anyway. I lunged in the doorway and grabbed him by the scruff of his neck. He scrambled to get away, but I gripped harder, and he yelped.

"Please!" he implored. "I—"

In one movement, I spun him around and swung. Before he was even done turning, my fist drove into his face. His head snapped back, and he stumbled. I hit him again. This time blood bloomed over his lower lip.

His eyes widened when he fell onto his ass in the center of the room. He sat there and dabbed at the blood.

"Get up," I growled. I didn't hit a man who was down. He could stand up and take it.

He shook his head like he was just going to sit there and be a pansy.

I picked up him, forcing him on his feet, then drove my fist into his midsection. He made a heaving sound and doubled over. As he was bending, I gave him an uppercut to the jaw.

He fell again. All the way down onto his back, blinking up at me from the carpet.

My chest heaved. Not from exertion, but from anger.

You're waiting for a description of this asshole, aren't you? The color of his eyes. The style of his hair and what kind of clothes he wore.

Here's my description of the guy who stole my wife's virginity when she was just a child: fugly.

I saw nothing when I looked at him. I only felt disgust.

His head lolled from side to side as he lay there and wallowed in pain. Christ, did he have no self-respect at all? I was kind of fucking shocked he was such a wimp. He hadn't even tried to hit me.

Braeden stepped up beside me and stared down. "Dude, you're a fucking pussy."

"Maybe," he said, dabbing at his lip. "But these bruises sure will look good on camera for the interview. Might even get me some extra cash."

I growled.

Braeden reached down and hauled him up, pinning his arms behind his back and serving him up to me like dessert. I didn't touch him. Instead, I shoved my face within inches of his. "Oh, there isn't going to be any interview." I motioned to B but spoke to Kane. "Have a seat. We need to have a conversation."

Braeden tossed him into a nearby chair. I stood in front of him, making sure I was close enough he had to look up.

Trent and Braeden flanked me. Drew was somewhere behind us. I still heard his fingers flying over the keyboard.

"Romeo," Kane said, dabbing at his already swelling lip. "I don't care what you say. I'm not walking away from that pile of cash."

"How much?" I asked. "How much is my wife's humiliation worth?"

"I still can't believe that mouse bagged an NFL player." He scoffed.

Braeden's hand shot out and slapped him upside his head. "Don't you fucking talk about my sister like that," he ground out.

Kane shrugged. "I'll admit she looks better now than she did at thirteen. Still don't have any tits, though."

I moved fast, so fast no one saw it coming. I swiped my leg out, knocked into his chair, and it toppled over with him in it. I ended up leaning over him, my face shoved in close to his.

"You say one more word about my wife and I won't be responsible for what happens after," I spoke, dead calm. Almost monotone. It was eerie, even to me. I didn't blink, and I didn't touch him again. I just stared. I let him see the full promise deep in my eyes.

He nodded.

I straightened but left him lying. I wasn't about to help the bastard up.

"Three-quarters of a million," he said once the chair was righted and his ass was in it.

I glanced at Trent and B. We all spoke without a word.

If he was only getting three-quarters, that meant the rest was going to Missy. By the time she was done, she would pocket well over a million dollars.

Guess that was a lot of money to help make her stupid #BuzzBoss website even bigger than it had already grown. Sure, I'd known Missy was still the #BuzzBoss. After we all left Alpha University, she kept it going, but instead of reporting on small-time campus gossip, she started going after celebrities. It took about a year, but eventually, the website had gone national and it became a legitimate source of gossip.

But knowing Missy, she wanted it to be even bigger. She liked power. She liked money... and she was willing to do whatever she had to do to get it.

If she wasn't a woman, I'd punch her in the face.

"You're not doing this story. You're going to walk out of here today and never talk to another reporter or gossip rag about me or my wife ever again."

He laughed.

My tongue slid over my teeth. "How much is this payday worth to you?" I tilted my head to the side.

"I already told you," he spat.

He was a dumb asshole. "Yeah, but that money, it ain't free. What's it going to cost you?"

"He has no idea what you mean, Rome. He's stupid," Braeden put in.

"If you give the interview, take the money, you'll never have another day of peace," I intoned, flexing my hands. "I'll always be around. Not physically, but you'll know I'm there. You know I can't stop you from selling your lies to the press, so you know you can't stop me from doing it either."

"I'm not lying. I popped her cherry."

"You got any proof?" I asked, wanting so badly to hit him again. The thought of this guy touching my girl made me want to kill. "Any evidence?"

"I have a picture."

I stilled.

Braeden made a sound and jumped forward, grabbing him up by the front of his shirt. "Men who take pictures of women in vulnerable positions make me sick." He reared his fist back.

Oh shit, this idiot went and triggered Braeden's memories of everything Ivy had been through.

I stepped forward in case I had to pull him off.

"She's got clothes on!" Kane screeched and winced, waiting for the hit.

"What?" Braeden paused.

"It's not from that time…" Kane slid his eyes to me. "It's a group shot of her with me and my friends."

Braeden dropped him. He sagged into the chair, relieved. Kane looked at me. "It's proof I knew her back then."

I shrugged. "So you knew her. Big deal. Doesn't prove shit. I have a lot of money, Kane. I have a lot of lawyers. I know people. I'll sue you so much and so hard you'll live inside a courtroom. Slander, harassment, falsifying information—I'll get you on it all."

Note: I didn't know if I could sue him for all that shit. I wasn't a lawyer, but he wasn't either, so whatever.

"Then there's the fact that you'll be labeled a sexual predator," Trent added.

Everyone looked at him.

Kane sucked in a breath.

"You were seventeen years old. She was thirteen. I'm pretty sure that's considered molestation, statutory rape... or at the very least, assault," I said, adding to Trent's words. "You know what the media will do to someone like you?"

He swallowed thickly.

"I'll make you burn through all that money in court fees, and then when that's over, you can live for the rest of your life as a registered sex offender."

"No," he said, his eyes wide like it never even crossed his mind.

"You know what they do to child rapists in jail?" Braeden asked quietly.

He paled.

"I know it seems like the press hates Rimmel right now, but they don't. She's their little darling. You come out with this, and they will turn on you faster than you even know is possible. She'll become a victim, and you... you'll be tried and sentenced before I even get you into court."

Beside me, Trent spoke. "Seven hundred and fifty grand don't seem like very much now, does it?"

"I'll ask for more," he said, angry. "I'll get it."

"Wonder how much I'll get when I leak your arrest record to the press," Drew mused behind us all.

Everyone turned to look.

He smiled from behind the laptop. "Breaking and entering, car boosting, assault, and... wait for it... solicitation of a minor."

Did you hear that sound?

It was the sound of the nail in his coffin.

I laughed. And laughed some more. "You're a fucking moron."

"How did you get ahold of that?" he demanded. "Those records are sealed!"

"Not anymore, they're not," Drew drawled.

"Drop the story," I intoned. "Or I swear to God, I will ruin you."

"I'll go to the press, tell them you threatened me! I'll tell the police!"

I grabbed my cell, lit up the screen, and held it out. "Want me to dial the cops now? When they get here, I'll tell them about your prior record and the fact you lured me here to try and blackmail me to keep you from telling your lies about my wife to the press."

"They won't believe you! Look at my face!" he yelled, blood splattering his chin from his busted lip.

"When Rome refused to pay your blackmail, you rushed him. He was just defending himself," Braeden said.

"That's what I saw." Trent agreed.

"Ditto," Drew replied.

"You gotta ask yourself: who they gonna believe? A guy with an arrest record that includes solicitation of a minor, or me, a quarterback at the top of his game, whose wife has been harassed relentlessly by the press and is now the victim of a sick stalker?"

"You're an asshole," Kane whined.

"I also make good on my promises."

His head hung onto his chest.

"Call and cancel the interview," I ordered.

He sat there debating for a long time. Well, it sure as fuck felt like a long time. Really, it was probably only minutes.

The silence was beginning to get to me. I was getting nervous he wasn't going to cave under the weight of my argument. For some people, that kind of money was a once in a lifetime.

But so was my wife, and I wasn't leaving here until he called it off.

"Dude, how many unpaid parking tickets do you have?" Drew asked, breaking the silence. "Did you know your driver's license is suspended?"

He slumped a little farther. "Fine."

"What was that?" I asked.

"I'll call it off."

"Do it now."

He took his sweet ass time pulling out his cell and calling up a number. When he pressed the phone to his ear, I made a sound.

"Put it on speaker," I demanded.

He did as he was told. He was learning.

"Hello?" a voice from the past answered.

"It's Jonathan."

"I'm on my way to the hotel now. You ready for the interview?"

Braeden began pacing at the sound of her voice.

"I changed my mind. I'm not doing it," Kane said and glanced at me.

I nodded.

"What!" Missy exclaimed. "You can't back out now!"

"Yes, I can. I have."

"If this is about the money…" She began.

"It's not. I just changed my mind." He glanced at me again, and I pressed a finger to my lips, indicating he better not say shit about me."

"Why?"

"It just doesn't feel right," he replied, and my eyes narrowed.

"They got to you, didn't they?" She accused.

"Who?" Kane pretended he had no idea.

"How the hell did they find out—Ah!" She gasped. "I never should have shopped it to *People*.

"Kane, listen to me—"

I dragged my finger across my throat.

He cut the connection and looked at me.

"Get your shit. You're checking out."

"I'm here until tomorrow," he insisted.

"Nope." Braeden argued.

I motioned for him to hurry up and then waited impatiently while he threw what little shit he had into a black duffle on the floor.

"Leave the room keys on the table," I instructed.

He put both keycards on the table.

"Don't bother going to the front desk. They'll check you out when they get the keys and send the bill to whoever is paying for this room." He didn't need to know I knew all about the #BuzzBoss.

We escorted him down the stairwell and out into the parking lot.

"I don't have a car here," he mumbled.

"Get in." I motioned at our rental.

He balked.

"If I wanted you dead, you would be already."

With a sigh, he got into the passenger seat, while me, Trent, and B squished into the back.

Drew drove him the airport and pulled up to the departure wing. "My plane doesn't leave 'til tomorrow," he whined.

"Change your ticket or sleep at your gate. I don't give a fuck. Now get out."

"Might want to clean your face up in the bathroom or TSA is gonna think you're the Unabomber," B cracked.

Kane spun in his seat. I saw the anger and hatred in his eyes, felt it brewing on his tongue.

Trent jerked forward, surprising us all, and grabbed him by the face, squeezing Kane's cheeks between his fingers. "You've been warned about talking about my sister. Don't say it," he growled. "'Cause this time I'll knock you the hell out, and we'll dump your unconscious pussy ass on the sidewalk and drive away."

"Fuck you," Kane muttered as he stormed out of the car like a five-year-old.

"You aren't my type," Trent yelled after him.

Drew drove off before he'd even stepped fully onto the sidewalk. I stared out the back window as he watched us drive away.

"You don't think he'll jump in a cab and go back to the hotel, do you?" B asked, his eyes watching him, too.

"Nah." I was sure we'd scared him enough. He knew I meant everything I said in that hotel room. He saw it in my eyes.

I would destroy him.

I would probably even enjoy it.

As Drew turned onto the on ramp to take us away from the airport and back to my wife, I glanced back one last time.

Kane was walking into the airport, on the way the hell out of our lives.

"Most anticipated celebrity births of the year! Who made the list?"

Chapter
Twenty-Four

YouCare.com

RIMMEL

Romeo Anderson was not the boss of me.

Neither were any of my three overbearing brothers.

So when he put me in bed and told me I had to stay there while he went off and likely did things I wouldn't approve of, my first reaction was to kick him.

Then I remembered I was tired.

And I didn't want to see Jonathan.

Maybe just this one time, I could appreciate his bossy, annoying behavior and not argue. Ivy seemed to be of the same mind, even though neither of us said it out loud. Besides, we had Nova to think about.

They were gone a long time… like hours.

We ordered food, but I didn't eat. I couldn't. My stomach was in knots. I drank some tea and picked at a muffin, but Nova ate more than I did.

After I'd glanced at the clock for like the millionth time, I glanced at Ivy. "Do you think they're in jail?"

"I really hope not," she replied. "What a bunch of boneheads."

● ● ●

Nova was napping between us on the mattress, and we both went back to watching some movie that was doing a terrible job at keeping our mind off things.

As much as I wanted Romeo not to go, I was sort of glad he did. I didn't want that story to come out. It would be humiliating. Even if I never confirmed it, even if it was embellished and not completely accurate, it was still terrible.

I would be so ashamed. My father would see. He would know it was true. It wasn't as if he were some picture of perfection—heaven knows he made more mistakes than me—but he was still my father.

My grandparents would see.

Everyone I worked with would see.

The entire world.

The press would run wild with it, and the coverage would be endless. I just wasn't up for it.

I was tired. I just wanted us to be happy and for the fresh start we worked so hard for to not be tainted with the past.

Ivy must have sensed my swirling thoughts because without a word, she reached across the bed, over her daughter, and grabbed my hand. I gave it a squeeze, thanking her for the silent support.

We sat like that until there was a knock on the door. Ivy and I glanced at each other.

"Think they forgot the key?" she whispered.

I shook my head.

"Me either."

There was another knock.

"Housekeeping?" Ivy guessed again.

I shrugged and slid out of bed and walked on what felt like unsteady legs toward the door. Ivy followed along with me. Both of us stopped at the door and listened.

I motioned for the peephole, and Ivy nodded. I leaned forward and squinted to look through.

I reared back like someone slapped me.

"What is it?" Ivy whisper demanded.

"Missy!" I whisper yelled.

Her blue eyes went so wide I could see the whites around her entire irises. *No way*, she mouthed.

Missy knocked again. "I know you're in there. Open the door."

Romeo told me not to open the door for anyone.

Remember how I said he wasn't the boss of me?

I opened the door.

She was standing there at the threshold like she owned the place. Her holier-than-thou persona made my stomach roll and my upper lip curl.

"What the hell do you want?" I snapped, my voice firm and angry, not one ounce of my exhaustion and stress showing through.

"I want my interview and my big payday."

I had to appreciate the fact that she cut right to the chase.

Hopefully, she would appreciate the fact that I was going to do the same.

I reared back and sent my fist forward with all the momentum I had. It slammed into her nose with really good accuracy. I actually felt the bone shift under my knuckle.

Pain exploded in my hand. I winced but otherwise sucked it up. I wasn't about to show weakness to this little bitch.

"Ow!" she wailed. Her head snapped back and blood began to pour from her nose. She pressed a hand over it immediately, pulled it back, and gasped when she saw all the red. "You hit me!" she exclaimed. "I think you broke my nose."

"Better get the hell out of here before I break something else," I snapped, shaking out my throbbing hand.

"You little bitch," Missy snarled and dropped her designer bag (which was now splattered with blood) onto the floor. The next thing I knew, she was coming at me.

I planted my feet and got ready for her. If she wanted a fight, then I would damn well give her one. She deserved an ass kicking after everything she'd done to my family.

Romeo wasn't the only one that could throw some punches today.

Just before she reached me, an arm snaked around her waist from behind, and she was dragged back. She continued to kick and hit and try to get at me even after Romeo lifted her clear off the floor.

"I told you not to open the door," he growled.

"You're not the only one who can protect this family."

"She broke my nose!" Missy exclaimed again.

"Maybe it will make you look better," Ivy called.

Missy started struggling again. Romeo looked bored and didn't even have to try to restrain her.

"I know you made him cancel!" she wailed.

"I have no idea what you're talking about," Romeo replied.

"You liar!" Blood was running out of her nose and into the palm of her hand.

"You should probably go," I told her. "Get that checked out."

"I'll call the police, have you arrested!"

As if on cue, hotel security walked onto the floor, out of the stairwell. "Are you the one who called?"

"That's us." Drew motioned for him.

"This woman tried to enter our suite. She's a reporter for #BuzzBoss.com. We asked her to leave, and she became belligerent. She tried to attack my wife," Romeo said. He was so calm, so reasonable even I didn't doubt what he was saying.

"She broke my nose!" Missy yelled.

The security officer looked at me.

"I'm afraid I did." I nodded. "She leapt at me, and I threw my hands up. My fist connected with her face."

"I saw the whole thing." Ivy nodded gravely. "I think she's a stalker."

Missy wailed in anger, and it only made her appear that much guiltier.

"I think she needs medical attention," I told the guard.

"I'll take it from here," he said, grim. "Sorry to have bothered you, Mr. Anderson."

"Romeo," my very charming husband corrected. He handed a still struggling Missy over to the guard and then moved by them so he and the rest of the guys could come in the room.

"I'm so sorry about your nose, miss," I called. "If you come near me again, I'm going to have to get a restraining order!"

Missy started screaming about lies, and I shut the door and threw the deadbolt. I leaned back against the door in relief.

"Way to bust her face, tutor girl," Braeden cracked. "She was bleeding like a stuck pig."

"Oh, nasty," Ivy muttered.

"You really let her have it, huh?" Romeo smiled. I heard pride in his voice.

"I'm so sick of that bitch," I muttered. "She had it coming."

"All that and more," he vowed.

I didn't ask him what that meant, because at the moment, I just didn't care. The adrenaline from seeing Missy at the door and from breaking her face was draining away. Suddenly, I felt more exhausted and woozy than ever.

Trying to push past the feelings, I turned all my attention to Romeo. "Well? Did you see him?"

"We saw him," Romeo muttered.

"Rome kicked his ass." Braeden cackled.

"Are you hurt?" I worried and shoved away from the door.

"I'm…" His voice fell away, like all sound totally faded out.

I stood there, swayed on my feet, and stared at him talking, not hearing a single word he said.

I saw my name on his lips. Concern darkened his incredible eyes.

There was some commotion around me, but it all disappeared. All I saw was Romeo…

Until he disappeared, too.

And then everybody died.

The End

Don't forget to leave a positive review online!

Cambria Hebert

Just kidding!

Story continues on the next page.

Gotcha…

Chapter Twenty-Five

Error Code 66
Page not found

ROMEO

I wasn't losing my shit.

For the most part. The only reason I was keeping it together was because she was in my arms, I could see the steady rise and fall of her chest, and I knew this was probably stress related. Rim was having a lot of trouble with panic attacks and anxiety, through no fault of her own.

I had no fucking clue if being panicked could make someone pass out, but it was what my brain was going with. It was the lesser of the bad shit running rampant through my mind.

No one ever told me falling in love so hard had the power to make a man feel so small. I wasn't used to this; I didn't think I ever would be. Everything I had was quite literally wrapped up in the woman lying flimsy in my arms.

Before Rim, I never realized just how much bigger everything around me was. How out of control in this life a man really was. We were all at the mercy of something greater… the universe, a god… luck.

I wasn't entirely sure.

• • •

I never worried before. It didn't matter what came at me in life 'cause I was in control

But I wasn't anymore. I hadn't been for a long time. Since that day at the shelter, when I saw Rim soaking wet from the rain.

Now everything for me hinged on her. On Rimmel.

She was the only thing I couldn't live without.

I found myself praying a lot, asking the force that was so much greater than us to just take care of her, to just please not take her away.

We were in the backseat of the rental when her eyelids finally fluttered.

"Rimmel," I said, turning her face so I could stare down. "Open your eyes; look at me."

She listened. There was a dreamy appearance to her gaze. Her full lips turned up, and she smiled at the sight of me.

She has my heart.

She has it all.

"Hey, handsome," she murmured, as if she didn't know I'd just been to hell and back.

"How are you feeling?" I asked, stroking her cheek.

Her brow furrowed, and the dreamy appearance vanished. I knew the second she remembered what happened, because she tried to sit up.

"Just lie still," I told her, gently pushing her back down.

"What happened?"

"You passed out. Guess knocking Missy into next week wore you out."

She rolled her eyes, and a lot of the worst worry I felt left me immediately.

"Where are we?" She glanced around the inside of the car.

"On the way to the ER."

"What!" She tried to sit up again. I restrained her. "I'm fine!"

"You just face planted on the carpet. You aren't fine."

"I didn't eat. I was lightheaded."

My mouth thinned. "I told you to eat."

"You tell me to do a lot of things," she muttered.

"Well, maybe you should listen."

"Maybe you shouldn't act like a caveman!"

"We're here," Drew announced, and the car came to a stop.

That was fast... 'Course, that was Drew's specialty.

"There's no need to be here. Let's just go back to the hotel," Rimmel said, sitting up to glare at the entrance of the ER.

"That's not happening," I told her.

Her eyes narrowed.

Only my wife would pass out one minute and then be ready to argue the next. Maybe I should watch my face; she was apparently pretty damn skilled at breaking noses.

"You scared the crap out of us, sis. Just go inside," Trent implored from the front seat.

Her shoulders slumped. "Fine."

"So you'll do what *he* tells you to do?" I muttered as I unfolded from the back of this lame rental and hefted her into my arms.

"I'm sorry I worried you. Again," she whispered, resting her cheek against my shoulder.

I grunted. I couldn't stay mad at her.

"I'll meet you inside," I called into the car at Drew and Trent, then strode through the wide double doors.

I was prepared for a fight to get a room right away. I wasn't about to fuck around in the waiting area for hours, all the while wondering what the hell was wrong with my wife.

Maybe it was some kind of complication from the car accident. Something no one caught when she'd been in the hospital the first time.

Thankfully, I didn't have to fight. The nurse at the station was a dude and a football fan. He recognized me even though we weren't in my home state.

"Right this way, Mr. Anderson," he said after I told him my wife passed out and needed looked at ASAP.

He showed us into a cubicle with curtains all around. Gently, I placed Rim on the generic bed and took up residence in front of her. "Our family will be in shortly," I told him. "All four of them."

B and Ivy had followed behind us in their car with the car seat.

He nodded and cleared his throat. "I need to get her vitals."

"Right," I said and stepped aside so he could get to her.

I didn't go far, though, and stared him down the entire time he was taking her blood pressure and her pulse.

"I'm sorry," Rimmel told the nurse. "It's not you. It's him."

The man and my wife shared a laugh.

I didn't think it was funny.

Once everything was recorded into his laptop, he left us to wait for a doctor.

"Stop being so mean to the staff." She admonished me. She looked better, more alert. Though her face was still too pale for my liking, and the circles under her eyes concerned me. Still, she looked pretty damn adorable sitting there with her legs dangling over the edge of the bed/cot thing. Her feet were bare because the second she'd dropped, I'd scooped her up, and we all piled in the cars.

Unable to resist, I moved back in front of her, balanced my palms on the corners of the bed, caged her in, and leaned close. "I'm not being mean. I'm getting results."

She kissed me.

She pulled back inches, her eyes on mine, and smiled.

"Stop that," I demanded, but it sure as hell didn't sound very forceful.

She kissed me again.

I let her, of course. I wasn't about to turn down some sugar.

"You like it," she whispered against my lips.

"That I do." I kissed her back. "How do you feel?" I asked, shifting away, scrutinizing her face.

"Not bad enough that I need to be here. I hate hospitals." She stuck out her tongue.

I tucked a loose stand of hair behind her ear. "What's not bad enough?"

"I'm just tired. I don't feel good... Threatening to have your sordid past splashed all over the internet will do that to a girl."

"He's not doing the story," I told her.

"Really?" Her eyes sparked with hope.

"Really. I already put his ass on a plane."

"How did you get him to cancel the interview? Who's to say he won't just agree to another one?" She worried.

There was always that slim chance, I supposed. But I really didn't think so. He saw how serious I was when I vowed he'd never get any peace. I'd blow up that fucker's world if he messed with Rim. "Don't worry about. I took care of it."

"Are the police going to be looking for you?" She sighed.

I laughed. "What do you think I am? An amateur?"

The curtain made an earsplitting sound when the doctor slid it open and strode in. With him was a nurse dressed in yellow scrubs with a lab kit in her hand.

"I understand you fainted," the doctor said, not looking up from her chart.

"Yes." She confirmed. "But I really don't think it's anything."

"People don't just pass out for nothing. There's usually a reason."

"Told you," I cracked.

The doctor looked up. He was probably in his late forties, with dark hair that was cut really short. "Romeo Anderson?"

I gave him my hand. "Hey, how are you?"

He shook, then looked at Rimmel. "This is your wife?"

No. It's my girlfriend. Idiot. "Yes. I'm hoping to find out why she fell over on me," I said instead.

"Jackie here is going to take some blood. Then I'll ask a few questions. I'll come back in when the labs come back, and hopefully we'll know what's going on."

Rimmel gave the lab kit and Jackie a dubious look. I caught her eye and lifted a brow, daring her to argue. I'd embarrass her. I wasn't above it, and she knew it.

With a sigh, she surrendered her arm and looked away when the needle poked her.

The doctor asked a bunch of questions, made some non-committal sounds, and then we were left alone to wait for the results.

Rimmel pointed dramatically to the giant cotton ball and tape on the inside of her arm. "Are you happy now?"

"I won't be happy 'til I know nothing's wrong."

My phone went off, and I pulled up the text and made a rude sound. "They won't let everyone back."

"It's not like we're doing anything anyway," she said, exasperated.

My phone went off again. *FYI: He got the website shut down. For a while anyway.*

Good. Missy, aka #BuzzBitch, never should have messed with us again. She'd get hers.

We'll be out soon, I typed out, then slid my phone away.

"You're okay, right?" Rimmel asked, her voice unsure.

I tilted my head to the side. "Why wouldn't I be?"

"Well, Braeden said you got into a fight with... *him*. And I'm sure he wasn't very nice to you."

Kane. The jackass.

"He's a loser." I scoffed. "He didn't even try to hit me. He knew it would be a lost cause."

"And seeing him?" She fretted.

Her concern for me always got me in the feels. How she always seemed to worry about me the way I did her.

● ● ●

That's what made this love thing so worth it. The feeling small and vulnerable. The being out of control... I wasn't alone.

Rimmel was right there with me.

We were in this together.

I went to her, cupping her cheeks. "Seeing him changed nothing between us, baby. You're still and always will be my before anyone else."

Her hands closed around my wrists. "You know the hip term for that these days is #bae."

I made a face. "That's just terrible."

"It actually means *poop* in Danish." She pulled back her hand, pressed it to her mouth, and giggled.

Her laughter was the sound of my everything.

"I guess I should be glad you didn't try to name Ralph that."

She swatted at my stomach, and I chuckled.

"Maybe we should just stick to the long version." She smiled. "I like the way it sounds when you say it anyway."

My arm slid around her back and pulled her to the very edge of the bed. Her thighs parted, and I stepped between them, brought my head down, and claimed her mouth.

I didn't lift my head, not at all. We remained fused together for one endless kiss. The sounds of a busy ER faded away until all that remained was her and me. The softness of her lips accepted me again and again; the feather-light way her mouth danced across mine made my heart thud heavily as full-blown thirst for more left me feeling dehydrated.

It wouldn't really matter how long we stood here and kissed. I'd still want more later.

• • •

A heavy clearing of a throat behind made me release her lips and glance over my shoulder. Rim ducked her head so she was completely hidden behind me, and I straightened a little farther to give her even more protection.

The doctor was standing there with the curtain in his hand and what I assumed were her lab results in the other.

"Doc," I said, acting like he hadn't caught me making out with my wife.

Dude was probably jealous anyway.

He stepped into the cubicle, the curtain falling closed behind him. "I have your results."

I glanced over my shoulder at Rim. She nodded, so I pivoted around to stand beside her. Both of us stared at the doctor expectantly.

"Did you find anything?" Rimmel asked.

"Actually, yes, we did." he said, and my stomach dropped.

My brain went into crisis mode, and I began creating a list of specialists and favors I could call in to be sure she got whatever the hell she needed. "What is it?" I asked, trying not to show how rattled I was.

"You're pregnant." He smiled, like he'd just dropped the happiest news bomb on us ever.

Our silence was not what he expected.

In fact, we both stared at him as if he hadn't spoken at all.

"I, uh, take it this is a surprise?" he asked when we still remained speechless.

Did he not read the papers?

"Did you just say I'm pregnant?" Rimmel asked, her voice shaky.

He nodded. "Changes in the body during the first trimester, like the blood volume in a woman's body nearly doubling as well as hormonal fluctuations, etc., can cause a woman to faint. That coupled with the fact you said you hadn't eaten and have been under some stress… well, that will do it."

"I'm pregnant," Rimmel echoed. "Romeo?" Her hand reached out blind, grappling for mine.

Her fingers gripped mine so tight it almost hurt. "Are you sure?" I asked.

"Positive. We ran it twice to be sure," the doctor replied.

I felt dizzy, shocked… so fucking thrilled.

Rimmel burst into tears. Like full-blown meltdown cry fest.

I picked her up, lifting her so her face was level with mine. Tears were trailing down her face as sobs wracked her chest. "You're having my baby," I told her, smiling so wide it hurt my cheeks.

Another sob ripped from her throat, and I pulled her against me. She clung to me and cried. The relief, the joy, the fear… it poured off her so heavily I felt it all. Even my own eyes started to get misty.

"I told you, baby," I whispered in her ear. "I knew this was going to happen. This time everything is going to be just fine."

She wiped her nose on my shirt and looked up. "A baby," she whispered.

"*Our* baby."

More tears slid over her cheeks, but she smiled before burying her face in my neck once more.

The doctor was very uncomfortable.

I didn't fucking care.

I'd never see him again.

* * *

He had no idea what this meant to Rimmel. To me.

God, we'd barely even started trying. She was convinced it would take months and months just like with Evie.

Bigger things are in control. Some things are just meant to be.

"When did you say your last menstrual period was?" the doctor asked, turning back to his chart, trying to move this along. "If you can get that down to the day, I could tell you with good accuracy how far along you are."

"I'm three and a half weeks." Rimmel lifted her head and said immediately. "Almost four."

I glanced into her damp eyes. "How do you know?"

"It was that first night," she whispered low. "I just know it."

Good enough for me. "Almost four weeks it is," I told the doctor.

He just wrote it down. He probably thought we were crazy.

"You'll want to see your regular OB when you get home," he said. "They'll be able to do an ultrasound in a few more weeks and give you an estimated due date."

Rimmel gasped and pressed a hand to her stomach. "Is everything okay? Did me passing out hurt the baby?"

Slayed.

Seeing her press a hand to my baby growing inside her just fucking slayed me.

"No, I'm certain your little one is just fine. All the other lab results looked great."

She didn't seem so ready to believe him. Doubt clouded her eyes.

"Do an ultrasound," I demanded. If that would make her feel better, then he was going to do one.

"At just under four weeks, a sonogram would show nothing," the doctor replied. "It's just too soon. I would recommend waiting until six weeks. Then you'll be able to see everything much clearer."

I was about to argue, but Rimmel put a hand to my cheek. "He's right. We'll wait a few more weeks."

"You sure?" I asked, searching her eyes.

She smiled and nodded. From within my arms, she glanced over her shoulder at the doctor. "Thank you."

"You're very welcome. If there isn't anything else, I'll have your paperwork waiting for you at the desk out front."

Rimmel nodded, and the doctor left.

She reached around, took one of my hands that was at her back, and guided it around to cover her flat stomach. A tear fell down her face.

"Are you happy, sweetheart?" I asked, rubbing against her stomach.

"So happy," she whispered. Soon as she said it, some familiar guilt crept into her eyes.

"Hey," I said. "It's okay to be happy. This baby deserves that."

It was like my words flipped a switch inside her; her eyes literally lit up.

"You're right," she mused. "This baby does, and I already love him or her as much as Evie."

I nodded once. "This is a lucky baby because he has a big sister watching out for him."

"Yeah." Her eyes softened. Then the rest of my words registered. "Him?"

I shrugged. "Or her. I'm thrilled either way."

"You gave me another baby," she whispered, lower lip wobbling. "Thank you."

My chest felt tight, and I hugged her close. "I love you, Rimmel." *So much.*

Her voice was muffled against my shirt. "I love you, too."

"C'mon. We gotta go," I said, sitting her down on the bed so I could crouch in front of her and offer my back. "Someone didn't feed herself today, so now I'm gonna have to stand over her to make sure she eats. Especially since she's eating for two now.

She laughed and climbed on, and I stood up. "I left my vitamins at home." She worried. "I didn't think… I should have brought them."

We were going home later tonight. It wasn't like it was a big deal.

But my girl wanted vitamins, and she would probably worry until she got them.

She was damn well going to get them.

"Vitamins and food," I said and started forward.

"Romeo?" She patted me on the upper chest, her voice right beside my ear.

"Anything," I told her and stopped walking.

"I don't want to tell anyone about the baby until I'm further along."

"No one?" I confirmed.

"Obviously we'll tell Ivy and Braeden. Trent and Drew," she said, like they didn't count.

They didn't. They were family.

"But no one else… I just want it to be ours for a little while."

"Whatever you want, baby." I agreed and started forward again.

We waited until we got back to the hotel to let the fam in on the good news. Rimmel cried again. Ivy cried. Nova clapped. All four of us guys stood over Rim while she ate an entire plate of food.

She complained.

I told her to get used to it.

I knew she was nervous. Hell, I was, too. It was probably going to be a long pregnancy; there would be a lot of emotions surrounding it. Good days and bad days.

But...

We were happy.

Celebrity News

Gossip +++ Buzz +++ Social Media Fre...

"Football Royalty Pregant Again! Will it be a Boy or Girl?"

—The Entire Internet

Chapter Twenty-Six

RIMMEL

At four weeks, we found out I was pregnant.

At five weeks, we decided not to find out the sex until he or she was born.

At six weeks, I developed a *very* strong aversion to Romeo's shampoo. (He got a new, less-smelly one).

At eight weeks, we first saw our little bundle growing inside me.

At twelve weeks, we made an announcement to all our family. (Valerie cried.)

At sixteen weeks, the press got undeniable photo proof of my bump, and the story went viral.

At twenty weeks, we felt the baby move inside me.

At twenty-five weeks, I actually started to let myself believe this time was going to be different.

Every single day of every single week, I thought of Evie. My love for her would never change.

Just like my love for this baby would remain.

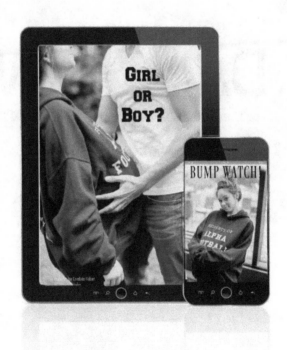

DAILY NEWS

MARYLAND'S FAVORITE COUPLE TELLS US ALL ABOUT THE BABY! *Plus* INSIDE THE NURSERY!

WHAT IT'S LIKE
@ Home with the Anderson's

Celebrity News

Chapter
Twenty-Seven

"#RomeoReveals:
2 mil bounty NIGHTMARE!
& #BuzzBoss true identity!"

"Media vows:
#BuzzBoss Banned!"

ROMEO

She glowed.

And I'm not just talking her typical, everyday kind of glow.

She held the kind of radiance that attracted attention, the kind that made it impossible to look away too long.

Rimmel cast a spell on me, the type that wiped my memory of what life was like before she literally stumbled into it. It wasn't a spell I wanted to break free from. I was blissfully bound, a willing hostage to everything our life together entailed.

The bad. The good.

The never-ending.

The knowledge her body literally cradled something we created, that she nurtured and grew with so much grace and courage… I didn't think it was ever possible. But it made me love her more.

Cambria Hebert

Celebrity News

Chapter Twenty-Eight

"The Most LUXURIOUS Baby Shower of the Year!" *Insider Pics Included!* –STYLE CYPHER

RIMMEL

I looked like a tennis ball with legs.

No really. My stomach was so big and round it was borderline alarming.

Ivy looked cute pregnant. Me? I looked like a beached whale.

Not that I was complaining. I wasn't. All I cared about was this baby was healthy and had everything he or she needed.

I had to admit, though, I was at times uncomfortable (at times = all the time), hormonal, and cried over silly things. Like when we ran out of pickles.

That only happened once.

Ever since then, Romeo and all four of my brothers brought home jars and giant individually wrapped pickles whenever they came home.

Literally.

Our fridge looked like a pickle market.

Naturally, it was a dream come true.

This time it was really happening. Sometimes I still struggled to believe it. At thirty-seven weeks, it was almost impossible not to believe someday soon I would be holding a baby in my arms.

And frankly, if you saw my gigantic stomach, you'd probably think it was impossible I was still pregnant and able to walk.

I was far enough along now that everything I put off (for fear of jinxing anything) was beginning to happen. Like a baby shower. *My* baby shower.

It was beyond over the top, but I figured Valerie earned the right for several reasons:

1.) I put it off for so long. After all, she had almost the full nine months to plan, which she took full advantage of.

2.) This was her first grandchild, something she thought she'd never have.

and

3.) We deserved this.

So here I was. Standing in the backyard of our compound, which had been completely transformed into some kind of opulent baby event.

Honestly? I thought this might put our wedding to shame. I took this as a total indication this baby was going to be spoiled beyond control by his or her grandma.

Yep, she was even going with the title grandma. She didn't want a fancy title or something that made her sound "less old."

Valerie didn't care. She just wanted a grandchild to love.

Despite the rocky way our relationship began, that was all in the past now. She'd been incredibly supportive of me during this pregnancy (almost to the point of hovering), and I knew without a doubt this baby would be loved.

I wished my own mother could be here. There was so much I wanted to share with her. I took daily comfort in the fact that she was with Evie, and it seemed oddly right that both my children have a grandmother where they were, since they both couldn't be with me.

I was standing in the shade, looking out over the massive event from underneath a giant white umbrella jeweled with what I sincerely hoped were not real crystals. I was afraid to ask Valerie. There were a ton of them; somehow Valerie had them suspended from all the trees and from some kind of frame she'd erected.

It gave the appearance they were floating in the sunshine, and the crystals sparkled brilliantly. With the umbrellas were also long strands of giant, clear glass beads, which hung at varying heights. Tables were scattered about, all round, all draped in white, with natural-colored wicker chairs around them.

Giant vases of white flowers were everywhere, along with an actual fountain for people to throw in pennies and make a wish for the baby.

The catering was so pretty it was almost inedible. White cupcakes were everywhere, and yellow-iced sugar cookies in traditional baby shower shapes made it into every guest's mouth.

Romeo and Braeden were standing with the Knights (the entire team was here with their significant others), and Ivy was chasing after Nova, who was chasing after a rogue clear balloon filled with sparkling glitter.

The second she learned to walk, she started to run, and her parents had been chasing after her ever since. Her laughter floated around as she scampered, dark curls bouncing around her head, and I knew her deep-blue eyes were sparkling with mischief.

Someone stepped up beside me, and my lips pulled into a wide smile when I saw who it was.

"Brought you a pickle." Trent extended the giant dill pickle Valerie had somehow managed to have specially wrapped.

I made a sound of deep appreciation and grabbed it to take a bite. "Mmm, so good." I groaned.

He laughed.

Trent and I had grown close over the past year. His quiet, understanding nature was a relief in the somewhat chaotic world we lived in. I never had to explain myself to him; it was as if he had this intuitive sense within him that tapped into whatever a person was feeling and he just knew. When Romeo was traveling, it was usually Trent I saw the most.

He was always my brother, but now he was more. Next to Ivy, Trent was my best friend. He'd become my confidant and someone I always looked forward to seeing.

"Whatcha got?" I asked him as I crunched. I leaned over and peered into the giant waffle cone bowl in his hand.

It was filled with some kind of cheesecake-flavored mousse with fresh berries and a honey sauce drizzle.

"This stuff is the shit," he said, shoveling it into his mouth. I swore nothing else would fit in there, but then he took a bite of the bowl.

"Valerie outdid herself." I agreed, focused on the pickle. It was really delicious.

He snorted, and it made me smile. "You think?"

"You know what's behind that giant white curtain over there?" I asked, motioning toward the huge display.

"Maybe." He shoved more food in his mouth, then paused in chewing. "You'll find out soon enough."

"Some brother you are," I muttered fondly.

He was laughing when Drew walked up and casually leaned down to take a huge bite out of the side of the bowl.

"Good thing I love ya, Forrester," Trent told him. "'Cause if I didn't, I'd kick your ass."

"Bring it, frat boy." Drew challenged and stole a berry to pop into his mouth.

"Quit hogging my sister!" Braeden hollered and injected himself under the umbrella. His arms wrapped around me from behind, and he kissed my cheek.

"It's a wonder you can even still do that!" I cracked, gesturing to his arms.

"You are looking mighty large today, tutor girl."

I slapped him in the head with my pickle.

"Ew! Pickle juice!" He jumped back and wiped at his face.

"What the hell are you doing to my wife?" Romeo demanded, his well-muscled arms wrapping around my shoulders and pulling me against him.

"He called me fat." I sniffed.

"I did not! I said you're large. There's a difference!" Braeden defended.

Trent and Drew snickered and continued to fight over the bowl of food. Why Drew didn't just go get his own I would never understand.

"You're not fat, baby," Romeo told me. "There's just more of you to love right now."

"I'm gigantic, and we all know it," I declared.

Romeo patted my belly, and right on cue, the baby kicked his hand.

"That's *my* baby," Romeo announced like that was all the explanation needed for the sheer size of me. He was very full of himself. Frankly, I think he enjoyed the fact I was blown up like a house. The bigger I got, the more pride he swelled with. Add in the fact that every time he touched my belly or spoke to our child, he was greeted with some kind of movement. It was a wonder his head wasn't as big as me.

"Daddy!" Nova yelled and came running up behind B.

He turned and caught her as she vaulted herself at him, and he held her over his head to make her laugh. "What are you doing, angel?" he asked.

Ivy panted as she joined the rest of us. Between her fingers was the balloon. "Your turn. I'm exhausted. I need shade."

Both Drew and Trent moved to the side, making room right beside me beneath the umbrella so she could cool off.

"Wanna see what's behind that curtain over there?" Romeo asked, his voice right next to my ear.

"You know I do!"

"You guys wanna give me a hand?" He directed the question to my three brothers, and they moved off toward the display.

I glanced at Ivy, and she smiled. "You're going to love it." She watched the three walk away. "I better supervise, because we both know how they can be."

"How's that?" Romeo asked, clueless.

Ivy and I laughed.

She bounded after them, and Romeo moved around so he was standing in front of me. "How's my baby momma doing?"

"My back hurts, my feet hurt, and my hands are so swollen I haven't been able to wear my wedding ring in weeks," I told him and smiled. "I'm so happy."

"That's all I've ever wanted, Rim. For you to be happy."

"I could never be anything but with you, Romeo." Even when I was at my darkest moment, when Evie slipped away from us, he was still the brightest spot I knew.

Romeo took my face and pressed our foreheads together. We looked at each other like we weren't in a place filled with people and noise. My stomach pressed against his, our child cradled right there between us.

"Before anyone else," he whispered so only I could hear.

"Always," I whispered back.

His smile was brilliant and charming when he pulled back. "Now don't be mad," he said, gently picking me up and cradling me against him.

"You're gonna hurt yourself!" I insisted.

He rolled his eyes. "Please, woman, have you seen my guns? Huge." As he walked and carried me, he flexed his biceps.

I laughed. As we neared the display, everyone stopped and watched us. The sounds of cameras going off filled the air, and people murmured about what a beautiful couple we made.

"What was it you were saying about not being mad?" I asked.

He glanced down. "I had to make a call, Smalls. That call involved some spending."

* * *

I groaned. "Romeo, what did you buy?"

"Nothing you don't need."

I groaned again.

"That's my baby in there, baby," he said. "You can't really think I wouldn't spoil you both."

He stopped in front of the white curtain. People gathered around. Valerie and Tony appeared beside us, and Romeo finally stood me on my feet.

The rest of our family joined us, and then Braeden hit a button on a remote in his hand.

The curtain dropped.

I gasped.

It was everything I'd ever even thought about buying for this baby. Some of the stuff I saw had been purely daydreaming.

All of it. Right in front of me.

Awws and ooohs went around the crowd, but I barely heard. It took a while for me to actually find my voice. "How did you know?" I marveled.

"Drew hacked your secret Pinterest board," Ivy declared.

I laughed.

Drew was entirely too handy with a laptop. Not only had he managed to keep the #BuzzBoss website down for several weeks after Missy's stunt in California, but he also erased a lot of the content from there permanently.

Afterward, Romeo leaked her identity to the press with an exclusive "tell-all" about what the press had now dramatically dubbed *the two million-dollar bounty*. Up until this point, Missy had been able to hide who she really was, but not anymore.

Her days of hurting people with personal details and secrets were over. No one in the business would trust her ever again.

And the public?

They tried and sentenced her a horrible person. I was hoping she'd move to another country. I knew I'd never see her again. And if I did?

I'd break her nose again.

I was no longer harassed by the press to the point of being in danger. We were back on the list of most well-loved and once again were known as football royalty.

I didn't care, honestly. I just wanted my baby to be safe.

But enough of that. Let's get back to the presents.

"I cannot believe you bought all this," I said, looking out over the huge display of stuff, which included a crib, a rocking chair, toys, teddy bears, blankets, and rugs. There was everything one could possibly need to fill a nursery and a closet.

"Well, we were starting to think this baby was going to be naked when he came home," Braeden joked. "We had to take a stand, sis. No nephew of mine will be seen with his boys dangling."

"Little boy babies don't dangle." Ivy admonished.

"Mine does," Romeo said.

"Damn right." B nodded, and then all four guys gave each other high-fives like the state of my potential son's dangly parts was something to be proud of.

I thought I might be traumatized.

"Roman Anderson," Valerie told him. "We have guests."

"Sorry, Mom," Both Romeo and Braeden mumbled.

Valerie looked at Trent and Drew expectantly. They apologized immediately.

Ivy and I laughed.

"It could be a girl," I said and caressed my belly.

"We all know it's a boy." Braeden argued.

Actually. We didn't. I refused to know the sex of this baby, something the techs at the hospital got pretty creative in hiding from us during our many ultrasounds.

I hadn't bought much either. I couldn't bring myself to do it. No matter how excited I got or how happy I was, I still didn't want to do anything that might jinx it. I mean, it was a little far-fetched and altogether dramatic to say this baby would be going home naked. I did have a few moments when I couldn't resist a stroll into a baby boutique, which always resulted in a few outfits here and there.

So yeah, here I was thirty-seven weeks pregnant, and we didn't even have a nursery.

Correction: we did now.

"It's not all from me," Romeo told me, taking my hand. "It's from all of us."

"You just leave it all to me," Valerie interjected. "I'll have all this moved into the house and the nursery all decorated and organized in no time. You just rest."

"Thank you," I told her sincerely.

"No, thank you," Tony said, coming forward to hug me. In my ear, he whispered, "This is the happiest I've seen her in a long, long time."

Babies had a way of doing that. "I'm glad," I whispered back.

"All the other gifts from the guests I'll have brought into the house, and you can open them later." Valerie went on.

I nodded. Just the thought of opening it all made me kinda tired. I was sure it would be a good job for Nova.

Absentmindedly, I rubbed my lower back as I stared over the haul of beautiful things. I recognized it all from my list. I had no idea how they tracked all that down from Pinterest. That had to have taken forever.

The next thing I knew, I was lifted off my feet. I gazed up at Romeo, who was looking at me with concern on his face. "Your back hurts."

"Just a little."

"When's the last time you ate?" he asked.

I sighed. "I just ate a pickle."

He glowered at me. "Something other than a pickle."

I groaned and pointed to my stomach. "Look at me, Romeo. There is no room inside me for a baby *and* food."

"Go sit." Valerie shooed us away. "I'll make you a plate, Rimmel."

Romeo agreed, like I didn't just say I wasn't hungry, and started toward our table.

"Let me down." I squirmed, uncomfortable. "I want to walk."

"Cranky," he muttered but stopped and placed me gently on the grass.

"You'd be cranky too if you felt like you were about to explode," I retorted.

"I know, baby." He caught my hand and threaded our fingers together. "C'mon."

On the way to the table, I tugged him toward the fountain. It wasn't small. It was taller than Romeo and very wide and round. Pennies littered the bottom already.

Once the shower was over and the fountain was drained, all the pennies were going to be taken to the bank and put into an account in the baby's name.

Romeo produced a penny from his pocket and held it out. "Wish?" he asked.

I shook my head.

"I'll make one for you, then," Romeo replied, accepting my superstition.

I nodded and smiled. He closed his eyes and put the penny between his palms. A few seconds later, he smiled and tossed it into the water, where it made a light splash and sank instantly to the bottom.

"It was a good one," he sang and took my hand so we could go sit.

A few steps later, I stopped, wrapping a hand around my belly.

"Rim?" Romeo said, spinning around with worry in his voice. "Rimmel." His hands were on my sides. I felt the fear in his stare, and I wasn't even looking at him.

Warm liquid trickled down the insides of my legs, beneath the white, flowy fabric of my dress.

I guessed all those Braxton Hicks weren't really after all. No wonder my back was hurting a little more than usual today and I wasn't all that hungry.

Romeo shuffled anxiously on his feet in front of me, and I straightened, still holding my stomach as nerves danced around inside me. "My water just broke."

His eyes flared. "Are you sure?"

I lifted the skirt so he could see my wet thighs. An uncomfortable feeling squeezed my middle, and I winced.

"Holy fuck!" he burst out. "That don't look right. What's happening?"

"I'm in labor," I told him, taking a deep breath. "We're going to meet our baby today."

"But it's not time," he demanded. "He's not supposed to come out yet!" He pointed at my stomach accusingly.

"I don't think he cares," I said as more pain squeezed through my middle.

"Okay, yeah." He panted, his arms hovering around me. "Okay, don't worry, baby. I'm right here."

He picked me up, and I made a small sound. He cussed, and I bit back a smile. He was the one worrying right now, not me.

"We're going to the hospital right now," he announced.

"But my bag, it isn't packed." I worried.

"Ivy!" he roared.

The entire family came running over, including Valerie and Tony. "We're going to the hospital. She needs all her shit. You can do that, right?" he asked, talking fast as he went.

"Rimmel, are you in labor?" Ivy burst out.

I nodded and glanced at Valerie. "I'm so sorry to ruin this gorgeous shower."

"Are you kidding? I've been waiting for this day! Don't you worry about a thing. I'll shoo everyone out of here, and then we'll be at the hospital right away!"

"Where the hell are my keys?" Romeo yelled.

"Probably in the house," I told him calmly.

"I'll drive," Drew announced. "Meet you in the garage."

And just like that, everyone burst into action. Ivy went to pack a bag. Braeden handed Nova off to his mother, and he and Trent flanked Romeo as he rushed me through the yard to my new Range Rover, Drew already in the driver's seat.

The second we were all inside, he peeled down the driveway like we were in one of his races.

I glanced up at Romeo, his face pale and wild.

I ducked mine into his chest and smiled.

"It's all right, Rim," he told me. "I'll make sure everything is fine."

He was so incredibly sweet. Even though I saw the nerves on his face, he was being the man I always knew him to be. Strong and capable.

Funny, I'd been so scared for this moment when I first found out I was pregnant again. Scared I'd never get here. Scared I would.

Now the moment was here… I wasn't scared at all.

There was an inner peace suddenly unlocked inside me, whispering everything would be okay and this baby would indeed be coming home with us.

With my head on Romeo's chest (I was still in his lap, getting him and me wet), I glanced across at the baby seat he'd just installed.

My eyes misted over.

We were finally having our baby.

"Hottest Dad Alive! Romeo slays fatherhood!"
-Starr Magazine

Chapter Twenty-Nine

ROMEO

Everybody in this hospital was incompetent.

I was going to sue them all.

It was like they were all just sitting around with their thumbs up their asses while my wife was in pain instead of getting my baby the hell out of her.

Rim was hooked up to machines with some band around her stomach and an IV in her hand. Even though she was bigger than usual, she still looked small in the center of the hospital bed, with that ugly-as-sin hospital gown covering her.

She was in pain. I read it on her face. When it got really bad, she bit down on her lip. I didn't like it. In fact, it made my stomach ache.

This was my fault. I did this to her. Why did I have to be so horny all the time?

"Hey," she said, holding out her hand.

I abandoned the pacing and rushed to the bedside, wrapping her hand in both of mine.

"I'm fine." She promised. "Stop freaking out."

"I'm not freaking out." I argued.

Her lips curved into a knowing smile.

"I don't like seeing you in pain," I grumped.

"It's not so bad," she told me. "Besides, I'm tough. I got this."

I chuckled, and the worst of my fear ebbed away. She *was* tough and she *could* do this.

There was a swift knock on the door before it swung open and a nurse strode in. I didn't like her. She was way too chipper and nonchalant about this situation.

"You have a parade in the hallway," she announced and motioned toward the door.

Braeden strode through, followed by Ivy, Drew, Trent, and my parents.

"Hey, sis, I knew you were gonna explode. Didn't I tell you?" Braeden said, stopping at the end of Rim's bed and grabbing her foot, which was underneath a blanket.

"She's not exploding," I growled and pointedly stared where he was touching her.

"Maybe not, but how close are you?" B said, pulling back his hand and giving me a wary look.

"I brought all your stuff and some extra," Ivy told Rimmel, carrying a large bag and setting it on a nearby chair. "And some outfits for the baby."

I stared at the bag like it had four heads. How much shit did she need? She wasn't going to be here that long—was she?

"Thank you," Rimmel told her as the nurse walked to the monitors and started checking stuff. I watched her like a hawk, wondering what she was looking for, if everything was okay.

"Contractions are closer now," she said. "Everything looks good."

"How much longer?" I asked.

"Could be several hours," she replied.

Hours? Oh, hells no. It had already been a couple hours.

Rimmel's hand went taut in mine, and her smile slipped into a mask of pain.

"Squeeze my hand," I told her, watching her face.

How long was she going to have to do this?

"That's a big one," the nurse said, reading the machine again.

"Can't you do something?" I snapped as Rimmel squeezed my hand with more force than I thought she had.

About a minute later, her grip relented, and she rested back against the pillows.

"Did you change your mind about an epidural?" the super unhelpful nurse asked.

"No," Rimmel replied immediately. "No drugs."

"Okay. I'll be back in a few minutes with the doctor to see how everything is progressing."

When she was gone, I looked at my father. "You see that negligence. We have a solid case."

He laughed.

"What the hell is so funny?" I demanded.

"We aren't suing anyone, Romeo," Rimmel declared.

I went back to pacing.

Braeden piped up from his position near Ivy. "Dude, you gotta tell the kid to hurry up. That's what I did with Nova. She came right out."

Ivy rolled her eyes, and my mom laughed.

"Rimmel, can I get you anything?" Mom asked her, stepping up beside the bed.

"No, thank you. I'm fine. Just a little nervous."

"Everything is going to be just fine." Mom assured her and brushed her hair from her face. "I can feel it."

Rimmel nodded and relaxed against the mattress.

The nurse came back into the room, followed by her new OB, who had already signed a NDA. "Should we see how things are coming along?" she asked as she went to check the machines.

"We'll be in the waiting room. If you want or need anything, you just have Roman come and get us. We'll be right here," my mother told Rimmel.

Rimmel surprised me when she grabbed my mother's hand and squeezed. "Thank you for everything."

"You're welcome, sweetheart," Mom replied, her eyes actually misty.

"See, Moms, I told ya Rimmel was a good one," Braeden said.

"You were right." She agreed as she and my father left the room.

Trent and Drew both went to kiss Rimmel and rub her belly for good luck (I glared at them both) before following along behind my parents.

The doctor glanced at Braeden and Ivy.

"I'm not leaving," Braeden announced. "That's my sister."

Rimmel sighed. "It's okay," she told the doctor.

"Go stand in the corner!" I ordered B. "Don't be looking at my wife."

B put his face in the corner. "Some things a BBFL don't need to see."

Ivy moved up beside Rimmel's head, and I did the same on the other side.

The doctor did her thing and announced Rimmel was almost ready to push. "We'll be back in just a little while, hopefully to have a baby!" the OB declared, then left the room.

The nurse adjusted her pillows as I glared at her, and Rim smiled sweetly. "Is he always like this?" she whispered, leaning down to my wife.

Rimmel giggled. "Sometimes he's worse."

"I heard that," I muttered.

"It's okay, Dad," the nurse remarked on her way past and patted me on the shoulder.

Dad.

Holy shit. I was going to be someone's dad.

Two things:

1.) I was going to be one sexy dad.

and

2.) I didn't know how to be a father.

When the nurse was gone, Rimmel was taken over by another fucking round of pain. I gave her my hand again, and she squeezed it until I thought my bones might break.

When it was over, I eased onto the side of the bed to take her stomach in both my hands. "You and me, we need to have a talk," I said. "Now I'm your daddy, and I say it's time to come out of there. Your mother has had enough." I leaned down a little closer. "Between you and me, I don't like the looks of the nurse, so you're gonna have to do some of the heavy lifting here. Don't worry. I'll be here when you get out."

I felt the stare of both girls, and I looked up. "What?"

They rolled their eyes.

I turned around to look at Braeden. He nodded. "That should do it."

"You two are idiots," Ivy muttered.

• • •

"I think I need to push," Rimmel said, her voice strained.

I leapt off the bed and yelled at B. "Go get the damn doctor, man!"

He rushed from the room. Ivy grabbed Rimmel's hand. "I'll wait in the hall. Give you two the first few minutes alone. Come get me when I can hold my niece or nephew."

She stopped and hugged me on the way past, then disappeared.

"Sometimes I thought this day might never come," Rimmel told me, holding out her hand.

I took it, kissing her palm. "It's here."

"I love you, even though this kinda really hurts."

"I'd take the pain if I could," I vowed.

"It's going to be worth it."

I leaned down and kissed her head. Her breaths came in short gasps now. My heart hammered in my chest, and my palms were starting to sweat.

The doctor and nurse came back into the room, closing the door behind them. After a look downtown and the second Rimmel's face pinched in discomfort, she encouraged her to push.

I stayed by my wife the entire time, I focused on her face, her hands... the sound of her breathing. I don't know how long she pushed—it felt like eternity—but then suddenly, the excited exclamations of the doctor and nurse and the sound of a crying baby cut into my concentration.

A squirming little baby appeared. The doctor placed it on Rimmel's chest.

"It's a boy!" she announced.

"A boy," Rimmel cooed and instantly wrapped her arms around him. "Hi there, little guy," she said, her voice hoarse with emotion.

He looked up at her like the sound of her voice was all he needed to hear. She started to cry and rubbed her fingers over his cheek.

I stared down at them, my wife and my son. I couldn't breathe. I couldn't think. My entire being went into looking at them, at the perfect picture they created.

"His eyes are blue, just like yours," Rimmel said, glancing up at me.

I swallowed.

"Romeo?" she said, a question in her voice.

I blinked, leaned down, and kissed her forehead. "God, Rim. You did so good. He's perfect."

"I'll need to see him for a bit," the nurse said, reaching out her hands.

I moved, using my body as a shield. "Don't touch my son," I growled.

Alarmed, she backed up. "I need to clean him up, get a weight."

"Dad?" the OB called. "Do you want to cut the umbilical cord?"

Behind me, the baby fussed. Rimmel made soft sounds to soothe him. I glanced at the doctor but kept my body taut.

"Romeo, let them do their job," Rimmel implored.

I crossed my arms over my chest and leaned toward the nurse. "She went through a lot of shit to have that baby in her arms." I warned. "Don't you take him from her yet."

"Another minute wouldn't hurt." She agreed.

I gave her a look I hoped scared her and stepped around to cut the cord. When it was done, I glanced back up at my wife. Her eyes were still on the baby.

"He's so beautiful," she told me. "Come see."

"I really need to clean him up." The nurse worried.

I glared at her.

"Oh, yes," Rimmel said. "I'm sorry."

Carefully, my son was transferred into the nurse's care, and she carried him to a small scale and began doing what she needed to do.

I watched but stayed near my wife. "Are you okay?" I asked. "Are you in a lot of pain?"

"I'm fine." She promised. "Go see him," she urged.

The doctor was talking to Rim, finishing with her, so I let them do their thing and went to see my son.

"He looks really healthy," the nurse told me. "Seven pounds, two ounces."

I peeked over her shoulder as she wrapped a generic blanket around him and added a pink and blue hat to his head. With care, the nurse picked him up and held him out to me. He was crying, and I knew it was her fault.

Without thought, I reached for him, pulling him into my chest, holding him as tight as I dared. "There now," I told him. "I got you. Everything is all good. We Anderson men are made tough."

The nurse laughed.

He was tiny, practically smaller than a football. What little bit of hair he had was light like mine. I brushed at a downy strand just beneath the brim of the cap. His one hand found its way out of the blanket, and it waved around. I slid my index finger against his palm. Instantly, his hand closed around it.

That's all it took. I fell so far in love with him there would never be any going back.

"It's better than I imagined," Rimmel said.

"What is?" I asked, still studying his little face.

"Seeing you with him."

"This is a good-looking kid, Smalls." I glanced up and smiled.

"I wanna see." She held out her arms.

I carried him over and surrendered him.

"We'll need to take him—"

"No," I growled.

"It's hospital policy," the doctor chimed in as she was taking off her gloves. "You can go with him."

The door opened, and Braeden's head appeared. "What the hell is taking so long?"

"It's a boy!" Rimmel announced.

The door flew open, and B and Ivy came in. "I totally called it."

"We'll give you just a few minutes, but then he must come with me," the nurse said, glancing at me.

I relented. "Okay, thanks."

She seemed surprised but didn't say so. She and the doctor retreated as Ivy and B rushed to see the baby.

"Oh my goodness, he's perfect!" Ivy said when Rimmel handed him over. Tears welled up in her eyes as she stared down at him. "So tiny," she mused.

"That's gonna be us soon," Braeden whispered as he looked over Ivy's shoulder at his nephew.

"What?" Rimmel gasped.

Ivy winced and glanced up at me, then at Rim. "We were waiting to say anything."

"You're pregnant!" Rimmel exclaimed.

Ivy nodded, and B grinned like he was the man. "We just found out. I wanted to wait 'til after the shower today to tell everyone."

"That's the best news ever!" Rimmel said, her eyes on the baby. "Congratulations!"

I held out my hand to B for us to shake. "Congrats, man. It's good news."

"I need to see him," Braeden said. "Uncle inspection."

"Watch his head," I demanded when he took the baby from Ivy.

"I'm your favorite uncle," he said, as my son stared at him wholly. "You got a few more, but I'm the best."

"Let me have him," Rimmel said. "They're gonna come back, and I want to kiss him."

Braeden slipped him into her arms and kissed her head. She smiled down at the baby, then looked up at me.

Unable to stay away from her another second, I climbed in the bed, squished right up against her on my side, and put my arms around both her and my son.

Rimmel kissed his head and adjusted his hat, then laid her head against my chest.

My chest was so full it felt tight. The amount of love and possession I felt in that moment was unsurpassed by anything else.

"Does he have a name yet?" Ivy asked.

I glanced at Rimmel. We hadn't discussed names very much because she was so superstitious throughout the entire pregnancy.

She nodded, almost shy.

I adjusted the black-framed glasses on her nose and kissed her temple. "Let's hear it."

"Blue," she said.

"Like the color?" I puzzled.

She smiled, looking up. "For the color of your eyes, the color of my favorite hoodie..."

"I can dig it," Braeden said.

"You don't get a say," I told him without looking away from Rimmel's upturned face.

She picked out a name that reminded her of me... What isn't to love?

"Blue." I tried it out. "I like it."

"Blue James Anderson." Rimmel went on and glanced back down.

He yawned like he was unimpressed.

"Love it." I agreed on the name, kissing her on the head. "I love you, too."

The nurse walked in, wheeling a clear baby bassinet along with her. I glowered.

Rimmel sighed. "Go with him, Romeo. And make them bring him back as soon as possible."

"Anything for you," I said and forced myself off the bed.

Instead of letting the nurse place him in the bassinet, I did it. He started crying almost immediately. Hell, I'd cry too if someone made me leave Rimmel's arms.

"Is he okay?" Rimmel worried, getting ready to vault out of bed.

"He's fine," I assured her.

As I was leaving, Braeden joined me. "Don't worry, sis," he told Rimmel. "I'll get Drew and Trent, too. No one is gonna bother our man Blue."

"There's more of you?" The nurse gasped.

"I apologize in advance," Rimmel told her sympathetically.

Ivy snickered. "I'm going to go tell Valerie. She's probably on pins and needles." She leaned down to give Rimmel a quick hug. "Congratulations," she whispered.

"Thank you," Rim replied with the familiar sheen of tears in her eyes.

The nurse went out the door with B and Ivy, but I hung back just a second.

"What are you doing?" Rimmel asked, staring after her son.

"Little Blue Jay is just fine, baby. I'll catch up with them in a few. But first, there's something I need to do."

She tilted her head to the side. "What?"

I surged forward, making fast work of the distance separating us. Careful of her body, I cupped her cheeks in my palms and kissed her soundly.

When I lifted my head, there was a dreamy quality to her stare and her lips turned up in a soft smile.

"What was that for?" she whispered.

"That," I said definitively, "was for breathing."

I kissed her again.

"And that was because I love you so fucking much."

"So fucking much," she echoed. "Now go watch over our son," she urged.

I held her hand until I had to let go to keep walking. Out in the hall, I jogged to catch up to my son, and when I looked down, I saw the perfect balance. Romeo and Rimmel, all mixed together.

He was tangible proof that two hearts could absolutely beat as one.

RIMMEL

The door remained closed.

Not locked, yet with an unspoken seal no one ever crossed.

Until recently that is. But not yet by me. Or Romeo.

Or the baby boy was cradled in my arms.

Blue was four days old and perfect in every way. You know how they say life can change in an instant, in the blink of an eye?

Whoever said that was probably a parent.

No love is ever so swift than the love that smacks you when your child is first placed in your arms. In that moment, everything shifted, everything changed.

The gravitational pull that held Romeo and me together spread to include our son. We already had a family, a big, crazy, loving one. Evie was part of that family; she always would be.

But Blue made it complete.

My heart belonged to Romeo, but now it orbited around our son.

His eyes were blue; they had the same kind of magic in them Romeo's held. Every time this baby looked at me, I felt engulfed, like the entire world narrowed down to just him and me. The only other person I'd ever met with so much power in just a single look was his daddy.

The light, downy hair barely covering his head was irresistible to the touch; his tiny, heart-shaped lips were pink and always begged for kisses.

He knew my voice and the sound of Romeo's. Those round, blue eyes would follow our sounds whenever we moved, and when he'd find us, he never looked away.

I won't lie. Sometimes when I looked at him and my heart swelled, I thought of my lost daughter, the one I never got to meet. I wondered if she would have the same eyes, the same hair, the same hungry appetite.

I wouldn't ever know the answers to those questions, but it didn't make me love Blue any less. If anything, it made me love him more because I understood all too well the fragility of life.

"This is your big sister's room," I told him softly as he gazed up at me. "I think she'd want you to have it, though. Are you ready to see?"

He didn't answer, but he didn't have to. It was more a question for myself.

Was I ready to go in, to face the past and the future all in one single moment?

Romeo was standing right beside me. He leaned over and wrapped his hand around the doorknob. I took a breath and nodded. The door swung in.

It felt like my heart caved in a little at the first sight of the room. I recalled what it had been before its glory now—a mostly empty space with a chair, a few stuffed toys, and a crib. This room always seemed cold to me. Empty. Sad.

It wasn't sad anymore. It was absolutely perfect.

In keeping with the house, the walls were light gray, soothing and soft, perfect for a sleepy baby. The hardwood floors were covered with two large area rugs, one patterned white and gray beneath the brand-new black crib, and a yellow one that looked like a cloud in the center of the room.

The wall behind the crib had a white stencil design, and in the center was a large, yellow wooden B. Everything was done in white and gray, but there were lots of yellow accents. The windows were draped with beautiful curtains, and the rocking chair was inviting.

No detail was left unattended. Valerie's stamp was everywhere.

Almost shy, I stepped into the room as my eyes roamed. "It's beautiful," I whispered to Romeo, glancing over my shoulder to see if he approved.

He gave me an ornery smile. "My mother wouldn't settle for anything less than the best."

I giggled. He was so right. She was so smitten with the baby in my arms. I didn't go a single day without seeing her in the four days since he'd been born. In fact, she'd probably be here later.

Rocking a little as I walked, I noted the closet, which was organized and stocked. There were even some blue outfits hanging among the mostly green and yellow I'd chosen before I knew he was a he.

"I don't know how they got all this done in four days." I was in awe.

"My mother and Ivy?" Romeo scoffed. "I'm surprised the whole house isn't redone."

* * *

I had to agree. I pivoted, noting the yellow dresser against the wall, and froze. Swallowing the lump in my throat, I wandered closer. My eyes never once left the picture sitting in a silver frame.

It was the only picture we had of Evie, her first and last sonogram.

They framed it. Added it to this room.

A sob caught in my throat as I stared at the tiny image. It was so fitting she was in here.

Romeo wrapped his arms around us from behind, his chin settling on my shoulder. "Feels right."

"Yes," I murmured. "It does." A tear slid down my cheek, but I didn't brush it away. I didn't have to. It was okay to cry about Evie. It was okay to be sad. It was also okay to be happy.

Life wasn't just any one thing. It was a combination… a melting pot of emotions, a mix of salty and sweet.

"You're being greedy," Romeo whispered. With one hand wrapped around me, he caressed the top of Blue's head with the other.

"He looks like you," I told him.

"My genes are more dominant," he declared, matter-of-fact.

I turned in his arm. "Is that so?"

"The proof is right there in your arms."

Well, I couldn't argue with that, now could I?

Romeo leaned forward, hugged us both against him, and pressed a kiss to the top of my head. "It came true," he whispered.

"What?"

"The wish I made right before he was born."

I tipped up my head to look at him. He held his arms out for our son. Gently, I handed the bundled baby over, taking care to cradle his head.

"I got him." He promised, concentration turning his handsome face serious.

I stepped away, watching as my giant husband tucked the tiny baby into his chest and fussed with the blankets, making sure he was warm.

He'd only been a father four days, but I knew without a shadow of a doubt exactly what kind of father he was going to be to Blue and to any other children we were lucky enough to add to our family.

Exceptional.

Exceptional (adjective): Not typical, unusual, uncommon, extraordinary, rare, unprecedented.

"I'm getting pretty good at this." He boasted, glancing up at me to grin.

"Yes, you are." I smiled, watching them.

"Romeo?" I asked as I wandered over to caress the soft pile of clean blankets on the end of the changing table.

"Yeah, Smalls?" he answered quietly, his face downturned as he studied our son.

"What was your wish?"

"For him to know your love, the kind of love I've only ever seen you capable of giving. The kind you give to me every day."

My heart did a cartwheel in my chest. "You're still my #bae, Romeo."

"Did you just call me a shithead?" He scowled, but his eyes danced with laughter and love.

"Don't use that language in front of my son!" I scolded.

He winced. "Sorry." Romeo glanced down at the baby. "Your momma says you can't say that word. I'll be sure to teach you worse ones when you're older."

"Roman Anderson!" I whisper yelled. "You *are* a poop head!"

"Aww, don't be like that, Smalls," he crooned and came closer, walking gently as he carried Blue.

When he stopped before me, he leaned down over the baby and kissed me soft. "You're still my before anyone else, Mrs. Anderson."

Love you, I mouthed, kissing him again.

Blue started fussing, and Romeo jerked back. "Hey there, Blue Jay. Tell your daddy what's the matter."

Ralph scrambled into the room with Darcy not far behind and rushed to Romeo's feet, where they sat quietly and stared up with wide eyes at the fussing new addition.

Ralph whined a little, and I patted him on the head. "Good boy." Even our two rambunctious dogs were wrapped around this little boy's finger.

"He needs to eat," I said, reaching for him.

Romeo stepped back, tugging his Blue Jay farther against him. "Don't be interrupting man time."

I put my hands on my hips. "He's hungry."

Romeo wagged his eyebrows. "You're sexy when you're bossy."

Well, it was a good thing I had that going for me, 'cause I was back to drowning in sweats, wearing the same Alpha U hoodie every day, and never combing my hair.

Who had time for anything else when they had a baby to love?

Well, Ivy did. She had some kind of magical powers.

"I'm gonna go make his bottle," I said. "I wouldn't want to interrupt man time."

Romeo crossed to the rocker and made himself comfortable. Both dogs lay at his feet.

When I was in the hallway, I heard him say, "About time she left. Now let me tell you about football…"

Little Blue Jay quieted down, and I knew he was listening aptly to the sound his daddy's voice.

All was right with the world.

I smiled.

P.S. Ivy had a little boy. They named him Jaxson, which made Blue and Jax less than a year apart in age. From the moment they met, they had an epic bromance, just like their daddies.

Blue James Anderson

Mommy & Blue

AUTHOR'S NOTE

It always seems impossible until it's done. True words, especially when it came to writing this book. This book was highly requested—as in almost on a daily basis, people asked me for a baby book for Romeo and Rimmel since the day *#Heart* released.

It got to the point it was all I was asked. I was never opposed to writing this book, but I didn't want to write it just for the sake of writing it. I wanted there to be a story in my head for it. Because I love this series so much, I wanted to be able to do it justice.

You know how you have a really great hair day and then you don't want to go outside because you know it will be ruined? Or when you actually get your house super clean and beautiful, but then you don't want to do anything to mess it up?

That's what it felt like to write this book.

The Hashtag Series started out as a single book. A single idea of a girl with glasses. I was inspired by hoodies, football, and cool weather. I never intended it to be eight books. I never intended to have an entire family come together and literally take over my life.

I guess the best things in life are unexpected (didn't Rimmel say something like that?) and this series has definitely been that. The success this series has had (and I'm not talking necessarily in units sold) blows my mind. The characters have become so well loved it's almost intimidating, even to me. Especially when sitting down to try and write about them.

How would I ever live up to the first seven books? How many ways can you make two people kiss without it seeming like an endless run-on of the same words over and over again? How do you maintain the magic that surrounds Romeo and Rimmel?

I know this book probably isn't what people were expecting. It has a lot more feels in it than I *think* were begged for. I think everyone wanted happy, happy, happy… But this is what Romeo and Rimmel told me. It's real, sometimes it's raw, but it's family, which is what they are.

And in the end, there were three.

A beautiful three at that.

#Bae was scary because I basically started out in the prologue with something deeply personal and painful for a lot of people. In one hundred percent honesty, I've never experienced a miscarriage or infertility problems. I debated (even now that the book is done) if I should do it. The last thing I want to do is offend someone with my portrayal of something like this. I don't want to hurt anyone or even try to lessen what those who deal with this feel.

All I did was try to write it to the best of my ability, with compassion, but also as the characters told me. Everyone deals with miscarriage and infertility different; some struggle WAY more than Romeo and Rimmel.

I just pray the story I wrote here does this series and this subject justice.

Also, I hope you as a reader got all the feels you longed for. I hope the magic was there for you and the love between this family shone through.

People will likely ask if this is really the end. Can you write more?

My answer is hard, but it's the only one I have. Yes. This is it. I could possibly keep writing, but it would ruin this "perfect" thing, and I don't want to do that. (I don't think this series is perfect in any literary or editorial sense. I hope you get what I'm saying here).

I leave you with this. We will always be #family. These words and stories will always be here for the true #nerds out there. I will be eternally grateful for everything this series has brought to my life, and these characters will forever be in my heart. I hope you revisit these books and characters often, as I know I will.

Thank you for coming on this #journey with me. Please keep spreading the word about this series, keep sharing the #love. Maybe someday it will grow big enough that we'll all be able to see it onscreen.

Next up for me is Arrow's book #*Blur*, and then after that… a new adventure is waiting. I'll see you all there.

XOXO,
Cambria

Cambria Hebert is an award winning, bestselling novelist of more than thirty books. She went to college for a bachelor's degree, couldn't pick a major, and ended up with a degree in cosmetology. So rest assured her characters will always have good hair.

Besides writing, Cambria loves a caramel latte, staying up late, sleeping in, and watching movies. She considers math human torture and has an irrational fear of birds (including chickens). You can often find her painting her toenails (because she bites her fingernails), or walking her Chihuahuas (the real rulers of the house).

Cambria has written within the young adult and new adult genres, penning many paranormal and contemporary titles. She has also written romantic suspense, science fiction, and most recently, male/male romance. Her favorite genre to read and write is contemporary romance.

Recent awards include: Author of the Year, Best Contemporary Series (*The Hashtag Series*), Best Contemporary Book of the Year, Best Book Trailer of the Year, Best Contemporary Lead, Best Contemporary Book Cover of the Year. In addition, her most recognized title #*Nerd* was listed at Buzzfeed.com as a Top Fifty Summer Romance Read.

Cambria Hebert owns and operates Cambria Hebert Books, LLC.

You can find out more about Cambria and her titles by visiting her website: http://www.cambriahebert.com

Cambria Hebert

CPSIA information can be obtained
at www.ICGtesting.com
Printed in the USA
BVHW080339160122
626297BV00006B/568

9 781938 857935